California Dreaming

The Davenports, Book 1

~ Archer & Tessa ~

Bella Andre & Nicky Arden

CALIFORNIA DREAMING
The Davenports, Book 1

© 2024 Bella Andre & Nicky Arden

Meet the Davenport family! Six brothers and sisters who call picturesque Carmel-by-the-Sea home. Successful, brilliant, and passionate, the only thing they all still need is the perfect partner in love and life.

Hotshot movie star Archer Davenport has never met a stunt he couldn't ace, a challenge he couldn't overcome, or a woman he couldn't have. When he breaks his leg during a dangerous stunt, the production company insists on hiring a live-in caregiver for him. He refuses the help... until he meets Tessa Taylor. She's not only caring and beautiful, she's also as tough on him as a drill sergeant.

Tessa knows all about confident men. She used to be married to one, and that didn't go well. Her only solace is her painting, even if she has no talent, as her late husband always claimed. Her biggest problem on this job, however, is that sexy, magnetic Archer makes her toes curl with desire every time he's near. She does everything she can to remain professional. But it gets harder and harder every day as she starts to fall for him—and for his amazing family—even though she'll have to leave him for her next client as soon as he's fully recovered.

Arch, however, has no plans to let Tessa disappear once his leg heals. In fact, as the sparks between them grow hotter and hotter, he's determined to show Tessa that she's not only the most incredible and loving woman he's ever known, she's also the most talented. And when a Davenport gives their heart away, it's forever.

A note from Bella and Nicky

Thank you so much for taking a journey with us to Carmel-by-the-Sea, a coastal city in California that we both think is one of the most beautiful places on earth. It's home to the Davenports, a loving family with six brothers and sisters who are all interesting, passionate, and single—until the right person comes along.

Whether they're out surfing in the early morning, enjoying a family birthday party, or just walking the dog on the beach, the Davenports are always there for one another. And when love comes along, it's always unexpected, but just right.

We hope you fall in love with this brand-new series as much as we've enjoyed writing each book.

Love,
Bella Andre & Nicky Arden

P.S. Please sign up for our New Release newsletters for more information on upcoming books: BellaAndre.com/Newsletter and nickyarden.com/newsletter

Chapter One

Archer Davenport gazed out at the beach below the town of Carmel-by-the-Sea and took a deep breath of the salt-tinged sea air. The waves were often huge, crashing into the shore, but today the water lapped gently on the sand. He didn't have much time in town, and he craved a walk on the beach before he had to leave his favorite place on earth and head back to Hollywood.

He pulled off his shoes and socks, rolled up the cuffs of his jeans, and let his toes squish into the soft, golden sand, just the way he had for more than thirty of his thirty-four years. He loved Carmel, loved it more than anything he could think of, except for his family. Coming home for his dad's sixty-fourth birthday party had given him the excuse he needed to get away from filming in LA for a couple of days.

Arch was at the point in his acting career where he could pick and choose his roles. At present, he was having the time of his life remaking a famous buddy Western with his real-life friend Smith Sullivan. Smith was playing the older, wiser gentleman train robber, while Arch was playing the younger, devil-may-care character who ran headfirst into danger and worried about the consequences later. Apart from the Western garb and the steam trains, it wasn't so different from their relationship in real life.

He grinned, watching the dogs running free on one of the few truly dog-friendly beaches in the US. Somehow, without it being explicitly said, all of the dog owners made sure to pick up after their dogs and also knew to bring only friendly dogs that wouldn't get into fights. Before Arch's career had taken off, he used to love to come down to the beach to walk the family dog, Buster, and soak in the joy of watching dogs running with their ears flapping in the wind and their tails wagging as they met other dogs.

He knew a few of the people on the beach by sight and took the time to say quick hellos. In most places around the world, he needed to wear a ball cap and sunglasses so that he wasn't constantly bombarded by requests for selfies. He was beyond grateful for his fans and knew it was the price he paid to be one of the hottest actors in Hollywood. But sometimes he just wanted to walk on the beach in peace. One of the best things about Carmel-by-the-Sea was that there were so many celebrities here—the legendary Clint Eastwood had been mayor for nearly a decade—and the town culture was to leave famous people alone. Amazingly, even the tourists mostly picked up that basic courtesy.

Just then, he heard the click of a smartphone camera and knew someone had caught on to his identity, but apart from that snatched photograph, he was left in peace. At least until a shaggy white dog spotted him, ran up fresh from the sea, and shook itself, depositing a spray of sandy seawater all over Arch. Then the dog dropped a slobbery red ball at his feet and barked an instruction for Arch to throw it.

Obeying the dog's command, he picked up the ball and lobbed it into the edge of the surf. As the dog went careening after it, Arch kept walking, giving a cheerful wave to its owner.

Coming toward him was a sprightly older lady with a cast on her arm. He had known Margaret Percy all his life. She owned one of the historic fairy-tale cottages built by Hugh Comstock that was a couple of blocks back from the beach. Margaret was one of Arch's favorite people in Carmel. In her early eighties, she was always off on some adventure or another. There might be a large age difference between them, but deep down they recognized each other as kindred souls.

They were both daredevils.

Margaret was walking with a much younger woman. A woman who made him feel like all the air had been sucked out of his lungs just from looking at her.

Arch mingled with celebrities every day. He

worked with some of the most beautiful women in the world, all of whom had makeup, hair, costume, and lighting designers to enhance their looks. But all of those famous women left him cold. Whereas this one, with her blue jeans and navy hoodie, her dark hair pulled back in a simple ponytail, had something about her that drew him. She hadn't done a thing to enhance her looks—in fact, the only thing on her face even close to makeup was a little gloss on her full lips. Her eyes were big and blue and framed by dark, spiky lashes.

And he couldn't stop staring.

When she turned her gaze on him, he saw the moment that she recognized him, because her eyes widened ever so slightly. A moment later, however, she seemed to realize she was staring and looked toward the ocean.

"Margaret," he said, turning his attention back to his friend. "Sorry to see you in a cast. Don't tell me you were performing with Cirque du Soleil again?"

Margaret chuckled, the laughter of a woman who clearly made it a point to enjoy every second of her life. "Don't give me ideas. That's something I've never done. At least, not yet. No, this is nothing so exciting. I was dancing the tango in Buenos Aires and tripped over my own high heels. Broke my arm."

"Ouch," he said. And then, "Although I'm pretty sure dancing the tango in Buenos Aires counts as something exciting." Though they had been walking in opposite directions, he turned around to walk with them.

"I take it you're back from Hollywood to celebrate your father's birthday?"

He laughed. "Was it the balloons, the massive sign hanging across the front of the house, or the sixty-four pink plastic flamingos on the lawn that gave it away?"

"Subtle is something you Davenports certainly aren't," Margaret agreed with a chuckle. "In any case, I was very pleased to get an invitation to the party. I'm looking forward to tonight." Then she turned to her companion. "What am I thinking? I should have introduced the two of you right away. Archer Davenport, this is Tessa Taylor."

Compelled to touch her hand and feel her skin against his, he offered his for a handshake. She hesitated just a moment and then clasped his outstretched hand. Her grip was surprisingly strong. Despite the fact that she was fine-boned and slender, he could see at a glance that she took good care of herself.

"It's very nice to meet you, Tessa," he said. "And call me Arch. That's what my friends and family usually call me."

"It's nice to meet you, too, Arch," she replied. Then she took her hand back, and the three of them continued walking along the beach.

Margaret was so busy telling him about her trip to Argentina that she barely looked where she was going.

He was worried that she'd break the other arm, but before he could steer her around a rock protruding from the sand, Tessa did it. He didn't think Margaret had even noticed how deftly Tessa had intervened.

"How are you managing with your broken arm?" He couldn't do much to help because he had to head back to Los Angeles after the birthday party, but he could make sure at least one of his brothers or sisters or parents dropped by Margaret's on a regular basis to check on her.

"Actually," she replied, "I'm being very well looked after." She glanced at her companion with real affection. "I honestly don't know what I'll do without Tessa. She's taken such good care of me."

He'd vaguely recalled Margaret talking about a granddaughter who lived in the east somewhere, so he asked Tessa, "Are you the granddaughter I've heard so much about?"

Margaret shook her head, but before she could answer, the young woman spoke up for herself. "I'm Margaret's caregiver."

The way she said it made it clear that she expected him to think less of her for having a job so many financial tiers down from his own. Instead, he was filled with gratitude that she had clearly earned Margaret's affection. It was easy to see that a real bond of friendship had developed between the two women. Which was particularly impressive given that Margaret could be extremely feisty, especially if anybody tried to get her to do something she didn't want to do.

As though reading his thoughts, Margaret said, "And don't think I've been an easy patient. I don't like being an invalid. I don't want to do my exercises, and the things Tessa won't let me do would make anybody crazy." She reached out with her good arm and slipped it around Tessa's back. "But she's a wonderful cook, excellent company, and bright as can be. I don't know what I'll do without her once I'm well enough for her to move on."

"Go back to Argentina and dance the tango, I'm guessing."

Margaret laughed. "No, Arch, the one thing I never do is repeat myself. Plus, I have finally realized that I've got to slow down. So I think I'll go on a walking tour of Ireland next."

He glanced over at Tessa and found her looking back at him, her beautiful blue eyes dancing. It was as though she was saying, *What can I do? She's a force of nature. I can't stop her.*

He hoped his silent nod let Tessa know that he completely understood. Margaret was a delightful and inspiring woman. She always walked her own path, and if she ever fell, she'd just pick herself up, dust herself off, and keep on going.

Margaret tapped her cast. "I'm getting this dreadful thing off tomorrow, and then with a couple of weeks of physical therapy, I should be as good as new."

"As long as you actually do your exercises," Tessa reminded her. Something about her tone let him know that she might look soft and sweet, but she was no pushover.

Then the inevitable happened. A couple of teenage girls giggled and started taking pictures of him. Though he truly appreciated his fans, right at this moment he hoped they'd be too nervous to approach him. He wanted a chance to learn more about Tessa.

But suddenly the pair came running up. "Are you Archer Davenport?" one asked him breathlessly.

"Yes, I am," he said. No point in denying it. At least they were too young to push their phone numbers into his hand or suggest they go somewhere a little more quiet, which had happened more times than he could count.

More giggling. "Can we get a selfie?"

He was about to agree when Margaret stepped forward. "Young ladies, don't you have any respect? Archer Davenport might be an actor, but he gets time off too. And the last thing he needs is to be bothered by a couple of impudent young stalkers."

They looked so shocked they took a step back. One of them mumbled an apology, and the other looked like she was about to cry.

But he knew they meant no harm. "It's okay. I'd be happy to take a picture with you both."

He stood between the girls as they snapped their selfies. He was careful not to put an arm around their shoulders. He didn't want their pictures showing up on the Internet, making it look like he was inappropriately touching teenage girls.

Once they'd taken their selfies, the bolder of the two said, "I loved you in *Morocco*. Are you and Sonia Montefiore getting married?"

How many times had he been asked that question? Sonia Montefiore had recently been named *People* magazine's most beautiful woman in the world. And she truly was beautiful on the outside. Unfortunately, she was also narcissistic and humorless, and the one time they'd had lunch together, she'd spent more time calculating the calories on her plate than having any kind of conversation with him. Still, they'd made a movie together, and they were both good enough actors that they'd managed to scorch the screen with pretend passion. But once the cameras cut, they'd headed to their separate trailers. He had nothing against the woman, but the rumors about their love affair were so far exaggerated it was ridiculous.

"I'm glad you enjoyed the movie," he replied, "but no, Sonia and I are not getting married. We're not a couple."

The quieter one looked quite happy with that clarification. Then she finally spoke up. "I've heard you live here? Is that true? Which house is yours? Is it one of the mansions over there?" She pointed toward Pebble Beach.

He shook his head. "I live in Los Angeles most of the time. Soon I'll be finishing shooting my latest movie." He didn't let on that he did have a house here.

Giggling, madly waving good-bye, the two girls ran off, all gangly legs and bouncing hair.

He'd been aware of Tessa watching him throughout that little interchange. He hoped he hadn't come across like a conceited movie star. It was a fine line to walk—keeping fans from getting too familiar and yet still happy to see his movies. Tessa didn't say anything, but Margaret piped up.

"You'd think they'd know better. I'm very glad you didn't tell them you lived just steps from the beach. That was good thinking. They'd be camping out on your doorstep." Margaret pointed and told Tessa, "That's Archer's place on Scenic Drive. Even though I've never been invited in," she added with a raised eyebrow, "I hear it's got its own screening room, and it's one of only a few houses in town that has a gym and an indoor swimming pool in the basement."

He got the heavy hint. "Margaret, if both you and I are ever in town long enough, I'll have you over, and that's a promise."

Though Margaret was in her eighties, she looked as pleased as the teenage girls had been when they got their selfie.

And this time when Tessa Taylor glanced at him, he was pretty sure he saw the warm light of approval in her eyes.

"Tessa," he said, "I'm assuming you'll also be attending the party tonight?"

When the Davenports celebrated, they often included their friends in town. His father loved a good crowd for his birthday, whereas his mother preferred to celebrate quietly with only family. No question it was going to be crowded and noisy tonight at the Davenport family home.

"Of course I will," Tessa said. With a smile, she added, "Otherwise, how could I make sure that Margaret doesn't get up on a table and show off her dance moves?"

"That's great news," he said, letting his gaze linger on Tessa's face until she blushed slightly and turned away.

His phone dinged, and his brother Finn's name popped up on the screen with a message. "Looks like I've been assigned the task of bringing a couple of big bags of ice for the party drinks."

"We'll see you soon," Margaret said as the three of them said their good-byes.

Though he would never have wished a broken arm on Margaret, he was very happy to have met Tessa and couldn't help wanting to get to know her better. Thanks to his father's birthday party, it looked like he was going to get that chance.

No question about it, this beach was magical. Particularly when a beautiful woman like Tessa had been walking beside him on the sand.

As he headed up the hill to the local grocery store for the ice, he realized he was grinning like a fool. Because even though he and Tessa had only just met, he couldn't help but hope she had also felt the sparks between them.

Sparks that were bigger and brighter than he'd ever felt with another woman.

Chapter Two

Tessa was both nervous and excited as she walked up the path to the front door of Howard and Betsy Davenport's house. She held on to Margaret Percy's good arm, but she wasn't sure if she was lending support so much as receiving it.

She still could hardly believe that she'd met and spoken with Archer Davenport. Not to mention that he'd told her to call him Arch, the way his friends and family did. It was such a gracious thing for him to have said to a total stranger, simply because she was working with one of his friends. Of course, he was only being polite, so he would remain Archer to her.

They passed the sixty-four pink flamingos prancing all over the front yard and the huge banner saying HAPPY 64TH BIRTHDAY, HOWIE, which they'd seen as they were driving by the house earlier that day. Now the garden was festooned with helium balloons and lit up with festive lights. It was impossible not to smile.

Though she was attending the party with Margaret to keep her from doing anything crazy enough to break another limb, Tessa was more nervous about coming than she wanted to let on. Margaret could clearly read her mind, however. She'd said to Tessa earlier, "You deserve a little fun tonight. And to be around people your own age. Relax, dear. Everything's going to be okay."

Tessa had never told Margaret her history, but somehow she felt the older woman had seen right inside her to the pain she carried, hidden behind her cheerful smile and efficient demeanor.

She took a calming breath before knocking on the door. She could hear music and the sounds of voices coming from the other side. In a minute, the door was opened by a woman who possessed both presence and beauty. She wasn't young, but her face expressed years of laughter and contentment. She smiled upon seeing them, and Tessa got the feeling that this was her natural attitude. Happiness.

"Margaret, I'm so glad you could come."

"Betsy, you're still as pretty as a picture."

The woman laughed as she waved them in. "I'm the same age as Howie. I'll be having my own birthday in a couple of months, but believe me, I won't be advertising it."

And yet, the easy way she'd admitted her age suggested to Tessa that she was perfectly comfortable with who she was, despite the years. Still, Tessa was shocked. She'd have guessed Archer's mother to be at least a decade younger. She was trim, her golden hair shoulder length and curled into a careless updo. Formfitting white jeans and a black top showed off a pretty spectacular figure for somebody who had given birth to six children.

"And you must be Tessa," Betsy said, reaching out to shake her hand.

Even though she was a paid caregiver, Tessa suddenly felt as welcome as Margaret, who'd known the family for decades.

Betsy said to Margaret, "You always look so glamorous."

Margaret made an annoyed sound and mock-glared at Tessa. "She wouldn't let me wear my high heels. I'll feel like an elf among all you tall Davenports, except for Erin."

She might not be able to wear high heels, but Margaret was wearing a black and gold sequined top over dark trousers and chunky jewelry, and she carried a fancy beaded purse. The only way Tessa could get her to abandon the gold stilettos had been to flat-out refuse to come with her unless she wore sensible flats. Still, Margaret regarded the Chanel ballet flats as though she'd been forced to go to a birthday party in hiking boots.

Tessa was wearing her best jeans and a sapphire blue sleeveless cotton sweater. She'd taken the time to do her hair so it hung loose in curls, and she'd even added a little mascara and lipstick. She'd tried to tell herself she was doing it out of respect for the birthday boy, but deep down she knew it was because she'd be seeing Archer Davenport again.

Even as she scolded herself for being so foolish, she felt fluttery with nerves. She'd had a crush on Archer Davenport ever since she'd seen him in his first movie, a teen surfing flick back when he'd been a teenager himself and she'd been twelve. In all her life, she'd still never experienced a celebrity crush like it. She'd seen every movie he'd ever made. So, to meet him in person, to be in his family home, was almost more than she could handle.

She'd have to keep a tight rein on her emotions. She didn't want him to think she was like those silly, giggling girls on the beach, drooling over him and grabbing selfies. No. She'd be cool, professional. He'd never know that being close to him made her dizzy.

A dog came bounding up and looked so delighted to see Tessa and Margaret that he could barely contain himself. "Buster, how did you get back inside?" Betsy said, trying to push the eager pup away.

Buster was no breed that Tessa could recognize. Shaggy, with straw-colored curly hair, big ears, and bright, intelligent eyes, he was a medium-sized dog with a tail that swept back and forth as he pushed against Betsy's restraining arms.

"Hello, Buster," Tessa said, squatting to accept

both a shaggy paw and a lick on her chin.

"Finn, call the dog, please!" Betsy called, and at the sound of a single whistle, Buster tore away again. "Everybody's in the great room and spilling out into the backyard," Betsy continued. "One of the boys will get you a drink. Have a good time."

Margaret twinkled at her. "I always do."

Tessa accompanied Margaret through the tastefully decorated home, checking ahead to see if there were any obstacles, changing levels, or cords she might trip over, but there was nothing to cause her alarm. They walked into a great room that immediately impressed her with its air of comfort. It wasn't fancy, but it was large and well designed. A peaked roof gave the ceiling height, and there were couches and chairs that looked made for comfort rather than design. It was the kind of room you just wanted to hang out in. And plenty of people were doing just that. Margaret was immediately pulled into a group of older people, all clearly golfers, who wanted to know when she'd next be on the course. Tessa stood slightly behind her while Margaret promised she'd be good as new in a couple of months. Knowing Margaret, it was probably true.

A tall man came over with a tray of drinks—white wine, red wine, and sparkling water with chunks of lemon. Margaret reached for a glass of red wine, and Tessa chose sparkling water. Maybe later she'd have a small glass of wine, but for now she felt she ought to keep her wits about her. Although Margaret had insisted that this was a night off, she intended to keep an eye on her client. And a sober one at that.

As she wrapped her hand around the glass, she glanced up at the man holding the tray and actually blinked as though her eyes might be playing tricks on her. Archer was movie-star gorgeous, but this guy was in a whole different league. Eyes that were dark and smoldering, with a black rim around the iris. Wavy dark hair that he clearly hadn't brushed, but seemed even more glorious for being messy. Beneath his can't-be-bothered-to-shave stubble, she saw the sculpted jaw, the perfectly bladed cheekbones. He wore jeans so old they'd worn through at the knees and were clearly too big, but somehow that only enhanced his build. Beneath an old gray T-shirt, she was aware of powerful muscles.

Margaret said, "Finn, good to see you. I see your dad's got you working as usual."

Finn chuckled. "I think that's why Dad wanted so many kids. He needed the free labor."

"Tessa, this is Finn Davenport. He's the good-looking one."

He flinched at the words, but Margaret had only spoken the truth. If she'd ever seen a more beautiful man, she couldn't remember where. Finn ducked his head, mumbled something that might have been *pleased to meet you*, and walked to the next chatting group with his tray of drinks.

Poor guy, he wore his looks like they were a curse.

People were ebbing and flowing, and while she recognized a few who'd either come by to see Margaret during her convalescence or had bumped into them on the beach, there wasn't anyone she really knew to talk to. She sensed, though, that Archer Davenport wasn't in the crowd.

She stood beside Margaret, listening to golf stories, noting how a couple of the older men seemed particularly attentive to her, and then she felt the air change. So slightly that only she noticed.

She glanced toward the patio doors that were wide open to the garden and watched as Archer Davenport came in. He was holding a beer in one hand and laughing, his arm slung around the shoulders of an older man who had to be his father. They were of a similar height, and one day she thought Archer would look very much like Howard Davenport.

As he walked through the door, it was as though everybody else in the room disappeared, as though they were in an alternative European movie. She was only aware of Archer. She ought to tear her gaze away, but she couldn't seem to stop staring.

He glanced up as though feeling her gaze on him. How embarrassing. She quickly turned to Margaret, mortified that he'd caught her.

But in only a minute, he was right there beside her.

"Tessa, Margaret, glad you could make it."

She couldn't believe he was talking to her. Of all the beautiful women in the world, of all the beautiful women in Carmel, of all the beautiful women in that room, he was talking to *her*. She was certain it was kindness. He must be aware she didn't know anyone, and he obviously had a soft spot for Margaret Percy. Still, for just a moment, she let herself indulge in the pleasure of having her twelve-year-old crush—that seemed to have turned into a thirty-two-year-old crush—standing there talking to her.

"You look beautiful."

As practiced as that compliment must be, in that moment as he gazed at her, she really did feel beautiful. And she wished quite suddenly that she wasn't wearing her best jeans, but some designer frock from Paris that she'd never be able to afford. That was the kind of woman he should be with. The kind who didn't totter in high heels and was on a first-name basis with couture designers.

She managed a soft, "Thank you."

"Margaret's obviously found her tribe. Let me introduce you to my family."

She was so surprised and speechless at the idea of Archer wanting her to meet his family that she let him lead her away. When she finally found her voice again, she said, "It's okay, I'm sure you have lots to do and lots of people to speak with. It's your father's birthday after all."

"Trust me," Archer said with a grin—one that was so sexy it made her heart beat even faster than it already was. "He's had his pound of flesh and more. He had me gardening this morning, and I've been fetching and carrying pretty much since I left you on the beach. Even I'm allowed a dinner break."

She hid her smile and decided that if he wanted to introduce her to his family, she wasn't about to argue. He led her first to where a tall, athletic-looking woman stood in a corner with a petite strawberry-blonde. The tall woman had hair so blonde it was nearly white. Tessa guessed that she must spend a lot of time in the sun—or in the beauty salon. But something about her suggested the former. Her toned shoulders and arms were set off to advantage by a short black dress. Her legs weren't slim, but they were muscular and gorgeous. She stood as though she were on the prow of a ship. No, as though she were on a surfboard. One foot slightly back, the other forward, her body inching ever so slightly toward the center of the room. She had eyes the color of the sea, blue-green, and was obviously in a good mood as she and her friend laughed together.

Archer said, "Mila, I want you to meet Tessa. She's new to Carmel."

The woman's eyes lit up as they shook hands. "New to Carmel as in looking for a house?" There was determination and focus in the gaze that assessed

Tessa.

Arch nudged Mila's shoulder. "We're not here to sell anybody a house. It's Dad's birthday."

She shrugged, not seeming at all bothered by his comment. "A Realtor's always doing business." Then she grinned. "That's how I got to be one of the top Realtors in Carmel-by-the-Sea."

"She's modest too," he said to Tessa with a fond shake of his head.

Tessa had never met anyone who seemed so fearless. Even though she felt intimidated by this dynamic woman, at the same time she wanted to know her better. Because Mila was so bold, she felt she could be too. "I'd have guessed you were an athlete."

For an instant, pure pain crossed Mila's beautiful face, and Tessa wished she'd kept her mouth shut. She knew all about private pain, but it was too late. The words were out, and she couldn't call them back.

"I used to be," was all Mila said.

Before the silence could grow more awkward, Archer said, "And this is my youngest sister, Erin."

For a second, Tessa was surprised that these two were related. Mila was so tall and muscular, while Erin was petite and not someone you would notice when you first walked into a room. At least, not when she was standing beside Mila.

Erin said, "I'm happy to meet you, Tessa. How do you like Carmel so far?"

She was pleased that she could say honestly, "I love it. I think Carmel-by-the-Sea is the most beautiful town I've ever been in."

Erin smiled in agreement. "What brought you here?"

She explained that she was Margaret's caregiver, but as Erin was about to ask another question, Arch stepped in. "While Mila here will try to sell you a house the minute you meet her, watch out for Erin. She'll interview you—just like she's already doing. Erin is a writer for the *Sea Shell*, our local paper."

Tessa was delighted. "I love the *Sea Shell*. I look forward to reading it every week." And then it hit her why Erin's name seemed familiar. "I really enjoyed your article about whale migration in the last issue. I learned so much."

Erin glanced at Arch, her eyes twinkling. "This one you can invite back."

Before they got any ideas, Tessa said, "Oh no, he's just being nice."

Then she was embarrassed she'd said anything so stupid and found herself blushing.

Archer said, "Don't mind them. Come on. Let's get something to eat."

As they walked away, she said, "I am so sorry. I didn't mean to bring up an awkward topic with Mila."

"It's okay. And you have a good eye. Mila's the best surfer of all of us—fearless and focused. She quit high school to go pro. She was one of the top surfers in the world when she suffered a career-ending injury. She still surfs, but she lost out on her dream."

"It's hard to let go of a dream," Tessa said softly.

Something else she knew about.

Chapter Three

Arch led Tessa to the buffet that had been set up in the big dining room. A long table that could easily seat twenty was piled with food. It smelled delicious and, despite her nerves, Tessa felt the beginnings of an appetite stirring.

At the end stood a handsome giant of a man carving a beef roast. Buster sat at his feet, no doubt hoping a chunk of meat would *accidentally* drop. His tail wagged hopefully while his eyes never left the man with the carving knife, who had to be a Davenport, but was bigger than any of them. He must be six foot four, with brown hair cut short, a beard trimmed close, and eyes the color of moss.

"Tessa, this is my big brother Nick. And I do mean big."

Arch was over six feet tall, but Nick towered over him.

Nick Davenport put down his carving knife and fork and shook her hand. "He means *older* brother, and it's nice to meet you."

Tessa had the impression of quiet strength in Nick Davenport. She got the feeling he was a caring, reliable man, but the gleam in his eye suggested he also had a sense of humor.

Looking at all the food, she felt a pang of guilt. She'd been so swept away by Archer Davenport talking to her that she'd forgotten all about Margaret. "I should get Margaret a plate of food," she said, "and make sure she's not doing anything crazy."

"Don't worry about Margaret," Arch said. "Half those golfers are in love with her. They'll be fighting over who gets to fetch her a plate. Don't spoil her fun."

Tessa had definitely noticed a couple of silver foxes charming the vivacious Margaret Percy, so after thinking it over for a few seconds, she decided it would be okay to take Arch's advice.

While they mingled, enjoying the food from the buffet, Archer introduced her to some of his family's friends and neighbors. People asked him how his movie was going, the way you'd ask anybody who was working on a business project. She didn't get the sense that they thought starring in movies was a bigger deal than building a house, or selling one, or writing an article for the *Sea Shell*. She really liked that about this group.

But then, a lot of movie stars had come and gone in Carmel over the years. She was pretty sure she'd seen the back of Brad Pitt once in the grocery store. He was just buying apples like anybody else.

While she savored every moment beside Archer, even more than she savored the delicious food on her plate, she managed to keep an eye on Margaret from across the room. Archer had been right—a gentleman had indeed fetched her a plate of food. When she seemed to be tired of standing, before Tessa could even move toward her, another gentleman, with a thick head of white hair, invited her to sit with him on one of the couches. It was so easily done, she doubted Margaret even noticed she was being cared for. She'd have loved to slip a cushion under the injured arm, but suspected Margaret wouldn't thank her for her trouble—or the reminder of her injury while she was at a party.

"He's having the time of his life," Archer said as his father came closer. "Dad," he went on, "I want you to meet Tessa."

Up close, Howard Davenport was the kind of dad she'd have loved to have. Big and big-hearted. Where everyone else in the family had shaken her hand, he enveloped her in a bear hug. She felt so comforted she'd have happily stayed cocooned in his big arms for longer. "Always happy to meet a friend of Arch's," he said.

"Happy birthday," she said.

"It sure is," he agreed. "But then, every day is a gift."

A man called, "Howie, we didn't come all this way not to visit with you. Get over here."

"My brothers," Howie said, and she followed his gaze to where five older men were huddled together. "And my best friends. Guess I'd better say hi, especially since some of them have come a long way to be here tonight."

He patted their shoulders, then headed off to where his brothers were gathered. Soon he was laughing, no doubt about old times growing up. "What a positive attitude your father has," she said to Arch.

"He doesn't just spout that stuff either—he really believes it." She saw the affection in Archer's gaze as his father joked with a neighbor. "He has high standards and expected all of us to work hard at school and life, but you'll never find a man with a bigger heart."

At a signal from Nick, Archer excused himself and left her side.

Betsy Davenport clapped her hands and immediately brought the room to attention. Tessa could see how very much she was respected by everyone, from her children to her friends. But it was the way Howie gazed at his wife that brought a lump to Tessa's throat. To think of being married for that long and still have a man look at you like that. She sighed. Until now, she'd never believed love could last that long. The marriages she'd been exposed to hadn't turned out so well.

Betsy spoke in a voice that commanded the room,

which gave Tessa the notion that she was either a teacher or had been at some point. Behind her, Arch and Nick dragged out a large flat-screen television and some speakers. Howard was encouraged to sit in a chair in the middle of the room facing the speakers, while everybody at the party gathered around him and Buster curled at his feet.

Were they all going to be treated to old family movies? Tessa kind of hoped they would be. It would be fun to see how these Davenports had behaved and what they'd looked like when they were kids.

Instead, Betsy said, "All our children are here with us tonight, except Damien. He's on tour with his band. But, Howie, he wanted you to know he's thinking of you." And then at her nod, the lights went out and the screen came to life.

Tessa knew who Damien Davenport was, of course. The whole world knew. A rock star, a pop idol—she'd heard him called both and wasn't exactly sure which was the correct term.

On the screen, he stood there holding a guitar. He had the curly hair in common with Finn, and he'd also inherited the slightly darker good looks. But there was a devil in that smile. She wondered whether he'd grown into the name or whether his parents had named him Damien with a sneaking suspicion of what his future would be like. Not that he was a bad boy exactly, but he had trodden his own path, that was for sure.

Damien said, "Dad, I wish I could be there with you tonight. But the boys and I want you to know we're thinking of you. I didn't write this song—two men way smarter than me did. But this one's for you." And then he began to play, and behind him, his band struck up.

As the familiar tune filled the room, everyone began to laugh. Damien looked up as though he could hear them, and with a grin, he said, "You may not know all the words, but I bet all of you know the chorus. I'm hoping you'll join in. If you don't, you know my mom will make you." And then they broke into The Beatles's "When I'm Sixty-Four."

Everybody loved it, but nobody more so than Howard. He clapped and laughed and sang along with the rest of them. And when it was over, Betsy said, "Now that you're all warmed up, I hope you'll keep on singing." And in walked five of the six Davenport kids, holding a huge cake flaming with sixty-four candles.

Howard took a massive breath and managed to blow out most of them. He took a second breath to get the rest, and then somebody called, "Speech!"

Howard Davenport didn't need to be asked twice. He stood and gazed at them all for a moment. "I look around me and wonder how I got to be sixty-four years old with so much to be thankful for. The road was never what I imagined it would be, but it was always right." He glanced at his wife. "I've been a lucky man—luckier than most, I know. I grew up in a good family, and my five brothers are still my closest friends. But the biggest stroke of luck was meeting Betsy. She was a young professor at Stanford. I was called in to build her some bookshelves. I'll never forget the sight of her, so young and so brilliant. And let's not kid ourselves—she was extremely easy on the eyes." There was a smattering of laughter, even some applause. He grinned at her. "Still is."

Betsy shook her head modestly.

Howie continued, "I'd always loved Carmel-by-the-Sea, but I wasn't sure Betsy would ever want to do more than make weekend trips here, given that her career was two hours away at Stanford. But once we started having children, she wanted to raise them here, and even though I've always felt she sacrificed her own career, we've been so happy. We've been blessed with six amazing, talented, beautiful children. But what I'm most proud of is that they're all fine people too. When I think about gifts, I look at you, my family, and I know you're the greatest gift of all." His voice caught on the last line, and Tessa felt her own eyes fill as he poured his love and genuine emotion into every word.

Betsy was the first to reach him, throwing her arms around him and saying, loud enough that even Tessa could hear her, "I never gave up anything. This was my choice, and I'd make it again and again."

Then all the kids came up, and Howard grabbed each of them in a bear hug. Tessa couldn't hear his words, but she was pretty sure he was saying *I love you* to every one of his children.

Not long afterward, the party started to break up. Conscious that Margaret was still recovering from her injury, Tessa gathered her employer's coat and the beaded handbag, not giving her much chance to argue. The silver-haired man who'd been sitting beside her helped her into one sleeve of the coat, then carefully settled the other side over her shoulder.

"That'll do, Carl—I'm not an invalid," Margaret snapped, but there was affection there too.

As they left, Tessa thought she'd never enjoyed a birthday party more. She'd arrived feeling like a stranger and left feeling like they had accepted her into their group of friends. As Howie had said, it was a gift.

It seemed Archer was leaving the party at the same time. Tessa found herself standing very close to him as he hugged his mother good-bye and then his father. "I'll call you from the set," he promised.

"Good luck, son," Howie said.

Mila, who was walking by, stopped. "Dad, don't you know it's bad luck to wish an actor good luck?"

"That's right, I always forget," he said with a light smack to his forehead. "Son, you go out there and break a leg."

As the three of them walked down the path, Archer

offered his arm to Margaret, who seemed thrilled to be escorted by a movie star, even if they had been friends for years. Then he offered his other arm to Tessa. It would have seemed rude not to take it, so she tucked her hand into his elbow, enjoying his warmth and the strength in his arm.

Buster the shaggy dog decided to tag along with them, so it was quite the entourage.

Archer led them to the car and helped Margaret inside. Then he opened Tessa's door for her. When was the last time a man had opened a car door for her? It must have been years.

He looked at her with such sudden intensity that she felt a quiver of longing shudder through her. He leaned forward and kissed her cheek. "Great meeting you. I hope to see you again next time I'm in town."

"I'd like that," she managed.

As she got into the car and he shut the door, the twelve-year-old deep inside thought she might never wash that cheek again.

Chapter Four

Arch was back on set in Death Valley before he'd even had time to reflect on how restful his weekend at home had been. Every time he visited Carmel, he felt the hold it had on his heart. There was nowhere like home and no one like his family.

Plus, there was something about Tessa Taylor that he couldn't stop thinking about. Not only was she gorgeous, but her kindness and gentle capability also shone through her beauty like a sunbeam. Since the night of his dad's birthday party, his mind kept flashing back to the tangible bond between Tessa and Margaret. How Tessa had managed to tame her feisty client and make a friend, too, was impressive.

What's more, the sparks between him and Tessa at the party had been undeniable. He remembered her blush when he'd held her gaze and a wave of electricity had raced through him.

He swallowed, trying to get a grip on himself. Especially now that he was worlds away in the desert, with an entire film crew waiting on him. Shooting for the buddy Western remake was running behind schedule, and everyone was showing symptoms of stress. What's more, they'd saved a tough stunt on a horse until the end of the shoot, and the crew was clearly on edge.

Arch didn't see what all the fuss was about. He liked to do his own stunts. It was one of the things that set him apart from some of the other Hollywood action stars, and he jumped at any opportunity to learn a new skill or try out a tricky sequence. But something about this particular stunt had the crew in knots, not least the stunt director. His name was Jesse Monroe, a seasoned director with a string of hit action movies under his belt and a reputation for running a tight ship.

Arch had been riding since he was a boy and was as comfortable in the saddle as he was driving his sports car, or riding the waves on his surfboard. But Jesse was still pushing for a stunt double, even though they needed to get this shot in the can. Arch figured a lot was riding on this movie and maybe Jesse was cracking under the pressure.

Jesse crossed the set, shielding his eyes from the harsh sun. He was short, with a weatherbeaten brow, but his wide shoulders and bold stance gave him a cocky air that he wore like a second skin.

"Are we ready to roll?" Arch understood that time was money, especially in the movie business.

"Frankly, I think this stunt is too difficult for you,"

Jesse said bluntly, the desert reflected in his Ray-Bans. He shook his head as if anticipating Arch's response. "I know you're going to argue with me, but I've got a stunt rider ready to go."

It was all Arch could do to stop his jaw from falling open. *Too difficult?* He'd been doing his own stunts for years. He had all the necessary experience.

He hitched up his jeans, hooking his thumbs through the belt loops and drawing himself up to his full height, easily channeling the devil-may-care attitude of his cowboy character. It was hot, hard work in full Western garb.

The tone of Jesse's voice had hit a nerve deep inside him, and he remembered being a young boy, held back by his mom while his older brothers went off together on big-kid expeditions. *It's too hard for you* seemed to echo in his head.

But he wasn't little Archie anymore. He was Archer Davenport. And anyone saying something was too difficult for him made him doubly determined to prove them wrong.

"I know my limits," he told Jesse, "and this stunt isn't anywhere close." He raised his stubbled jaw and set his lips in a firm line. "I've never had a problem with a horse before."

Jesse inched forward, asserting himself. "There's a first time for everything," he said. "I'm in the business of calculated risks, and I'm telling you this one isn't worth it. That leap across the river is too much."

Arch searched for his longtime friend and co-lead, Smith Sullivan. Smith knew Arch better than anyone else here. He might be older, but the two of them had a natural friendship that ran much deeper than most of the other Hollywood relationships Arch had formed during his years in the limelight. Smith would back him up.

As if sensing the need for support, Smith Sullivan made his way over to the two men, the heavy thunk of his boots audible on the dusty ground. Smith's dark eyes turned to Arch, silently asking what was going on. His strong jaw was covered with the stubble the director wanted for them.

But to Arch's dismay, Smith didn't look fully sold on the idea as Arch explained his decision to go ahead with the stunt.

"Are you sure about this?" he asked. Beads of sweat gathered at Smith's temples, and he wiped them away with the back of his hand.

Arch was disappointed that Smith also thought this stunt might be beyond him. But then, Smith had written, starred in, directed, and produced his last film. No doubt that was making him hesitate. If anything, the doubt coming from all corners made Arch all the more determined. In the movie, his character was the doer; Smith's was the thinker. It was time to live up to his character.

"Hell, yeah, I can do it. Just watch me."

Jesse looked to Smith for his reaction, and the older actor gave a brief nod. Arch knew Smith respected his abilities, and he was determined not to let him or the movie down.

Arch tipped his hat and made for his horse, a beautiful brown stallion named Bracing Bill with impressive muscles that rippled as he galloped. Though the horse was known to be highly strung, Arch and Bracing Bill had bonded during filming. He was pretty sure they respected each other. Apart from a couple of minor mishaps, they'd worked well together—a fact that made Arch more than a little proud.

He stroked his faithful companion. "You love to run, don't you, my friend?"

Bracing Bill leaned into his touch, and Arch murmured encouraging words, preparing them both for the task ahead. He'd always been good with animals. And it gave him a well-founded confidence the others didn't seem to share. He whispered to the horse for a few minutes, until everything was ready.

After the makeup artist did a final touch-up, he felt the familiar surge of excitement as he contemplated the challenge of the scene ahead. The rest of the cast and crew swung into action around him.

Last-minute costume and sound checks over, he placed one boot in the stirrup and mounted, comfortable in the saddle's smooth, worn leather. The stunt involved riding his horse hard across the desert and jumping a river, pursued by lawmen. Arch bent low to whisper again into the horse's ear. "This is it, buddy. Let's show them everything we've got."

He settled himself. Straightened his back and pulled down the wide brim of his hat to shield his eyes. Then he nodded.

When the director called, "Action!" Arch went for it—one take. With only a nudge to the flanks, the horse took off.

Hot wind blew in Arch's face, and the sheer speed of the animal sent his heart thudding pleasurably in his chest. He felt completely alive on the back of the horse, keeping rhythm with Bracing Bill's elegant stride. He might be surrounded by people with several camera lenses trained on his every move, but he was able to tune everyone, everything out. Nothing existed except him and the horse riding in unison, the glare of the sun, the glimmer of the river ahead.

Smith was waiting for him on the other side. Arch could just make out his friend's broad silhouette astride his horse. The leap over the water was the trickiest part of the stunt, but the rest of the scene was simple. Once the river was behind him, the two cowboys would lead the lawmen in different directions and get them hopelessly lost before meeting back at the old farmhouse.

As he reached the river's edge, he and the horse

were one. This was what he was born to do.

He could feel Bracing Bill gathering speed, ready to propel them both across the water. They were going to nail this stunt in a single take, even though Jesse and Smith had thought the horse too nervous.

Inwardly, he smiled. Outwardly, he gritted his teeth and let his eyes close to a squint against the sun. The horse reared up, ready to make the leap. It was poetry in motion.

Then a sudden boom crashed across the ravine.

Arch knew that sound. Prop dynamite. Loud, convincing, and thoroughly unnerving. Particularly for a horse.

Time slowed as Arch felt the horse spook beneath him and then stumble. They were going down. And fast. There was no guarantee Arch wouldn't end up crushed beneath the beast.

He had to act.

As the horse lost his footing, Arch propelled his body through the air, determined to make it across the water. He could see the other bank—so close—his hat flew clean off his head. Just as he thought he was nimble enough to clear it, something held him back.

His boot. Caught in the stirrup.

Time whirled back to normal speed, and before he knew what was happening, he was on the ground, his leg pinned under the horse. He heard an ominous crack.

Shock coursed through Arch's body. No pain yet—

With a panicked whinny, Bracing Bill rolled to his feet, away from Arch. At least the horse had emerged from the fiasco unscathed.

Unfortunately, Archer couldn't say the same.

Closing his eyes, Arch saw stars. The pain struck, lightning hot.

He lay there, stunned, then felt a rough hand on his shoulder. "You okay there, buddy? That was some fall."

Smith.

Arch tried to speak, but his throat was dry. What had happened?

He lifted his head, winced with pain.

"Easy now," Smith said gently.

Arch struggled to get up and fell back. He swallowed. "Is the horse okay?"

"The horse is fine," Smith said. "In a hell of a lot better shape than you."

Arch turned his head and saw Bracing Bill had trotted back toward his trainer. The horse was clearly okay, if a bit shocked.

Smith picked up Arch's cowboy hat, flattened by the horse. "Dude, this could have been you. I thought for a minute this buddy movie was going to end up short one buddy." Though Smith spoke lightly, Arch knew his friend was dead serious.

The director called, "Cut!"

Arch felt the surprise ripple through his pain-ridden body. The cameras were still rolling? As if the moment couldn't get worse, he now knew his failure had been caught on film.

But any thoughts of the movie faded as the medics appeared at his side. Smith stepped out of the way. Arch gritted his teeth as the doctor examined him. When the doctor's sturdy hands pressed against his shin, he let out a yelp of pain.

"The bad news is you've broken your leg," the doctor said. "The good news is it looks like a clean break of the tibia. I'll splint it for now, but you just bought yourself a helicopter ride to the hospital."

★ ★ ★

When Arch woke, it was to an all-white room and a brightness that felt unnatural. It took a few moments before it all came flooding back. The loud boom. The spooked horse. And then the *crack* as his leg snapped. He blinked a few times, eyes adjusting to the light made of an unearthly blend of hospital halogen and afternoon sun. He looked down at his legs. There was a thick cast on his left leg beneath the flimsy sheet. His broken leg felt both heavy and absent at the same time. The pain, though—that was objectively bad. He breathed deeply, desperate for a cool glass of water.

Just then, the film's director, Martin Miller, rushed into the room.

"There's my hero," he cried.

For a director who'd just lost one of his leads, he looked pretty jubilant. After the necessary inquiries about how Arch was feeling, Martin let him know why. "We captured it all on film. You never slipped out of character. And then Smith rushed in—he got to you first. You tried to get up, couldn't. He showed you the smashed hat. It was a stroke of genius. We can use most of it in the movie. We couldn't have written the scene any better than what actually happened out there."

Arch's head felt fuzzy as he tried to follow the excitable Martin's words.

"It's a quick rewrite of the end," he continued. "I'm already working with the screenwriter. Your character's leg is broken. You're in bed, with a gorgeous woman taking care of you. We've even got the last line. Smith looks at you being waited on hand and foot and says, 'Some guys get all the breaks.'"

It was the corniest line Arch had ever heard, and he had to stifle a groan, but if his director was happy and not yelling at him for ruining his expensive movie, Arch could live with that.

Martin patted him on the shoulder, and Arch tried not to wince. "Where am I?"

"Hospital. You were airlifted to Los Angeles."

Arch didn't remember any of it. The drugs the doc on set had given him had definitely worked.

"Get some rest, cowboy," he said, "and we'll call you back to film that last scene or two in a couple of weeks."

Arch watched him leave, shaking his head as Martin chuckled and murmured to himself, "Some guys get all the breaks."

Chapter Five

Back home on Scenic Drive, Arch was in a rotten mood. While on set in Death Valley, he'd bemoaned having to leave Carmel-by-the-Sea. But now that he was back in the town he'd always loved so much, he was cranky. Not even the unspoiled view of the ocean could raise his spirits.

His home was a peaceful retreat, designed around the view, which made the ocean feel close enough to touch. Clean lines, neutral colors, and tiled floors gave it a laid-back vibe that usually bred calm and creativity.

But right now he didn't feel calm. Or creative. He shifted his weight in the huge leather armchair he'd set up in the open-plan living area to admire the view. His left leg was elevated, but he couldn't get comfortable. His skin itched and his muscles throbbed. And to make things worse, his agent was telling him off. Julius Malone ("Call me Jay") was one of the top agents in Hollywood, and Arch owed him a lot. Still, it was no fun being on the receiving end of a tongue-lashing.

"You could have been killed." Jay shook his head.

He'd been Archer's agent since the beginning of his career and was one of the most powerful players in the business. He could make or break an actor's career with a simple nod of his balding head, which he kept close-shaved. He looked more like a tough character actor than a wheeler-dealer. Jay *was* tough, but he was also shrewd, and there was a whole lot of warmth in his steely gray eyes—you just had to know where to look for it. Most important, Jay was trustworthy. A quality often hard to come by in Hollywood.

Arch knew he'd taken a risk performing the stunt himself, but it had been a calculated risk. He frowned and said, "I had it. The stunt was going perfectly. We were about to jump. It's not me you should be yelling at, it's the fools who let off the dynamite early and spooked the horse. The exact same thing would have happened to the stunt double."

Arch shifted again in his seat as he waited for Jay to respond. He didn't want to admit to himself—or anyone else—how close he'd come to serious injury. If the horse had fallen just an inch or two in either direction…

But he wasn't going to dwell on the what-ifs. He'd been able to throw himself almost clear, and he was lucky he'd suffered no more than a broken leg. All Arch needed was a little time to recuperate, and then he'd be back on his feet and a hundred percent again.

Jay folded his arms, and the gold cufflinks on his

crisp white shirt caught the light. "The stunt double can be replaced. The star of the movie not so much. You knew better, and yet, you still made the decision to do the stunt, even though it could have cost you not only the entire movie, but your life, as well."

Jay was right. Deep down, Arch acknowledged he probably shouldn't have performed the stunt. But he was too stubborn to admit it, even now. Besides, apart from Arch himself, everyone on set was happy about how the whole thing had played out. He told Jay how the director loved it and was currently rewriting the end to fit the new direction.

But Jay wasn't impressed. "Yeah, I heard. They want you back in six weeks to film the final scenes. And, probably so you don't do something stupid before filming resumes, they're hiring you a full-time caretaker. Sorry—care*giver*."

Arch sat up, alarmed—then winced, still not used to his body's new vulnerabilities. "You're kidding, right? I'm not having either one living with me. I'm fine."

Jay didn't even blink. "Great. If you're so *fine*, then get me a glass of water."

Clearly, his agent and friend had come prepared for some pushback. Well, Arch could push back as well. He started to lever himself out of the chair, wincing even as he tried to hide the pain, but Jay immediately placed a firm hand on his shoulder to keep him down.

"Don't be a fool, Arch," he said, shaking his head. "You don't have anything to prove. And you need the help. Otherwise, how are you going to manage doing even the simplest things, like getting a glass of water?"

"My family will help." Obviously. His mom and dad were close enough to come over every day if it was really necessary. And his siblings too. That was what family were for, right? He said as much to Jay, but it was like talking to a brick wall. Jay was adamant that they should follow the studio's instructions.

"I don't want to risk another setback," Jay said, taking a seat on the sofa. "It's not just about you, Arch. This movie is too big, too important, for your ego to get in the way."

"My ego?" Arch echoed. "This isn't about my ego. This is about the studio wasting money on something I don't need."

Jay scoffed. "Since when do you care about the studio's budget?" His voice was low and rough.

Arch swallowed. He had a point. The studio was spending millions on this highly anticipated Western remake; what was a caregiver's wage for a few weeks? He changed tack. "Okay, then, it's about my privacy. Carmel is my home. I'm pretty much left alone when I'm here. I like it that way. I want to protect this space."

Jay fell quiet. Their relationship was such that he knew Arch was earnest about protecting his privacy. It was something all his clients wanted, but usually couldn't manage.

Arch watched him thinking things through and thought he'd won the argument until Jay finally said, "I understand. You know I do. But too much is riding on this. Filming is already behind schedule—the crew have to move on to other projects. It's in your best interest to comply."

Jay would always protect his best interests. But a huge part of his job was negotiation. He was a pro at keeping relations between film studios and movie stars mutually beneficial and knew all the right things to say to both—even if they were the opposite things at the same time.

Arch scratched at his cast distractedly. He wasn't used to being immobile. If he was honest with himself, he also wasn't used to not getting his own way. "I don't care what the studio and the producers think," he said. "It's not their life we're talking about. They can't control everything."

Jay sighed. "It's not about control."

"Sure sounds like it from where I'm standing." He looked down. "Sitting."

Jay lowered his voice to a dangerously even tone. "Arch, this is a question of good faith. They need to know you're going to be able to finish their film on time."

Arch stayed silent. He was good at that. When he

was younger, it seemed like all his siblings got their way by shouting the loudest. Not Arch. When he needed to make a point, he fell silent. And stayed that way. For as long as it took. In that sense, he had infinite patience. Or stubbornness, depending on how you looked at it.

The silence stretched between the two men. Arch watched the ocean, the foam of the waves as they crested and then fell away. There were a few surfers bobbing around like seals, waiting for the next ride. He took a few deep breaths, in and out, and tried to ignore the impulse to stick something inside the cast and scratch his leg.

But Jay was wise to all of Arch's moves. They'd known each other too long, been through too much. No amount of the silent treatment could shake him.

"To be honest," Jay said, leaning even farther forward and forcing Arch to meet his eyes, "I can't believe you went for the stunt on that horse in the first place. Doesn't he have a reputation for being nervous? What were you thinking?"

Arch felt heat rise within him. His agent knew that it was in his contract for Arch to do all his own stunts. He'd negotiated it, for heaven's sake. And Arch could have performed that stunt. Why was he the only one who could see this? How many times did he have to explain it? "It would have been fine if the horse hadn't been spooked by faulty props. I almost cleared the river."

"Okay, let's agree that you almost cleared it. Let's also agree that you almost died when you *didn't* clear it."

How easily Jay had gotten him to break his silence. They really had known each other too long. He scowled. "The director loves the new footage," he reminded Jay.

"Sure he does." Jay nodded, finally sitting back in his seat. "At least you and Smith stayed in character. They're cutting out Smith's last line, ending the scene where he shows you the flattened hat and reminds everybody, including you, that you could have been killed."

Arch leaned forward and then immediately groaned. His leg ached unbearably. "Wait, you've already seen the rushes?"

Jay didn't grin, but came as close to a smile as he'd managed all morning. "I'm not happy I nearly lost one of my best clients, but I'm not going to lie and say it isn't a great scene."

Arch was relieved. Jay's taste never wavered. It was good, it was instinctive, it was dependable.

Nonetheless, Arch was not to be distracted from the point at hand. "That's great news. But I'm still not having a caregiver coming into my private sanctum to baby me."

Jay shook his head. Arch couldn't tell if he'd won

this battle or not. He waited for a sign. But if Jay was going to concede, he wasn't about to admit it. "If you hadn't aggravated me so much, Arch, I would already have told you the other reason for my visit. I actually came with good news."

Arch smiled. "Go ahead. Clearly, I could use some good news."

"You've been offered the lead in a huge action movie that starts shooting in ten weeks. It's going to be *major*, with a paycheck to match. It's called *Shock Tactics*."

Now that *was* great news. Their petty disagreement about an in-home caregiver disappeared. "Seriously? The futuristic action-hero pic?" He'd heard something about *Shock Tactics*, but he'd been too busy shooting the buddy movie with Smith Sullivan to think about it too much.

"That's right. You can be the next big action hero with no audition and a huge paycheck. Or you can be the hero in the nice little romantic comedy you've also been offered, where you can sit down for most of it. If you're not going to do everything you can to heal properly, maybe we should take the rom-com offer." Jay paused a beat. Then two. Finally, he shrugged and said, "Unless you're willing to have a live-in caregiver for a few weeks. Up to you."

And that was it. Jay had played his power card. Arch had to hand it to him—the man knew how to strike a deal. Obviously, Arch wanted the action movie. If it went well, it could be the beginning of something huge. He knew how important these franchises were. The news that he'd been offered an action role somewhat mollified him, but he was still really unhappy about the idea of being stuck in a cast with a caregiver helping him get around inside his own home.

Giving Arch a few moments to think things through, his agent got up and went to the window. "I sure love this view. Must be one of the finest in the world." Then he grinned over his shoulder at Arch. "You keep doing the big movies I get for you and with the money I make off you, I might buy one myself."

Arch laughed. Jay had already made plenty of money from his string of A-listers. Peace had been made between them. And he had to admit, life was always better when it was peaceful.

While Jay turned back to take in the view once more, Arch suddenly had a brilliant idea. Now that he'd thought of it, he couldn't believe it had taken him all this time to come up with it. If he had to have a full-time, live-in caregiver, there was only one person he'd consider.

Tessa Taylor.

She'd been on his mind ever since they'd met, and this would be the perfect opportunity to get to know her better. He would just have to think of a way to convince her to split her time between him and

Margaret. He was sure Margaret would thank him, given that she liked being taken care of even less than he did. He smiled to himself, remembering how gorgeous Tessa had looked when they first met on the beach and then again at his dad's birthday party.

The warmth in Tessa's eyes had captivated him. It had been a long time since he'd felt sparks like that. Sparks that fizzed and crackled with all the heat of a late-night campfire.

So he said to Jay, "If I have to have a caregiver, there's only one I want. Her name is Tessa Taylor."

Chapter Six

"You're not ready," Tessa said, placing both hands on her hips to show Margaret she meant business. "I can't leave you."

The two women were in Margaret's kitchen, stubbornly facing each other across the oak table. Between them, a pot of steaming black coffee and a plate of bagels and cream cheese lay untouched. When Tessa's agency had called to say she'd been requested for work elsewhere in Carmel, she'd been surprised, having been scheduled for another week with Margaret. Margaret must have encouraged one of her many male admirers to put in the call. It was just the kind of devious plan her mind was capable of conjuring.

Over the weeks they'd been working together, Tessa had grown genuinely fond of Margaret. Not only did she admire her whip-smart mind and zest for life, but she's also seen her softer side. *The marshmallow in all of us*, Tessa liked to call it. Some people were better at disguising it than others, but deep down, everyone had something soft and squishy about them. Margaret was no different. But she also knew how to put up a fight. She was an inimitable sparring partner.

But then they'd told Tessa the client was Archer Davenport, who had broken his leg while filming. She couldn't have been more surprised, couldn't imagine such a strong, vital man wounded. Her first instinct had been to rush to his side, but then her sense of self-preservation kicked in. Given that she clearly hadn't overcome her embarrassingly big schoolgirl crush on the man, was it really a good idea for her to work with him? Especially given that she wouldn't just be making meals for him. Heck, just getting him up the stairs to his bedroom would involve more touching than she could imagine without feeling hot all over.

Margaret leaned across the table, lifted the coffee-pot, and poured them both a cup. She was dressed as impeccably as ever—chunky silver jewelry around her throat and wrists, white hair swept back off her face. She was fully made up and dressed for the day, no matter if it was only ten o'clock. Tessa had forced her patient through her morning exercises, and a leisurely late breakfast was supposed to be their reward. But now the plate of sliced bagels couldn't have looked less appetizing.

Margaret took a long sip of her coffee, eyeing Tessa the whole time. "I'm so much better now. That horrid cast is off, and I'm doing my exercises. I'm already looking online at walking tours of Ireland."

Tessa let out a great sigh. Would she ever be able to get through to Margaret? *One step at a time* was Tessa's tried and tested motto, but Margaret took that one step and ran with it to a hundred. There was no way she was ready for a walking tour of Ireland. It was true she had made remarkable progress given her years, but grit would only get you so far.

"You can't rush healing," Tessa said gently.

The change of tone did the trick. Margaret's sparkling eyes softened. She reached for a sliced bagel and placed it delicately on her floral china plate. "The agency called me to check that I no longer needed you. I said you've done a marvelous job and I now have the energy and agility of my forty-year-old self. Maybe even thirty. My dear, you've helped me heal, but your job here is done. Someone else needs you now."

Tessa rolled her eyes. "Flattery will get you nowhere."

But Margaret was not to be swayed. "Working for Archer Davenport will be the perfect next job for you. You can stay in Carmel, so I'll be able to see you when I'm in town. I'll let you give me a little check-up every now and then, just to prove how well I'm doing." Margaret bit into her bagel, clearly pleased with herself. After she swallowed, she said, "I'm going to miss you, but it's time for you to move on. Arch called me personally last night to make sure that I could manage without you and that you were the kind of person he could work with. I gave you a glowing reference."

Tessa's eyebrows shot up. *The kind of person a movie star could work with.* Who was that, exactly? Tessa had grown accustomed to spotting a few movie stars and celebrities during her time in Carmel, but she wasn't exactly used to the limelight. Or helping them put on their shoes.

What would Archer Davenport be like as a boss? From their brief meetings, he'd seemed about as down-to-earth as someone that good-looking and famous could be. She recalled the way he'd chivalrously opened the car door for her as she left his father's party. How he'd leaned in so casually to kiss her cheek, with no idea of the effect he'd had on her.

Just thinking about it sent a quiver of longing through her. But it was quickly followed by another stab of concern. All she currently knew about his injury was that he'd broken his tibia doing a stunt. Whether it was a clean break, or shattered in a more complicated fashion, she'd yet to find out. Either way, he was going to need some intensive physical therapy to get him back on set. The problem was that Tessa wasn't sure her mind could remain clear—or clean—enough to be that therapist. Just the thought of Archer Davenport made her tremble with desire that wasn't the least bit professional.

Tessa realized Margaret was still waiting for her to

respond. "I'm not convinced you're fully healed," she said, taking a sip of her coffee.

Margaret made a clucking sound. "I'm out of my cast and doing my daily exercises."

"Which I have to nag you about every day," Tessa reminded her. "Goodness knows what bad habits you'll fall into without me around to annoy you." Tessa flashed her best cheeky smile.

But her winsome grin was lost on Margaret. "You're not giving up the chance to shack up with a movie star to keep me company, which we both know is all you're doing at this point." She paused and gave Tessa an inquiring look. "Most women would jump at the opportunity to work with Archer Davenport. What's stopping you?"

Tessa blushed. Trust Margaret to call her out. But it wasn't like she could articulate the sense of unease that weighed heavily on her chest. "I've seen his movies. He's so alpha. What if he won't listen to me?" She left out the bit about how he made her feel weak in the knees… and how a childhood crush on a big star could never end well for a normal woman like her.

Margaret laughed and unconsciously smoothed her glossy chignon, though not a hair was out of place. She'd finished one bagel slice and was already halfway through another. At least she had her appetite back. Maybe Margaret was doing better than she'd thought.

"If you can make *me* listen to you, Archer Davenport will be a piece of cake. Believe me. I've known him since he was a boy. You won't find a sweeter nature." Margaret smiled devilishly. "Plus, I daresay he's a lot easier on the eyes than I am."

Tessa shook her head, although she couldn't quite conceal a little smile as she said, "Can't say I noticed."

"You're not fooling me," Margaret replied. "I saw the way he looked at you when we were at the party. He spent most of the evening with you. There was definitely a twinkle in his eyes."

Tessa blinked hard. What was Margaret suggesting?

Okay, so Archer had been kind enough to show her around his family home, but she was an outsider, and he had simply been a good host. Rather than continue to deflect Margaret's insistence, she changed tack. "I'm surprised you had time to notice anything while you fended off your many admirers." She grinned, recalling how the older gentlemen had swarmed around Margaret, fighting over who would fetch her a plate of food. But Margaret was impervious to flattery. She had enough inner confidence for them both.

Despite the churning in her stomach, Tessa reached for a bagel—more for distraction than out of hunger. But Margaret wasn't to be swayed. She tapped her French tips on the table, waiting for a response. Patience wasn't one of Margaret's virtues.

Tessa said, "You and I both know he was being

nice, that's all. There was no twinkle. He's a movie star. His last girlfriend was Sonia Montefiore, for heaven's sake. She was voted the most beautiful woman in the world by *People* magazine."

But Margaret simply huffed, as if to say, *What does a little beauty poll have to do with anything?* "The twinkle in that man's eyes was undeniable. I've been around for over eighty years, and I've never been wrong about a twinkle." She flashed Tessa a charming twinkle of her own before her voice softened. "Even though you like to play it down, Tessa, you're a beautiful young woman, and there is no way that boy could miss it."

Margaret's words were meant to soothe her, she knew, but they had the opposite effect. Tessa's heart began to beat double time, and she set the bagel back on the plate. Of course, she felt drawn to Archer, too, so to have Margaret suggest the feeling was reciprocal was almost too much to hope.

They fell silent for a moment, a comfortable silence between two people who'd learned how to live with each other peaceably over several weeks. Tessa finally bit into the bagel and chewed thoughtfully. How was she going to get out of this situation without offending anyone?

But despite Tessa not speaking any of her thoughts aloud, Margaret seemed to catch some of her feelings, which must be written all over her face. "Archer Davenport is a real gentleman. He takes after Howie. I am absolutely positive he would never do anything to make you feel uncomfortable. In any way. And his enormous family keep him as down-to-earth as they come."

Tessa would have loved to get a word in edgewise, but Margaret was on a roll. She couldn't decide if Margaret was intent on getting rid of her or playing Cupid. Maybe it was both. But clearly she was concerned that Tessa not be blinded by his movie-star good looks.

"Don't get me started on all that nonsense you read in the tabloids about Arch and Sonia Montefiore. You heard him on the beach—they never were a couple. It was just Hollywood hype. Those magazines love to speculate on A-list romances because it sells copies. But *I* saw the way he looked at her outside of the love scenes, and not only was there not a twinkle in sight, it was the opposite of love."

Margaret was still trying to reassure her, but it was hopeless. Tessa's worst fear was to make a fool of herself by falling head over heels for a man she could never have. Archer Davenport was her celebrity crush, not her patient or even her employer. Twinkle or not, they lived in completely different worlds.

She looked down at her watch and found that her fingers were worrying at the leather strap. Alarm bells were going off inside her. She had made a promise to herself never to be with a man who made her feel small. Never again. Arch was literally larger than life. She was used to seeing his handsome face on giant movie theater screens and billboards. He was a star and she was a caregiver. It was no match at all.

Margaret sat back in her chair, clearly satisfied that she'd won the argument and the conversation was over. But Tessa would go into the agency this afternoon and speak to her manager personally. She'd come up with a good reason why she couldn't take the job and ask to be placed elsewhere.

Then this whole issue would go away.

* * *

It wasn't a long drive to Monterey, where the agency she worked for was located, but Tessa still tried to enjoy the views. After all, it might be the last time she could soak up the gorgeous scenic coast. She would miss the beach, that much was certain, with its golden sand and dreamy, flaming orange sunsets.

When she arrived at Helping Hands, the receptionist said that Nina Patel was just finishing a meeting and would be with her shortly. Nina was the owner of the agency, and Tessa had never met her; they had only spoken on the phone before today. Tessa took a seat on the leather couch and waited nervously, feeling like she was in a hospital waiting room. It was a relief when the receptionist finally called her name, and she made her way along a magnolia-painted corridor to Nina's office.

Nina Patel was a formidable-looking woman in her fifties, smartly dressed in a gray skirt suit and pearls. She greeted Tessa warmly, offering her a seat and a glass of water, which Tessa took gladly.

"Congratulations on bringing such a great client to the agency," Nina said. "I understand Mr. Davenport asked for you personally, having witnessed how good you were with your current client, Margaret Percy. We're very pleased with your excellent work. There will be an NDA to sign, of course, to protect Mr. Davenport from the press."

Wait—what? Tessa felt the first stirrings of panic. She hadn't even accepted the job, but everyone around her was acting like it was not only a done deal, but that it was the best thing that had ever happened too.

She cleared her throat. "I'm flattered, of course, that Mr. Davenport thinks I would make a good live-in caregiver as he recovers from his injury, but I imagine you have someone else on your books who would be better suited to the position—someone with celebrity experience?"

Nina's brow furrowed. "The client has requested you personally. Who could be better?"

Tessa swallowed. She had to think fast. And then she remembered—she'd had a request last month to help a mother with a newborn. She reminded Nina that once her time with Margaret Percy was over, she was supposed to go to Los Gatos, a town ninety minutes north of Carmel.

Nina frowned again, and even before she spoke, Tessa felt like she was back in school about to receive a lecture from a disapproving teacher. "Mr. Davenport understands how valuable you are as one of our best caregivers," she said. "That's why he offered a higher salary to compensate. This will be a lucrative assignment for you. We've already found someone for the Los Gatos job. No need to worry about that." Nina paused and said, "And of course you'll receive a finder's fee for bringing Mr. Davenport to our firm."

Tessa's heart pounded. Everything was moving so quickly. And yet—a higher salary was a tempting offer. Plus a bonus? She needed the money. When it came down to it, Tessa didn't care where she lived or what she wore. She had very few possessions and enjoyed life that way. There was only one thing that was truly important to her. Only one thing that she lived for.

Her art.

No one in Tessa's life knew that she spent every minute of her free time painting and went without luxuries in order to buy professional-quality paints and brushes. She knew she wasn't very good, but she was determined to keep going and get better—even if it was all in secret. She'd fantasized about a weeklong workshop in Santa Fe with Mylene Fraser, her idol. It cost three thousand dollars… a sum that until this moment had been out of her reach.

She could sense Nina growing impatient.

"If you're really averse to such a good proposition, Tessa," Nina said, all the warmth vanishing from her voice, "then I can't imagine what better opportunity we'd be able to offer you here at Helping Hands."

Tessa understood. Her fate had already been sealed by the agency. If she wanted to feed her passion, she would have to follow the money. "Of course. I'm happy to accept the position."

Nina was all smiles again. "Excellent. I'll just get you to sign the paperwork, and you'll start with Mr. Davenport this afternoon."

So soon?

Then again, what was the point in putting off the inevitable? Fate, a horse, and Margaret Percy had somehow conspired to put her in Archer Davenport's home. What could she do but follow the path she'd been shoved onto?

She shook Nina's hand and told her she'd head back to Margaret's house to pack her few possessions. She'd traveled around so much these past few years that she was a pro at packing. All it took was one suitcase with clothes and toiletries and a backpack full of art supplies. She'd managed to keep her painting from Margaret's beady eyes and would have to find a suitable spot to hide her easel at Archer's place on Scenic Drive, though she didn't think that would be a problem in a movie star's spacious home.

What was a problem—a *huge* problem—was how her heart thudded as she thought about his blue eyes and wide grin.

No question about it, she would have to keep a tight rein on her feelings if she was going to survive living with the heartthrob of her dreams.

Chapter Seven

Tessa parked her twenty-year-old SUV in the driveway and switched off the engine. She didn't move. She couldn't.

A stone's throw from the beach, Archer Davenport's house was even more fabulous than she'd imagined. In the years she'd been a caregiver, Tessa had been used to visiting, and living in, all kinds of houses, from modest to grand. Her job had taken her far and wide, and she'd thought she'd lost her greenness when it came to spectacular homes. And yet, coming from Margaret's historic fairy-tale cottage, this place was a modern masterpiece of glass and sharp angles. Its crisp white paint practically sparkled in the sun.

She recalled Margaret saying it had its own screening room and was one of the few houses in town that had a gym and indoor swimming pool in the basement. The kind of luxury Tessa still had a hard time imagining. She took several deep breaths, trying to convince herself that this was just a job like any other.

She got out of the car, still trying to slow her racing heart, and took her two bags from the back. The front door was built like Fort Knox, an intimidating dark gray with a series of security cameras around the buzzer that immediately made her feel self-conscious, and an electronic keypad.

She smoothed back tendrils of her long hair, which was tied in its usual ponytail. She wore jeans and her white uniform shirt and jacket, her name stitched across the breast in royal blue. Should she have dressed smarter? But no, if Archer Davenport wanted her to be his caregiver, then he was going to have to take her as she was.

She swallowed again, avoiding the eye of the camera. It was to be expected, she supposed, that a movie star would place a premium on privacy. She thought back to their first meeting on the beach, when she'd been out walking with Margaret. It had taken, what, two or three minutes before their conversation had been interrupted by those young fans? She couldn't imagine what it must be like to lose your anonymity so completely.

Setting her bags on the step, she took another deep breath and pressed the buzzer.

To her surprise, the door swung open seemingly of its own accord.

And up there was Archer Davenport, a sheepish expression on his face, sitting in the middle of a grand staircase, his crutches in a heap on the tiled floor below.

Tessa gasped and raced over to the stairs. "What happened?"

Archer's cheeks turned slightly red. It was totally unexpected, and completely adorable. "Looks like you arrived just in time," he said, half grinning, half grimacing. "I needed something upstairs, but lost my balance."

She gave him her most reassuring smile in return, trying not to gaze too intently into his deep-blue eyes. Archer tried to stand, but she stopped him. "No, hold on to me. Don't put any weight on that leg." She gestured at his cast.

Archer scratched at his sun-streaked hair. "I don't want to sound patronizing," he said carefully, "but are you going to be able to take my weight?"

Tessa reached for him. "If I couldn't, you would have made a real mistake in hiring me. Fortunately for both of us, I'm stronger than I look."

She slipped easily into caregiver mode, carefully maneuvering Archer until he reached the bottom of the stairs. She handed him his crutches, and he made his way to a big leather recliner in front of the bay window.

As soon as she'd seen him stuck on the staircase, it was amazing how quickly she'd forgotten that she'd seen every film Archer Davenport had ever made.

Then again, since her heart was still racing, maybe she was just fooling herself that she was ready to deal with him as anything but a massive movie star.

"Glad you got here when you did," he said. "I guess I need help more than I thought."

With relief, she noted how good-humored he was. Or maybe, after weeks of living with Margaret, she was just used to more resistance.

Tessa couldn't help but notice how strong he was and how good he smelled. He smelled like summers in Italy… or at least what she imagined summer in Italy would smell like, given that she had never been abroad.

The view of the ocean took her breath away. The blue sky seemed endless, and the beach begged to be walked on. The furniture was minimal and expensive looking. Lots of leather and steel, but comfortable cushions and throws. Several huge, leafy, potted plants softened what could otherwise have been stark. She hoped she'd get a chance to spend time studying the paintings on the walls.

Archer's taste—or his decorator's—was exceptional, and she longed to study each of the priceless artworks that felt as though they'd been chosen for their beauty rather than their investment value. At the same time, his home was definitely straight out of a magazine spread.

The minute she guided Archer into his leather reclining chair by the window, with his broken leg properly elevated, she shook her head at him. "Attempting the stairs without help was a foolish move. What were you thinking?"

Archer blinked at her, clearly shocked. "Nobody speaks to me like that," he said.

Tessa's heart plummeted to her sneakers. Of course no one scolded Archer Davenport: He was a world-famous celebrity. He was used to people asking for his autograph and telling him how good he was at his job. And now here she was, a nobody, telling him off like he was a school kid. With a flash of panic, she realized she was about to be fired from a job she'd barely started. She had no doubt whatsoever that Nina Patel would never work with her again because of all the money she'd lose the agency if Archer sent her packing right this second.

But before she could think of an appropriate apology, Archer broke into a cheeky grin. "Hey, don't look so serious. I kind of like it." His eyes flashed playfully with mischief.

Oh my. Margaret might have been right about that twinkle. Because if Tessa had admitted to alarm bells about this man before, now they were jangling louder than ever. And when he laughed, an infectious, joyful sound, she swore her knees actually went weak. She'd thought that was something you read about in books. But nope, here she was, doing her best to stay upright.

All because of his twinkling eyes and wonderful laughter.

She tried to calm down. This spark between them was nothing. Archer was a movie star, schooled in the art of flirtation. He probably wasn't even aware that he'd switched on the boyish charm.

But no. The longer she held his gaze, the more she was convinced there might actually be a real connection between them. Because despite her inexperience with dating since her husband, Lewis, had passed away, the attraction was undeniable.

Tessa smiled nervously. Okay, so she wasn't about to be fired. But if she was going to be living here for several weeks, she couldn't let herself fall for this man. It would be bad for her on every level. Which meant she needed to come up with a strategy to keep her heart safe.

The first thing would be to look as plain as possible. Wearing her uniform was a good start, and she definitely wouldn't wear any makeup around him—but she also made a mental note to switch from contact lenses to glasses and to sweep her hair into a practical bun each morning. She'd been told that her hair was her best feature, so it wouldn't do to wear it in a girlish ponytail like she had today. And she certainly wouldn't let the curls cascade down her back, as she'd done at the birthday party.

She composed herself and gave Archer her most

professional smile. "No more going upstairs unsupervised. Promise?"

But he wasn't listening—he was staring at her chest. She looked down in surprise, unable to stop the blush from spreading across her cheeks.

He raised a brow. "Why does your shirt have your name on it?"

She breathed out. He was only reading the embroidery. Of course. It was crazy to think he'd been checking out her curves.

"It looks like a nurse's uniform," he added.

Something inside her firmed up. She was going to have to look past his movie-star good looks and remember her position. "I am here as a professional caregiver," she reminded him. "This is my uniform."

Although the truth that she'd never tell him was that she'd abandoned her uniform while working with Margaret. She had allowed herself to relax and enjoy her company as if she were living with a long-lost aunt. A tough but benevolent long-lost aunt.

But Archer Davenport was no relation, even a pretend one, so Tessa cleared her throat, straightened ever so slightly, and checked her watch. "I understand you're still on pain meds. What's your medication schedule?"

Archer frowned ever so slightly and she wondered if her tone was a little too nurse-like. Well, he would just have to get used to it.

"No. I'm good. But do you have to wear a uniform? I feel like I'm back in the hospital."

"A hospital that took great care of you," she reminded him, before listing a long regime of exercises that would help to heal and rehabilitate not only his leg, but his core and back as well.

This was when she allowed herself to glance at his chest in return. She knew from several of his movies that under that black T-shirt were impressive pecs and tanned, rippling abs. When she looked up at Archer's face, she saw a scowl at her mention of a strict routine.

How did she always end up with the most reluctant clients? Had he thought they were going to be the way they'd been at the party—relaxed—and just spending time in each other's company?

Not on her watch.

Undeterred, she continued, "I'll also be in charge of your nutrition, which is a vital part of your recovery. Are there foods you can't eat due to an allergy? Or that you just don't like?"

She imagined he was used to the Hollywood lifestyle of green juices and sashimi and grain bowls. So she was surprised when he said he wanted comfort foods. "Pizza and spaghetti and ice cream sundaes."

Now it was her turn for her eyebrows to shoot skyward.

He laughed. "I'm supposed to be training for an action movie. They have a production nutritionist to help us prepare. She gave me a meal plan. It's on the sideboard. And unfortunately, there isn't a single pizza or ice cream sundae on it." He made a move to get up to grab it for her, but she shook her head, and he stayed put. "There's a card with the key code, too, in the bowl there."

She went to the sideboard, noting its sleek walnut top, and found the list. As she'd suspected, it recommended a lot of green, leafy vegetables, lean meat, and fresh fish. "This is a very healthy diet."

"Tell me about it," he said sadly. "Like I said, not a fry or a hamburger in sight."

She smiled in sympathy. "Don't worry. I know how boring meals like this can be, so I'll try and make them as tasty as possible. I can work magic with kale, I promise."

He grinned. "I'm willing to believe there's magic in those healing hands of yours."

She blushed, flustered for a moment. So much for staying professional.

"Anyway," he continued, "it's only ten weeks. I can put up with eating super healthy for that long."

"Ten weeks?" she repeated, confused.

When he explained that shooting on his next film started in ten weeks, she couldn't keep the shock out of her voice. "But a fractured tibia takes *four months* to heal."

He shrugged, unfazed. Clearly, he was used to getting his own way. "Well, this one is going to take ten weeks."

She took a deep breath. She was good at her job, but she wasn't a miracle worker. "Then you'd better do all your exercises and follow the doctor's orders. And mine."

She grabbed a pen and added a few items to the nutritionist's list before telling Archer her first job would be to buy groceries. Then she could set about designing a meal-prep schedule for the week.

Again, she couldn't help but notice he looked disappointed.

"Okay," he said. "But before you leave, would you mind changing out of your uniform top? I never know when photographers are staking out the house, and I don't want anyone to know I'm stuck at home with a broken leg." He paused, a playful look returning to his face. "Besides, like I said before, it makes me feel like an invalid. Your regular clothes will be just fine."

There went her plan to make herself look more professional and plain. But she agreed to change into a different shirt to go shopping. Privately, she decided to wear her uniform most of the time when she was in his house, to remind them both that she was his paid caregiver.

"I'll just grab my luggage and take it to my room before I head out."

Again, Archer made a move to get up.

"No, you stay right where you are," she said. "I can handle my luggage on my own—and certainly better than you could right now."

She could see he was struggling with not being able to help. Having met both of his parents, she could guess that Archer was an old-fashioned guy and no doubt considered it his duty to help carry heavy luggage. It could be more difficult for men who saw themselves as the chivalrous type to allow other people to come to their aid. But she'd have to show him she was perfectly capable of doing it herself, even if privately she thought the attempt was sweet.

"I've moved my bedroom to the ground floor," Archer said. "There's a guest bedroom next to mine. You can set up in there. It's very comfortable."

She blinked at him. Share a bedroom wall? *No way.* If she was going to keep things professional, she'd have to sleep as far away from Archer as possible. She couldn't spend her nights lying awake, imagining she could hear him. "Are there any bedrooms on the upper floor?"

His expression turned petulant, and her stomach flipped as she noted the adorable way his bottom lip jutted out.

He shrugged. "There's two. But what if I need you in the night?"

She swallowed as the words *need you in the night* immediately turned into a sexy scene inside her head.

She really needed to stop thinking about him this way! "If you need me, call my cell, any time, day or night."

With that, she excused herself and hauled her bags upstairs. She nearly gasped with pleasure when she reached the upper floor. The floor-to-ceiling windows showed off Carmel's glorious beach, with dozens of happy dogs running around, playing with one another, and bounding in the surf while their owners looked on with smiles. Facing the window was a telescope, as well as a comfortable seating area and bookshelves full of books and treasured objects, all of which she'd inspect later, along with the art on the walls. She recognized the work of a couple of artists she followed herself who were becoming famous.

She chose the bedroom with the ocean view, assuming there wouldn't be any other guests staying, and rapidly unpacked her clothing. She set the backpack containing her painting supplies against the wall.

Then she changed into a plain white T-shirt and headed back downstairs. Archer was sitting where she'd left him, reading what looked like a script. "Can I get you anything before I leave?"

He shook his head, but she went to the kitchen—a gorgeous gourmet space that had her fingers itching to start cooking—and poured him a glass of water. She set it beside him with a reminder to drink plenty of fluids, then took the grocery list and the credit card he offered her. He told her to pick up anything she liked to eat as well, which was nice of him.

She paused for a moment in the driveway, studying the house. She couldn't quite believe this was going to be her home for the next ten weeks and Archer Davenport her constant companion.

She was thrilled and apprehensive in equal measure. But she was determined to do her best to bring him back to the peak of health. She was, after all, very good at her job.

And if there was a little flutter in her pulse when they were working close to each other, no one had to know but her.

Chapter Eight

The house felt weirdly silent after Tessa left. But that wasn't the only reason Arch could hear his own heart thumping. When she'd appeared at the door, she'd looked like an angel sent to help him just when he'd needed her most. After he'd gotten over the initial shock of how beautiful she looked and the deep blue of her concerned eyes, the nurse's uniform had snapped him back to attention. There was something surprisingly sexy about it—librarian sexy—and he couldn't help wanting to pull the ponytail band from her hair, shake loose those dark curls, and kiss her senseless.

But instead of his wooing her with his smooth moves, she'd discovered him on his backside, trapped halfway up the stairs. What an embarrassing way to kickstart their working relationship. And since he was currently imprisoned in his lounger with his aching left leg raised, he didn't have much else to do but recall that moment.

Tessa hadn't hesitated, however. Not even for a second. She'd rushed to his side, and with impressive strength considering she was so much smaller than he was, she had helped him back to his chair.

Then, once she knew he was safe and comfortable, she'd told him off. In that moment, she'd been sexy nurse, librarian, and high school gym teacher all rolled into one.

He'd liked her style even as he realized he was *actually* being told off. She wasn't playing the sexy nurse. Not playing at all, in fact. More like a drill sergeant. And the truth was that he'd been impressed she'd had the gumption to speak to him that way. People usually talked to him as though he was special.

But Tessa hadn't. And her confidence in her position as his caregiver had impressed him. It was yet another sexy thing to add to his list….

Jay had sent over the new script for *Shock Tactics*, and Arch wanted to read it through, but before he could reach for the binder containing the script, there was a knock on the front door. It swung open, and he figured Tessa must have forgotten something.

His heart leaped a little, and in a flirty tone, he called, "Miss me already?"

When his mom walked through the door, he cringed.

Betsy Davenport raised one eyebrow, one of her classic mom moves. She was already on to his crush on the new caregiver.

"Just me, Archer," she said, entering the sunny living room with a smile on her face and a grocery bag in her arms. "Sorry to disappoint."

Arch greeted her warmly, but strangely, he *did* feel a sense of disappointment. He loved his mom more than anything, but he was already missing Tessa's eyes and the dark curls he longed to free from her ponytail.

"How are you feeling?" She put down the bag and came to give him a hug.

Arch let himself feel comforted by the familiar scent of his mom's lotion and the tight grip with which she hugged all her children.

"It's not too bad." He didn't want her to worry, but in truth, the leg ached constantly. It hurt far more than he'd let on to anyone. And he planned to keep it that way—otherwise he ran the risk of his family and friends smothering him with offers of help. He appreciated that he had a wonderful circle of people who cared about him, but for the time being, he wouldn't mind some alone time with Tessa. Not to mention the fact that he absolutely *hated* feeling like an invalid. He'd always been strong and able to take care of himself. It still rubbed him the wrong way that he'd managed to get himself injured. If only he'd been a little quicker off the horse, then none of this would have happened.

"I've brought you a fresh batch of oatmeal cookies," his mother said, "still warm from the oven." She gestured at the paper grocery bag. "And a tub of rocky road ice cream. Before you say anything, I *do* know you movie stars are supposed to watch your calories, but a little comfort food won't hurt."

Arch grinned and thanked her. Oatmeal cookies had been his favorite sweet treat as a child, and he was touched. She knew exactly how to comfort him.

"You're not teaching this afternoon, Mom?" he asked as she put the ice cream in the freezer and set about brewing tea.

"I had morning classes," she answered. "My students were quite excitable today. We were reading the Greek tragedy *Antigone*, and, well, let's just say that opinions were divided, and the discussion got heated."

Betsy Davenport had been a brilliant Stanford professor before she moved to Carmel and a quieter life, but she never seemed to regret giving up her highbrow academic career. In fact, she was always happiest when all her six children were home—which she complained wasn't often enough since they all had busy lives and demanding jobs. When she wasn't being the world's best mom, she taught Classics at the community college in Monterey and California State University Monterey. Arch was proud of her and knew that her students adored her.

Betsy set the brewed tea and a plate of cookies on the glass coffee table, shifting it so Arch could reach. Then she paused to gaze out the window. "That view of the ocean. You just can't beat it." She stood watching the waves.

He eyed the cookies hungrily. Just one wouldn't hurt. He'd have to act fast, before Tessa returned to give him another scolding.

"So, how are you really feeling?" His mom took a seat on the leather couch opposite him. "We joked about you breaking a leg at Howie's birthday, but you didn't have to take it so literally." Her blue eyes, which matched Arch's own, twinkled with humor, but he could tell he'd really worried her.

At last, he admitted that his leg hurt quite a bit. He just couldn't keep the truth from his mom, even if that had been his initial plan. "But the real pain is how foolish I feel for messing up the stunt."

His mom squeezed his hand and then gently let it go. There was tenderness in her eyes, but also a firmness to her mouth that meant he was about to get a talking-to. For the second time today. He steeled himself.

His mom took a breath—a rather shaky breath. "Arch, you could have died."

He shook his head. "No, I was fine doing the stunt. It was the prop dynamite that spooked the horse. That's why he went down. I've tried to explain this to everyone, but no one seems to believe me." But instead of calming her, his explanation only seemed to make things worse.

"Please, Arch," she said, "all I'm asking is that you let the professionals do the really dangerous stunts in the future."

He was about to defend himself again when she held up her hand.

"Don't answer me now. I feel bad for even asking you to consider this—it goes against who you are. But I'm your mom, and I can't help myself. So just promise me you'll at least *think* about not doing the dangerous stunts." Her voice cracked as she added, "Because you're still my baby, and I don't know what I'd do without you."

Arch felt his heart plummet to his toes. It would break his mom and dad to have one of their kids seriously hurt, let alone to lose one. But he had to live his own life. And that meant playing by his own rules and trusting his instincts—just as they'd raised him to do. At the same time, he understood that he needed to find a way to live life on his terms while avoiding taking foolish risks. The issue at present was that he wasn't exactly certain how to do that.

His mom seemed satisfied now that she'd said her piece. She turned the subject back to her morning class, but Arch's mind wandered a little as she spoke. She would never have known how bad his accident had been if his emergency contact—his big brother Nick—hadn't called the family and let them know Arch had been hospitalized. He would have to speak to Nick about not worrying their folks unnecessarily. It caused too much anguish.

He was about to help himself to another cookie when the door buzzer sounded. His mom stood to answer it, but before she could get there, the door opened. His sister Mila called, "Anybody home?"

Which was clearly her idea of a joke, because they all knew he was marooned in his house, recuperating.

Mila appeared in the doorway, a bunch of grapes in one hand, flowers in the other, and her hair still dripping wet.

"Been surfing, sis?" he asked.

Mila waved the flowers. "No. I was getting a manicure." She paused a beat before giving a little laugh. "Of course I was surfing."

Arch knew he should have laughed, too, but he was struck with a sudden, overwhelming envy of her ability to dive into the cool ocean and ride the waves, when he was in a cast. "Do you have to rub it in? Showing up here all sandy and windblown when I'm stuck in this chair for ten weeks?"

Mila shared a look with his mom, clearly both thinking, *What's he so annoyed about?*

But Mila had learned something about patience herself over the years—especially considering *her* injury had ended her career, whereas once his broken leg healed, his career could continue without any issues. So, in a calm voice, she said, "I'll just put these flowers in water."

Mila placed the grapes on the coffee table next to

the cookies. Arch eyed the fruit—he would have to stick to a healthy diet and keep working out if he was going to be in shape for *Shock Tactics*. But his mom's oatmeal cookies were irresistible. He reached for one, telling himself that he had the willpower to train extra hard when he needed to burn off some cookie calories. The buttery dough all but melted on his tongue, and he chewed the raisins, enjoying the bursts of sweetness.

His mom sent him that look, the one that said, *This is not how I raised you, Archer Davenport*, so with his mouth still half full, he said, "Thanks for the flowers, and sorry about the bad mood—but don't you think I want to be surfing?"

Mila turned back from the kitchen cabinet, her blue-green eyes flashing. "Then you shouldn't have done a stunt that nearly got you killed. I heard that horse rolled over onto you and nearly did you in."

Arch felt the color rise in his cheeks. Why did everyone seem to think it was his fault? He was tired of explaining that it hadn't been. The prop department had screwed up. It happened. And now he had to listen to everyone in his family tell him he'd been an idiot.

"I'm changing my emergency contact to somebody who doesn't tell everyone my business," he said in a grumpy voice. "Nick's nothing but a blabbermouth."

Mila put down the vase she'd been filling with water a little too abruptly, and some liquid splashed over the side. "Arch, you know we don't keep secrets in this family. There's no way Nick wasn't going to tell us what happened. It would be the same no matter which of us was your emergency contact."

He sighed. Mila was right. There were no secrets among Davenports. He knew he was being difficult. But he was in pain and felt like a fool sitting there with his leg elevated while his mom and sister fussed over him. Plus, if he was honest with himself, the biggest reason he was in a bad mood was because the warm, fascinating woman he'd met on Carmel beach and gotten to know better at the birthday party seemed to have been replaced by a cool model of efficiency.

More often than not, his mom could read his mind, and his siblings' minds too. In her most gentle tone, she said, "I know you're in pain. I can see it on your face. Is there anything I can get you? Do you need more pain meds?"

He told her he was up to date with his meds, and in return she told him that the pain of a break was always worse in the first few days. "Now, I'd appreciate it if you would explain the injury to me in more detail."

"I broke my tibia. It's a simple fracture."

She tousled his hair. "I'm glad it wasn't something worse. You kids always have healed well from injuries. Still," she added with a sigh, "it's a broken leg. That's what, four months for a full recovery?"

He felt his mood grow cloudy again and scowled. There was no hiding anything from his mom. She had spent so much time in the emergency room with six athletic kids that she was almost as good at giving a diagnosis as a seasoned ER doc.

"I start shooting my next movie in ten weeks. I need to heal in eight. Ten is the absolute max."

His mom wasn't surprised that he was pushing the timeline of his recovery. He had always played by his own rules, and if there was one thing she understood, it was that her kids were ambitious and driven. He was certain he could begin filming in ten weeks.

Betsy smiled and said, "Well, if anyone can heal that quickly, it's you. And there's no question in any of our minds that you'll do all your exercises. I hear from Margaret Percy that Tessa's extremely strict with her clients, especially when it comes to physical therapy."

His scowl deepened. "She showed up here in a lab coat with her name stitched on the pocket. I feel like a science experiment."

Mila snorted with laughter. "I *love* that! She's letting you know who's boss right from the get-go. I knew I liked that woman the moment I met her."

Again, he recalled the way Tessa had scolded him when she'd first arrived. But Mila's comment made him even more determined to keep the upper hand when his all too attractive companion returned from the store.

Mila brought over the vase of flowers and sat next to their mom. The flowers were perfectly arranged—a trick of the trade from her real estate business. She helped herself to an oatmeal cookie and then asked, "So, is she sleeping in the guest room down here?"

Their mom turned to her. "Mila, what are you suggesting?"

"Nothing, really," she said with a shrug. "I'm just glad that when I sold Arch this house, it came with two beds on the ground floor as well as a gym and pool in the basement." She turned to him. "It's almost like I knew the day would come when you'd need water therapy and a gym within a thirty-second walk."

Argh. His sister really knew how to push his buttons. Granted, all six of them knew exactly where to push one another to get a reaction. Which was why he tried not to show that she'd gotten to him as he replied, "I told Tessa she should sleep on the same level as me, but she chose a bedroom upstairs. Hauled a couple of heavy bags up there too. I couldn't even help her."

"Why did she do that?" his mom asked. "What if you need her in the night?"

Arch felt vindicated. "That's *exactly* what I said. But she insisted that she'd keep her phone on and said I could call if I needed her."

Mila laughed. "She's probably worried that your snores will come through the walls and keep her awake. Besides, she doesn't need to be on call twenty-four seven. She'll need her space." She paused a beat before adding, "I really do like her a lot, by the way. She seemed smart and intuitive when we met at Dad's party."

"And very pretty too," his mom added.

He couldn't believe it. Was his mother actually matchmaking? Arch knew there was nothing she wanted more than to see her kids happy and in love. Normally, his feathers might have been ruffled at the idea of his mother trying to set him up. But the truth was that in this specific case, he wouldn't mind a little meddling, if that's what she wanted, to encourage Tessa in his direction.

Arch felt Mila's eyes on him again, but he refused to meet her gaze. He wouldn't be able to hide the truth of what he felt for Tessa from his sister—or from any of his family, most likely. The truth that they could all clearly see was that he found Tessa overwhelmingly attractive. It was the real reason he'd asked Margaret Percy if she could spare her caregiver. And his family all probably knew it.

Without a moment's hesitation, Mila said exactly what he was thinking. "If you ask me, Arch noticed exactly how pretty Tessa is. That's why he's in such a bad mood. Mr. Famous Hollywood Star thought he was getting a sexy new playmate. But he ended up with a professional nurse instead."

Arch scowled at Mila—he especially didn't appreciate the Hollywood star stuff—then turned stubbornly to look at the view. But it was pointless to deny the obvious truth, especially when she put a comforting hand on his shoulder. When he finally met Mila's gaze again, it was as playful as when she'd teased him when they were teenagers.

Still, he couldn't let her get away with teasing him, especially when she was right. He grabbed the nearest cushion and swatted his sister.

"Ow," she said, even though he could see she was hiding a grin. "This family can only deal with one invalid at a time."

Arch grinned back and readied himself. "Bring it on, li'l sis."

But before Mila could retaliate, his mom called a stop to the energetic cushion fight she could see brewing with a simple lift of her hand. "And where is Tessa now?"

The door buzzer sounded.

Mila said, "Right on cue."

But instead of Tessa, his sister Erin appeared, clutching a bag from the local bakery.

"Hey, big bro," she said, coming over to give him a kiss on the cheek. "Brownies for the broken."

She opened the bag and added six brownies to the plate of cookies. By the smell, they'd just been baked and would still be warm. His mouth watered. What was Tessa going to think when she came back with bunches of kale and found him pigging out on sweets?

Erin took a seat on the couch. Next to Mila, Erin was tiny. "How are you feeling?" she asked. "I heard your stunt was pretty messed up."

"I feel fine," he lied in a slightly irritated voice, "and please don't print that I was at death's door."

Erin glanced at the other two. "What's gotten into him?"

"He's grumpy because Tessa isn't falling at his feet," Mila replied.

Erin shot him a grin. "Good. I knew Tessa was full of good sense the minute I met her. I was wondering if the day would ever come when a woman would be able to resist you." The grin turned slightly wicked. "I'm very pleased to know that day has arrived." Erin might be the quietest of the six of them, but she could also lay out the sharpest words when the occasion called for it.

While Erin might have thought she was being provocative, Arch instantly saw her statement as more of a challenge than anything. Because if there was one thing he knew, it was that when he wanted something badly enough, he made it his mission to get it.

If Tessa was wary about giving in to the obvious chemistry between them, then he simply needed to show her how good they could be together. It shouldn't matter that their worlds were different. He was nothing more than a guy who thought she was drop-dead gorgeous and wanted to get to know her better.

Now he just needed to figure out how to get her to want him as much as he already wanted her.

It was true that he hadn't ever had to deal with this before—all his previous girlfriends had pretty much fallen at his feet. And they'd been nice to spend time with, mostly.

But none of them was anything like Tessa. He already knew this deep within himself. She was the kind of woman who finally made him understand why so many of his friends had stood at the altar and pledged to love the woman in front of them for the rest of their lives.

He'd waited a long time to find someone who made him believe that maybe happily ever after didn't just belong in fairy tales.

He was already falling for Tessa.

Now he just had to find a way to make her fall for him.

Chapter Nine

Tessa set the brown paper bags on the doorstep and fumbled in her pocket for the door code, which she hadn't yet memorized. It had been fun shopping for Archer, even if it had taken a while to shake off the tingle she felt every time she remembered who her new client was and that she'd sleep in his house tonight.

Opening the door, she called out what she hoped sounded like a professional hello, picked up the bags, and walked down the hallway to the open-plan living area. She'd gone to town on the leafy green veggies and chosen only the best cuts of organic meat and fresh fish to help Archer get the protein he needed to heal. Later, she'd sit down and make her own comprehensive meal plan, but first they needed to get through his daily exercises. She had a feeling that Archer wasn't going to be the most patient of clients. Nonetheless, she felt confident she could handle him.

The sound of laughter popped her out of her thoughts. Was Archer entertaining his Hollywood buddies already? She couldn't leave him alone for a moment. Didn't he realize that he needed to actually rest while he recuperated? Otherwise, his already ambitious healing target of ten weeks was going to be impossible.

She entered the room, mentally preparing a professional but firm lecture—his second of the day!—but was shocked when she saw three of the Davenport women seated around Archer, drinking tea and indulging in treats.

For a split second, a pang of longing shook her. If only her family was like that. Tessa had one older sister, Cheryl, who was very successful. She was married with three daughters. But these days, Tessa rarely saw her sister or her sweet nieces.

Since Tessa had been widowed, and then had run into money troubles, her sister acted like her dire financial situation was a virus she could catch. Rather than supporting Tessa through a difficult time by actually being around to talk things through, Cheryl sent care packages of her cast-off clothes. It was nice of her, but given that her sister's taste was expensive and fancy—all silk dresses and ruffled shirts that were no use to Tessa at all—she'd started taking the designer clothes to thrift stores for store credit. It was the only way she could keep her wardrobe updated, while allowing any spare income to be saved toward a watercolor workshop. Over time, however, she had come to love thrifting. It had become the gift her sister didn't know she'd given.

"Hi, Tessa," Mila said. "We were just talking about how good working with you is going to be for Arch."

There was a kind and respectful note to Mila's voice that made Tessa feel certain they hadn't been gossiping about her in an unkind way.

Archer said, "They were reminding me I have to do exactly what you tell me."

She could see the visit from his female relatives was doing him good. In fact, now that he looked more cheerful, he looked even hotter. Seriously, she needed to get over her crush—and her hormones—ASAP.

Betsy got up and gave Tessa a warm hug, then said, "Let me help you with these groceries." She helped carry the bags into the kitchen, all the while talking about how pleased she was that her son was going to get such excellent care. "Margaret speaks so highly of you," Betsy said as she unpacked the healthy food with an approving look.

"I grew very fond of her," Tessa said. "And she made excellent progress."

"All down to your expertise, I'm sure." Betsy opened another grocery bag and showed Tessa where everything was kept in the kitchen and the separate pantry. Clearly, Archer's mom was over here a lot.

When they'd finished, Erin called her over. "Come sit with us." She patted a seat next to her on the sofa.

"We brought some freshly baked goods. Well, at least Mom and I did. Mila brought grapes, because she's always super conscious about good nutrition."

"Rightly so," Mila said. "Arch needs actual nutrients, not chocolate chips."

When Mila gave Tessa a warm smile, any discomfort she felt at suddenly finding herself in the midst of the female side of Archer's family melted away. But she shook her head at the invitation to sit and instead offered to make the women more tea.

Mila stood. "I've got to make some calls." She turned to her sister. "Don't you need to get back to the paper? Or do hard-nosed journalists keep their own hours these days?"

Tessa could tell that Mila meant no malice toward her sister. There was such warmth between them all that Tessa felt her heart ache again at the knowledge that she'd probably never have anything like that kind of relationship with her sister. And then there was Archer, still looking super hot, even with cookie crumbs in his lap.

"We should all be going," Betsy agreed. "We don't want to tire Arch out."

With that, the women gathered their things. But before they left, Erin turned to Tessa and said, "Mila and I have coffee every Tuesday morning. It's a nice way to catch up with each other. We're meeting tomorrow, and it would be lovely if you could come too."

Erin named a fancy coffee shop Tessa had often walked past but never entered, and a thrill raced through her just from being invited to join Archer's sisters. It was as if she already belonged in their fold. She smiled and thanked her. "I'd like that a lot," she said, "but I might be needed by Archer."

Of course, as soon as the words left her mouth, he told her to go.

"You need time off too," he said. "I can get by for an hour on my own." He gave a mischievous grin. "After all, I *have* been coping on my own until now. And please call me Arch, Tessa."

Tessa nodded at his request, even as she held back a sigh. He certainly hadn't been coping so well when she'd first arrived and found him stranded on the stairs, but at least she had gotten things off to a good start with a no-nonsense approach—even if she felt gooey to the core every time she glanced his way.

The Davenport women said their good-byes, and Erin pressed a business card into Tessa's hand. "Text me," she urged, "so I have your number."

Tessa smiled down at the business card for the *Sea Shell*, Carmel's weekly newspaper. She'd been in town for weeks, and was close to Margaret Percy, but it felt like she'd just made her first friend her own age.

After the women left, she offered Arch one more chance to take something from the plate of goodies before she put them away. "You're not going to bust me for eating junk food?" He sounded surprised.

"No. Seeing your mom and sisters did you good, I can tell. And a couple of cookies aren't the end of the world."

She could tell from his physique that he kept himself in prime shape. She did not need to give Archer—or rather, Arch—a lecture on eating well and avoiding junk. Besides, she wasn't a complete purist about food. She understood that sometimes a treat helped a patient as much as a well-timed visit from people they loved.

He patted his flat belly anyway. "I'd love to get straight back to the gym, or at least the pool," he said, "but I know I'm not strong enough yet. The physical therapist I saw in the hospital wrote me a daily workout plan. It's at the back of the file with the nutritionist's notes."

Tessa pulled out the workout plan and read through it. She'd helped enough patients heal from broken bones that she had a pretty good notion what the exercises would be. As she'd expected, this was a more rigorous plan than someone of Margaret's age and strength would receive, but she could ensure Arch did the exercises properly. She offered to gather the equipment he needed and bring everything up to the ground floor.

To her relief, Arch didn't attempt to dissuade her from lifting anything or try to haul himself downstairs to the gym.

"Why don't you change into your workout gear, and I'll meet you back here in ten minutes? I'll set up the mats." But as soon as the words left her mouth, she realized her mistake. "Or do you need some help changing?"

She was trying so hard to be professional, but at her own suggestion of helping him off with his clothes, she felt heat rush to her cheeks.

It was so difficult to talk to him as she would with Margaret, whom she frequently helped with her clothes, or any other of her countless patients who had needed that same level of care. It wasn't even like Arch was the first handsome man she'd worked with. And yet, all her cool flew out the window at the very suggestion that she might assist him in unzipping his pants.

The truth was, she was afraid of getting that close to him—as if one touch would be all it would take for her to lose the battle. To not fall completely under his movie-star spell. Although, to be fair, he didn't act like an entitled movie star. She waited with bated breath for his reply, hoping against hope he could handle his pants himself.

★ ★ ★

Arch stared at Tessa, trying to read her neutral expression. Was that a flush of color across her tanned cheeks, or was he only seeing what he wanted to see?

He was tempted to reply that he *did* need her help getting changed into workout gear. Just the thought of her hands on his skin filled him with warmth. As did super sexy visions of the two of them tangled together on his bed, pleasure humming through every part of their bodies.

But the truth was that he didn't need help. He'd managed to dress himself the last few mornings, and he could easily pull on a pair of shorts. Plus, he didn't want to overstep his boundaries with Tessa.

At least, not yet.

He sensed that winning her heart was going to take time. So he would have to move slowly and respect that she was in his house as a professional.

What's more, there was a vulnerability to Tessa that she did a good job of hiding beneath that efficient exterior. But he could still sense that she had been hurt in the past. Not physically, but emotionally. Her guard was up.

At one time or another, he had seen something similar with his sisters. A short burst of fury went through him at the thought that someone had hurt a woman as precious as Tessa. He'd been pleased when Erin had asked her to join her and Mila for coffee. Their letting another woman into their tight circle was a big deal, and he was glad for Tessa that she was going to have two of the coolest women in Carmel as new friends.

He couldn't help but feel a little glad on a personal level too. Because if she started hanging out with his sisters, maybe they'd put in a good word for him. His sisters might tease him, but they knew him better than anyone else, and they knew he'd never deliberately hurt anyone, least of all a woman living in his home to do a job.

Tessa was still waiting for an answer, so he shook his head. "I'll manage getting into my workout gear just fine." With that, he took his crutches and maneuvered as well as he could into his bedroom to change.

He dug out a pair of red shorts and took his time slipping them over his cast. When he got back to the living area, he found Tessa on her hands and knees, unrolling his green yoga mat. She had set out varying pairs of free weights in neat rows and two resistance bands.

She hadn't noticed him, which allowed him to observe her luscious backside for a moment.

It was a great moment, even if he did feel a little bad for drooling over her when she wasn't looking. Then again, he *was* just looking. Not touching, no matter how desperate he was to do just that. No, he wouldn't dare touch her in a sensual way unless she told him she wanted it too.

When she stood, she went to the fireplace where one of his favorite paintings hung. He'd started collecting art when he signed his first big Hollywood contract. He loved to find unusual pieces and support up-and-coming artists.

Tessa stood still, gazing up at the piece in wonder. It depicted swaths of blue water the artist had captured in motion, bubbling and rippling, the suggestion of a shimmering body swimming beneath all that blue. Tessa didn't give it a cursory glance, as most of the people who came here did. Instead, she stepped closer, then away, giving the painting her full attention.

"It's a Lawles," he said to Tessa's back. "She had a small solo show in LA last year, and I fell in love with this piece."

She turned, clearly surprised to find him back in the room already. "Kalinda Lawles, yes, I know her work. I love how photorealistic all her work is," Tessa said dreamily. "At the same time, there's something so free, almost abstract, about the brushstrokes." She continued to gaze at the painting in awe, before adding, "I don't know how she does it."

Arch was impressed. "I don't know many people who would have recognized her name, let alone known so much about her work." Eager to get to know this fascinating woman better, he added, "You must really like art."

But instead of getting into a subject they were both clearly passionate about, she laughed off his comment and told him to come to the mat.

He obeyed, happy to get closer to her. But as she settled him on his back to begin a mobility warm-up, he found he couldn't concentrate on her instructions. He was too aware of her—her pretty floral scent, her seemingly delicate but strong wrists as she gently took hold of his good leg. And then he noticed a smudge of green on her thumbnail. Nail polish she hadn't managed to completely remove? But she didn't strike him as a woman who had weekly manicures—not like Mila, whose nails were always polished. She always said she kept them that way so she could picture herself signing the biggest real estate deals in Carmel with beautiful hands.

He closed his eyes and took a deep breath to force his concentration on the workout, not on Tessa. Keep his focus on the exercises. Build up his strength. Make it on set in ten weeks for what was sure to be a blockbuster action movie.

Tessa helped him circle his ankles, open his hips, stretch his spine. He was torn between enjoying every minute of her touch and the pain in his leg.

Then she started him on straight leg raises with the injured leg, staying close by to spot him.

"Is it aching?" she asked, reading his mind.

He opened his eyes and found her own trained on his. She blinked and then looked away. "A little," he confessed. "But this is helping."

"Let's move to your upper body," she suggested,

choosing a medium-sized pair of dumbbells. "Before you say anything, I'm sure you can press more than this, but let's start light, okay? Your body has been through a trauma, and it's normal to take time to get back to your usual strength."

He accepted the weights from her outstretched hands and tentatively began chest flies. Without a word, she shifted position so that she could spot him. He relaxed as she counted his reps in a calm, soothing tone, hovering behind his head.

His gaze naturally rested on her white T-shirt, and he wondered if she knew what a pleasant view he had. It helped to keep his mind off of the ache in his leg. "Your top is nice," he said, bringing the weights back to his pecs.

She let out a short laugh. "It's just a white T-shirt I got in a thrift store. I get a lot of my clothes by thrifting."

"Really? Maybe I shouldn't admit this, but I've never been inside a thrift store."

She laughed again, this time with her whole body. "Clearly, you don't need to thrift shop."

For the first time, he felt like he'd put his foot in it. He didn't want Tessa to feel bad for not having the same financial resources he did.

Besides, he liked new experiences. "Maybe some time you can take me to one?"

She looked down at him as though she thought he

might be teasing her. Then, realizing he was serious, she shrugged. "I'd be happy to."

★ ★ ★

Tessa was having trouble focusing, which she never did when she was working with a client. But with Arch, everything was different. Her hands were going through the motions, helping with his workout, but her mind was on his muscles as they rippled beneath her touch. She felt the heat of his flushed skin, was stirred by his nearness and the sound of his breath as he lifted the weights, each movement wafting his fresh, delicious scent to her.

Little beads of sweat gathered at his temples, and she wanted to wipe them away, smooth back the brown hair that curled there. Her heart was beating so uncontrollably that she was worried he might hear it.

She had never felt this attracted to someone before, let alone someone she hardly knew. Her husband had certainly never made her feel this way.

Lewis had been really unpleasant toward the end of his life—throughout their entire marriage, really. She still felt bad lusting after Arch in a way she never had with the man to whom she'd said her vows.

Plus, she didn't know how to respond to his request to go with her to a thrift store. At first, she'd thought he was teasing her, but no. He'd been serious. No doubt he'd use what he learned to create one of his movie characters, because he certainly didn't have to worry about finding bargains in real life.

Luckily, she was saved from answering by the ring of Arch's phone.

He put down the weights with a thud and apologized. "I bet I know who that is," he said, clearly annoyed that his workout was being interrupted.

She helped him sit up, although his core was clearly strong enough for him to do it alone. She allowed herself a moment to imagine his perfect, tanned six-pack—which she knew she'd likely see in the very near future during one of his workouts—and shivered a little.

"Would you mind?" he asked, gesturing to the glass coffee table where his cell vibrated.

"No problem," she replied, trying not to seem flustered. She fetched the phone, wondering if the caller was Sonia Montefiore. He'd told the girls on the beach that they were not a couple, but had that just been to throw them off the scent? Margaret had sounded one hundred percent certain that they weren't. But then, if it was his girlfriend calling, she didn't think he'd seem so annoyed.

Not wanting to intrude on his privacy, she didn't look at the screen as she passed the phone to him. Nonetheless, she was immediately relieved to hear a male voice on the other end of the line. Which was ridiculous, given that whether he had a girlfriend or not had no bearing on her work with him as a client. She couldn't imagine a world in which someone totally normal like her would end up with someone as famous and larger-than-life as Archer Davenport.

"Hi, Jay." Arch listened, his expression turning downcast. "I see." And then, "You know I don't want to do that." More silence. Arch was actively frowning now. "Yeah, I know you're just doing your job, but can't you buy me some time?" He listened some more and then snapped, "Got it."

The call ended abruptly, and Arch shook his head as he placed his cell beside him on the floor.

Tessa waited, not wanting to pry, but she couldn't help wondering who had upset him so much.

"That was my agent, Jay Malone," he explained without her needing to ask. "Someone with a big mouth alerted the media to my injury. There's a bunch of talk online. The studio wants to control the story, so a news crew is coming by to interview me later. Obviously, I don't want to speak to the press, but it seems like I don't have a choice. All part of the job."

"Who would do that?" she asked. "Who would leak something so personal about you to the media?" She couldn't imagine having her privacy invaded that way.

"People who want to make a quick buck. People who talk too much." He shrugged, though he was clearly still irritated. "Could have been someone on set, someone working at the hospital. Who knows?"

And then it occurred to her that the news crew would be coming to the house. Panic gripped her. She deeply valued her anonymity. "Do I have to be on-screen?"

"No. I'll keep you out of it, don't worry."

She relaxed a little. She'd never taken care of anyone famous before, and at first glance it sure seemed like a lot of work. Considering Arch was still in considerable pain, it didn't seem fair that now he had to give an interview on TV just so the narrative of his accident didn't spiral in a way that was undesirable to the studio.

"They say all publicity is good publicity," he told her, "but I've never believed that."

She'd never thought she'd feel empathy for a movie star—after all, they always seemed to have everything they ever wanted and more—but now she realized things weren't that clear cut.

Because right now, she most definitely empathized with Arch in this situation. Any normal person would be able to take a long nap right now. But he had to work out, eat really clean, and do media interviews—all while enduring the pain of his body working to heal.

No, she thought, she would *never* want to be famous.

"Let's forget about it for now and finish."

Chapter Ten

Somehow, Tessa managed to get through the rest of their workout without short-circuiting from being so close to Arch. She whipped up a nutritious, kale-packed lunch, which he wolfed down.

Arch might be restricted by a cast, but he still managed to keep himself busy. There were more phone calls with his agent and a press agent from the studio, who went through the questions he could expect from the TV interviewer. The press agent asked if Arch needed her there, and he laughed. "I'm an old pro at this. I'll be fine. Don't worry, I won't get tricked into saying anything I shouldn't. Who's doing the interview?"

Tessa strained her ears. She wasn't a big TV watcher, but she knew *Celebrity Tonight*, a daily show that highlighted what the stars were up to, the good and the bad. They promoted the new TV shows and movies and were quick to report when a famous marriage or relationship broke up or a new one began. If a star was in trouble, the news wouldn't take long to show up on

Celebrity Tonight. The co-hosts were Roxy Thanton, a former supermodel, and a guy who'd once been in a boy band. His name was Ben. Tessa couldn't remember his last name. All she knew was that they were both easy on the eyes and constantly upbeat.

"Yeah, that's fine," Arch said. "I've worked with Roxy before. No problem." He sounded resigned rather than thrilled that the co-host herself would be flying up to interview him. Tessa was no expert, but even she knew that the stories the hosts covered themselves were always the leads.

Arch didn't seem bothered by the fact that he'd have a TV crew in his house in a few hours. Tessa, however, was on edge. She tidied the already tidy house, straightening the cushions and running the vacuum cleaner around.

From his chair, Arch cocked an eyebrow. "What are you doing? I have cleaning staff."

"I don't want the TV people reporting that you live like a slob," she said with dignity.

"It's the crew who will make the mess," he retorted. "They'll move the furniture and track sand in. I'll get the cleaners in tomorrow to clean up after them."

Even so, she made certain the downstairs rooms were spotless and was pleased Mila had brought Arch flowers, as they made a nice centerpiece on the coffee table.

The crew were coming at three p.m. At two, Tessa

asked Arch what he was going to wear. He was currently in a pair of board shorts and a T-shirt that had seen better days. He glanced up at her from the script he was reading, looking amused. "You're as bad as the studio's PR people. I'm supposed to wear a T-shirt in a solid color and loose trousers so that I look relaxed, but not like I'm letting myself go."

She was almost positive the PR rep hadn't said anything like that. Probably, she'd told him to look strong and sexy, which was what every female viewer would want to see.

"Maybe you should start getting ready now," Tessa suggested. It was going to take him longer than it usually did. He seemed surprised at her suggestion and then glanced down at his cast.

"Right. Thanks. I forgot that even changing clothes is a workout now." He got himself to his feet, grabbing the crutches she held out for him. His biceps bulged as he worked the crutches. She had never, *ever* thought she'd find crutches sexy.

But then, that was before she'd met Archer Davenport.

What was the protocol with a TV crew? Should she make coffee? Would they want snacks? Should—

Arch called, "Tessa, can I get an opinion?"

She walked into his bedroom and found him in a pair of black cotton trousers that were loose enough they'd fit easily over his cast.

But his torso was bare.

She'd known this moment would come, but she hadn't expected it just then, and the sight of all that gorgeous skin and muscle had her feeling all fluttery inside. My God, he was gorgeous, with defined pecs, an impressive six-pack, and those incredibly well-built arms that she'd noticed earlier.

More than anything else, she wanted to place her lips right at the vee of his collarbone. A rush of heat went through her as she imagined the taste of his skin.

"Tessa?" His voice pulled her back from her fantasy with a start, which was when she saw what she hadn't before. His bed was covered in T-shirts. "Can you pick one?"

Black, gray, red, pale pink, and several shades of blue. She picked up two, one navy and one the blue of the ocean on a stormy day, and held them up against his chest. She tried to ignore the heat coming off his body, the pull she felt from standing so close to him, and use her judgment.

"This one," she said, choosing the shirt the color of the ocean. She didn't say that it brought out the color in his eyes.

He pulled the shirt over his head, and she stood back, giving the final outfit a critical once-over. She nodded. "You'll do."

Which was the world's hugest understatement, considering she couldn't imagine a better looking man.

Even the other brother she'd met at the party, the one Margaret had called "the good-looking one," couldn't hold a candle to Arch right now. At least in Tessa's eyes.

The shirt fit perfectly, showing off his amazing physique, along with bringing out the gorgeous blue of his eyes. But the overall look was relaxed. Archer Davenport might have a broken leg, but the image he exuded was that he was fine and recovering rapidly. It was exactly what she believed his agent and his PR team wanted the outfit to say.

"Thanks, Tessa," he said. "You've got a good eye for color."

Mmmm. The sound of her name on his lips. So… well, so sexy. Mentally, she gave herself a shake. She really needed to stop thinking like that! All he'd done was say her name. It wasn't like he'd begged her to let him strip off her clothes to make love to her, or anything crazy along those lines.

At three p.m. sharp, the doorbell rang.

She turned to check that Arch was completely ready. He was in his big chair, a glass of water on the table by his side and his crutches out of sight. He'd insisted on that.

At her questioning look, he nodded. "Let's get this over with," he said with a grimace.

She opened the door to find Roxy Thanton standing there.

By first becoming a super model, then co-hosting *Celebrity Tonight*, Roxy had become a celebrity herself. Her image was often splashed across the gossip pages of magazines with various hot Hollywood heartthrobs, or she was being praised for her great fashion sense.

In person, the woman was a bona fide knockout. She had long, highlighted blond hair, a tan, and glowing skin made even brighter by her tight white dress. Her makeup was so perfect, Tessa felt like she was looking at a photograph.

"Hello," Tessa managed, feeling slightly starstruck. Behind Roxy were three men and one woman with cameras and other equipment.

Roxy Thanton walked past Tessa as though she weren't even there. "Arch? Where are you?" she called in her sexiest voice.

The crew were a lot nicer. One of the guys asked Tessa where he could park the van, and another asked about the power supply. The woman said, "Hi, I'm Shay. This won't take more than an hour, which we'll edit down to about five minutes."

"I'm Tessa," she said. "I'm Arch's caregiver, but I'll do whatever I can to help."

The noise and activity of a TV crew was a stark contrast to the intimate atmosphere she'd enjoyed with Arch so far. She never could have predicted he'd be so knowledgeable about art, for example. The way he described being moved by a painting or photograph had had her captivated. She was slowly beginning to realize the sensitive way he saw the world. It was probably what made him such a good actor. He was able to empathize and use his intuition to get straight to the heart of something. Or someone.

What surprised her was how real he was, how he talked to her like her opinion mattered to him, which was the opposite of the way Lewis had treated her. Arch didn't take himself too seriously, and quite frankly, that was almost as attractive as his gorgeous face and killer body. She would need to double her efforts to stay professional to have any chance of keeping her heart from being ripped to shreds.

Like right now, when she had to watch the gorgeous blond TV host flirt shamelessly with Arch as they put the final touches to the rearranged furniture for the interview. The crew had all but wrecked the minimalistic calm of Arch's living room, setting up lighting, two cameras, and what she learned were boom mics.

Tessa kept out of their way as much as possible, taking the opportunity to get settled in her bedroom and put away the rest of her possessions. The act of hanging up her clothes made her realize this really *was* going to be home for the next two and a half months. The room was more luxurious than any hotel she'd ever stayed in.

When she couldn't find a reason to stay upstairs

any longer, she went down to find everything set up. Roxy was sitting across from Arch and chatting away as though they were old friends. Maybe they were. The crew were doing sound and light checks around them.

One of the crew had knocked a painting crooked when setting up the rigging. Luckily, it wasn't damaged, but she felt aggrieved on Arch's behalf. Couldn't they see that these paintings were precious? An accumulation of hours and hours of work? She moved over to where the painting had fallen sideways and slid the frame upright on its hanging wire.

"Can we keep the household staff out of frame, please?" Roxy said, her friendliness gone in an instant.

Tessa felt as though she'd been stabbed by an icicle. She was about to apologize when Arch spoke up. In a firm tone, he said, "Roxy, I'd like you to meet Tessa Taylor. She's a professional caregiver, and I'm very lucky to have her here to help me recuperate."

She'd wanted to stay out of the interview completely, but she understood that Arch was sticking up for her, and a part of her melted.

Roxy suddenly flashed Tessa a sparkling white smile. "This must be an exciting placement for you, looking after a celebrity of Archer Davenport's caliber."

Inwardly, Tessa squirmed at the patronising tone. But again, Archer spoke before she had the chance to.

"All in a day's work for Tessa," he said. "Besides, there are no celebrities in this household. I'm just a regular California guy who got lucky at his job."

Roxy let out a tinkling laugh. "I love how you still insist on this 'I'm just a regular guy' spiel. Everyone in the world knows your name. And your face. Not to mention those abs of yours." She laughed again and then reached over and put her hand on his belly.

Tessa wanted to reach out and swipe Roxy's hand away. How dare she touch him? She was here to interview him, not put her hands on him. It was completely unprofessional.

Somehow, Tessa managed to hold herself back *and* hold her tongue. She didn't want to embarrass Arch. But she did train her gaze on him, wondering how he'd respond to this kind of behavior. In the short time she'd known him, Arch had never once seemed like a Hollywood movie star.

To her surprise, Arch ignored Roxy's comment. He simply laughed and suggested they get started. And Tessa also noticed that he subtly shifted his torso out of Roxy's reach.

Arch had been interviewed by Roxy before. Many times, probably. Tessa had seen a couple of the interviews on TV. There was an ease to their exchange that made Tessa's stomach feel funny.

But then Arch turned to Tessa and gave her such a warm, genuine smile that the sick feeling in her stomach disappeared and was replaced with a little flutter instead.

"I'll get started on dinner prep," Tessa said, hoping that her voice sounded more natural than she was really feeling.

"That's great," he said. "You did an amazing job with lunch. I can't believe you make veggies taste so good. This interview shouldn't take too long, and then I can give you a hand."

Tessa laughed. "I'm here to help you—not the other way around. I've got this covered, so you don't need to worry."

She retreated to the kitchen, which had a spacious prep station where she could work in peace. She couldn't wait to get away from the film crew. Not least Roxy and her shiny hair and too-perfect makeup and figure.

The pantry off the kitchen was bigger than some of the bedrooms Tessa had slept in and was lined with fitted cupboards and drawers stocked with dry goods. For someone who traveled as much as Arch did, he sure had a lot of food at home. She looked for the brown rice she'd purchased, trying to get her thoughts in order.

Despite Arch's kind words, the annoying thing was that Roxy was completely right: Tessa was utterly overwhelmed by Arch's life and career. Watching him slip so easily into conversation with the TV crew, effortlessly switching on the charm, obviously accustomed to the bright lights and being a huge celebrity, brought home the differences between them. She couldn't pretend she was used to working around film crews and famous TV hosts. Despite all her experience, everything about her current job here felt alien, whereas Arch and Roxy seemed to have great chemistry. They were from the same world. Tessa could feel the stirrings of an unwelcome jealousy.

She shook her head. She'd been here only a day and look how quickly she'd succumbed to feeling like a teenager with a crush again. She was better than this.

She could still hear them chatting and laughing in the other room. It was yet another reminder that Arch's place was out there in front of the camera and the millions of people he reached. While hers was in the kitchen and the gym, tucked away and anonymous, doing her best to get him healthy again.

Still, she enjoyed cooking, and having such a range of wonderful ingredients at her fingertips made her feel like she was running a Michelin-starred restaurant in a glitzy corner of Hollywood. She tried to ignore the hubbub of the crew and focused on what she knew best.

Arch's voice carried, though. He was amiable, playful even, answering Roxy's questions about the horse stunt with self-effacing laughter.

Tessa couldn't help but creep to the archway of the kitchen to listen as Roxy said, "I've seen the footage of that stunt. Arch, do you have any regrets?"

Tess knew that the prop dynamite had spooked the horse, but would Arch tell the world that? It would likely only get the person who had accidentally set off the dynamite shoved into the public eye for doing something that had nearly ended Arch's life. No, she doubted he'd say anything about it. Because he wasn't the kind of man who would blame anyone for an honest mistake. Even one that had broken his leg—and nearly broken the rest of his body too.

He said, "I'm really proud of the movie we're making. Doing my own stunts brings a little more reality to the production. But it's also true that it was a dangerous stunt, and it didn't go perfectly. Honestly, I'm glad it was *my* leg that got broken and not the horse's."

What a great answer. She felt so proud of him.

He continued, "My body is usually a fast healer, and I have a great team looking after me. I'll be back on set before you know it."

As Roxy moved on to rumors that Arch had been chosen as the lead in *Shock Tactics*, Tessa went back to her meal prep.

Following a tried and tested healthy recipe that had won even Margaret's approval, Tessa allowed herself to get lost in the rhythm of cooking. That was, until she heard Roxy's honeyed voice say, "I'd love to interview your caregiver too—get her thoughts on how you're doing."

Tessa dropped the knife she was holding on the

cutting board, and her palms started to sweat. The word *no* ran repeatedly through her mind. Arch had said they wouldn't need to interview her. Surely he must have noticed how on edge the very idea of them being in the house had made her. She waited with bated breath for his answer.

"No," she heard him say firmly. "She doesn't want to be on film. We've got to respect that."

Tessa let out her breath and peeked into the main room. She could see Arch and Roxy across from each other, see the cameras trained on the pair of them. The TV host's carefully penciled eyebrows were raised. Clearly, she hadn't expected to be told no. And not so bluntly. So far, Arch had been easygoing with her questions. But Tessa could well imagine that not many men said no to a woman like Roxy.

Roxy let out a little laugh. "Quite the firm answer," she noted. "A little protective, maybe? Is there possibly a budding romance between the star and the nurse?"

Tessa gasped. Had Roxy somehow seen through her and guessed at the crush she was trying so hard to conceal? The very idea that Arch would get involved with his "nurse" was ridiculous, despite all the movies and books with that plot. But once the rumor mill started churning, she could imagine being crushed by it. She felt sick to her stomach.

But Arch took the question in stride, shutting it down with a simple, "Come on now, Roxy. You've already got what you need for your exclusive, right? We don't have to involve innocent bystanders."

Tessa could sense that beneath the friendly tone, Arch was warning Roxy not to push things too far. She'd gotten her scoop, was here inside *his* home, and, as he'd reminded her, *Celebrity Tonight* had an exclusive interview.

To her credit, Roxy got the message, quickly redirecting the interview to his real-life friendship with on-screen buddy Smith Sullivan. Tessa ducked back into the pantry, relieved. She was very grateful to Arch for keeping her out of the limelight. She enjoyed hearing him speak so enthusiastically about his friend. "I've learned so much from Smith. I'm in awe of his talent—and any day you go to work with a good friend, with a great script, and a good crew, it doesn't even feel like work."

Tessa baked chicken breasts with olives and tomato, and chopped vegetables and fresh herbs for an accompanying salad. By the time she heard the film crew packing up their equipment, she had everything ready for dinner, as well as a batch of healthy overnight oats for breakfast in the morning.

Tessa didn't return to the living room until she heard the last good-bye and the slam of the front door. Although she wanted to check on Arch immediately, she gave him a few minutes to decompress after what had surely been far too much activity for someone who needed rest—especially considering they'd done some physical therapy before the interview. Plus, she wanted to make sure that everyone had really left.

A little while later, quietly entering the living room, she found Arch staring down at his elevated foot, flexing his toes. Even though he was much fitter than the majority of her clients, there was no way a fractured tibia wouldn't be causing him pain.

She took in his pain meds and a fresh glass of water and put them on the table beside him. "Did the interview go well?" she asked, as if she hadn't heard most of it from the kitchen. The crew had replaced the furniture where it had originally been, and apart from a bit of gaffer tape and a few grains of sand, there was no evidence they'd ever been there.

Arch turned to her and smiled. "Part of the job. One of my least-favorite parts, if I'm honest, but they went easy on me." He didn't mention that Roxy had wanted to put Tessa on camera, and she didn't bring it up. All the same, she was grateful he'd spared her that ordeal.

He motioned to the couch across from him. "Sit," he said. "You've been on your feet too long."

Tessa hid her smile. She was used to working long hours, much of it on her feet. Looking after the self-sufficient Arch was no hardship.

"I'm doing just fine, thank you," she said, but she did take a seat. "It's you I'm worried about. You've got to be worn out. We had an intense workout this morning, and the interview must have zapped the rest of any energy you might have had. Can I get you anything? Do you need a nap?" Margaret had napped every afternoon, complaining like a cranky toddler each time her body proclaimed her fatigue.

But Arch shook his head, smiling. "I've got to get to work learning the new script."

She had to admit, watching Arch try to mask his pain tugged on her heartstrings. "Take your pain meds, Arch. Maybe those will help get you in a napping mood."

He grinned and swallowed the pill without protest. "I guess you know what's best for me," he said, a cheeky note creeping into his voice.

"I certainly do." Unable to prevent an answering smile, she added, "I'm glad you've finally seen the light. And if you're ready to be a good patient, then I suggest you take a catnap before you open that script again. Recharge. A lot of healing is done during rest."

But Arch just scoffed. "I haven't napped since I was two years old."

She rolled her eyes. His body would let him know what he needed to do, despite his protests.

"A little reading isn't going to finish me off," he insisted. "And I'll feel much better for getting on top of my work. What I really want is for you to take some time to yourself to unwind before dinner… and pass me that binder you'll find in the drawer so I don't have to hobble over there myself."

Though she still thought a nap was in order before he worked, she understood wanting to stay on top of things. So she fetched the script. "Whatever you do, stay reclining with that foot elevated," she said, just to remind him who was boss. "I'll check on you in a bit. And make sure you keep your phone in your pocket in case you need me."

Earlier, she'd almost felt too intimidated to open the door to his house, but after a few hours in Arch's home and around his family, she already felt comfortable enough to boss him.

Still, it was a shock all over again to walk into her bedroom. It was so exquisite. On the same side of the house as the living room, a huge window offered a sweeping vista of the ocean and blue sky. Gauzy white curtains floated on either side. The walls were painted a soft cream, the floors and wardrobes of a light wood that seemed to reflect the golden afternoon light. The king-sized bed was made up in oatmeal linens and looked so welcoming she was tempted to nap herself.

But no. She should acclimatize, but she couldn't forget that she was working.

This wasn't her home. Or her life.

Even if the idea did seem tempting every time Arch flashed his perfect smile.

Chapter Eleven

Tessa went to the big window. The view really was breathtaking. The golden beach, kids making sandcastles, teens catching the last of the sun. She watched the walkers and runners, dogs greeting one another and chasing after balls, surfers riding the waves on the horizon. It was truly idyllic. She couldn't believe that this was where she was going to wake up each morning.

She tore her eyes away from the scene, and her gaze fell on the one bag she'd yet to touch. Although she was alone, she surreptitiously hauled the backpack into the open room that was set up like a library, with a telescope pointed out the huge picture window. She unzipped it cautiously, her heart hammering in that familiar way. Nothing gave her the kind of sweet anticipation that taping a fresh sheet of toothy watercolor paper to the easel and filling her pans with paint provided. She pulled out a drop cloth to protect the floor from any drips. She set up by the window and then admired the scene before her.

When Arch was a bit stronger, she'd go outside to paint, but today she wanted to stay within calling range in case he needed her.

Somehow she knew that he would respect her privacy. Besides, it would be really difficult for him to get up the stairs without her help. If he needed something, he would call. Which meant she could finally relax and do her favorite thing in the world.

First, she mixed her paints, trying to re-create the golden tones of the sand below. The blank paper didn't intimidate her. Just the opposite. She loved the feeling of a fresh start. The moment where anything could be put on the expanse of white. A whole world of possibilities opened up before her.

The first brushstrokes sent shivers of happiness through her body. She felt most herself while painting, even though she kept it secret from everyone. The very fact it was a secret was a large part of what made it so liberating. She didn't need to worry about technique or style—or even her color palette—because no one would ever see the painting.

It was just for her.

Creating art was a compulsion, not a choice. It was how she made sense of the world and processed her emotions. It was a totally personal enterprise, and as far as she was concerned, it would always stay that way.

Her husband had always said that she had no talent and that her paintings were amateurish, but she'd painted anyway in secret. It was her art that had helped her through the difficult times when he was so ill and demanding. No patient she'd had since had been as demanding… or as angry. It was as though he'd blamed Tessa for his illness.

Painting had been a calming influence on her *and* a way of getting all her emotions out.

Unfortunately, his words still rang in her ears: *You might have gotten the love for painting, but you sure as hell didn't get the talent to go with it.*

But as the paintbrush began to guide her movements, she allowed herself to question whether Lewis had been right. There was a part of her, way down deep inside, that wondered if there was more to her work than he had realized. Sometimes she looked at her paintings and felt proud of the work that had come out of her, unguided by any training or schooling. There was something truthful in the art she made. Put most simply, it was the way she uniquely saw the world.

But those proud moments never lasted long, not when her husband's harsh words still rang in her ears and down into her heart too. He might have died, but she had a feeling his cruel words about her passion for creating art never would.

She thought now of the artwork Arch had so informally hanging in his house. There was the gorgeous Kalinda Lawles they'd talked about, of course. But she was sure she'd also spotted an original Chagall in the downstairs guest room and a Georgia O'Keeffe above the stairs. And she hardly dared believe that the small, square canvas hanging in the living room might be a Picasso… could it?

Of course, she'd never be that good—those artists were true masters of the craft—but Tessa had made her peace with her private painting a long time ago. At least, that's what she always told herself.

She thought again about Arch's collection. He had a keen eye, not just for painting, but for all art. There was a blue and pink Tracey Emin neon sign in the hallway, which she'd yet to see lit. Tracey Emin was a British artist, and she was impressed that Arch had her piece on his wall. The handwritten words *You Loved Me Like a Distant Star* had made her swoon just looking at them.

Considering the telescope by the window, did Arch ever sit up here, looking up at the sky?

He was just downstairs. With a shock, she realized that she had found it peaceful working while he was in the house. She usually preferred to paint alone and never quite felt comfortable hiding her activity in clients' houses. But this felt different. Something about being here felt comfortable. Like everything was just right.

She checked her watch and was startled to see that two hours had passed since she'd opened her box of paints. She'd been utterly engrossed in her work all this time. Hoping Arch was okay, she took the painting off the easel and found a shelf in the closet where it could lie flat to dry. She washed her brushes and her hands in the en suite so that no trace or smell of paint was visible on her skin and headed downstairs, annoyed with herself for losing track of time.

But when she entered the living room, she saw that Arch hadn't moved an inch. He was deep into reading the script. She smiled. Like her, he'd been so absorbed in what he was doing he hadn't noticed the time passing.

"Hi," she said quietly.

He looked up, surprised. But as soon as he saw her, warmth flooded his face, and his eyes twinkled. Just the way Margaret had teased her about.

He put down the script and replied, "Hi."

He stared at her, a look that seemed almost to be wonder, and she worried for a moment she had paint on her face or hands or clothes. But no, she was thorough in hiding her time painting. She didn't make mistakes like that.

"It's almost seven," she said. "I think we both may have lost track of time."

He nodded. "This script is good. Plus, I found that I liked knowing you were in the house, even though you were upstairs." He flashed her a way-too-sexy grin. "And I didn't even call you back down here for no reason… though the thought crossed my mind once or twice."

She found herself laughing, even though he was laying on the charm way too thick. She should be putting up bigger walls to protect herself, but instead, she said, "I'm glad you're a fast learner. I wouldn't have taken kindly to a prank call."

"Oh yeah," he said. "I'm *definitely* a fast learner."

She pretended not to notice the sexy undertones or the mischievous twinkle in his eyes, even as her face grew warm. Instead, she swiftly changed the subject and asked if he was ready for dinner.

That twinkle undiminished, he replied, "Oh yes, I'm hungry."

For food?

Or for *her*?

The thought was *way* too potent for her to linger on. Forcefully shoving all thoughts of being touched by Arch out of her head, she said, "*Celebrity Tonight* will be on soon. I can bring you a tray so you can stay on your lounger with your leg elevated, if you'd like to watch it."

"Only if you're eating in here with me."

She looked at him. She'd eaten all her meals with Margaret, but Margaret hadn't made her pulse pound. She needed to keep her distance from Arch if she was going to protect her heart, so she said, "Oh no, I'll eat in the kitchen."

He burst into laughter. "You're joking." But the laughter soon faded when he saw she was serious. "Come on. You can't leave me to eat all on my own. It's... well, it just doesn't seem right. Especially when we're going to be living together for so many weeks. I don't want you to feel like 'the staff,' forced to eat in another room." He paused for a moment. "And also, I'd really like your company."

Giving him a small smile, she nodded. "Okay, then I'll eat with you from now on, if I'm not out grocery shopping or taking care of something else for you."

While she was still determined to keep her emotional distance as much as she could, she understood how lonely it could feel to eat alone. Her husband might have grown more cruel as he'd become more ill, but after his passing, she still remembered how alone she had felt sitting at the table eating dinner by herself.

A few minutes later, she brought in their meals. "This looks amazing," he said, staring in wonder at his plate. "It's a work of art."

"Thank you," she said. "Not as good as your mom's oatmeal cookies, I'm sure, but definitely more nutritious."

Arch nodded and then took the first bite of his food. After he had swallowed, he told her it was delicious. She glowed at the compliment. It was always nice when your cooking was appreciated. Most people didn't realize how much time and care it took to prepare something that tasted good while also being good for your health.

"So, we know my mom's specialty is cookies. Now tell me about your mom. Is she more into health food like this?"

Tessa blinked. She never spoke about her family or childhood with clients. It was a wall she'd firmly put up when she started working as a caregiver, and she'd never once allowed it to come down. Not even with Margaret, who'd felt like a kindly aunt.

"I'm self-taught," she replied, hoping he didn't realize she hadn't exactly answered his question. "Once I started learning how healing the right foods could be, I really got into it."

Arch nodded. "Makes sense. I already feel better after eating a few meals you've made." Arch managed to turn everything he said into a compliment. It was disarming.

For some reason, Lewis's voice slid into her mind again, criticizing her food. His dinners had no flavor, he'd always complained. Of course, by then he was on so many meds it could have been true, but those last few months had been incredibly difficult as he'd turned his anger about his illness against her.

"So, tell me more about you, Tessa," Arch said. "You've met my entire family. Is yours as big? Or are you an only child?" He put down his fork and trained those sparkling eyes on hers.

She looked away, because holding his gaze—especially when he asked such personal questions—made her stomach flip.

Strangely, it felt like they were on a date. A very intimate first date. Her gaze darted around the room, from the view of the sunset to the gorgeous art, before landing on the enormous TV. She finally remembered he was about to show up on the TV screen.

Thankfully, it was the perfect way to avoid his personal questions. "Your interview will be on in just a moment." She reached for the remote and hit the On button.

As the screen flickered to life, Arch's face appeared, smiling and looking relaxed in the very same lounger he was sitting in right now.

"Oh man," he groaned. "I hate watching myself on TV." She was surprised, but found it endearing that while millions of people paid to see Archer Davenport on-screen, he clearly didn't share their pleasure.

It was surreal to be sitting next to the man on the TV. He seemed so much larger than life up there on the screen, all tanned skin and white teeth. He was laughing now, the sound booming from the surround speakers rigged in every corner of the room.

"We really don't have to watch this," he said. "In fact, we don't have to watch anything. I'd much rather get to know you better. We'll be roomies for the next couple of months after all."

But Tessa wasn't about to start talking about herself. "If it's okay with you, I'd like to see how the interview turned out. I could only hear snippets from the kitchen." She shot him a quick smile and then turned back to the TV.

Roxy's voice rang out as she asked him about his injury, touching his arm in concern. Tessa felt her own skin prickle. The chemistry between them on the screen was just as palpable as it had seemed to her in real life.

"It was my choice to do the stunt," TV Arch was saying. "I've always enjoyed doing my own stunts, so I've had a lot of practice."

Roxy nodded. "Like in *Way Back in the Wilderness*."

Tessa recognized the name of the film that had shot Arch to stardom.

On-screen, Arch nodded back. "Exactly. I've had a lot of training, so I'm pretty confident with all kinds of stunts."

Even though she'd heard quite a lot of the interview, it was interesting to see how they'd edited it down. They'd kept in the part about him being happy working with Smith Sullivan, and there was a clip showing the two of them in cowboy garb, obviously taken on the set of the film before Arch's accident.

Then the camera was back on Arch and Roxy, who said, "And a little gossipy birdie told me that you're all set to be the new star of *Shock Tactics*."

Tessa shot a look at the real Arch beside her. That was the script he'd been reading? *Shock Tactics* was the next huge futuristic action-hero movie—the latest in a blockbuster series. She'd read about it online.

Arch was already famous, but this kind of role would propel him to the next level.

On the TV, Arch raised a teasing eyebrow. "It seems like you know more than I do about casting in Hollywood. I don't believe any announcements have been made."

Roxy let out her girlish laugh. "One thing I know for sure is that your star is continually on the rise, my friend. Why don't we take a look at your journey so far?"

The interview cut to a montage of Arch's career. Tessa recognized footage from his best-known roles as they flashed across the screen, as well as a few smaller movies he'd made. Of course, she had seen every single one.

Watching the short movie clips in order, she could observe how he had grown up. First the teenager who'd melted hearts all over the world and then maturing into the chiseled cheekbones and sun-streaked hair of a man who'd grown only more fascinating with time.

It was overwhelming to see these career highlights, especially sitting beside the real man. But instead of feeling giddy at her unique position, Tessa felt the gap between their worlds grow even bigger. Arch was so normal here at his home, nothing about him suggesting he was any different from the handsome guy who served her cappuccino at the coffee shop. But the truth was that he *was* different. His life was camera crews and news scoops and red carpet premieres.

She had to remind herself not to get caught up, no matter what.

Arch was not a man she could fall for. Not unless she wanted her heart smashed to smithereens. She'd already been through that with Lewis. No way was she ever going to sign up for it again.

The montage of his career in the movies ended, and the camera cut back to Roxy asking Arch about his rehabilitation routine and caregiver. Tessa's heart leaped into her mouth. Earlier, she'd heard him make it clear that she wouldn't be filmed, but what if he'd spoken about her?

She stared at the screen, frozen, waiting for Arch to reply.

"I've got great help from the best available. I'm truly grateful. And it means I'll be able to get back to work very soon."

She looked at Arch and smiled, appreciating that he hadn't let her become part of the narrative. It felt like he respected her wishes, and she liked that. Especially given that her husband never had.

And then, despite his leg, he reached across to the

couch for the remote and switched off the TV. "Honestly, Tessa," he said, his solemn expression a far cry from the outgoing and confident man she'd just watched, "I hate seeing myself on-screen. It makes me cringe."

"I'm sorry. I shouldn't have made you watch it just because I was curious."

"You have nothing to be sorry for," he replied. "I just thought you should know."

As she nodded to make it clear that she understood, she finally saw that he'd finished his dinner, while she'd been so caught up in watching the interview she'd barely tasted her own. When she got up to clear his tray, he told her to sit down and finish.

"I ate too fast," he said. "You're a really good cook. I don't know how you managed to make something that healthy so delicious. You could make a fortune as a personal chef to Hollywood stars. Everyone I work with is always watching their weight. And all of them—me included—hate feeling like we're eating rabbit food."

Tessa never knew what to say when someone complimented her. But she was pleased that he'd noticed she was good at something, even if it was just cooking healthy, tasty food. And he wasn't wrong. The meal *was* good.

"Thank you," she said. "I'm glad you're enjoying my cooking." And then, because she wasn't used to being regarded in such a positive light—especially with Arch's beautiful sea-blue eyes gazing into hers—she quickly changed the subject back to him. Most people were only too happy to talk about themselves, and she was happy to let them.

"Even though you don't like watching yourself on-screen, I thought the interview went really well."

He shrugged. "I got the right sound bites in and avoided saying anything I or the studio would regret. All in a day's work." Then he turned the spotlight back to her, though she'd yet to answer any of his previous questions. "How did you get started in the caregiving field?"

She couldn't find a way out of answering no matter how much she racked her brain. "I sort of fell into it."

Before Arch could ask her any more questions, since she'd finally finished her meal, she took their empty plates and headed for the kitchen. "Time to do the dishes." She enjoyed clearing up after a meal, resetting the kitchen, getting it spic and span before she made the next thing. "Then I'll bring out dessert." It was fresh fruit with a little yogurt, both tasty and healthy.

But as she turned on the faucet, the sound of crutches against tile made her spin around. "What are you doing up?" she exclaimed. "You need to get back into the chair and keep your leg elevated."

"Not a chance," he said. "You cooked this delicious

meal. The least I can do to say thank you is run some soapy water over a couple of plates. I'm the one in the family who washes the dishes, because I can handle delicate things without breaking them."

He delivered this in his sexy, playful voice, and though she did her utmost to ignore any possible innuendo, she couldn't stop imagining what it would be like to have those big, capable hands on her.

As he took the plates and Tessa saw that he was intent on winning the dishwashing battle. "Okay, you can wash. But I'll dry."

With that, Arch tossed her a dishtowel, and they embarked on cleaning up the dishes in an amiable silence. As she dried the china plates, Tessa realized this simple act of domestic cooperation was a million times sweeter than any moment with Lewis at home—who would never have done the dishes even if she'd offered him a zillion dollars. And it was made even sweeter because the movie star, with his hands currently in soapy water, was the last person on earth she would have thought would insist on washing up after dinner.

No doubt about it, Archer Davenport continued to surprise her—in really good ways—at every turn. It should have felt great. But she couldn't help but fear that one day her walls would fall around him. If they did and she let him into her life and heart, there was no possible way that the massive celebrity and the caregiver would make it as a real couple in real life.

Things like that happened only in the movies.

Chapter Twelve

Arch lay in bed, staring up at the ceiling. Somewhere above his head was Tessa. On her bed. Maybe naked beneath the sheets.

Of course, in his fantasies, she was *definitely* naked.

Being this close to her and yet with an entire floor between them was torture. He couldn't stop thinking about her smile, her knowledge and taste in art… and her skill at batting away personal questions.

The more he got to know Tessa, despite her reluctance to open up to him, the wilder she drove him. She was both mysterious *and* sexy. It was a deadly combination. His entire being was aflame just thinking about her.

The sensation was a welcome distraction from the throbbing pain in his leg. He put on a brave face with work and his family, but he did know that a broken tibia wasn't the same as a hangnail. He had the pain to prove it. Tessa was the only one who saw his discomfort, but she didn't nag or fuss. She simply handed him pain relief when he needed it.

They'd completed another round of exercises after dinner, and though the exercises were far less strenuous than earlier in the day, he could still feel the ache in his bones.

Immediately understanding how he was feeling without his having to speak, Tessa had changed tack as his muscles tensed. She slowed down the movements, helping him maneuver into stretches that sent a rush of release through his limbs.

It was like she had a sixth sense for his needs. She made his whole body feel good.

It might be true that she hadn't been quite as relaxed and sociable as he'd hoped, but he couldn't deny that Tessa Taylor was an excellent caregiver.

And an excellent cook.

And had a smile more beautiful than any he'd ever seen on another woman.

And there he went again.

All he could think about was that smile, those pink lips… and how badly he wanted to brush them with his own. He was insanely attracted to her, and something about the way she often looked flushed in his presence—especially when she was having to touch him during their therapy sessions—made him fairly confident that she felt the same undeniable chemistry.

Even if she was going out of her way to act like she didn't.

He tried to shift position, but it was useless. He was

stuck on his back, leg raised on pillows. It was extremely irritating. Plus, he knew *exactly* what would make him feel far better: some fantastic sex with the woman he couldn't stop thinking about. And, of course, he'd make absolutely sure Tessa enjoyed every blissful second.

He allowed himself to close his eyes for a moment and imagine what it would feel like to have her here beside him. Her mouth on his. His hands running over her delectable curves.

His eyes snapped open, and he stared at the ceiling. She was just a flight of stairs away.

He felt like he had to see Tessa. Maybe she was feeling the same frustrated longing he was. She'd given him her cell number for emergencies. But it wasn't like he could explain over the phone what he truly needed. He cast his eyes around the softly lit room. When his gaze landed on his crutches propped against his bedside table, he knew what to do.

Shifting to the left of the bed, he grabbed their handles and tossed them out of reach. "There," he said aloud, feeling satisfied that being stranded without his crutches would qualify as an emergency. "Now I'm stuck."

He reached for his cell. It was midnight. Would she already be asleep? It had been a long day for them both.

But he decided to take his chances and scrolled through his contacts. His heart leaped anew just at the sight of her name. He hit the number and waited, aware of his heart still pounding in his chest the way it had when he was a teenager and had called the home of his first crush, hoping her dad didn't pick up the phone.

Tessa answered after three rings. "What happened?" she said, not even bothering with a hello.

"I need you," he replied.

He didn't have time to explain why. Tessa disconnected, and within seconds, he could hear her feet on the stairs as she raced down to him.

He set his cell on the side table and tried to arrange his features into the most innocent expression he could muster. He probably should have put on a T-shirt before he called—he slept only in his boxers—but it was too late now. Besides, she was used to touching his near-naked body during their workouts.

The door burst open, and there was Tessa, panting in the doorway, a worried expression on her face. But when she saw him sitting up in bed, she frowned. "What's wrong?" she asked. "What do you need help with?"

Her dark hair flowed down her back, just as he'd seen at his dad's birthday, the curls still bouncing from her dash downstairs. She was wearing a pair of linen shorts and a loose white tank top. He could just make out the swell of her breasts beneath the fabric, and that alone made him feel like his grasp on his attraction to her was about to slip.

Somehow, he managed to tear his eyes away from her gorgeous figure to give her a sheepish look and then pointed at his crutches, which he realized now weren't nearly as far from the bed as he'd thought.

"I can't reach my crutches." And then, realizing that she was probably going to call him out on that, he changed his tone to sound a little cheeky. "Or maybe I just wanted to see if you would really come downstairs if I called."

She looked at him, a little incredulous, but then a smile began to play around those luscious lips. Calmly, without rushing, she walked over to his side of the bed, picked up the crutches, and propped them against the table once more. He could tell she was slightly amused, but he could also see that she was irritated too.

"How did your crutches get all the way over there?" she asked, clearly questioning his motives, even though he was pretty sure she already knew the answer.

She was so close now that he could smell the scent of her coconut shampoo. Unable to come up with a believable fib, he decided to admit the truth.

"I tossed them over there, hoping that if you came downstairs, you'd give them to me… and maybe stay a little while."

At that, Tessa took a step backward. She folded her arms across her chest, and the playful expression instantly disappeared.

Damn it! He'd said too much too soon. He just couldn't help himself. And now he couldn't take it back.

The damage was done.

She moved the crutches even closer. "Why do you want me to stay? Are you in pain?"

Phew. She had given him the opportunity to explain his flirtatious comment.

He nodded and then said, "My leg is hurting. A lot." He paused and looked into her sparkling eyes. Before he could stop himself, he added, "But the truth is, I can't stop thinking about you."

She looked both vulnerable and a bit irked. So the last thing he expected her to say was, "You've got a broken leg. You can't possibly have sex."

Arch chuckled, pleased that she had read his mind. Which also made him wonder, yet again, if she'd already been thinking the same thing.

"I have no doubt that we could find a way to work around that." He hoped his voice sounded as sexy as he found Tessa right now.

But it was as though she hadn't heard him. "Also, I'm your caregiver, not your girlfriend. Or your one-night stand. I think you're forgetting that. Tonight, I'll excuse it because you're not used to taking such strong pain pills. But if you pull something like this again, I won't be so understanding."

But despite her strong words—damn, she was sexy when she was mad and lecturing him—her cheeks had flushed a charming shade of pink.

Was she going out of her way to act like there was no attraction between them? Yes, she most certainly was. But Arch knew she was just hiding from the truth of the heat between them. He'd never felt anything like it. Not until he'd first laid eyes on Tessa on the beach.

Her arms had dropped to her sides, and her chest rose and fell beneath her thin tank top. Neither of them spoke. And then he saw her lips part, ever so slowly, and for one wild moment he thought she might actually let their magnetic connection pull her toward him. He threw back the bedclothes so that she could climb in, revealing the rest of his torso.

But to his horror, all that did was make her mood palpably shift. He watched, aghast, as she literally shut herself down in front of him.

She cleared her throat. "As I've already said, the next time you call me, it had better be for a good reason, or I'm going to have to call the firm I work for and let them know you need someone else to work with you."

He knew he should let it go, but he'd never felt an attraction this strong before. He'd been drawn to her the minute he set eyes on her, and now she was in his home, half dressed, and he was hurting and lonely, and all he wanted was to put his arms around her and feel her skin against his own.

In a gentle tone that held no pressure or cajoling in it, he said, "I know you're here for work. But you're also single. I'm single. We could have a lot of fun together."

She hesitated for just a moment and then said, "Yes, I'm single. But I'm also a widow. I'm only here to be your caregiver, nothing more." She paused a beat. "Good night."

She turned her back on him and left the room.

As the door clicked shut, he stared at the spot where she'd just been standing, feeling like the worst jerk in the world. He hadn't missed the pain in her eyes.

A widow.

He'd been coming on to a woman who'd lost the love of her life, robbed of happiness by death.

Way to completely blow it, Arch.

He let out a big sigh. Ten minutes ago, it had seemed like such a good idea to call Tessa down here. He'd so badly wanted to see her face, to let her know he was thinking of her.

But now he regretted the decision. Somehow, he'd let his emotions get away from him and override his common sense.

He twisted uncomfortably to turn off the bedside lamp. The room was thrown into darkness, leaving him once again staring at the ceiling. Sleeping was hard enough with his leg needing to be elevated all night, but even if his leg had been in perfect condition, he still wouldn't get much sleep tonight. Not when he was utterly furious with himself for pushing Tessa's boundaries.

And especially for not realizing that her tough exterior was hiding a world of pain.

Tessa had been married, and her husband had died. Though he didn't know anything more than that, it had to be a lot to come back from. And jumping into bed with him to have "fun" was surely the very last thing on her mind.

From this moment forward, he vowed, he'd be a better man.

Even if it hurt like hell to still want her this bad, knowing he would likely never have her body… or her heart.

Chapter Thirteen

As he had predicted, Arch slept badly that night. It was impossible to get comfortable with his leg in the cast, and the open windows bringing in the soft ocean breeze did nothing to cool the heat in his body after seeing Tessa in her skimpy pajamas.

For what seemed like hours, thoughts of Tessa raced through his conscious and then his dreaming mind. The dark curls of her hair. The deep blue of her eyes. How soft the skin between her breasts had looked when he caught a glimpse.

Now it was eight a.m., and he was not rested.

Slipping on a T-shirt and shorts, he made his way on crutches to the kitchen. From the hallway, he could hear Tessa tending to breakfast. He paused in the doorway for a moment and watched as she made coffee. It was hard to predict how she would greet him. Like nothing had happened? Or would she be back to that matronly strictness that had been a major disappointment yesterday morning? He hoped not.

At the same time, he felt guilty for coming on to

her last night. He owed her a massive apology.

Tessa still had her back to him as she made her way around the kitchen. Something in him softened as he watched her. She looked like she had been made to be part of his home and had been living here for months. He'd always loved his Carmel-by-the-Sea house, but suddenly it really felt like *home*. All because Tessa was here.

But when she turned to pour the coffee and saw him standing there, her whole body tensed, and she became stiff. Her long hair was pulled back in a practical and very nurse-like bun. She was wearing her uniform shirt again. The one with her name stitched across the front. Obviously, he had made her uncomfortable, and now she was redrawing the boundaries between them.

Not a good sign.

And it was all his fault.

Yet again, he inwardly cursed himself for his behavior. He'd always thought he'd escaped the curse of the totally self-involved celebrity. But from the way he'd acted last night, he suddenly felt like he was its poster boy.

He swallowed and said in his best lighthearted voice, "Morning. Something smells good."

"Good morning," she replied, sounding like a hotel receptionist about to check him out of his room. "I'm making buckwheat pancakes with fresh strawberries."

Without a hint of a smile, she continued to lay the table. With one place setting only.

She didn't intend to join him for breakfast. His heart sank, even though he couldn't blame her.

He walked over to the table and, resting his crutches against the marble, turned to face her. "Tessa, can you stop for a moment so that I can speak with you about something really important?"

She frowned. And he knew she wasn't going to make this easy. He'd have to bite the bullet and lay himself bare to her.

"I am so sorry about last night. I didn't mean to upset you. I didn't know anything about your past, but even if I did, I had no right to hit on you." He took a deep breath. If there was one thing his parents had taught him, it was that if you were going to apologize, you should do it properly. "I also wanted to say that I'm so sorry you lost the love of your life."

But to his surprise, Tessa made a face and shook her head. "Lewis Taylor was my husband… but he wasn't the love of my life."

"He wasn't?" Arch was so surprised he stared at her.

Tessa sighed, then sank into one of the kitchen chairs. Arch took the one across from her and waited. Whatever she needed to say, he was there to listen.

She stared down at her hands in her lap. "I guess I thought that at first. That he was the love of my life. I mean, that's why I married him." She sighed. "But let's just say his initial charm wore off pretty fast." She paused again, and he waited, surprised to feel his own heart thudding in his chest. He couldn't bear the image of her at the altar, dressed in a beautiful white gown, waiting to marry someone who wasn't him.

Considering marriage had never before crossed Arch's mind, this proved he had it *bad* for Tessa.

"And then when he got sick with early Parkinson's…" She trailed off. The silence grew. Finally, she said, "That's how I fell into caregiving."

He could see that she didn't plan to say more. He watched her face. She hadn't said it outright, but from the little that she had said, he got the sense that her husband had been controlling and not a very nice man.

Arch felt instinctively protective. More than that, he wanted to punch the guy. Even though he had died from a terrible disease.

After he'd gathered himself, he said, "It must have been really difficult caring for him."

She nodded sadly, still not meeting his gaze. How Arch longed to look into her eyes and tell her that she didn't have to worry about men being jerks anymore. He wanted to treat her the way she deserved. The way she should always have been treated.

But after the way he'd acted last night, he was afraid it would only sound like another come-on.

She took another deep breath, and he suddenly realized that maybe she'd never told anyone about her husband before. He leaned across the table and took her right hand in his. Not in a sexy way, but in a comforting one.

Her skin was soft. Their touch electric. But he only squeezed her hand gently and then let it go. It was his way of showing her that she was safe here. No harm was going to come to her under his roof.

What's more, it meant so much to him that she was finally opening up. Especially in the wake of his behavior last night. He cursed himself again for ever suggesting she climb into his bed. He wasn't a hormone-ridden sixteen-year-old anymore. He should have known better.

Thankfully, Tessa seemed to get the message as she gave him a small smile, then began to speak again. Her husband had been in financial services. "After he got sick and couldn't work, he started day trading." She made a face. "I had no idea what he was doing—he only said he was working on a project, and as he was so bitter about losing his health, I was happy that he took an interest in something." She blew out a breath. "I didn't know that he was making crazy bets. I want so badly to believe that his illness and the meds made him irrational, but all I know for sure is that he lost all our hard-earned savings." She raised her eyes to his. "I ended up widowed *and* broke."

"I can't imagine how that must have felt. Didn't he

have any life insurance?"

"He cashed in the policy to keep trading."

"How could he do that to you?" Arch couldn't hold back his incredulous tone.

"Like I said, I try to blame the illness and not him." She took a breath and pulled her shoulders back, clearly working to brush off the past. "Anyway, it turns out that looking after sick people is something I'm very good at. So, I made it my career."

He was impressed by how brave she'd been. How brave she still was. Because underneath that tough exterior was a woman who'd been dealt a seriously rough hand.

Clearly, her husband had made her lose her faith in there being any good men out there, and then Arch had proved her right by coming on to her the first night she was in his house.

What a fool. Right then and there, he decided that nothing would get in the way of his showing her not only his deepest respect, but also how a man should treat a woman he cared about. The way his dad had always treated his mom.

If his leg hadn't been broken, Arch would have kicked himself. After his antics the night before, he was surprised she hadn't packed up and left already.

But the very fact she was still here—making pancakes, no less—gave him hope. Hope that they could be friends, at the very least. And, deep down, he still harbored a hope that she was as drawn to him as he was to her, even if she hid it well.

He couldn't say anything that would make last night up to her, so his actions would have to be louder than words. Starting right now.

When she brought over his plate of pancakes, he picked up his knife and fork and then cut his pancake stack clear in half, pushing one side in Tessa's direction. "We're equals," he said, "right down to the pancakes. This stack is enormous, and working with me—especially on the therapeutic movements that I don't want to do because they hurt so much—means you need your strength as much as I need mine."

To his relief, Tessa smiled, and he immediately felt like he'd conquered a tall mountain, simply because he'd made her smile again.

"Okay," she said. "These pancakes are actually good enough that I'm not going to object."

She got herself a plate and cutlery, though he wouldn't have minded sharing the same plate. Or fork. Maybe even feed her the pancakes himself—

Just then, his cell buzzed. It was Jay. Though he wanted to tuck into his warm and delicious-looking pancakes, he picked up.

"Arch, my man," Jay said, his voice way too loud for this time of the morning, "how are you feeling? Nursed back to full health yet?"

Arch grimaced. His agent loved to win an argument. He should have known that Jay would be unbearably smug at getting him to accept a caregiver. Well, little did he know just how wonderful that caregiver was. If anyone was getting the last laugh, it was Arch.

He told Jay that his exercises were going well and he was being fed like a champion.

"That's exactly what I wanted to hear. I just got off a call with the producer of your movie with Smith Sullivan. He was thrilled with your interview last night. They figure they should ride the wave of interest a prime-time splash like that will have generated, so they've arranged for you and Smith to present an award at Moonrise."

"Wait—what?" Arch said, incredulous. "The prestigious indie film awards?"

"The very same," Jay said, sounding pretty pleased. Next to presenting at Sundance, Moonrise was it on this continent.

Arch caught Tessa's eye, and she raised a brow as if to say, *Impressive*. She could hear every word, Jay's voice was so loud.

"But that's in two weeks," Arch said. The producer must have pulled some serious strings to get them that slot so late in the day. "I'll still be on crutches."

"Exactly," Jay replied. "That's part of what they love about doing it this way. It's such great promo for the film, with fans getting to watch their favorite actor heal and come back to life before their eyes. I'll be in touch with the details soon. Stay healthy, cowboy."

And with that, Jay ended the call.

Chapter Fourteen

Tessa made her way to the coffee shop to meet Mila and Erin, feeling as nervous as if it were a first date. She had changed into one of her favorite shirts, a designer piece that she'd picked up for a few bucks at a thrift store. She'd let down her hair from its tight bun.

She'd immediately liked Arch's sisters when they'd first met and hoped they felt the same way about her. At the same time, as she had said to Arch, they'd probably invited her only to be nice. But he had assured her that his sisters wouldn't do that unless they genuinely liked her. She could tell he was pleased that they'd invited her, which made her all the more nervous for this to go well.

But if she was being completely honest with herself, that wasn't the only reason she was feeling nervous. Truth be told, the last twenty-four hours had been a total emotional whirlwind.

After Arch had suggested she share his bed last night, she had swung between two conflicting reactions. To her mortification, her first instinct had been to jump on in. He had looked so incredibly hot sitting up in bed, shirtless, with that sexy look in his eyes. It had been torture to tear her eyes away from his rippling, tanned abs.

But she had promised herself to stay professional. Professional was the only way to protect her heart.

At the same time, his easy charm—and his obvious expectations that he could show her such a good time that she wouldn't regret sleeping with him—riled her up the wrong way. Clearly, her movie-star client was used to getting what he wanted.

Margaret had assured her that Archer Davenport was a real gentleman, just like his father. And in the end, he had been. But only after she'd rejected his invitation to be the flavor of the week.

So, she had picked up his crutches, which clearly had only been a ploy to get her down there in the first place, and fled his bedroom.

Only to find that when she got back upstairs and into her own bed, it felt cold and lonely. And then she couldn't help wondering whether Arch had anything on beneath the covers over his hips. All of which were *very bad* thoughts for her to have about a client.

Needless to say, she did not sleep well.

That wasn't even the worst of it, though. Out of nowhere, she had told Arch about her husband. She never talked to *anyone* about Lewis, let alone a client. Even Margaret knew almost nothing about Tessa's past.

But at breakfast, she'd found herself opening up to Arch with an ease that was both surprising and frightening. There was something about him that made her want to tell him things she'd never tell anyone else. An openness and an interest in her—but also a distinct feeling that he'd never judge her for her actions or thoughts.

And then, after they'd shared the stack of buckwheat pancakes she'd made, he'd helped her with the dishes again. She found it so endearing. And that was all it took for her to wonder what it would be like to feel his hands on her skin…

The devil on her shoulder told her she'd been an idiot to turn down his offer to join him in bed. Thank God the rational part of her brain won out in the end.

Getting involved with a client was a *massive* no-no. She could get fired over it. But more than that, if she did become intimate with him, she'd leave with a broken heart as soon as their affair was over. Because how could she not fall for him? And how could he stay for long in Carmel after his leg healed, when he would need to return to his real life in Hollywood? He already had more films scheduled.

His life was so far away from her own that it truly was unimaginable that anything could ever work out for them long term.

Not that he'd been asking for long term last night.

She was so lost in her thoughts, she almost didn't notice that she'd stepped onto Ocean Avenue, where so many of Carmel's restaurants and high-end boutiques lined the streets. Tessa didn't have the money to go inside most of them. Her usual coffee place was down a little side alley, but Erin had said to meet them at Saint Anna's, a beautiful coffee shop with European-style *pâtisseries à la crème* arranged in rows in the window.

She stared at the gorgeous array of delicacies, took a breath to steady her nerves, and went inside.

The shop was bustling with customers, each circular table occupied. She soon spotted Mila and Erin, who had already secured a table in the corner and were chatting with the couple at the neighboring table. Tessa smiled. These two were so friendly and open, they probably knew everyone in town.

Erin spotted Tessa and waved her over. She was wearing a silk blouse and tailored jeans, and Tessa was glad she'd made the effort to change out of her uniform before leaving the house.

"Morning!" Erin said, bright as anything. "We saved you a seat. Don't you look pretty. What are you having?"

Tessa sat next to Erin and said she'd love a cappuccino. She definitely needed another coffee after the sleepless night she'd had. Although she wasn't about to tell Arch's sister that.

Erin waved the waiter over and ordered Tessa's coffee, as well as a refill for herself and a plate of the assorted French pastries that she said Saint Anna's was famous for.

After saying hello, Mila, who looked all kinds of fabulous in a beautifully made pale gray suit, told Tessa, "This is Estelle."

At the next table, Estelle was dressed in a glamorous cream linen two-piece, a single strand of pearls at her throat. Her white hair was swept back from her face with a velvet band. She extended a hand to Tessa, and they exchanged hellos.

Estelle turned to Erin. "I'll email you an update to my obituary this afternoon. It was so nice talking with you both." She stood and placed a tip on the table for the waiter.

After she left, Tessa asked Erin if Estelle was ill.

Erin nodded. "No, but she's very organized. The obituary section of the *Sea Shell* is read by everyone in town. It's not uncommon for people like Estelle to make sure I'm aware of all their accomplishments. They even send updated lists of loved ones when a new grandchild or great-grandchild is born. I'm used to it, obviously, and I really enjoy learning more about the people in our community here. The life stories of some who have lived in Carmel-by-the-Sea for fifty-plus years are amazing, and it's an honor to write and publish their stories."

"Okay, enough about the *Sea Shell*," Mila teased. "Let's focus on Tessa. Beginning with where you got that gorgeous top."

Tessa grinned and touched the ruffled collar appreciatively. "At a thrift store."

Both sisters looked surprised at first, but then surprise gave way to amazement. Tessa guessed neither of them had ever set foot in a thrift store—just like their brother.

Erin said, "Wow, that's an amazing find. I can never find anything when I go thrifting. Although I read a lot about hidden designer gems in those packed racks. The funny thing is that I've written articles about thrifting even though I've never had any luck in real life."

"It's a bit of an art form," Tessa said, laughing. "You have to know which store to go to on which day of the week, along with what time the new inventory comes in—then throw in a lot of patience, and bingo—you have what I like to call a *find*. Oh, and another important key is to look up. Some of the best treasures are on the highest shelves, because people get focused on the racks of clothes and never think to see what's lining the walls. I'll take you both one day, if you like."

The waiter arrived with the coffees and Danish pastries. Tessa took a deep sip of her coffee, which was frothy and dusted with a fine layer of cocoa. Delicious.

Mila went straight for an apricot Danish, which

Tessa thought looked too pretty to eat.

"You're clearly brilliant at thrifting, but you'll have to count me out," Mila said. "Not because I don't think you can find great clothes in thrift or resale stores, but I would have nightmares about bumping into a client wearing one of their old dresses. I don't think it would help me sell high-end homes."

Erin wrinkled her nose at her sister. "You're such a snob. How is buying and selling a used house any different than buying and selling a dress that no longer fits or that you're just ready to get rid of to open up space in your closet for something new?"

Though Mila had explained her aversion to thrifting clothes in the nicest possible way, Tessa had still been feeling slightly embarrassed that she'd actually gone and invited the two women to join her on a future thrifting trip. But then Erin had come back with a pretty good rebuttal.

Still trying to relax with Arch's sisters, Tessa accepted a raspberry pastry from the plate Erin offered her. It was such a treat to be sitting in a coffee shop, chatting and eating delicious pastries on a Tuesday morning. Tessa couldn't remember the last time she'd done something like this.

Mila wiped a smudge of apricot jam from the corner of her mouth. "I'm too busy to go thrifting anyway." She leaned forward, an excited glint in her eyes. "Jay Malone, Arch's agent, called me this morning and told me he's looking for a place."

"That's great," Erin said, although she had sounded more impressed by Tessa's thrifting skills. Or maybe that was just what Tessa wanted to believe.

In any case, Tessa, who figured Jay would have a big budget as a top Hollywood agent, said it sounded like an exciting new client for Mila.

"It is," Mila replied. "And nice for Arch, too, to have his agent nearby. Especially since they're close friends as well. Speaking of which…" She gave Tessa a broad smile that she figured was supposed to look innocent but seemed anything but. "How are you getting on with our dear brother?"

Erin added, "It's been about twenty-four hours, so I figure he's already driving you crazy. Am I right?"

Both women were entitled to be the tiniest bit nosy, given how close all the Davenport siblings were. Tessa decided to remain neutral. "It's going fine," she said. "And his house isn't only beautiful, it's also so comfortable and full of warmth."

"So the setup is working for you?" Mila pushed.

Tessa nodded, though after last night and this morning, she was having bigger and bigger doubts that she could keep her growing feelings for Arch under wraps for the next two months and protect herself from heartbreak.

"Good," Mila said. "Just don't let Arch push you around. He's too used to getting things his way."

Tessa's cheeks flushed as she thought about the proposal he'd made the night before. She took another sip of coffee, hoping neither sister would notice her reaction. "I've been a caregiver for long enough, fortunately, that I'm not so easy to boss around," she said at last, putting down her cup. "He listens to me, at least so far. He also does his exercises without complaint, and he's eating well and even seems to enjoy my cooking."

"That's good to hear," Mila said. "I thought he'd be pretty resistant to working with a caregiver. Then again, I hadn't counted on someone like you. Clearly, you're the reason he's willing to follow instructions, rather than doing things his own way, like he normally does."

Tessa was surprised to find herself wanting to defend Arch—and also to deflect the spotlight from herself. "I think what's driving his motivation to heal as quickly as possible is that he still has a couple of scenes to shoot with Smith Sullivan to finish that movie. He's also really excited about his next action film. He knows he needs to be in top physical shape for both. I just hope I can help him fully heal in the compressed time frame he's insisted on."

"Arch can be easygoing a lot of the time, but he also has a stubborn streak," Mila said. "If he wants something badly enough, he won't stop until he gets it."

Erin laughed. "Sounds a lot like you, sis."

To her credit, Mila took the teasing in stride. "It's true. Stubbornness runs in the family. Though I like to call it determination. We Davenports don't give up easily when we want something."

For a millisecond, Tessa wondered if Mila was referring to the possibility of a romance between her and Arch. But she was pretty sure she hadn't given away her budding feelings for him.

At the same time, Tessa had a prickling sense that if Arch was truly determined to entice her into his bed, she'd have a hard time resisting. Even now, the image of him bare-chested and grinning flashed into her mind.

But no. She was determined to stay strong. She'd had a lot of practice in her lifetime; now was the time to use it.

To her relief, the two sisters turned their attention from Arch and returned to the topic of his agent's house-hunt. Mila was clearly excited—she'd already lined up three fabulous places for him to view.

Tessa enjoyed listening to their easy chatter. She was surprised how comfortable she felt in their company. It was like the three of them had been hanging out for years. She couldn't imagine how nice it must be to have a built-in best friend for life in your sibling. She finished her pastry and then checked her watch. Already an hour had gone by.

Erin mirrored the gesture. "I have to get to work."

"Me too," Mila said. "But this was nice."

Erin turned to Tessa. "I loved having you join us today. And I can't wait to go thrift store shopping with you on a day when you can take a little more time off from working with Arch."

Tessa felt herself glow at their comments. "Thank you so much for inviting me. I often get so caught up in my work that I forget about socializing."

"Well, we can't have that," Mila replied. "Let's make this a regular thing. Please come along next Tuesday too."

As they left the coffee shop, Tessa felt like she'd made two friends in town.

If only her relationship with their brother was as uncomplicated.

Chapter Fifteen

Tessa and Arch soon found a routine that worked for both of them, and as the days passed, it started to feel as though she and Arch had always lived and worked together. It was strange to think it had been only a week since she'd first arrived, full of nervous energy about working with a movie star.

Rising in the morning at the same time, Tessa made them both a healthy breakfast, showered, and then helped Arch through his exercises. He performed them diligently, working his muscles to the point that she sometimes wanted to tell him to slow down, but she knew how important it was to him to stay in top physical condition. She admired his dedication and tried to stay cool and professional every day while secretly admiring his incredible physique.

He spent mid-mornings reading over his script while she prepared lunch, using her skill and imagination to add flavor and interest to his extremely healthy diet. Whatever she made, he complimented her. After she'd been married to a man who'd had only complaints, it felt strange to receive so much praise, but she loved the way he appreciated her cooking. It made her work even harder to do a great job for him.

After lunch, she completed a short workout of her own in the home gym or took advantage of the pool. She loved the cool feeling of the water on her body as she breast-stroked through thirty laps, letting her mind wander.

Which of course led to thoughts about Arch. Since the night he'd come on to her and sworn that from then on he'd be a perfect gentleman, he hadn't broken his word. Why then, in the moments they were apart, did she so often find herself daydreaming about him pulling her in for a kiss?

What's more, when she woke in the night, she always imagined going downstairs to him. While he'd kept his promise not to try to get her into his bed, he'd also made it very clear that she'd be welcome anytime she chose to come to him.

She could so easily—too easily!—imagine the way he'd brush her hair out of her eyes and gently caress her cheek. She could almost feel the sensation of his lips on hers, tender and yet firm. His fingers traveling down her spine, making her shiver.

And every time she went down this road, her sexy thoughts felt like a betrayal. Because she knew better. Not only was falling for a client *verboten*, but they could never work as a couple in real life—and Tessa wasn't the kind who could be satisfied with a fling.

In the afternoons, Arch's friends dropped by, and one—or several—members of his family usually made an appearance. She'd finally stopped jumping out of her skin when she discovered another Davenport in the house. It became clear they all knew the key code and rarely bothered to knock. It took some getting used to, but she found that she loved how comfortable and casual the family were around one another. She'd never experienced that kind of family closeness before.

Between visitors, Arch was constantly on his phone or laptop, catching up with people and keeping on top of business. She'd never realized how much work went into being a movie star.

He had people helping with his social media, people coordinating his public appearances—and she also discovered that he spent a lot of time and money on charity. She tried to coax the devices away from him when she could, reminding him that rest was an important part of his recovery. Sometimes she was successful, other times not so much. But it seemed Arch was aware of his stubborn side and tried not to let it completely control him. In those small moments of victory, she felt real pleasure.

And then her mind would linger on the word *pleasure*, and she'd succumb to yet another forbidden fantasy…

★ ★ ★

With every day that passed, Arch found himself more intrigued by Tessa. She had created a simple but very effective routine for him that he'd never have guessed he'd enjoy so much.

Normally, he liked to work hard and play hard. And yet, the last week, which mainly involved eating well, working out, and focusing on his recovery, felt like one of the happiest he could remember. He woke every morning looking forward to the day ahead.

Something deep inside told him that his anticipation to greet each day was less about the day's activities and more about the company. Tessa made everything seem great. She never pushed him too hard, but he found himself working harder than he'd believed he could, simply because she was there to support him.

His dad treated his mom like she was everything in the world to him, and that was how he wanted to treat Tessa. She lit up a room from the moment she walked into it. It was just a shame there was one room where she never ventured…

Thankfully, by now he believed he had earned her trust. Because he'd kept his promise. Since the night he'd pushed things between them too far, Arch hadn't made a single move on Tessa. It wasn't for lack of wanting her. He still stared up at the ceiling every night, hoping she'd come down. In fact, he'd spent hours imagining how her body would feel beneath his, beside his, over him...

But if anything ever did happen between them, the next move had to be hers.

However, while it was extremely unlikely that she'd ever make a move on him—he could practically see the walls she'd put up around her heart and body, at least where he was concerned—this didn't stop her from constantly occupying his thoughts. Especially when she was out of the house, as she was now, and he could flash back to the feel of her hands on his body as she'd helped him stretch earlier in the day. Or the sweet scent of her light perfume as she sat down to eat a meal with him. Or how incredibly gorgeous and sexy she looked coming out of the pool after her daily swim.

Tessa often went out in the afternoons, when he was resting or working on his script, leaving with a backpack and returning a couple of hours later, flushed and happy. He was deeply curious about what she was up to during her off time, but a voice inside his head told him not to ask. Tessa was a private person. She had already opened up about her love of art and the bad way things had ended with her husband. He didn't want to push her for more too soon. If she wanted him to know where she went each afternoon, she would tell him. And it would be all the sweeter if she opened up to him of her own volition versus his dragging the information out of her.

As he gazed out the window, wondering when she would return, it suddenly hit him. He was falling for Tessa. Hard.

He'd always been career-driven and had dated women who worked in the same industry, since he was so busy there wasn't time to meet a woman outside of work. But something about breaking his leg, and meeting Tessa, had literally stopped him in his tracks and made him reevaluate his life. The truth was that he was enjoying his forced vacation more than he could have imagined.

But more than that, he was enjoying Tessa in his life in a way that was different from anything he'd ever felt.

Could it be that he'd been waiting all his life for this woman?

Sitting with the questions for several long moments, he realized that instead of frightening him, the idea made him happy.

He picked up his script. The plot was great—full of action and surprising twists and turns. But right now, he was reading a romantic scene between his character and his character's quiet assistant and love interest. Arch couldn't help imagining her with Tessa's dark hair and vivid blue eyes—

"Daydreaming, little bro? Bet I can guess about whom."

He jumped, jolting his leg so it smarted. When he

looked up, Mila was standing there, looking at him with a knowing expression.

"I was working," he said, knowing better than to sound defensive, but not quite managing it. "Daydreaming is part of being an actor." She looked as though she doubted his word, so he added, "At least it is when you can't do more than sit in a recliner all day." Finally giving her a smile, he said, "It's good to see you." Maybe his sister could take his mind off Tessa. He set the script on the glass coffee table.

She slumped onto the sofa across from him, looking a little worn out, which was strange for her. "I've been working some serious overtime trying to find your agent a place he'll fall in love with."

He knew Jay was looking for a beach house in Carmel. It would be great to have him in town, but it also made him feel more determined than ever to be strong enough to shoot *Shock Tactics*. What if Jay was depending on his commission in order to afford one of the ridiculously expensive houses in Carmel? What if his leg didn't heal in time and they decided at the last minute to replace him?

"Is he a tough customer?" Arch asked, guessing at why his sister had a slightly frustrated look about her.

"Let's just say that Jay is... discerning." She sat up straighter on the couch and drew her shoulders back. "But you know me—never one to back down from a challenge. In fact, I thrive on them. Just like you."

Clearly, his sister's natural competitive streak had been activated. She'd always been that way and then found the perfect outlet in professional surfing. When that had ended in tragedy, Mila's thrill in chasing the perfect wave had transformed into closing the sale on the perfect house. It was what made her one of the hottest Realtors out there.

"So how are you feeling?" Mila asked, her tone serious now. "Is the pain still bad?"

Arch shrugged. He could feel himself getting stronger by the day, but the ache in his left leg throbbed often enough to remind him he was still healing. "It's okay," he said.

"Which means it hurts like heck," Mila replied knowingly, given that she'd been in even worse physical shape after her career-ending injury. "And I know what you're like. Too proud and stubborn to admit when you need help." A sly look came into her eyes. "Except when it comes to Tessa."

At just the mention of her name, his heart beat faster. But he didn't want to risk any more teasing from his sister. "You know I had no choice about a live-in caregiver. That was all the studio's doing."

"Yet you managed to snag the prettiest caregiver around."

Arch grinned. "All part of the healing process," he joked. "But seriously, she's amazing at her job." Suddenly, he had an idea. "Did you drive here?"

Mila nodded. "Why?"

"Tessa's been so great with me that I'd like to buy her some flowers to say thank you. It'll be a surprise for when she gets back."

Mila raised an eyebrow, but he could also see she approved. "I knew I pulled in here for a reason rather than just driving by. Sure, let's go."

"By the way," he said, "Tessa said you guys made her feel truly welcome at your Tuesday coffee. I think it meant a lot to her."

"I enjoyed her company. Tessa's one of the most grounded people I've met in a long time," Mila replied. "*And* she can resist your charms. What's not to like?" She helped him to his feet and handed him his crutches. "Let's go."

A cool breeze blew in through the windows of Mila's Range Rover, and Arch closed his eyes and breathed in the fresh sea air. Apart from sitting in the garden a few times, he'd barely been outside the door. For someone used to being on the go all the time, it had been frustrating at first. But now he was getting used to the slower pace. Still, it was nice to be out, knowing he'd have a lovely surprise waiting for Tessa when she got back from whatever it was she did in the afternoons.

Mila was normally a fast driver, but as if she could read his mind, she slowed down her racer style and drove along the coast road slowly enough that he could take in Carmel-by-the-Sea's beauty as if through fresh eyes. Since his career had taken off, life had been go, go, go. But getting out of his house reminded him of Carmel's gentle pace and the pleasure of seeing families and couples enjoying their afternoons on the golden sand and in town.

Mila pulled up at a red light. She was humming along to an old country song on the radio, tapping the beat on the steering wheel.

And then that's when he saw her.

Tessa.

She was standing a ways back from the beach on a flat rock. In front of her was an easel, and she was frowning in total concentration as she painted the landscape in her view.

So *this* was where she disappeared to when she had some time off. She was a painter! And from what he could see from the car, her work was excellent. She had an extraordinary eye for color and composition.

As the light turned green and Mila accelerated, he twisted his neck to catch the last glimpse of Tessa and her easel just to make sure he hadn't been hallucinating.

But no. It was definitely Tessa. Her incredible knowledge and appreciation of contemporary artists all made sense now, along with the dreamy yet satisfied look in her eyes when she returned to the house after her time alone.

Now that the mystery of her afternoons off was solved, he had even more questions. The main one being, why on earth did she keep her talent a secret? If he'd been able to paint, he'd want to show his work to as many people as possible. Not hide it away.

But maybe that was the difference between him and Tessa. While he had always loved an audience, even as a little kid putting on one-man shows for his family in the backyard, Tessa clearly kept her passions inside herself, nurturing them without an audience.

Though he had a zillion questions for her about her paintings—in particular why she was working as a caregiver instead of getting her work into galleries—he decided then and there to respect that painting was Tessa's private work.

If she wanted him to know about it, she'd tell him. At the same time, a part of him couldn't help but feel he was lying to her by omission. Which was why he really hoped that one day in the very near future, she would trust him enough to share her passion for making art with him.

Because he never wanted her to think that he would lie to her.

Chapter Sixteen

Tessa always felt revived after a couple of hours spent painting. Even better, she'd stopped in at a thrift store on her way back to Arch's home and found a retro crochet dress in cream that fit perfectly and cost next to nothing. So, she arrived feeling utterly content. Lately, she'd taken to painting outdoors whenever she had time off, and she'd been working on a beach landscape that was going particularly well.

Flushed and, if she were truthful, excited to see Arch again after some time apart, she called hello, and then went straight upstairs to drop off her backpack, her easel, and her new dress, and freshen up.

It wasn't until she'd splashed some cold water on her face that she realized she hadn't heard Arch reply.

Surely he couldn't have gone out alone? Maybe one of the Davenports had dropped by. But when that was the case, he usually left a note by the door.

She raced downstairs and into the living room.

To her relief, she found him sitting in his usual spot in the reclining chair. His laptop was open in front of him, and she frowned. He was supposed to be taking an afternoon nap while she was gone, not working.

She was about to give him a talking-to when she noticed the expression on his face. His usually sparkling eyes were full of anguish. Immediately, her heart pounded with worry. He was so stoic, but by now she knew when he was hurting. It broke her heart to see it. But this was something more than just his aching leg.

She rushed over and asked, "What is it, Arch? Something seems really wrong."

After what seemed like forever, Arch looked away from the screen and up at Tessa. He swallowed hard. "The director sent me a video of the stunt from the buddy movie. The one that landed me in this." He gestured to the cast on his leg.

She walked around behind him, and he tapped Play. A golden desert scene appeared before her, the dust in the air dancing in the sun's rays. The camera panned across the impressive landscape, over a glistening river, and then in the distance, she saw Arch on the back of a horse in full Western cowboy gear.

He looked so handsome and strong up there, she almost gasped. This was the Archer Davenport, gorgeous and magnetic, she had swooned over as a younger woman. The man she still swooned over.

Then, with a speed that wowed her, the chestnut-colored horse took off at full speed, and she watched, riveted and horrified in equal measure, as the huge, powerful animal galloped across the screen toward the river. Arch rode well, his body in rhythm with the animal's, but then—

A terrible explosion sounded. Even though she'd known from his description of the accident that it was coming, her body still jerked. The horse spooked just as it was about to jump over the river.

And then the fall.

Oh God… the fall.

Arch's body tumbling in slow motion, down, down. And then a closeup of the horrific pain on Arch's face as the horse rolled over his leg.

Tessa cried out.

She couldn't help it.

The camera moved to the hat lying on the gravel.

Arch's fall had been terrible, and before she knew what she was doing, she put her hand on his shoulder and heard her own voice tremble as she said, "I'll never be able to unsee that in my head." She looked at her hand. She was actually shaking. "You could have been killed."

He put his hand over hers as if to give her comfort. "You're not the first person who's told me that."

She pulled away and came around to sit opposite him. All of a sudden, she was furious.

Angry because Arch had misled her about the accident and downplayed the whole thing.

Upset because the idea that he could have been

killed turned her world upside down.

The two emotions battled for precedence, and to her dismay, she found tears pricking her eyes. She cared about him so much already, despite the lies that she'd been telling herself.

The awful truth was, he wasn't just another client.

"Tessa," Arch said softly.

He had noticed her tears, and she lowered her eyes, embarrassed. "Why? Why would you do a stunt that's so dangerous?"

She wasn't judging him. She just couldn't understand why he would put himself in so much danger. Too many people loved him for him to be so reckless.

If she had that many people who loved her—or even one man who truly adored her, heart and soul—she would never have taken such a risk.

★ ★ ★

Arch gazed deeply into Tessa's eyes. He couldn't believe how much worry he saw there, and he felt terrible about showing her the clip. He'd upset her, and that was the last thing he'd intended. He swallowed and decided to tell her the truth.

"I love my family so much," he began, "so don't get me wrong when I say this. Nick is three years older than me. Finn is two years older. They were bigger, tougher, and could do the things I couldn't. I wasn't the tallest or the toughest, but whenever I heard 'it's too hard for you' from one of them, or my parents, it was like something inside me went crazy. I'd have to prove to everybody that I was big enough, tough enough. It got so ingrained in me that I still react that way."

Tessa looked to be deep in thought. "Mila says everyone in your family is stubborn and determined."

"She's right," he conceded. "Although Mila's even worse than my brothers. She's only a year younger than me, and when we were kids, she was tougher than any of the boys. She still is. So, if I wasn't trying to keep up with my big brothers, I was trying to keep up with one of my little sisters. And even Erin, in her quiet way… sometimes I wonder if she's the toughest of all of us."

Tessa turned her gaze away from him and back to the screen. For a moment, they both stared at the frozen shot of the flattened hat on the ground.

In a gentle tone, she said, "You don't have to prove anything anymore."

Arch let out a small laugh. "You sound like my mom. And Mila. And, frankly, everyone else who's talked with me about the accident."

But Tessa didn't crack a smile. She still looked deeply worried, and it hurt him to see the pain etched across her forehead.

"I know I have no right to tell you this," she said, "but I can't keep it in. Please don't do another stunt like this one." There was a painful pause. In a husky tone, she said, "Your mom's not the only one who cares about you. I do too."

He searched her face, her eyes. She was sincere, as always. Tessa was the most down-to-earth person he'd ever met.

Instinctively, he leaned toward her. She was so close that he could catch the scent of her. His stomach somersaulted.

She wanted him to kiss her. He could feel it. And, man alive, he had thought about this moment enough. He turned his head and was about to press his lips to hers when she pulled away.

He stared at her, shocked. Had he read the signs all wrong again? But no. There was desire in her eyes. She couldn't hide it.

She wanted him as much as he wanted her.

But clearly, she wasn't ready, and he respected that. Instead, he would store away the information she'd let slip.

She cared about him. *I do too*. Never had three words meant so much.

He cared about her too. In fact, he wanted nothing more than to admit to her that he'd seen her painting—and that she no longer had to hide any part of herself from him. Earlier, he'd decided to wait until she felt comfortable enough with him and trusted him enough to tell him that she was an artist. But though that did make sense, when he did finally tell her he knew, would she be stunned and hurt by the fact that he hadn't come clean right away?

So instead of mentioning her painting, he wanted to give her what she'd just said she wanted from him. "I won't do another stunt like that." And he meant it.

It was a promise he hadn't even been able to make for his mom. But he couldn't stop himself from making it for Tessa.

At this, she gave him the most beautifully radiant smile he'd ever seen. "Good."

And for a moment, every single thing in the world felt just right.

"I'd better start dinner," she said, and he felt a jolt of happiness when she walked into the kitchen and exclaimed, "Oh, how beautiful," when she saw the flowers.

He'd bought a crazy-huge bouquet that included everything from sunflowers to daisies to roses and had Mila place it in a large vase on the kitchen table. He'd taken his time choosing the perfect thank-you card and could tell from the heavy silence that Tessa was reading it.

"Oh, Arch," she said, coming back toward him, the card in her hand. "You don't have to thank me for doing my job." But he could see how pleased she was.

"As I said in there," he reminded her, "you make my life better in every way. Flowers are the least I can do to say thank you."

Oh yes, there were so many ways he wanted to thank her... but he'd vowed that she had to make the next move. So until then, he'd wait and dream of this woman.

The one he was falling more head over heels for every second of every day.

Chapter Seventeen

The following day, Tessa smiled contentedly as she swung her backpack to her shoulder and headed out for the afternoon.

Arch had completed all his exercises that morning without complaint. He was getting stronger every day—she felt the evidence in her hands as she guided his rippling muscles, trying hard not to tremble with need at the sensation of her hands on his skin. And then they'd shared a delicious lunch of fish tacos before Arch excused himself politely to work on learning his lines for the new movie.

She admired how diligent he was, how much he loved his job, and wondered if he would ever ask for her help in reading lines with him. Just the thought made her flush with warmth. She could picture the idyllic scene: the two of them on opposite ends of the couch, two glasses of wine, the sun setting through that huge window.

But no. She shook her head, letting the dark curls tumble over her shoulders. Her romantic daydreams were getting out of control. For starters, neither of them was drinking alcohol at the moment—Arch for health reasons and Tessa because she was trying so hard to stay professional. She couldn't get tipsy and risk saying something she'd regret. Besides, the more she stayed out of his movie-star world, the better.

One huge upside to Arch having such a creative drive was that she could indulge in her own. While Arch learned his lines, she spent a couple of hours each day painting. Since she'd moved onto Ocean Drive, the ocean had become an even more prominent source of inspiration, and she'd taken to painting in a secluded spot by the beach.

This was a new move for her. For so long, she had hidden her painting away, seeking out isolated rooms in her clients' homes, trying her best to paint the outside world from memory without actually being in it. But in the last ten days, something had shifted inside her, and with Arch safely resting at home, she saw no harm in following her passion to paint *en plein air*.

It was the only passion she *could* indulge in while she was living with Arch.

After saying good-bye as she left the house, she slung her pack and easel in the back of her car and headed for the remote end of the beach. Her belly fluttered with anticipation as she considered how close she was to finishing her current piece.

There was nothing like laying down the final stroke

of paint, then standing back to observe what had somehow flowed from her fingertips.

It was magic every time.

And there was something different about this new painting, something more sophisticated than she'd ever managed before. She wasn't sure what it was, exactly. But she liked it.

It was rare for her to feel proud of her work, but it felt good. Almost as good as Arch's abs had felt that morning…

The afternoon light in Carmel-by-the-Sea was gorgeous, and she put on her sunglasses to shield her eyes. Since arriving in Carmel, she never tired of driving through its streets and soaking in the atmosphere. Although she'd never traveled abroad, she felt as though Carmel had a European feel to it, with its blooming flowers and the scent of the sea that rode on the breeze from the beach to the forest in the mountains above them. She could easily imagine she was in a charming village in the Netherlands or Switzerland, with cobblestone streets, quaint hotels, and laid-back charming inns.

But it was the beach that most captured her imagination. Golden sand like flawless sugar and stunning blue water, which appeared to melt into the blue, cloudless sky. She parked, then carefully carried her materials to the secluded spot on the rocks where she'd been painting all week. Her fingers itched to get started, and after she set up her easel and taped the unfinished painting to it, she mixed her colors.

She heard footsteps coming across the rock and turned in surprise.

In all the days she'd been painting here, she hadn't encountered a single person. But now she saw a woman wearing a multicolored loose blazer over a swirling green skirt that danced in the breeze, as did her curling gray hair. Chunky jewelry in silver and turquoise caught the sun as she approached, carrying her own easel. Tessa never painted in anything but a T-shirt and jeans, so she admired the woman's bravery in not worrying about ruining her expensive clothes.

Uneasily, Tessa watched the woman set up nearby. She looked vaguely familiar, and Tessa wondered if she'd seen her around town. Tessa wasn't used to painting around other people, but after they both smiled and exchanged a nod of greeting, the woman angled her easel away from Tessa, and she breathed a sigh of relief. The stranger wasn't going to chitchat; she was there to work.

Before putting paintbrush to paper, she made sure to set her alarm to remind her when to stop. Otherwise, she might become so lost in her painting that the concept of time would melt away. As hard as it was to stop when she was in the flow, she couldn't take really long breaks while working for Arch. She hated the thought of not being there for him if he needed her.

But she comforted herself knowing that her phone was always on, and Arch would call.

Now she just had to empty her head of all things Archer Davenport and actually concentrate.

She turned her gaze to the beautiful ocean, tracing the trajectory of the waves as they lapped against the shore. From her vantage point, it felt as though Carmel were showing off its best features today, just for her painting. She had returned to focus specifically on one of the classic Carmel cypress trees in her sightline and to add detail and shadow to the craggy rocks. She loved these finishing touches.

Soon, her thoughts melted away until all that was left was color and the movement of her rigger brush among the rocks. Tessa fell into a pleasant meditative state, so she jumped when her alarm suddenly sounded its urgent call. *Zing! Zing! Zing!*

She reached for her phone and turned off the alarm. While she'd been painting, she'd completely forgotten about the other woman painting nearby. But now she caught the woman's confused expression. Tessa smiled apologetically, and the woman set down her brush and came over.

"I'm sorry," Tessa said, meaning it. "I set an alarm to keep track of time. Otherwise, I'll just stay here until nightfall. But I didn't mean to disturb your own painting. I hope you'll forgive me."

The woman laughed, showing a set of pearly-white

teeth. "I know the feeling. But would it be the worst thing to while away a few more hours?"

It would be bliss, but she didn't have that luxury. "I have to get back to work."

At that, the woman looked confused again. "Oh, I'd assumed you were a full-time artist. I see you out here most days." She smiled and then, to Tessa's horror, walked around the easel and peered at Tessa's work.

It felt as though a stranger had walked in on her in the shower. Her instinct was to throw herself at the easel to protect it from prying eyes, but instead she went beet red, the woman's words ringing in her ears.

I'd assumed you were a full-time artist.

Tessa couldn't imagine anything close to that life.

The woman studied the painting so intensely that Tessa blurted, "I know it's not very good, but I love how I feel when I'm painting, so I do it anyway."

The woman looked up with a quizzical expression. "It's excellent," she said simply.

Tessa stared at her in confusion. "I'm sorry?"

"Yes, excellent," she said. "I suspected just by watching you work that your heart and soul were pouring out onto this paper. And now that I see the results, I know I was right. Not only do you have the technical talent with those layers of glazes, you also have a unique understanding of color." She paused and motioned to the horizon on Tessa's painting. "Those blues simply melt into one another. It's wonderful."

Tessa didn't know how to respond. The only person who'd ever seen her work was Lewis, and he'd never had one nice word for it. But now here was a complete stranger, a painter no less, who believed the exact opposite.

"Y-you like it?" Tessa half stuttered in disbelief.

"Very much," she replied. "In fact, I think you should enter the Carmel-by-the-Sea *plein air* competition."

Tessa's mouth dropped open. "You're kidding." It was a statement rather than a question.

She couldn't believe the woman was being serious. Carmel had a well-known art festival every year. It was a huge event in town, with live music and VIP events. The *plein air* competition was a big highlight, and some of the most renowned artists entered each year.

Tessa couldn't believe this woman thought her painting would have a chance. At the same time, she could see from her expression that the woman wasn't joking.

"I have a few flyers for the competition with me," the woman said. "It outlines all the rules and how to enter." She gestured at her expensive-looking handbag, casually set on a rock by her easel.

Tessa followed her, dumbstruck. But that was nothing compared to her surprise when she set eyes on the quarter sheet taped to the easel.

She would know her work anywhere. This was

Mylene Fraser. *The* Mylene Fraser, a famous local artist and a jurist for the American Watercolor Society who had exhibited all over the world. Even Arch owned one of her paintings—she'd admired it on the living room wall. Tessa couldn't believe it.

"You're Mylene Fraser," she blurted.

The woman laughed. "Why, yes, I am. And you are…?" She extended a hand, and a silver and turquoise bracelet flashed. She had paint on her fingers.

Tessa managed to introduce herself and then quickly added, "I'm a big admirer of yours, Ms. Fraser." This was the artist whose weeklong workshop she was saving up to attend. It felt like meeting her on the beach must be a sign.

Mylene smiled her lovely smile again, her hazel eyes filled with warmth. "That's very kind," she said graciously. "And I of you. Promise that you'll enter the competition."

Tessa was overwhelmed that a famous artist had complimented her work, but she was also such a fan that she knew she couldn't let this moment slip from her grasp. How many times in life did a person ever come face-to-face with their heroes?

She accepted the competition leaflet from Mylene, who looked pleasantly bemused at Tessa's fangirling. *It's now or never.*

"I don't suppose you have any pointers for me?" she finally managed to say. "I'm sorry to ask—it's not every day that an artist one admires so much compliments one's work. I've never been taught—I'd love to learn how to get better."

Mylene touched Tessa on the shoulder. "Just keep following your instincts. You've got everything there already. The only piece of advice I could give you is to paint with more confidence. Load that brush with more color and less water. You aren't auditioning to be a painter, Tessa. You already *are* a painter. And, I predict, one with a brilliant future."

Tessa could hardly take it in. She thanked Mylene profusely, feeling like she was glowing from the inside out, before excusing herself to pack up. "It's been a real pleasure to meet and speak with you," she said.

"Likewise," Mylene replied. "Just make sure you enter that competition. Have faith in your talent. And if that feels like a stretch, then maybe it will help to remember that *I* have faith in your talent. I remember what it was like just starting out. The doubts. The fears. But you are way past those early days, Tessa. You're capable of wonderful things—you've only to believe it yourself, and your paintings will soar even higher."

Tessa headed back to the car, feeling like she was already floating on air.

But by the time she had packed her kit in the trunk and hit the road, doubts had begun to creep in. Mylene was probably just being nice. Or maybe she was one of the organizers of the festival, and they needed more people to pay the competition entry fee to fund the rest of the events. Still, it had been nice to talk about art with another painter.

By the time she returned home, she had decided to put Mylene's compliments out of her mind, even though there was a *huge* part of her that wanted to tell Arch everything. But what if he acted the way Lewis had? Or worse, what if he pretended he thought her painting was good? No, it was safer just to keep it a secret.

She raced upstairs, packed away her easel and art supplies, and made sure to clean up thoroughly in the en suite bathroom before Arch saw her.

When she finished, she ran a brush through her hair, wound it into a neat bun, and went to find him.

But he wasn't in his usual spot in the living room. She called his name. Nothing. Maybe he'd gone for a nap, she thought, and was still asleep. She walked down the hallway in the direction of his room. But no. His door was ajar, and the bedroom was empty. She began to panic. Had he taken a fall?

Louder this time, she called his name again. But all she heard was the sound of her own blood rushing in her ears. Drat him—had he wandered off for a walk along the beach? She wouldn't put it past him to try to manage on his own before he was ready.

Then she heard a grunt. And another.

Coming from the basement.

She rushed down the stairs, and there he was, back pressed against a leather bench, working on his upper-body exercises in the gym. He was shirtless, tanned abs and triceps rippling as he shoulder-pressed with a couple of heavy dumbbells. Watching his stern reflection change to a smile in the mirror when he noticed her, Tessa found herself swooning. She knew better, but…

He caught her eye in the mirror and held her gaze as he lifted the weights above his head.

Her mouth was dry, desire bubbling up in her, but she managed to say in as neutral a tone as possible, "Those dumbbells are too heavy for you right now."

Arch laughed and then set the weights on either side of the bench. "I have to up my game if I'm going to be ready for an action flick." He took a swig of mineral water. "But I made it down here all by myself, so I took it as a sign I'm getting stronger."

"You are," Tessa had to concede. "But that's exactly why you shouldn't push yourself too soon and possibly set yourself back."

Arch shook his head as though he couldn't believe she wasn't throwing him a thousand compliments about his incredible physical prowess right now. "Don't worry, I know my limits. Besides, I'm getting my cast off tomorrow. And I saved the rehab exercises for when you got back."

The truth was, she couldn't stop thinking about the offer he'd made that fateful night, when he'd thrown back the bedsheets and patted the space beside him.

With his half-naked body now so casually displayed, she couldn't help wishing that she'd thrown caution to the wind and leaped right in.

Chapter Eighteen

Arch didn't know what was more exciting—getting the cast off his leg this morning, or the surprises he had planned for Tessa later.

There was something so incredibly sexy about the way she drove as they made their way to the hospital. Maybe it was the way the breeze from the open windows ruffled her usually primly tied-back hair. Or the casual way she turned the leather wheel with the palm of her right hand.

He'd never felt so intoxicated by something so ordinary.

All he knew was that he had it bad for Tessa.

Real bad.

It helped that it was a beautiful morning for a drive. So peaceful. Right now, it felt like only he and Tessa lived in Carmel, in a bubble of pure sexual tension.

He stole another glance at her. How did she make a blue shirt and jeans look so damn good?

As if sensing his attention, Tessa gave him her bright, genuine smile and then returned her attention to the road.

"You're going to feel like a new man with that cast off," she said. "You're playing it cool, but I can tell how excited you are. I imagine you were a nightmare as a kid at Christmas, up at dawn and racing downstairs to rip open your presents before anyone else was awake."

Arch laughed. She'd hit the nail on the head. *Why wait when you can do it right now?* had always been his motto.

But she was wrong about where the bulk of his excitement lay. Yes, he was glad the cast was coming off… but if only he could tell her that ninety-nine percent of what he felt right now came from the simple pleasure of being beside her as she drove.

Tessa pulled up at the hospital. After she parked, she told him to stay put and got out first, coming around to his side to open the door and help him out.

Although he loved it when Tessa manhandled him, he wasn't going to miss feeling helpless and uncoordinated with his crutches.

Together, they entered the white building, and he gave his details at reception. He was wearing a baseball cap and dark glasses, but at the mention of his name, the receptionist's head snapped up, as if she needed to confirm it really was him. Thankfully, he wasn't the only celebrity who'd ever been treated here. He really did owe Clint Eastwood and Doris Day a debt of gratitude for living in Carmel; people had become much more relaxed about celebrities.

The receptionist directed them to the consulting room, and the doctor came in shortly afterward.

"Morning, Archer," Dr. Reid said. "How's the leg?"

"Stronger every day." He nodded toward Tessa. "Tessa has been a massive help with my physical therapy. And nutritionally as well—I've never eaten such healthy food that tastes so good."

The doctor looked at Tessa more carefully now. "That's quite high praise. Maybe you could share some of your recipes with us at the hospital for our other patients."

Her cheeks were flushed with her pleasure at the compliments, and she nodded. "Of course. I'd be happy to share my recipes with anyone who wants them."

With that, Dr. Reid asked Arch to lie back on the bed so that he could remove the cast and examine the leg.

"Don't have to ask me twice," Arch replied, accepting the doctor's help to straighten out his lower body.

The doctor cut the padding and stockinette with shears and then began to pull apart the cast with a shiny instrument. The sensation of cool air on his skin after being in the cast for so many weeks felt incredible. He breathed out an audibly happy sigh of relief.

"Feels good, doesn't it?" the doctor said, smiling. "Now, just let me take a look at how you're healing, and then we can get your walking boot fitted. You'll find it much more convenient. It's easy to unstrap, so you'll be able to shower more easily. Plus, it's much lighter and more comfortable to wear."

The doctor's words were music to Arch's ears. The only issue was that he would have to be a bit more inventive if he was going to keep Tessa's hands on his body during workouts. He didn't want to give up the way she spotted him with the weights, or took his arm when he tired of walking with crutches.

"You're healing well," Dr. Reid said as he asked Arch to do a few movements with his left leg. "Faster than I would have thought."

It didn't take long before he was walking out, with a set of instructions on how to continue healing and a warning not to overdo it.

Tessa was waiting for him and gave him a thumbs-up when he got closer. "Good job," she said.

Receiving her praise, Arch felt as good as if he'd just accepted an Oscar.

As they left the hospital, he turned to her. "My quick healing is definitely down to your care, Tessa."

She flushed a little. "That's kind," she said, "but you're also more determined to heal than anyone I've ever known." She paused a beat. "I never know how things are going to go whenever I take on a new client, but we've been a good team, you and I."

"We certainly have." And then he added, "I hope you don't have anything planned for the rest of the day."

She raised an eyebrow. "I had planned to take stock of which new exercises you can move into now that the cast is off—then make sure you get a really good workout with the new plan."

"We will definitely do that," he agreed, "but I have a few things arranged for us to celebrate my being out of that cast."

"You do?"

He nodded. "If you're okay with putting off my therapy for a little while, I was hoping to take you to a few of my favorite places."

To his alarm, Tessa looked flustered. Had he pushed it too far? She didn't know he'd been planning this day for an entire week. He wanted to share the beauty of his home with Tessa, wanted her to understand why he so loved this place. It was the best way he'd come up with to let her into his world. Not the Hollywood world where he had to dwell now for work, but his real home. The place where he'd been raised so lovingly by his folks and which he shared with all his siblings.

He wanted her to see the real Archer Davenport. But more than that, he wanted her to feel as special as she really was. And hopefully, the more he opened up to her, perhaps she might open up more with him too.

He flashed her his most charming smile. "I've got it all figured out. Let's go!"

In the car, he insisted on giving her directions without letting her know where they were headed. So when they arrived at the Monterey Bay Aquarium and parked, Tessa pushed her sunglasses onto her head and turned a beaming smile his way.

"I did not peg you for an aquarium fan," she said.

"Are you kidding? I *love* this place. The ocean is magical. I've been coming here since I was a kid."

"I've been wanting to stop in. I've heard this aquarium is one of the best in the world." She paused and smiled before adding, "And knowing it was the model for the *Finding Nemo* movies makes it seem even more special."

He reached over and, without thinking, took her hand in his. "Thank you for letting me whisk you away for a few hours. I've been wanting to do something nice for you. You've been amazing."

She visibly swallowed, but held his gaze until her dark lashes fluttered against her cheeks.

"I thought we'd start with the sea otters," he said as he walked through the entrance with her, working to get used to the new boot, "since they're about the cutest creatures on earth."

"Otters, huh?" she said, as though happy to discover something new about him.

"Did you know otters keep their paws out of the water to stay warm?" It was a random fact he'd learned on one of his excursions here.

"I didn't know that, but it's adorable." Relief flooded him as he realized Tessa was going to enjoy this as much as he'd hoped she would.

"A friend of ours works here, and I'm a member, so we're getting VIP treatment."

He'd arranged everything ahead of time with Avery Chandler, who worked in community outreach, and they went straight to the second floor of the sea otters' exhibit to watch them swimming. Avery was there to meet them.

Avery Chandler was one of Finn's friends from high school, but she'd become a family friend too. She'd had a tough time in her teens, getting pregnant in high school and choosing to keep her son. Finn had stuck by her, and they were still very close. Arch couldn't imagine how hard it must have been for Avery, starting out as a janitor at the aquarium and working her way up. She had always felt like another sister to him, so he gave her a big hug when he saw her.

"Ave. How's it going?"

Avery was a redhead with big brown eyes and a wide smile. Her chin looked determined, and it didn't lie. There wasn't much Avery Chandler couldn't accomplish if she put her mind to it.

She returned his hug. "How's my favorite movie star?"

"Doing much better now that my cast is off." He

immediately went on to say, "I'd like to introduce you to Tessa Taylor. She's been taking care of me ever since I got injured."

"It's lovely to meet you, Avery," Tessa said. "And I really appreciate you giving up your time for us today."

Avery grinned. "There isn't much I wouldn't do for the Davenports," she said. "They're like family." She pointed to the otters. "They're all rescues," she explained as the creatures turned somersaults in the water. "They can't survive in the wild anymore. Some of them have survived shark attacks. We even have these surrogate mothers who take care of orphaned pups."

"They are adorable," Tessa said, her lively eyes trained on the water and her cheeks pink with pleasure.

Arch thought *she* was completely adorable, but he held his tongue. They had all day together after all. And there was so much more to come. He couldn't wait to surprise her even more.

Avery took them to see the Open Sea exhibit next, to catch a glimpse of the sea turtles and the brilliant jellyfish as they pulsed through the water. Together, they stood before the ninety-foot window and watched as the hypnotic underwater scene played out before them.

"Better than any movie, don't you think?" he said, whispering into Tessa's ear so as not to disrupt the calm atmosphere. At this time of day, the aquarium was quieter than usual, and he was thankful. He inhaled and caught the delicate scent of her coconut shampoo. His lips brushed her earlobe for a split second, and he thought he saw her shiver.

She turned to him with a twinkle in her eyes, then whispered back, "I can think of some movies that compete with it."

He loved knowing she thought so much of his movies, but it made it nearly impossible not to kiss her. Somehow, he held himself back, knowing the time wasn't quite right for kisses. Not yet.

After they watched the turtles, he told Tessa, "Avery's giving us a private, behind-the-scenes tour. Just you and me. She's going to take us through all the areas usually off-limits to anyone who's not staff so that we can learn more about how the animals are cared for. In fact, we're going to help the staff feed the puffins at lunchtime."

Tessa's lovely eyes widened. Clearly, no one had ever surprised her like this. She was absolutely glowing. And beyond gorgeous.

He couldn't believe that he was the lucky man who had put that smile on her face.

But then she looked down at his booted leg and said, "Are you sure you can be on your feet for so long? I don't want you to push yourself too hard today."

"Don't worry," he replied. "I'll let you know if I'm in any pain."

"Promise?"

He nodded. "I promise."

He thought he could see a glint in Avery's eyes as she watched. Then she said, "Archer and his family are big supporters, so it's a pleasure to show you some of the important work we do here in marine conservation. Follow me."

But as they turned, Arch was spotted. Despite the baseball cap and shades, it was bound to happen, but he had really wanted to shield Tessa from this part of his life and take her out for the day like any other person. To make things worse, the fans were three young women, freshmen in college, they told him, who flirted with him shamelessly as he signed their notebooks and quickly posed for a selfie.

Tessa stood back from the scene, her face neutral. He couldn't figure out what she made of it all. After the girls left, he apologized for the holdup, but Avery said, "If those selfies end up on social media, and they mention the aquarium, it's a win for us."

While he appreciated Avery's outlook, the truth was that some days he'd happily give up his fame for a little while. Just to be normal for a few hours in a world-renowned aquarium with his friend and a woman he was falling hard for.

The two women chatted like old friends. Tessa was so warm and down-to-earth when she was off duty. He'd noticed that she could make friends with anyone and put them at ease. It was a quality he admired.

Avery talked about the role of the aquarium in combating climate change and plastic pollution and encouraging sustainable seafood. She was passionate about her work, and Tessa asked intelligent questions as they walked.

Then he piped up, "We're off to feed the puffins!" His excitement was a little uncool for a grown man, but he couldn't contain himself. Having seen Tessa with the otters, he knew she was going to flip over the puffins.

"This is a special treat," Avery said with a warm smile. "We don't let many people this close to the puffins, but I've known Arch long enough to make an exception. I know you'll be quiet and respectful too, Tessa."

Arch grinned and inwardly thanked Avery for the extra boost to his status. He was a man who could be trusted around puffins.

He hoped that would help Tessa accept that she could trust him too.

Avery explained, "Adult puffins mostly eat small fish, such as sand eels, herring, hake, and capelin. Puffin diets vary from colony to colony because of the variety of fish around the breeding islands. But they all seriously love feeding time."

They arrived at the puffin sanctuary, and Arch watched as Tessa carefully followed the staff member's instructions to help feed the brightly colored birds. He got more pleasure from watching her than the puffins—she was so careful with the birds and so delighted when they took the food from her hands.

When feeding time was over, she turned to him and said, "Honestly, Arch, I don't think anyone has done something this nice for me before. Ever."

The way her eyes were shining, he thought his heart was going to burst out of his chest. He felt a huge grin spread across his face. Her words were music to his ears.

From what she'd told him about her husband, he'd had a hunch that the man hadn't treated her the way she deserved, and now he was absolutely certain he was right.

Tessa deserved everything in the world. And he planned to give her just that. But since he still didn't want to make the mistake of coming on too strong, too soon, he kept that sentiment to himself. Instead, he said, "That was just for starters, Tessa Taylor."

She looked incredulous that there could be more. "What do you mean?"

"We're off to our next stop."

She looked confused. "Wait, there's more?"

He thanked Avery for her time and asked her to come to the next Davenport family brunch. The redhead groaned. "I know, I keep missing them, but I'm so busy with work, and now that Josh has baseball practice, I barely have time to scarf a piece of toast for breakfast on the weekend, never mind come for brunch."

"You should both come," he urged her. "We miss you."

"I'll try," she said, giving him a hug good-bye and then pulling Tessa in for a hug too. "I hope to see you again soon."

"Me too," Tessa replied.

He was glad that the two women seemed to have formed a bond so quickly. Because if he could ever convince Tessa to be with him, it would be nice to know that, in addition to his sisters, she would have another friend in Avery.

As she settled behind the wheel of his car, she said, "Are you sure your leg is up to more fun and merriment?"

He grinned. "I'm feeling great so far."

"Okay, then." She grinned back. "Where to now?"

"We're off to an escape room."

★ ★ ★

Tessa wasn't at all sure about an escape room, but Arch seemed so excited about the idea that she pretended to be more enthusiastic than she was. She'd read about escape rooms and always thought they sounded more like a terrifying ordeal than a fun activity. They were an interactive, immersive, live-action game played in a variety of strange locations—like a real-life game of Clue. Yet she'd never been able to imagine what an escape room looked like, let alone what it would feel like to spend an afternoon locked inside.

However, when they got there, her nerves soon evaporated. He'd booked the Alice in Wonderland experience for them. How had he guessed that it had been one of her favorite stories as a kid? She loved the upside-down world of Wonderland, its curious and chatty creatures, the topsy-turvy tea party. The decorations and puzzles in the escape room didn't disappoint. Their escape was from a hotel located in the former house of Lewis Carroll, the author of Alice's many adventures, and they had to make sure to catch the tail of the white rabbit and work together to get out of the rabbit hole.

She was still a little worried that Arch was going to hurt himself. It was the longest he'd spent on his feet since the accident, and he was only just getting used to the boot. But he really did seem fine. More than fine. Both fit and playful and, to her delight, incredibly good at teamwork and communicating with her to escape the room.

Maybe it was all that time spent on film sets with different personalities, juggling different visions.

Or… maybe they actually were a good team.

No, there was no *maybe* about it. They *were* a great team.

And it was the most fun she'd had in years.

★ ★ ★

By the time they were back outside, she was ready to head home and prepare dinner, especially when Arch said, "I don't know about you, but I'm starving." He turned to her with his gorgeous smile, the one that lit up a movie screen and made her heart skip. "I would like to take you to one of my favorite restaurants."

"But, Arch, I'm not dressed for a fancy place." Celebrities could eat at the finest restaurants in the world in old jeans and get away with it, but she didn't want to do that.

He laughed. "You don't dress up for this place." He put an arm around her. "Come on, trust me."

The tiny fish-and-chips place on Cannery Row felt like the perfect end to a perfect day. He chatted with the owners, who had reserved them a table, then left them alone to enjoy the best fish and chips Tessa had ever tasted.

More than ever, she wanted to give in to the urges she'd been fighting from the moment she first set eyes on Arch. All day long, he had touched her, little brushes of his fingertips on her hand, her arm, on the small of her back. His touch was delicate, light, almost innocent.

Except that she knew it was anything but innocent. Especially given that she was no longer able to hide her attraction to him, no matter how hard she tried. Especially when he didn't hide his attraction to her at all.

And then there were all of his little flirty comments. Some so subtle that she wondered if it was all accidental. Maybe Arch was just a friendly, outgoing, charismatic person, no matter who he was with.

But no, she knew the truth: He was doing it to torture her because he could see through her carefully composed exterior and knew that she wanted more. *Way* more.

She wanted to feel the heat of his skin next to hers in the worst way. So much that it made it hard to concentrate on the amazing things he'd lined up for them to experience together today.

If only he realized she would have been just as happy with him at home. Naked, preferably.

Day by day, moment by moment, she had felt her resolve to stay professional turn to mush. But today? Well, today the walls she'd barely managed to keep up were coming down. Fast.

On top of that, it was fascinating to see how well Arch dealt with the fans who came up to him all day long. First, there'd been the giggling freshmen at the aquarium and then countless requests at the escape room venue. Through it all, he remained friendly, especially to the teens and little kids. Actually, he was just plain great with everyone. And so normal. So easy to be with.

And, most of all, so ridiculously sexy!

Arch took another mouthful of perfectly battered fish and dipped a fry in ketchup. She was already full, but couldn't resist another deliciously crunchy fry.

He had given her the most memorable and wonderful day of her life. Every element had been so carefully planned, put together with such thought, that she couldn't believe someone had it in them to be that romantic—let alone for *her*.

She caught his gaze across the table. There was so much warmth and affection in his eyes—as though she were the only woman in the entire world. It really had been the perfect day, and now there was no denying it: She was falling hard for Arch.

The thought scared her, for all the reasons that she'd been telling herself while she'd been working with him. But today, falling for Arch finally felt so right.

She had never felt like this with anyone else. Which meant that now she had no choice but to make a decision about her feelings—and her actions.

Would she risk everything to be with him for as long as it lasted? Or would she keep trying with all her might to keep her walls up until her assignment with him was over?

She lifted her glass of water to her lips, all the while holding Arch's penetrating gaze. And that's when she knew.

She wasn't going to play it safe anymore.

After today, she wasn't sure she'd be able to keep up the charade of being nothing but a professional with him.

Arch was well and truly under her skin.

And she wanted him to stay there.

Chapter Nineteen

Tessa realized that Arch was far more romantic than she could have dared to dream. Maybe Margaret had been right and Arch was more like his chivalrous father than she'd first thought.

When they'd eaten their fill, Arch suggested they take a slow stroll down Fisherman's Wharf… maybe get some ice cream… watch the sunset. Again, she checked in with him to make sure he wasn't overdoing it and feeling pain. But when he assured her again that he was feeling perfectly okay, she found herself nodding eagerly. Accepting his outstretched hand, she allowed her fingers to link with his.

After such a romantic day with him, it felt totally natural for them to hold hands. The electricity that sparked as their skin touched felt just right too.

Their romantic vibe intensified as they stepped outside and she saw the last of the sun's glorious reds, pinks, and oranges streaking the darkening sky. She gazed at it dreamily, wishing she had her paints and could capture the scene. Immortalize the moment.

Create a physical memory.

He guided her along the promenade, where families and couples weaved in and out of the shops and stalls, kids begging their parents for saltwater taffy and churros.

The water lapped gently on the shoreline as the last of the sun disappeared, and the fairy lights that flickered on in front of every restaurant and store made everything seem like a scene from a movie.

And here she was—with the actual leading man. She could hardly believe this was her life.

"I thought we could head up there." Arch gestured to the end of the wharf, where a few slightly secluded benches looked out to sea. Even as he did, he didn't let go of her hand. And she was glad, because it really did feel so right to be this intimate with him.

"Looks like the perfect spot," she said, relishing the opportunity to sit with him alone for the first time today.

She shook her head at the offer of ice cream, explaining that she was too full from dinner… although the real reason was that her stomach had been turning somersaults since she'd admitted to herself that she was falling for Arch.

Big-time falling.

As they walked in step, she shivered.

"You're cold." He stopped and slipped off his navy sweater. "The wind off the water can really kick up at this time of evening."

He was right—the wind was stronger, and she was a little cold. But that wasn't why she'd shivered. It had come more from the thrill of having spent the perfect day with the perfect man, but she wasn't about to admit to that.

She laughed when he asked her to hold up her arms so he could slip the sweater over her head. "You're getting a taste of what it's like to be a caregiver," she said as he gently pulled the sweater down over her body.

With a slow and sweet sweeping motion, Arch smoothed her hair back from her face where it had become staticky from the fabric. "The only person I want to take care of is you," he said.

His voice was deep and gruff with emotion. And, to her surprise, she believed him.

She believed him because she felt *exactly* what he was feeling—that they were made to take care of each other.

When they reached the bench, she instinctively sat close to Arch so that her right thigh touched his left. Although they weren't far from the hustle and bustle of the promenade, it felt like they were the only two people in the world. Just them, the sound of the sea, and the breeze that ruffled Arch's hair.

She gazed out at the horizon, where white sailboats coming into harbor bobbed on the waves, and took a deep breath. "There's something I want to tell you about me." She felt him grow instantly alert beside her, though he didn't say a word. Previously, she hadn't been sure that she could tell him something so personal, but she knew she had to if they had any hope of a future together.

She took a deep breath and blurted, "I paint."

He didn't miss a beat, just turned his head so he was looking at her profile. "I know."

She sat back, more than a little stunned. "You know?" When he nodded, she said, "Then why didn't you say something?"

He looked so sincere as he said, "Because it was clearly something *very* personal to you. Of course, I hoped you'd tell me about your art at some point, and yes, there's been a big part of me that felt like I was lying to you by omission. A couple of times, I could barely keep from telling you that I knew. But I couldn't shake off the sense that saying something too early might make you uncomfortable. So in the end, I justified it by telling myself that you'd tell me more about yourself and your passions when the time was right." He smiled. "You don't know how happy I am that right now is clearly that moment."

Though he had kept the knowledge of her painting to himself, how could she be mad at him for that? It was clear that he had only been trying to give her the space she needed to tell him something she kept secret from everyone else.

"Thank you for explaining that," she said, meaning every word. "It helps me understand why you waited to tell me that you already knew I was painting in the afternoons." She paused. "And if I'm being totally honest, had you told me earlier, I don't know that I would have reacted well to your finding out my secret passion."

He looked utterly relieved that she wasn't angry with him. "I do have a question for you, though," he said. When she nodded for him to go ahead, he said, "Why did you feel you needed to hide it from me?"

She looked down at their clasped hands. "Because it's just a silly hobby. A time-wasting indulgence."

When she looked up into his face, he was frowning. "Why would you say that? Especially when it's clearly something you're very passionate about."

His calm and encouraging responses made her feel bold enough to answer his question by revealing yet another part of her life that she'd kept secret from everyone.

"My husband—he used to belittle me. He thought I had good taste in other people's art, but I couldn't transfer it to my own work. He said it was no good. Amateurish." She shook her head at the memories of all the times he'd said such cruel things, the old sense of shame flooding her. "But even though I had no encouragement, I couldn't stop." She hesitated. "I think it's how I make sense of the world. When I'm painting, it's like I go somewhere else and inhabit a new reality, one where everything seems so much clearer."

She paused again, surprised at how open she was being—*and* how good it felt, even if part of her felt foolish admitting so much. She turned to Arch and found his expression rapt.

"Tessa, what you've just described—that's *exactly* how I feel when I know I'm nailing a scene. Like I'm being totally open and honest and unafraid of what people might see me do… or be." His smile was full of admiration as he added, "Clearly, when you paint, you're using your authentic voice."

She smiled back at him. But it was more than just a smile on her lips. It felt like her whole body was smiling.

Her *authentic voice*.

That was it exactly. She'd never been able to articulate so clearly how she felt when she had a paintbrush in her hand and a clean sheet of paper coming to life in front of her.

It was amazing to realize that she and Arch understood each other on a deeper level. And maybe a part of her—one that she had shoved way down deep—had always known this would be the case. When it came to Arch, this was what scared her—and thrilled her—the most. She'd never known that fear and joy could be such close bedfellows.

"Are any of your paintings at the house?" He sounded eager to see them.

"Yes…" She paused again, checking in with herself to see if she trusted him enough to let him see them. Finally, she admitted, "But I'm not ready to show them to you."

"Well, whenever you do feel comfortable showing me, I know I'm going to love them," he said.

She shook her head. "Please don't say that. Don't get your hopes up. I'm mediocre at best." Mylene Fraser's compliments jumped into her head, but she instinctively shoved them away.

After so many years of believing she had no talent, it was extremely hard for Tessa to switch to thinking that she *might* have some.

But even as she was warring inside herself over whether she did or not, Arch said, "I knew the minute you talked about the paintings in my house that you had a special understanding of the craft. And now I feel I've spent enough time with you to know that you can see underneath the surface of life and the world around us, which is what really great painters do."

She blushed and found she couldn't tear her eyes away from their hands, which were still intertwined. There was something so perfect about the way their fingers fit together.

She felt secure. And, for the first time in forever, sexy.

It was a combination she'd never experienced before.

"I love the art on your walls," she said. "In large part because you don't just have a Picasso and a Cézanne. You also have a bunch of up-and-coming talents who will be huge one day. That's the mark of a great collector. You can see the beauty of the past, but also the present and the future." She shook her head, her mouth turning down a bit at the corners, not in self-pity, but what she believed was self-awareness. "Trust me, my paintings can't compare with what's on your walls. I'm never going to be Georgia O'Keeffe or Mylene Fraser."

He squeezed her hand, and she looked up to see him smiling. "Why would you want to be anyone but yourself?"

His soft question stopped her in mid-breath. She'd been too busy comparing herself to other painters and listening to the echo of Lewis's negative comments to see her own work as being unique—and for that uniqueness to be a good thing.

Arch's simple question hit her hard, not just in her heart, not just in her gut, but throughout all of her—mind and body. When she was with him, she felt more herself than she had in years. Maybe ever.

"Thank you for saying that." She fell silent again for a few moments, listening to the distant sound of families enjoying themselves and the gentle lapping of the water. Arch still gripped her hand. "No one has ever believed in me. Or just let me be me." Then she finally smiled and said, "I love what you just said. I love the idea of being unique, of creating paintings in my own style. And I love that you've helped me to see my paintings in a new light. In fact, that one simple question—'why would you want to be anyone but yourself?'—has just now made me stop caring if people don't like them. Even you."

Arch laughed and then, with his free hand and a light touch of her cheek, turned her to face him. The breeze whipped strands of her hair from its sensible ponytail, and he tucked them carefully—sensually— behind her ears. "Now you sound the way a great artist should. If you ask me, all artists, whether they're painters or dancers or actors, should take a page out of Picasso's book. He didn't give a damn what other people thought of his work. In fact, I think his brazen confidence only made people love it more."

"Thank you, Arch," she said softly. It was the sincerest thanks she had ever given. "Thank you for making me see *my* art in a totally different way than I ever have before."

"I think I'm the one who owes *you* thanks."

Now it was her turn to look confused. "For what?"

"For opening up to me. It means the world to me, Tessa. Knowing that you trust me enough to tell me about your past. And also that you've taken my words to heart. You *are* an artist, even if no one ever sees your work but you."

Just like that, time seemed to stop. It was just the two of them on that bench, the pier's fairy lights twinkling, the last of the light disappearing into an inky blue.

He let go of her hands, then cupped her face, gently stroking her cheeks. Her heart beat double time as she let her eyes flutter closed.

But he didn't make a move to kiss her, even though she could feel his breath on her lips. And that was when she realized he was waiting for her to make the first move. And it only made her want him more to know he cared enough to not just assume she'd be dying for his kiss.

She leaned in just the slightest bit and touched her lips to his. It was an invitation from her to him and one that promised so much pleasure. His soft, full lips on hers, the taste of him, their tongues finding each other, almost overwhelmed her. They both moved gently at first, then passion overtook both of them, and yet again, she was the one making the decision to grab the back of his head, to thread her fingers through his thick hair, to pull him closer. He wrapped his arms around her, and she let herself melt into him.

It was the softest, most gentle, most tender kiss she'd ever had. And somehow, it was also the most passionate, most urgent kiss she'd experienced.

She didn't want it to end.

She wanted to stay this close to Arch forever.

Chapter Twenty

Later, when they got back to Carmel, he suggested a moonlit stroll on the beach, as though he didn't want this perfect day to end. She didn't either, but she also knew he'd spent more than enough time on his feet for the day. As she walked into his house, the whole day seemed like a dream.

But it was real.

Her lips still felt pleasantly bruised from the intensity and urgency of their kisses. They had just kept kissing and kissing and kissing, wanting more and more.

Her head—and body—were swirling with sexy thoughts mixed with deep emotions. Had Arch encouraged her deepest and most secret desires to paint and then also kissed her senseless? Kissed her with an intensity she had never dared to let herself dream of?

Once they were inside, she said, "Why don't we get you back to your chair and elevate your leg for a while? You've had a long day."

"I've had the best day, Tessa. I swear there's no

better medicine than you. I honestly don't feel any pain in my leg at all."

Though she was charmed and extremely flattered by his words, she had to be firm. "Still, I know it's a struggle walking in that new boot."

Arch shrugged. "I'm just happy to have the cast off. Plus, I need to get all the practice I can walking with this thing before I have to climb the stairs unaided at next week's awards ceremony."

She nodded, remembering how thrilled Arch had been to receive the invitation to present an award at the Moonrise Independent Film Festival in Moab, Utah.

"I was wondering if you'd do me the honor of being my plus-one?" He looked a little nervous, which wasn't something she'd seen in him before. "It's a small indie film festival, but it's become one of the most respected ones around. Remember Jay saying that Smith Sullivan and I would be presenting the award for best feature film? It's a good opportunity to do some advance publicity for the buddy movie." He looked so hopeful as he added, "It would be way more fun with you there."

But instead of feeling excited about being asked, Tessa felt all the wonder of their day together rush out of her body like air escaping a deflating balloon.

Pure panic set in. One extremely hot, long kiss, and suddenly he wanted her to be his plus-one at an industry event? It was her idea of a nightmare. All she wanted was to stay safely in the small world she'd created for herself. Not be seen on the arm of one of the world's most visible and photographed men.

This was exactly what she'd been afraid of—that she'd fall for Arch, and the entire world would be the audience to her heartbreak.

She swallowed hard. "I'm not sure about that, Arch," she said carefully. "I am still your caregiver, after all, and going as your date would be really unprofessional. If my company finds out I've been romantic with a client, I'd probably get fired. And possibly never be able to work again in this industry, because you're so famous, and everyone would always associate my fall from grace with you."

Saying it out loud made her realize the truth of it and what a precarious situation she'd put herself in. She was too good at her job to lose it. She'd lost everything once before, when her husband, the man she'd foolishly trusted, had gambled all their money away. She'd built herself back up, slowly. She didn't have much in the way of savings, but she had a little and a job she enjoyed. She couldn't allow herself to be that vulnerable ever again, and yet, here she was, on the road to potential disaster.

Arch's face fell. He'd obviously thought she would jump at the chance to attend a film festival with him. But then, his eyes lit up once more. She could almost see a lightbulb go on over his head. "But doesn't coming with me count as work? Like, what if I trip on the red carpet? Wouldn't that be the perfect reason to have my caregiver with me? To prevent further injury?"

"Wait, there's a red carpet?" Now she was even more horrified. It didn't sound like the small awards ceremony he'd made it out to be.

He shrugged, as though it were no big deal. "There's always a red carpet."

Of course red carpets were no big deal to him—he walked them all the time. He knew how to pose for the hundreds of cameras flashing in his face. How to deal with being stopped to sign autographs. She'd witnessed firsthand how he took fame in stride. Being approached by strangers was nothing to him.

But just the thought terrified her.

"I can see you're worried," he said, "but if I let the Helping Hands agency know that you're going to accompany me for work, will that be okay with you?"

She should say no. But he'd just made it so easy for her to justify saying yes. He was still her client, and he was still healing.

After a long pause, she finally nodded. "All right. I'll go with you. But not as a romantic plus-one. Only as your caregiver."

She barely had time to take her next breath when he bent down to kiss her.

And with that kiss, all her fears were forgotten. At least for the moment—when all she could think about was how much she wanted him.

★ ★ ★

Though they'd had a big, long day together out and about in Monterey County, Arch wasn't the least bit tired. On the contrary, he was full of energy.

And it was all down to being with Tessa.

With her brilliant care of him and his broken bone, she had returned him to himself. But it was more than that. The way she'd kissed him on the pier had been so damned good. He'd never been happier knowing that she wanted him as much as he wanted her. That was why he'd forced himself to wait for her to make the first move—so that he'd have no doubt that she felt their connection too. It was also a massive deal to him that she'd confided in him her passion for painting.

Tessa flicked on a lamp, then went to get them both ice water. When she came back, he was no longer in his solo lounger, but on the couch.

"Why did you move?"

"So that there would be room for both of us." He didn't need to add *and so we can kiss more*, because some things were so obvious they didn't need to be spoken out loud.

It all felt so natural, being in his home with her, holding her in his arms, kissing her.

But if he wanted things to go any further, he was going to have go out of his way not only to be truthful with her, but also to apologize if he did something that put him in the wrong. If he didn't want her to hide anything from him, he had to be the same way.

"I need to say something to you. Something important."

Tessa stiffened. Inwardly, he cursed himself. He'd put her back on her guard—that same guard he'd worked so hard to take down. He made a mental note to think more carefully about the way he phrased things, not just blurt them out.

Tessa's eyes were wary, as though she was mentally running through a whole host of awful things he could have done. "What is it?" she asked. "You're not secretly married to Sonia, are you?"

He grimaced. "No, of course not. I know we already talked about this on the pier, but I'm just really sorry that I didn't tell you earlier that I knew about your painting. I don't want you to think I'll do it again—that I'll keep things from you in the future. I want you to know—to believe—that I'll always be honest with you."

Relief rushed over Tessa's face. "Thank you for saying that. I was glad when you told me on the pier, but hearing you say that you'll never keep things from me again... Well, that's a really big deal to me."

With every word she spoke, he was glad to see her

grow more and more trusting. Clearly, she'd been expecting something *much* worse. He figured it was because she'd been let down so badly in the past.

As her body relaxed next to his on the couch, he saw he was forgiven for keeping his knowledge of her painting from her—and he hoped it also meant she was giving him her full trust as well.

But he knew it for certain when she said, "Although I told you on the pier that I wasn't ready to show you my paintings, I've just changed my mind."

Though he was dying to see one, he had to ask, "Are you certain?" Because she hadn't been so sure out on the pier. In fact, she'd flat out said she wasn't ready.

She smiled at him then, and he found himself lost in Tessa's smile.

Her smiles were so seductive. As were her kisses.

And he couldn't believe how sensual her touch was, the passionate way her hands sought out the hair at the nape of his neck and tugged him against her as they wound their bodies closer.

She nodded. "I'm sure."

Could it really be true? She was going to let him see her paintings?

She took a deep breath. "This is a *huge* deal for me. But given what I said on the pier about how I no longer care what you or anyone else thinks about my painting, whatever your reaction is, I'm determined to be like Picasso."

He grinned at her wonderfully courageous words, but then noticed that her hands were trembling. Despite her amazing resilience, Tessa was still vulnerable, and he had to tread carefully.

He followed Tessa's lead upstairs to her bedroom. He tried to keep the sexy thoughts out of his mind as her hips swayed up the stairs ahead of him, but it was darned hard. She had no idea how attractive she was—one of the many things that got to him.

They entered the guest room, and she flicked on a lamp. He glanced around for any signs of her private life—her little habits or personal items. But the room was as neat as the cleaning service had left it. The only personal possessions that he could see were a tube of hand cream on the nightstand, on top of a book about twentieth-century female artists.

She went to the wardrobe and opened both sets of doors. There were very few clothes hanging inside and a modest stack of T-shirts and knitwear on the shelves. Most of the generous space had been given over to a backpack, some boxes that must hold art supplies, a black portfolio, a small folding wooden easel, and a folding stool like a backless director's chair.

She turned and flashed him a nervous look. He gave her an encouraging smile, but that was all. He didn't want to come across as pushy, even though he was dying to see one of her paintings up close.

She drew out the portfolio and unzipped it with

trembling hands. He wanted so badly to wrap his arms around her so that she would know she was safe. But again, he fought the urge. It was important to let her deal with her emotions and fears without his interference. And also for him to stay steady and calm and show her he could be trusted that way.

Being here, in her room, he could see more than ever how Tessa wasn't like any of his past girlfriends. He was used to starlets who had never heard the expression *traveling light*. Actresses and models who went from venue to venue with glam teams and stylists and an entourage of "friends."

Whereas Tessa was the very definition of unfussy and private. It reminded him of the way his own mother was.

And he loved it.

At last, she turned to face him as she pulled out the sheet he'd seen her working on when he'd driven past with Mila. She lifted it carefully and brought it over to the light.

He tried not to gasp. But it was nearly impossible when her painting was *astonishing*.

He'd caught a quick glimpse before, but up close he could see that she'd captured something so special about the ocean and the beach that he was simply awestruck.

Although it had some modern touches—the way she'd mixed her colors, for example, and their loose, flowing layers—her artwork also paid homage to the great *plein air* artists before her.

He loved the mix of tradition and innovation, but mostly he loved the way she saw the world. It was the Carmel-by-the-Sea that *he* saw too. The elegance and the purity and the sheer breathtaking beauty of the blue sky and golden sands. And even more than that, she'd captured the warm and wonderful feeling of *home*.

He wanted to tell Tessa all this, but at the same time, if he told her exactly how impressed he was, she might not believe him.

She was looking at him expectantly, her nerves probably at an all-time high. So he simply said, "It's wonderful, Tessa. Just wonderful." He could hear in his own voice the deep, genuine awe he truly felt as he set the painting in the portfolio.

A look of relief washed over her, and then she came to him, throwing her arms around his neck and kissing him deeply.

He pressed his body into hers. Now that they were standing up, rather than sitting on a bench, he could feel just how perfect a fit she was for him. He pulled her in even tighter, kissing her deeply. Arch was utterly lost in her.

When Tessa finally drew back for air, her eyes were cloudy with desire. His must look the same. It took all of his willpower not to unbutton her shirt then and there.

But no. He needed to be a gentleman. And just as he had wanted her to take the lead on their kisses, if they were going to sleep together, she would have to take the lead there too. Simply because he couldn't bear the thought of taking something from her if she wasn't ready to give it freely to him.

He stepped back and looked at the painting again. It really was incredible. "Your talent is amazing. You should be exhibiting in the finest galleries." He paused. "I'd be proud to hang your work on my walls."

He wanted to offer to buy it, but would she be offended? Would it make him seem patronizing?

She looked surprised by his reaction, but thrilled at the same time. "If you really do like it—"

"I really, really do *love* it."

She smiled again. "Well, then, in that case, you can have it."

"Seriously? You're *giving* it to me?"

Her grin grew even wider as she echoed, "Seriously. I'm giving it to you."

Just in case she changed her mind, he picked up the painting and walked with it back downstairs and into the living room, carefully navigating the stairs in his boot with help from her hand on his arm to make sure he didn't trip.

"Wait, are you hanging it right this minute?"

"You bet I am."

He unhooked a painting from its position over the fireplace. It was by a successful up-and-coming artist, but he didn't like the work nearly as much as he liked Tessa's. He set the framed painting down and then balanced Tessa's on the mantel, its thick, toothy paper giving it enough stiffness to lean upright.

He stood back, admiring her work. And when he looked over at her, she was the one who looked awestruck this time, her eyes sparkling and her smile wider than he'd ever seen it.

It gave him such joy to see her so happy. "I'm going to get that framed tomorrow. It looks great right there."

"You've got to be kidding me." She shook her head and gave him a look that made it clear she thought he'd lost his mind. "You can't put it in the same room as a Picasso!"

"Of course I can," he replied, still grinning. "You're being Picasso, right?"

She shook her head in disbelief and then let her hair down from its tie so that it fell like a curtain over her shoulders.

"I was already a sure thing tonight," she said, her voice so low he had to strain to hear. "You don't have to do that."

"We both were," he replied. Then he added two things he really wanted her to know. "But hanging this painting here doesn't have a damned thing to do with making love with you. It's here because it's where it belongs." He drew her in against him. "And you and I are together tonight because it's where *we* belong."

Chapter Twenty-One

Tessa stood beside Arch's bed. It felt like a year since she'd fled this room after he'd called her down under false pretenses and lifted the covers to welcome her in.

Now everything was different.

Her mind reverberated with the echoes of their passionate kiss in the living room. It was as if every lustful feeling she'd been holding back had come rushing out of her all at once.

She couldn't get enough of his skin, his smell, the taste of his mouth. What's more, she felt his body responding in the same way.

Their passion was in perfect sync. It was *intoxicating*.

And now here they were in his bedroom, both of them flushed with desire. She was nervous and excited in equal measure. She held his gaze as he crossed the room to come to her. Every thought he was having about her was written across his face.

And she knew each and every thought involved her being naked… and filled with pleasure.

All her nerve endings fired as he gently swept her hair away from her face and kissed her tenderly on the lips.

"You're so beautiful," he said in a voice thick with desire. "I've thought so from the first moment I saw you walking on the beach. And I've been wowed at every stage of getting to know you and living with you here." He took a breath that shook slightly from the emotion he was clearly feeling. "You're so special, Tessa. I want to show you just how special you are."

When she nodded eagerly, he began to unbutton her shirt. He took his time. As each button revealed more of her skin, she felt herself growing more and more sensitive, every inch of her crying out to be touched.

He kept his eyes on her until the last button was undone and the fabric fell open to reveal her simple white lace bra. Only then did he allow himself to cast his gaze over her breasts.

She couldn't help it—she trembled as she felt his eyes undress the rest of her.

Out of nowhere, he said, "If you want me to stop here, I will. We don't need to rush anything. We have all the time in the world."

But she shook her head. "I couldn't bear it if you stopped now." She took his hand and laid it on her chest. "Please, keep doing exactly what you're doing." She let a wicked glint enter her gaze. "And more. So much more."

With that, he kissed her again with such deep passion as his mouth sought hers hungrily. She wanted him with every fiber of her being. She couldn't remember ever wanting anyone, or anything, more.

He slipped the shirt from her shoulders, kissing her neck as he went. His lips were so soft on her skin that she shivered with need.

Part of her wanted to beg him to rip off the rest of her clothes. The other half wanted to savor every single second of his kisses, his caresses. To follow the slow, erotic trace of his fingers down her spine and then around to her stomach.

He stopped there and pulled away to look at her again.

"Please," she whispered, "please don't stop. I want you so badly, Arch. You have no idea."

"Oh yes, I do. Because I want you just as much. But I'm trying to control myself," he said huskily. "I want to take it slow. To savor every single inch of you."

His arousing words made her feel bold enough to reach for the hem of his T-shirt and pull it up, over his gorgeous abs. He lifted his arms, and she slipped it off.

"My jeans," she managed to say. "Get them off."

From the look on his face, he hadn't expected her to be so bold. She had surprised herself too. She'd never felt this urgency before. And she'd certainly never felt so appreciated. Or as though she could vocalize her desires to her lover without fearing she'd be laughed at or pushed away.

His breathing quickened as he slowly, tantalizingly, pulled down her zipper. The sound echoed between them like a promise.

He groaned at the sight of her white lace panties. A part of her wished she owned fancier, sexier lingerie. But Arch certainly didn't seem to care that her underclothes were no fancier than her T-shirts and jeans.

"This is where I'd love to pick you up and throw you on the bed," he said. He looked down at his boot. "But I don't want to undo all the physio you've given me. As hot as it would be, somehow I don't think you'd forgive me for screwing up my leg again."

She laughed. "How about I help you, then?"

She went to the bed, the crisp sheets cool against her hot skin, and lay back. She couldn't help adding, "Maybe this is the kind of help you'll actually be happy to accept."

Arch removed his boot and knelt at the foot of the bed so that his head was level with her zipper. Carefully, he lifted her hips and, inch by inch, slipped the jeans down her legs until she was just in her bra and panties.

And then heaven began.

He was kissing his way up her body, beginning with her calves and inching up to her thighs. The feeling was electric, and she relished every sensation as pleasure rolled through her in waves.

She couldn't believe how gentle his touch was. The depth of his tenderness. And how sexy, how sensual, how full of pleasure he made her feel.

It was everything she could have wished for, if she'd been bold enough to make that kind of wish.

His hands slid up and across her curves. He touched her slowly, still so gently, and then she felt her panties being peeled from her skin. It was exquisite torture.

She raised herself onto her elbows to look at him. His tanned skin, the mop of sun-licked hair, and the rippling of his biceps made her breath catch in her throat. She'd never known sex could be like this.

He was driving her crazy making her wait for more... but she was desperate for it. And it took everything she had not to beg him to go fast and hard.

★ ★ ★

Tessa's white lace panties were pooled beside him when he felt her gaze. He raised his head and took in the sweet sight of her nearly naked on his bed.

"You're even more beautiful than I could have imagined." And he meant every word. She was gorgeous beyond his wildest dreams.

She sat upright then and held out her arms.

He went to her without so much as a moment's pause. She was irresistible. And he needed to see all of her.

To explore all of her. Inch by glorious inch.

Even though the effort to go slow was nearly killing him, he took his time unhooking the bra and releasing her full breasts.

Sweet Lord, she's beautiful.

Now that she was fully naked, it was going to be a nearly impossible task to be gentle and to keep taking things slow. But he was determined to do just that.

He could barely wrap his head around the fact that he had taken off her clothes, let alone how much she obviously wanted him. And now here she was, a total knockout. Her curves were divine, her skin soft as butter.

Tessa Taylor deserved this kind of worship.

And he had never been happier in his life than he was right now, knowing that she was giving him the chance to do just that. To worship all of her, inside and out.

Carefully, he lowered himself over her and covered her smooth belly with kisses, which soon became teasing licks around her navel. She moaned in pleasure, and to his ears, the sound was like a rhapsody of angels.

He felt so lucky that *he* was the one she'd chosen to give her the pleasure she deserved. He gripped her hips and felt her lift up toward him, urging him to go on, to take more, and to give more.

He stopped to unzip his jeans, but she said, "No, you're not getting away that easily."

He raised an eyebrow. "Is Nurse Taylor making an appearance again?"

She laughed, joyful and sexy, and then in an impressive feat of fitness, managed to roll him onto his back and straddle his hips.

She gently bit his left earlobe and whispered, "It's *my* turn to tease *you* now." She eased the zipper of his jeans over his rock-hard erection.

He moaned at her touch, just as he'd wanted to do every time she'd touched him during their exercises, or when her skin had brushed his. He already knew she had healing in her hands, but even in his most wicked imaginings, he hadn't known how good they would feel as she caressed him.

Tessa was blowing his mind.

"You. Me." He paused to try to think straight, which was nearly impossible with her naked and straddling him in his bed. "I've never felt like this before, Tessa. Like we're two halves of a whole. Like we can read each other's minds."

As she slid off his lap to pull off his jeans, she said, "I've been dreaming of this moment. I always have."

He was stunned. Did this mean that she had felt the same spark on the beach that first day?

But he didn't have time to contend with questions when she was undressing him as slowly and as sensually as he had her. And he loved it.

Once she had him naked, he decided enough was

enough—it was time to take back the control and show Tessa the pleasure he could give her. He grabbed her by the waist and rolled her over so that he could reach her soft lips.

He parted her lips with his tongue and then gently stroked it over hers. She moaned into his mouth, and he relished the sound. Laying her down, he returned to worshipping each part of her body.

She had given him the most incredible day, had shared her private passion for art with him, and now he wanted to show her what all this meant to him. What *she* meant to him. He wanted her to have all the bliss she deserved, and more.

"Tessa," he murmured, then took her breast into his mouth. She shuddered in response, and he teased her sensitive skin with his tongue, feeling it harden at his touch. She arched her back, and he used the space to draw her even closer. As he drew small circles around the taut peak of her breast, she moaned, and when he moved to the other breast, he heard her whisper his name.

"Archer," she breathed.

Never had he responded so strongly to the call of his name. He cupped both breasts now, showering them with kisses. He longed to hear her say his name again. Louder, stronger. He wanted her to cry out his name in utter ecstasy as she climaxed for him, over and over.

She rocked her hips beneath him, and the sensation of their bodies moving in sync made his heart pound. He gasped as she clasped her hands around his lower back and urged him to move closer to her.

"I want to feel you," she whispered.

He wanted to feel her, too, but he couldn't let himself give in to the temptation just yet. He needed to taste her first.

He moved down to slip between her legs, and now it was his turn to moan as she parted her thighs for him, offering herself to him in the most intimate way possible.

He kissed her sex, slowly, gently, feeling her warmth and inhaling her sweet scent before allowing himself a taste. Her moans spurred him on, and he felt like an Olympic champion accepting a gold medal for making her feel so good.

When he finally used his tongue, he lost himself in her honey elixir. Her thighs trembled around his ears, and he let himself go, touching her in every way he knew possible, determined to feel and hear her climax.

Only when her hips rocked against his mouth, and her shudders became stronger did he use his hands as well. And then he felt her grip him with all her might, and he knew she was about to tip over the edge.

"My God," she cried out. "Oh, Arch, yes! More, please. I need more!"

He gave her everything he had, following the

waves of her orgasm until her body calmed and her muscles relaxed. Once he knew that every ounce of pleasure had flowed through her, he moved back up her body, stroking her hair away from her forehead. Slowly, she opened her beautiful eyes, wide with wonder.

"That was…" She trailed off. "So good. I don't even have the words to tell you how good I feel."

He smiled and brushed her flushed cheek with his hand. "You don't need to say a word for me to know. I felt it in every shudder. I heard it in every moan. I don't think I'll ever be able to get enough of you, Tessa."

As if his words had sparked even more passion, she pulled him in for another long, hot kiss. And although it took every ounce of self-control, he wouldn't let his animal instincts take over. Instead, he leaned across and opened his bedside drawer, where he'd stashed a packet of condoms in hopes that this moment would happen.

He ripped open the package, but then she took it from him to slowly slide protection onto his erection.

And then, straight out of his dreams, she took him into her hands and guided him into her.

Again, he wanted to ravage her, but he held himself back, wanting the pleasure to last for both of them. He moved slowly so that she could feel every inch of him.

"You really do have a gentle touch," she whispered into his ear. "You know when to be gentle, and you know when to take control." She gave him a small smile, one that was full of lust, even as she said, "Just like when you're washing dishes."

He smiled, too, then, and knew it was the moment to take her fully.

In one hard thrust, he was inside of her. It was, he thought wildly, the only place he ever wanted to be again.

She cried out his name, and they moved together in a unison he'd never experienced before. He kissed her mouth passionately, and their lips stayed locked as he felt her inner muscles tighten around him. Only once she climaxed so beautifully beneath him did he give in to his own pleasure.

His mind was utterly, completely blown. He'd never felt so good in all his life. Not until Tessa had found her way into his home, his heart, and now his bed.

When the sensations subsided, he opened his eyes to find her gazing dreamily at him. He kissed her nose, her cheeks, and her mouth again before he rolled onto his side to face her.

Tessa looked completely dazed in the aftermath of their lovemaking. It was adorable and deliciously sexy all at the same time.

"I never knew sex could be like that," she said in a soft voice.

He brushed the backs of his knuckles over her

cheek. He felt the same way, and he wanted to tell her that what they'd just experienced together wasn't just sex—they had made love to each other. But he instinctively knew that hearing the word *love*, even in the context of hot sex, would freak her out. And he didn't want to ruin the moment by accidentally moving too fast.

So he swallowed down the words and simply said, "Neither have I. You're so special, Tessa. So damned beautiful and smart and talented… and amazing in bed too."

She wriggled closer to him and slipped her arms around his neck, stroking his skin with her fingertips. Her lips met his, and she whispered against them, "You're the one who's amazing, Arch." Then, to his surprise, she said, "And I can't get enough."

Despite all his exertion, he felt himself getting aroused again. He wanted more of her, and she wanted more of him, and so they began to make love, slower and more tenderly this time. They explored and enjoyed each other's bodies in a way he could only have dreamed of before tonight.

And already he couldn't wait for more of her.

Chapter Twenty-Two

The morning sun shone through the gauzy curtains, and Tessa turned her face toward it, letting the warmth touch her face. She'd never awakened with such a feeling of peace. And then she remembered why… and shivered with pleasure.

Arch had been the perfect lover, beyond her wildest dreams. She'd given every inch of herself to him, and he'd kissed it, licked it, caressed it. He moved in ways she'd never experienced before.

He'd known what she needed more than she had herself.

And now here she was, naked in his gigantic bed, watching him sleep.

How did I ever get so lucky?

He looked beyond sexy with his dark hair against the pillow, one tanned, well-muscled arm behind his head.

Unable to help herself, she kissed his neck, tasting his salty skin and inhaling his scent.

Slowly, he opened his eyes. When he saw her, he

grinned. "Well, good morning."

She matched his smile and said, "It *is* a good morning."

He pulled her down for a kiss, and although she suddenly felt shy despite everything they'd shared the night before, she parted her lips to let his tongue tangle with hers.

The kiss was heavenly. Heck, every single thing about Arch was heavenly.

When they finally pulled away, he rolled out of bed.

"Hey, where are you going?" she teased. "I'm not sure I'm done with you yet."

He flashed her a saucy grin. "You make me coffee every morning. Today, it's my turn. Except you get to drink yours in bed." He pulled on a pair of boxers and his leg boot, then turned at the doorway to waggle a finger at her. "Don't move!"

She nodded, letting herself fully enjoy the sight of his perfect physique walking away.

She lay back in sheets rumpled by their lovemaking and stretched. She couldn't remember the last time she hadn't been shaken from sleep by an early alarm, let alone the last time someone had fixed her morning coffee. She didn't even know what time it was.

The feeling was *bliss*.

Within minutes, Arch came back, carrying a wooden tray. She sat up, propping herself on the plump pillows.

"Your coffee, madam," he said, gently setting the tray across her lap. On it was a latte with a heart swirled into the foam and a bud vase holding a white rose from the bouquet he'd bought earlier in the week.

"It's so pretty!" she exclaimed, thanking him. "I wish I could sketch it and remember this moment always."

Arch grinned again, and her heart leaped as she knew that she was making him as happy as he was making her.

"Your wish is my command," Arch said and disappeared again.

She took a tiny sip of her coffee so as not to disturb the foam heart just yet and sighed in contentment. It was delicious.

When Arch returned, he was carrying her backpack of art supplies. Sheepishly, he said, "I didn't know what you needed, so I brought it all."

The caregiver in her wanted to scold him for carrying something so heavy on his own down the stairs, but considering the way he'd thrown her around the bed last night, he was already a lot stronger than she would have thought. And she hadn't warned him to take it easy when he was sending her straight to heaven, again and again…

She put the tray on the bedside table, pulled on his T-shirt—feeling his eyes on her naked skin the entire time and loving his obvious appreciation of her body—then stepped out of bed to get her sketchbook and watercolor pencils from the bag.

Arch sat on the bed, watching her with a soft expression she didn't dare interpret as anything more than a happy morning-after-good-sex look. As she sketched the breakfast tray, all she could think was that no one had ever taken care of her this way. Or cared so much about what she wanted or needed.

She caught the light behind the rose and the contrast of the coffee, the heart still floating on top. The sketch wasn't a masterpiece, but still, she lifted it up to show Arch. "What do you think?"

He gave her a look of disbelief. "How did you capture that so quickly?"

She shrugged and laughed. Had she really believed, even for a second, that Arch would criticize her little sketch's shortcomings? "For some reason, I'm feeling pretty inspired this morning." She let a little wickedness seep into her tone.

"Inspired enough to consider being my date to the Moonrise awards ceremony?"

Just like that, Tessa's good mood faltered. She really did not want to be in the limelight, even if it meant being on Arch's arm. Why was it so important to him that she attend this event? "Exactly how big is this ceremony going to be?"

"It's an indie, not one of the big ones," he explained. "So although there's a red carpet, it's not like the whole world is watching."

But even as he traced a finger down her arm, making her shiver with need, she knew with utter certainty that if she showed up on his arm at an event, regardless of the size, the entire world would definitely take note. She'd bet money on the fact that her picture with him would be plastered across the Internet and in the press. She could already see the headlines: *The caregiver and the star. An unexpected love story? Or a disaster waiting to happen?*

"It's no big deal, really," he went on. "I'd just feel better with you by my side." His expression softened. "After last night, you surely must know how good being around you makes me feel, Tessa."

She nodded, unable to argue with that, and replied quietly, "I feel the same."

"So you'll come?"

She knew she was walking into the danger zone, but how could she say no to him after all they'd just shared? After he'd just told her how much it would mean to him if she went?

"Okay, I'll come," she finally replied, and although every fiber of her being was terrified at the prospect, she could see how happy it made him. But in the next moment, a new worry flashed through her mind. "I have nothing to wear!"

"Tessa, you'll be the most beautiful woman there

even if you show up wearing a painting smock."

Because it was such a sweet, if untruthful, thing to say, she showered his face with kisses.

When they finally ended the embrace, she decided she'd better visit a thrift store to look for a dress during her break this afternoon. She'd seen plenty of amazing gowns turn up in stores after being worn just once for a special occasion and had often marveled at how inexpensive they were considering their designer labels. She'd never had a place to wear a fancy dress before, but now, for the first time ever, she could let her best thrifting instincts run wild.

Arch's phone buzzed, and when he looked at it, he groaned. She thought he might have missed a bunch of important business calls or emails, but to her surprise, he said he was going to be late for a meeting with his family. "We have a weekly breakfast date, for whoever's in town," he explained. "Otherwise, I'd be making you my scrambled eggs on toast right now."

"There's always tomorrow," she teased. She loved the idea of a weekly family breakfast. It was so cute and cozy. "Besides, I should get myself ready for the day." She stretched her arms over her head, feeling sore in the best kind of way.

"Do you have plans this morning?"

"Only to take care of you once you're home and hopefully get some painting done too."

"Perfect. I can't wait for you to reconnect with my

family and to meet Damien. He's back from his tour."

She froze, thinking she'd misunderstood. "Wait, what? You want me to come to breakfast? With your family?"

"Of course. Everyone loves you. And my mom makes a mean French toast."

Tessa felt panic grip her. Everything was moving so quickly. First, the sexiest night ever in Arch's arms, then agreeing to attend an awards ceremony with him, then being asked to join an intimate family gathering?

She didn't even know what they were to each other yet. It was too much. Without thinking, she blurted, "But I don't want your family to know about us."

From Arch's disappointed expression, she realized he'd been thinking the exact opposite.

"Why not?" he asked.

Hating that she'd hurt his feelings, she simply said, "This. You and me and what happened between us last night… It's all so new." She inhaled deeply, then blew out a shaky breath. "Can we keep what's happening between us a secret for now?"

Arch didn't reply, and she recalled his sisters telling her just how stubborn he was known to be.

Suddenly, a sly look came into his eyes. "Okay," he said. "We can keep this between us, but will you come to breakfast with me anyway? In a professional capacity?" He lifted his leg as if to remind her the walking boot was on it. "After all, I'm sure they'll be expecting you to accompany me as my caregiver. And you don't want to disappoint my mom, do you?"

She laughed even as she said, "That's emotional blackmail, Archer Davenport." But looking at his sweet, hopeful expression was enough to melt her resolve. "Okay. But I'd better freshen up and put some clothes on before we head over."

Arch checked his phone again. "We've got a little time first…"

He reached out, and she fell into his arms, kissing him with all the passion she had, just the way he was kissing her too.

★ ★ ★

Forty-five minutes later, as Tessa stood nervously at the door of Howard and Betsy Davenport's home, she recalled how different she'd felt the last time she was here. Then, she'd been Margaret's caregiver and painting in secret. Now, she'd just had mind-blowing sex with the man of her dreams and shown him her paintings. He hadn't belittled her or criticized her work. Quite the opposite—he'd been supportive and encouraging.

Everything was different now.

Arch smiled and squeezed her hand. "It's going to be great," he said, obviously sensing her trepidation. "My family already adore you. There's nothing to worry about."

He pushed open the door, and Tessa quickly dropped his hand and allowed herself to be welcomed in by Betsy. Buster pushed past her, tail wagging so hard that his entire body wagged along with it. He seemed as excited to see Tessa as he was to see Arch, rubbing his body against them and demanding as many pats and greetings as he could wrangle.

"Be careful, Buster," Betsy admonished. "If you trip poor Arch and he breaks his other leg, you'll really be in trouble." But the dog gave a single woof, as if to say, *I would never trip my human brother*, and went back to being blissed out as Arch rubbed his head.

"So good to see you again, Tessa," Betsy said warmly, and Tessa could feel that she really meant her kind words.

She marveled at how effortlessly glamorous Betsy looked in a blue linen shirt and jeans and was thankful that she had put together her own outfit carefully. It was thrifted, of course, but she knew that her shirt with the crocheted edges was a particularly rare find and worked well with an A-line cotton skirt she'd had for years.

"Everyone is in the kitchen," Betsy said. "You're the last to arrive as usual," she said playfully, hugging Arch. "And you can't even blame your crutches anymore."

Arch grinned and said, "It's Tessa's fault this time, not mine. She put me through my paces with exercise this morning."

Tessa froze. Didn't he realize that his voice was laden with flirtatious undertones?

If his mom noticed, she didn't let on. Tessa prayed that Betsy had no clue that they were anything but client and caregiver. But something told her his mom was *way* smarter than that…

"That's her job," Betsy said, then turned to Tessa. "And clearly you're very good at it if Arch is already out of his cast."

"Thank you for the compliment, but Arch is exactly the kind of client a caregiver dreams of." Belatedly realizing how that might have sounded, she quickly added, "He always does his physical therapy exercises without complaining."

With a smile, Betsy excused herself to fetch eggs from the pantry, and before they entered the noisy kitchen, Tessa pulled Arch aside. "You agreed to keep us private," she whispered.

He frowned. "What did I do?"

"When you talked about me putting you through your paces this morning? You made it sound so… sexy."

Arch grinned. "If that's the case, then I'm not the only one, with you calling me the kind of client a caregiver *dreams* of." Then he added, "Don't worry, Mom didn't cotton to our little sexercise."

Tessa frowned this time. "I'm serious, Arch. Please

respect my wishes to come across to your family as nothing more than your professional caregiver. It's all I'm asking of you. Is it really too much?"

At that, Arch's whole demeanour changed from teasing to serious, and he apologized immediately. "I won't do that again. I promise. I am, after all, an actor. For example, I can pretend I don't want to rip your pretty shirt open right now and taste your skin." With that, he leaned in and gave her a quick kiss that sent her heart and body spinning like crazy, just like the night before. "Last kiss until we get back to my house after breakfast. Scout's honor."

With that, he opened the kitchen door, and they walked into the boisterous hubbub of a family gathering, where everyone was talking at once. Erin stopped slicing a melon and came to hug Tessa hello, and Mila waved as she paused in her job of making coffee.

Finn was frying bacon, and Nick was squeezing oranges. Both greeted her as though she were one of them.

Then Arch took her to meet Damien.

The Davenport men were all gorgeous, but Damien had a brooding sex appeal that probably sold as many albums as his husky voice. He was even better looking in person, in ripped Levi's and a black concert T-shirt. But despite the rock star's sexy good looks, Arch was the only man who could ever make Tessa feel weak at the knees—or make her heart beat wildly from nothing more than a smile.

"Dad put me on toast duty," Damien said, pointing at a gigantic eight-slice toaster and rolling his eyes. "Last week, I played Wembley Stadium. This week, I'm buttering whole wheat toast for this motley crew." He looked at Tessa. "I also have sunflower spread if you're vegan."

Tessa shook her head. "Butter's fine."

"Welcome back to real life." Arch laughed at his brother even as he gave him a hug hello.

Betsy joined them, and Tessa asked if there was anything she could do to help.

"Oh, you're a sweetheart," Betsy replied. "Would you mind setting the table? Howie is about to get started on his famous omelets, and then we can all eat."

Tessa smiled and followed Betsy to the dining room. Buster came along as though to supervise. As she took the silverware from the drawer and laid each place, she already felt more like a part of this giant, friendly family than a guest. And though it was dangerous to let herself feel that way—as though she were actually part of Arch's life in a permanent way, rather than just until her contract ran out—she couldn't help but give in to the sweetness of being with his family. All her life, she'd dreamed of being part of a family like the Davenports, so for this one precious morning, she would let herself enjoy every minute of it.

Chapter Twenty-Three

Looking around the huge dining table laden with breakfast, Tessa marveled at the good nature of the Davenport family. They were warm and loving, a truly good group of people. Sitting next to Arch, after a night of the most intense and connected sex of her life, she felt like she was starring opposite him in a movie.

A super sexy, extremely satisfying movie.

It was almost too good to be true. And yet, this was her life right now. She could pinch herself.

She watched Betsy and Howie and wondered how they'd worked together to build such a loving bunch. Their deep love and affection for each other after so many years of marriage felt like something out of one of Arch's early romantic comedies. She hadn't thought such happy-family scenes existed in the real world.

"This all looks delicious," she said. "Thank you so much."

It had been a long time since she'd attended any kind of big meal, let alone a family one where each person had contributed. Howie's omelets looked incredible—steaming hot and oozing with melted cheese. The bacon was crispy and smelled divine. The fresh fruit glistened, and the toast was perfectly browned.

She didn't know where to begin. It was so nice to be cooked for. After so many years of looking after others and thinking about their nutritional needs, to be offered an array of food so expertly cooked was a true pleasure.

"You're very welcome, Tessa," Betsy said. "It's nice to have you here. I know this meal isn't nearly enough, but we're all *so* thankful that you're doing such a great job of looking after Archer."

"I can't believe you managed to get him out of that cast so quickly," Mila added. She should know, given her personal knowledge of recovery from injuries. "I know how pleased he is."

Tessa flushed. It wasn't the only way she'd managed to please him. She had to work to push the dirty thoughts out of her mind as she said, "He's a good patient."

"I don't believe that for a second," Damien said. "He's one of the most stubborn of us Davenports. And that's really saying something."

"Hey!" Arch said. "That is not true. I'm not even in the same league as Mila."

At that, the whole family burst into laughter. Mila joined in good-naturedly. Clearly, they were all used to being teased and took it with good humor. Plates of food were passed, and Tessa helped herself to a small portion of everything.

As she tucked into a perfectly crispy piece of toast, she realized that by inviting her to his weekly family brunch, Arch was letting her see yet another side of him. The softer, more vulnerable family man.

She felt honored.

"Now that you're out of your full cast," Finn said, "you've no excuse to get out of dishwashing duty."

Tessa smiled, thinking once more that despite Finn's being shockingly handsome, the only Davenport brother who did it for her was Arch. Until now, she'd remained quiet, but she couldn't stay silent on this one. "At home, Arch has already proved himself to be pretty good at dishes. Cast or no cast."

The entire table trained their gazes on Tessa. She tried not to turn pink.

"Are you saying that Arch actually helps around the house?" Erin asked, clearly surprised.

"It's true!" Tessa slowly eased into the Davenport banter.

"I'd need to see it to believe it," Erin replied.

"I'm a gentleman," Arch said. "And enough making fun of the guy with the broken leg. Why don't we ask Damien about his tour? I bet he's got some stories."

"Good point," Howie said. He turned to his youngest son, whom Tessa was doing her best not to fangirl over. She loved Damien's songs. "Do you have any stories that won't make your old man blush?"

Damien laughed. "Life on the road is not nearly as rock-and-roll as you might think, Dad. It's not the eighties anymore," he teased.

"Ouch!" Howie exclaimed. "I might be silver-haired, but I'm still pretty with it for an old guy," he replied in the same teasing tone.

Tessa thought Howie and Betsy were the most youthful set of parents she'd ever met, but she didn't want to interrupt Damien's story. He was telling them about the night one of their amps had an electrical issue onstage during the concert.

"That was in Madrid. Or maybe Paris. Rob, our guitarist, just went with it," Damien said. "Like it was part of the stage show. There were sparks flying in every direction from the amp, and he just went over to it, dropped to his knees, and started riffing and rocking out."

"Was it dangerous?" Betsy asked, a frown forming on her forehead. Clearly, Tessa noted, it didn't matter how old your kids were. You still worried about them.

Damien shrugged and speared some melon with his fork. "It was just a minute or so, and then the roadies took the faulty amp away and replaced it with a new one."

"Well, I love you all too much to enjoy stories like that," Betsy replied. "I worry about you now just as much as I did when you were newborns." It was almost exactly word for word what Tessa had been thinking.

"She's not kidding," Howie added, reaching for more bacon. "Sometimes she sits bolt upright in bed at night because she's forgotten to remind one of you kids to renew your car insurance."

Betsy laughed good-naturedly, and again Tessa saw that this kind of teasing was an expression of love and affection among the Davenports.

Then Betsy said, "That was just once, Howie. And you promised not to tell."

Howie shot his wife a loving look and a wink.

Tessa bit into her omelet thoughtfully. There was so much love here in the Davenport family home, so much care. Little wonder Arch had been so considerate with her on their date. And why, even when he was doing wickedly sexy things with her in bed, she had still felt so safe with him.

This was the real world he'd grown up in—not Hollywood. She could see that now. So why was it that he'd never been in a relationship for more than a year?

Before she'd even met him, because he was her super secret star crush, she'd followed his relationship status in the press like every other woman who had a crush on him. He'd had a string of beautiful girlfriends, of course. And been linked to countless models and actresses he'd probably never even met in real life, but who were the perfect clickbait to get you to a Web page full of ads for washing machines or tennis shoes.

But as far as Tessa knew, no woman had been around for more than a year. Having spent so much time with him, she couldn't understand why. Arch was absolutely everything a woman could desire in a man—hot, thoughtful, hardworking, sensitive, and fun. Not to mention absolutely sensational in bed. So what gave?

All she could think was that it was Arch who didn't want to commit, that he was the one who left those relationships with women who were a million times hotter and more successful than Tessa.

So what chance did that give her?

The silent answer to that question—*zero*—made her tremble inside. She was already so attached to him, so caught up in passionate and tender feelings that she couldn't deny any longer.

Tessa had never given herself to a man lightly. If she slept with a man, it meant something.

What's more, she loved being here with his family. Listening to their easy chatter and feeling so welcome made her heart feel full to bursting. But once he tired of her, she wouldn't only lose Arch, she'd lose his family too.

Arch turned to whisper in her ear. "You okay?"

She must have gone quiet—and her smile must have faded without her realizing it. His face was full of genuine concern, and despite her doubts, it made her melt.

"Of course," she whispered back and gave him a smile. But it was a slightly careful smile, because even the thought of not being with Arch and his family made the whole situation feel even bigger than it already was.

When she looked around, she saw that Betsy had caught the moment between the two of them, and she mentally kicked herself. So much for keeping up professional appearances. She wouldn't believe for a second that Betsy couldn't see the deep connection she and Arch had formed. Heck, for all Tessa knew, his mother was already feeling sorry for her, simply because Arch didn't do long term with anyone. No matter how beautiful and successful that woman was. And especially if that woman was just a caregiver who dabbled in painting.

Thankfully, no one but Betsy seemed to notice anything, because Damien was still the center of attention. Which made sense, considering he'd just returned from a European tour.

"How does it feel coming back to earth with the rest of us mere mortals after being cheered on by thousands of fans night after after night?" Erin teased. "All of whom are holding up signs saying how much they love you."

"You know me. I love touring, but I'm always happy to be home," Damien replied. "I'm desperate to get in some surfing while I'm here. I've missed Carmel. Of all the places I've been, there's no other place like it."

Mila piped up again. "You should come to my weekend beginner classes for a refresher."

Damien laughed. "It hasn't been *that* long since I caught a wave, sis." He took a sip of coffee. "Besides, I couldn't imagine anything worse than you as my teacher. You're so impatient."

Mila leaned across her mother to pinch Damien on the arm.

"Ow!" he said, but with a small smile. "See? You're still a bully! Just like when we were kids."

"I'll have you know that my students rave about me," Mila informed him. "I'm an excellent teacher. Everyone thinks so."

"Come on, you two," Howie interrupted, shaking his head. "Play nice. Tessa already knows we're a stubborn bunch—she doesn't need any more insight into just how competitive we are."

But Tessa wasn't surprised. The Davenport siblings were all so successful in their individual ways—of course they were competitive. It was par for the course of wanting to do better. She was about to say so when Finn cleared his throat.

"Hey, why don't we all head to the beach tomorrow morning? A little sibling surf session. And we can keep an eye on Damien," he joked. "Make sure he doesn't drown."

The family broke into happy chatter, each of them talking about how long it had been since they'd all surfed together.

Arch grimaced. "Aren't you forgetting something?" He pointed down at his leg with its walking boot.

Erin put her hand on Arch's arm. "Don't worry, you can still come and watch us crush it on the waves. You could even score us."

Arch rolled his eyes. "How kind of you."

Tessa laughed and told him, "You'll be out on the waves again before you know it. And a morning by the ocean inhaling the salt air will do you a world of good. You've been cooped up indoors for too long."

"See? Doctor's orders," Erin said. "You have to come now. We'll buy you breakfast after."

Howie let out a deep chuckle. "I love how you kids are already planning tomorrow's breakfast while you're eating today's."

The siblings laughed, and Tessa joined in.

"I hope you can come too, Tessa," Erin added. "Do you surf?"

Tessa was filled with gratitude—it was so nice the way Arch's sisters included her, as though she was part of the family. "I'd love to come," she said, "but I have to admit I don't know how to surf."

Mila almost choked on her slice of bacon. "What?" she spluttered. "That's a tragedy. I'm going to give you a one-on-one lesson. Watching you walk, and by the way you hold your body, I can tell that you're a natural athlete. I could teach you to surf in no time."

Tessa didn't know what to say, but Arch did. "I'll teach her, Mila. When I'm mobile. But I'll do my best to convince her to come with me to score you guys on the waves tomorrow morning."

His voice was gentle but firm. And rather than protesting, as Tessa thought she might, Mila simply nodded.

Clearly, something unspoken had just passed between brother and sister.

Breakfast went by quickly as the family caught one another up on news, and before she knew it, Tessa had cleared her enormous plate of food and Arch had volunteered for the dishes.

"Let me give you a hand," Damien said.

Mila busied herself collecting plates. And then the three of them disappeared into the kitchen.

Betsy suggested the rest of them move into the living room to finish coffee, and Tessa followed. The room looked even larger than she remembered from Howie's party. The cream sofas were plush and comfy, and she sank happily into a seat, belly full, feeling the warmth of family love all around her.

★ ★ ★

Arch began the mammoth task of rinsing all the

breakfast dishes, then handing them one by one to Damien so he could stack them in the dishwasher. Mila took out her phone and began tapping away.

"How full are your plans for the week, sis?"

"My week's looking pretty relaxed, apart from a few surf lessons here and there and continuing to look for a house for Jay."

Perfect, he thought. "In that case, how does an afternoon of shopping sound? On my credit card."

Mila's head snapped up, and Arch grinned. It was so easy to get his sister's attention when he wanted it. "I have an awards ceremony coming up, and Smith and I have been asked to present. I have to travel, and since I'm still not all that steady on my feet, I've asked Tessa to come and make sure I don't make a fool of myself falling on the red carpet. I'd like to get her a dress and shoes for the event."

Mila's eyes narrowed, and Arch waited, wondering if his actor's training had made his half lie—that Tessa would go as his caregiver rather than his lover—sound convincing. But it was one hundred percent true that he wanted to buy Tessa the most gorgeous gown in the world, so she would see what he already saw—that she was the most beautiful woman in the world.

"That's nice of you," Damien said.

"You want to buy an expensive dress and shoes for Tessa," Mila repeated.

He nodded. "So she fits in on the red carpet. And

also to say thank you for all she's done to help me heal this well and this quickly." Arch braced himself for some snarky comment from his sister.

A mischievous look danced across Mila's face, but to Arch's surprise, she simply said, "Sure. You'll have to find out her dress and shoe size, but an afternoon spending your money? I could happily do that."

Arch thanked her. He didn't want Tessa going thrifting when she didn't have to, even though she always looked great, whatever she wore.

He had loved watching her at breakfast, admiring the ease with which she fit into his boisterous family. She got along so well with everyone, just as he'd known she would.

The only thing that he hadn't loved was her sitting by his side pretending she was just his caregiver. How badly he had wanted to blow their cover and let everyone know that she was *his* woman and that he cared deeply about her. It was a surprise to him how strongly he felt this urge to tell his family—and the whole wide world—just how deeply he cared. He'd brought home two women in his entire life, at their insistence, even though he always preferred to keep his romantic life private.

But now he felt exactly the opposite.

He wanted to stand up and announce to one and all that he was smitten. That Tessa had stolen his heart from the moment he'd first seen her. And that as each day passed, he'd fallen harder and harder for her.

He was so proud of Tessa. She was beautiful, caring, great at her job, and also an incredibly talented painter. What's more, she had no idea how special she was.

So far, they'd had only one date and spent one smoking-hot night and morning together, but he already wanted more. *Way more.*

But for the first time in his life, he wasn't sure what to do to get it. Tessa wasn't like any other woman he'd been with. She was vulnerable and, at the same time, strong as steel. He didn't want to lose her by rushing in like a bulldozer and overwhelming her. She'd had a bad enough time with her husband without Arch accidentally screwing things up.

Dishes done and the kitchen set to rights, he rejoined the rest of the family. Most of them were ready to leave and get on with their day.

"Thank you so much for having me," Tessa said to his parents. "It was a delicious breakfast. And the warmth of your family was wonderful to be a part of too."

Howard enfolded Tessa in one of his legendary bear hugs. "You're welcome to our family breakfast anytime, Tessa, even when you're not looking after Arch anymore."

Arch could see that Tessa was really touched, and the urge to take her hand and tell her how much he wanted her to be part of his family was nearly overwhelming.

Chapter Twenty-Four

Betsy closed the door behind Arch and Tessa and walked back to the rest of her family, who were still chattering away, despite making plans to leave ten minutes ago. In the living room, Mila was holding court.

"Could you see how hard they were trying to be casual?" Mila flicked back her long blond hair.

Erin didn't say anything, but her lips curved in a smile.

"You're talking about Archer and Tessa, I assume," Betsy said, though it was obvious.

"Of course they are," Damien said, rolling his eyes. "No wonder the poor guy never brings a woman home."

Mila ignored her brother. "They might as well have worn matching neon-pink signs saying, 'I want you and I need you now.'" She flashed a cheeky smile as she quoted one of his songs. "Surely even you can see that."

Damien held up his hands in mock defense. "Hey,

I've been away. I don't know what's been happening. To me, they just looked like two people who work together and like each other."

At that, Howie let out a chuckle. "Come on, son. Even I can see that those two have chemistry." He put an arm around Betsy. "Kind of reminds me of when we first met and were trying to hide our feelings and play it cool."

"How did they even meet?" Damien asked.

"You really have been away a long time. It's a good story," Betsy said. "Want some more coffee before I tell you?"

Her children all said yes, apart from Nick, who had to get going. They settled themselves on the sofas. Even though everyone but Damien knew the story, they clearly wanted their mother's take on it.

Betsy took a sip of her coffee and smiled to herself in that mysterious way that her children called her *romantic dreamy face*. "Tessa was Margaret Percy's caregiver. Remember we told you she had an accident dancing the tango in Buenos Aires?"

Damien didn't always remember everything that happened in Carmel, even though he liked to be kept up with local news and gossip. "Sounds like Margaret, all right. Is she okay?"

"She tripped over her high heels and broke her arm. But you know Margaret—she doesn't let anything slow her down. Not even a broken bone."

"A bit like Arch," Erin added.

Betsy nodded. "A lot like Arch. That's why those two have always gotten along despite their age difference. In any case, Margaret needed a caregiver, and that's how Tessa came to Carmel-by-the-Sea. And from what Margaret tells me, when she and Tessa bumped into Arch on the beach, there was instant chemistry. I believe Margaret described Arch as having 'twinkly eyes.' She claims that he was taken with Tessa as soon as he met her."

Damien nodded. "But how did she end up being *his* caregiver?"

"His stubborn streak," Mila offered.

Damien looked confused.

"He insisted on performing a dangerous stunt in that buddy movie he shot with Smith Sullivan and got himself a broken leg," Betsy explained. She sighed deeply, still troubled by her actor son's stubborn streak. "I know he told you it was no big deal and that he's healing, but the truth is that Archer could have died. He was almost crushed under his horse. He's lucky he got away with nothing more than a broken tibia." She cleared her throat as she made an effort to hold back tears. It still upset her that her boy could have been fatally injured.

Erin put a reassuring hand on her shoulder. "He's fine, Mom. And I really think he's learned his lesson this time."

Betsy nodded. "He promised me that he'd be more careful in the future. And I think his recovery time and being stuck in a cast have shown him the consequences of listening to the daredevil who lives inside his head. Anyway, Margaret's arm healed, and Arch was instructed by his agent to get some proper care at home so he could recover in time to begin shooting a new movie. Some big action thing that Arch is desperate to do. And..." She paused meaningfully. "He would only agree to it if Tessa was his caregiver."

Finn said, "I like her. She seems so normal. Nothing like some of the women Arch has been with over the years."

"I *really* like her," Erin said. "And it's clear that she's just as besotted with Arch as he is with her. Her eyes turn dreamy every time she looks at him—when she thinks no one is watching." Erin looked a little troubled. "But I don't want Tessa to get hurt. We all know Arch's track record with women. He seems to lose interest pretty quickly. And he's never been serious about anyone before."

"That's true," Betsy said, "but maybe it's because Archer has never been with the right woman. He might not realize it yet, but he's fallen for Tessa. Hard."

The Davenports made murmurs of agreement. Tessa was a great match for Archer.

"What's funny," Mila said, "is that Arch asked me

to go shopping for Tessa, to find a dress for some red-carpet event. The poor sap tried to convince me he was only accompanying him so he didn't fall over and make an ass of himself."

The entire family burst out laughing.

Mila scoffed with continued amusement. "I mean, he's a good actor, I'll give him that, but he clearly doesn't want Tessa with him just because she's his caregiver. You ask me, he wants to let the world know he's found The One."

"How will you know her dress and shoe sizes?" Betsy asked.

"Arch is going to get them," Mila replied, shrugging. "I bet he's already got a pretty good idea, given the way he's constantly undressing her with his eyes."

"Mila," Finn said with a shake of his head. "I don't need to envision my brother in bed with someone."

"I agree," Damien said. "You're in too-much-information territory now."

Then Erin said, "It's not just about the dress for these kinds of events. What about her makeup and hair? Tessa is so naturally beautiful she never wears more than mascara, from what I can tell. But there will be a certain expectation for Arch's date to look Hollywood glam. I'd hate for her to feel out of place."

"You're right," Mila said. Frowning slightly, she added, "I'm not sure she knows what she's let herself in for."

"Why don't you two offer to do her hair and makeup?" Betsy suggested. "You both have the know-how, and I'm certain that Tessa will feel more comfortable with you than a professional."

Erin's eyes lit up. "That's a great idea, Mom."

Mila agreed it sounded fun. "Imagine what we could do with those eyes. She'll be even more gorgeous when we're done with her."

"We'll make her the belle of the ball," Erin added. "Arch won't know what hit him."

"You guys are such schemers," Damien told them. "From what I can see, their budding romance doesn't need any help. Those two have found their way to one another without our interference."

"But it's so much more *fun* to interfere," Mila argued.

Betsy looked at her husband, who had stayed uncharacteristically quiet during all this chatter. "Honey," she said, "what are you thinking?"

Howie glanced up with a serious expression. "I'm thinking that if everything goes well, he might marry her. And I for one think Tessa would be a wonderful daughter-in-law."

Betsy reached over and patted his hand. "You're even more of a romantic than I am. But don't get too far ahead of yourself. We aren't even certain they're dating yet."

To everyone's surprise, Howie replied, "Oh,

they're more than dating. When I see the way he looks at her, it reminds me of the way I've always looked at you."

Erin leaned forward. "Did you know straightaway with Mom? Like Margaret thinks Arch did with Tessa on the beach that day?"

Howie nodded and began to tell the story the kids knew so well—but always loved to hear again—about how the two of them almost didn't get together.

"I was too shy to ask your mother out," Howie said. "She was so beautiful and intelligent and so composed. I'd never met anyone like her. And so I just kept taking longer and longer to build her bookshelves, trying to buy myself some more time to work up the courage."

Betsy laughed. "At the same time, I kept trying to find new places to squeeze in more shelves in my office, simply to give him a reason to stick around. I knew he liked me, and I liked him. But I couldn't work out why he didn't do something about it."

"Because you were as beautiful then as you are now," Howie replied, and she melted inside. "It was intimidating! But I think I knew, even before either of us showed our true feelings, that you were the love of my life."

The kids groaned, just like they always did, and Howie laughed his belly laugh. "Okay, that's clearly enough nostalgia for the kids. Damien," he said, "now that you're back, you can make yourself useful. I noticed some fencing out back needs re-doing."

"Always leaving the best jobs for when I get home," Damien complained good-naturedly, stretching and getting to his feet. But before anyone left the room, he said, "I know you're all having a great time playing matchmaker, but there's one thing you're forgetting."

Erin frowned. "And what is that, oh guru of love?"

Damien shook his head as if they were missing the obvious. "I don't get the sense that Tessa cares much for the limelight."

Of course it was the other hugely famous Davenport who would pick up on that.

"Even if that's true," Erin said, "love can conquer any mountain."

Damien's eyes looked a little haunted, and Betsy's maternal senses prickled. He shrugged and said, "Well, if it is true love for them, I sure hope it works out." Then he and the other men headed out to deal with the fencing.

Betsy looked at her lovely daughters, of whom she was so proud, and asked them to help clear the coffee things. They moved into the kitchen and worked together in friendly silence until the dishwasher was completely full of breakfast dishes and Betsy started the cycle.

Mila and Erin didn't seem to be in a hurry to leave,

and soon the girls returned to the subject of Arch and Tessa's romance.

"When do you think Arch is going to realize he's in love with her?" Erin asked.

Mila shrugged. "I don't know." Then she added, "And when do you think Tessa is going to realize she's in love with him? I get the feeling she's as strong-willed as he is."

Betsy smiled warmly. "I was just thinking about being in the same position all those years ago when your father was building my bookshelves. I feel for Tessa. I remember how it was so tantalizing and frustrating at the same time, having feelings for Howie, but not being certain that we could make our lives work together. The chemistry between us was undeniable and growing by the day. And yet, neither of us did anything about it because we were both so scared of not being able to make it work." She shook her head at the woman she had been. "We could have blown everything if on the last day we hadn't realized we'd fallen in love with each other. Your father was packing up his tools, and I was just racking my brain trying to think of another project to make him stay."

Buster wandered in to see if there was any new food being cooked that he should know about. After sniffing the air hopefully, he gave up and curled on the floor beside Betsy. She leaned down to pat him, still lost in the past.

"Howie was lingering in my office, and I could tell

he didn't want to leave either. And then we both said it at the same time. Just blurted out that we'd fallen for each other."

Betsy smiled, and she was sure the girls' expressions matched her own. It might be a familiar old story, but it was a good one.

Erin asked, "Do you think we need to help them along a little?"

Frowning, Mila added, "And do you think Damien's right? Everything that comes with Arch's fame could be a problem for Tessa?"

But Betsy shook her head. "Damien's concerns about Arch's fame and Tessa's potential aversion to it could very well be valid. But even if they are, you put it beautifully, Erin, when you said that true love can take what looks like an impossible situation and make it possible."

"That what you and Dad did," Erin pointed out. "He thought you'd never want to leave Stanford to live and teach here, in such a small town. But you did."

"And I've never regretted that decision for a second." Betsy paused. "As for giving them a little help, I think it's always better if two people in love figure it out for themselves, in their own time. Just like me and your dad. I have faith that Archer and Tessa are going to open their eyes and then their hearts to one another very soon. Remember your dad's favorite saying."

That's how love works. One day you're building bookshelves, the next day you're building a family.

Chapter Twenty-Five

Breakfast had left Tessa with a warm glow that she hadn't felt for a long time. Spending time with Arch's family was like being cocooned in a warm bubble bath. She felt comfortable and relaxed—as though she was doing something good for her wellbeing rather than just surviving.

The more she considered it, the more she realized she could be herself around the Davenports, without having to pretend that she was tougher, stronger, funnier, or more successful than she really was.

The Davenports were so different from her own colder, smaller family, but it was like she'd always known them. Like she belonged. She never felt she'd said the wrong thing, or worse, had nothing to say at all. Instead, she slipped right into the flow of their easy conversation, teasing and all, and she never wanted to leave.

The thought was as thrilling as it was frightening. All afternoon, while she spent her free time painting at her usual spot on the beach, she hadn't managed to sustain her usual concentration. Her memories of last night and this morning were so distracting. Her mind kept returning to his strong hands and to how naturally he'd found her most sensitive parts, caressing and worshipping them.

But great sex with Arch wasn't entirely responsible for her distraction, even if it was hands down the best sex of her life. Honestly, though she'd had a massive crush on the movie-star version of him before they'd ever met, the fact that he *was* a movie star wasn't exactly a plus in her mental pro-versus-con columns. What *was* a plus, however, was the flesh-and-blood man with a family who kept him grounded. And who welcomed her into their home.

Breakfast had been proof of how well she fit into his family. All the worry about how different their lives were faded into the background as long as she was surrounded by the noisy but loving Davenports. However, as soon as she was away from them, any future with Arch felt impossible.

She was well and truly torn.

And that did not make for a good mindset in which to paint.

After working slowly and without much progress for a couple of hours, she decided to call it a day and return home to Arch. He needed more time to learn his lines, but she wasn't about to let him slack off on his exercises. Not when he was so close to making a full—

and super quick—recovery.

She parked, then called a hello as she entered the hallway, carrying her backpack and easel. Despite the medley of conflicting emotions she'd had all afternoon, her heart leaped with anticipation at seeing Arch.

She needed to get a grip. It had been, what, a couple of hours since they'd last seen each other? Yet here she was simpering like a teenager at the mere image of him waiting for her on the couch, script in hand.

As she headed up the stairs to wash her brushes, put away her backpack, and freshen up, she was surprised to bump into Arch coming down.

He flashed her that killer grin. "Hello, you."

"Hi there, yourself," she replied. "What are you doing up on the second floor? I was expecting you'd have your head buried in your script."

"I was, but for some reason I found it harder to concentrate today than usual." Arch shrugged, holding on to the banister. "So I gave up and went to watch the surfers on the beach through the telescope."

Something about his glib explanation felt forced. But it was his house, so why shouldn't he wander it at will?

Well, at least they were both equally distracted today. She was glad to know that it wasn't only her. "Me too," she said softly.

Arch took her backpack and easel and set them on the stair above her, brushed the hair from her face, and then kissed her. His passion took her breath away, and she felt herself yield to his embrace.

How could one man's lips—not to mention his hands and every other inch of his incredible body—make her feel so darned good?

"It might sound crazy," he said, drawing back, "but I missed you while you were painting."

Tessa smiled, feeling her heart flutter. In a half whisper, she said, "I missed you too," and kissed him again.

Their embrace was deep and heated, and it took all of her willpower not to undress him right there, halfway up the stairs.

When they finally pulled apart, she looked into his soulful eyes. "Did it bother you?" she asked, the thought only just occurring to her. "Watching people surf when you can't join them?"

Arch stroked her chin with his thumb. "I'd be lying if I said I didn't feel a little jealous. But every day, my leg feels stronger. I'm healing, and it's all down to you."

"Thank you for saying that, but we both know that you've been a surprisingly excellent patient," she said. "I can't take all the credit. You work hard, and you're determined, and you have a positive outlook. That's why you're getting better so quickly."

As soon as the words left her mouth, it dawned on Tessa that Arch *was* healing at a remarkable rate. Just watching him navigate the stairs and how easily he had lifted her backpack—not to mention her body last night—was proof of how well he was doing with the walking boot.

It felt like a punch to the gut to realize that he wasn't going to need her much longer. Her heart was going to break when that day came, regardless of how sweet he'd be about letting her go.

Though her heart already felt like it was breaking from nothing more than the thought of a future without Arch, she pulled herself together. "But that doesn't mean you can start slacking. It's time for your afternoon exercises," she said.

"Are you sure you don't want to swap exercises for sex?" he suggested. "I've read that it's surprisingly aerobic."

Of course she wanted that! She was *desperate* to rip off his clothes right there and then. But she couldn't put her own desires ahead of his recovery. "Do all your exercises first. Then we'll see if you've got enough energy left."

Arch gave her a wicked smile. "Don't you worry, I'll have *plenty* of energy left."

He waited for her while she put her kit away. When she followed him down the stairs, she saw how well he navigated each step. She had to make a choice. She could either borrow worries about that day in the future when she and Arch parted. Or she could enjoy every minute that she had with him and accept that when this job was over, life would return to normal.

Once she was gone, this would all feel like the dream that it was. She'd move on to another client; Arch would go off to shoot his new movie, and it would likely propel him to even greater fame than he had now. His real life was in Hollywood. Not here in Carmel with her. *Of course* they would part ways, no matter how well she got on with his family or how at home she felt here.

It made her ache deep inside to think about leaving him, but they were from such different worlds she truly didn't see how they could work out long term. Which was why her best option was simply to enjoy every second she still had with him as much as she could.

"I was thinking," Tessa said as they entered the kitchen, "now that you're out of your cast, we can switch up your exercise routine and work on building back some of the muscle in your leg. How does warming up with some laps in the pool sound? Then I've got some water rehab exercises for you."

Arch's eyes lit up. "I would love to get back in the water," he said. "I've missed it so much."

"I thought that might make you smile." She went to the fridge and poured him a tall glass of coconut water. "Drink this. It's important to stay hydrated, and this is full of electrolytes. I'm going to get changed, and then I'll join you."

"In the pool?" Arch asked, a sexy look coming into his eyes.

"Nope, I'll be able to check your form from the sidelines," she said firmly, but unable to hold back a shiver of longing.

Upstairs, she slipped off her skirt and shirt and changed into leggings and an oversized T-shirt, her usual uniform for working out.

She was glad Arch liked her suggestion of getting back into the water. Swimming was the perfect exercise for this stage of his rehab, and she enjoyed knowing that she could introduce small pleasures back into his day. There was nothing like looking after the wellbeing of someone you cared for deeply.

Down in the basement, she watched as Arch performed a confident front crawl. Soft spotlights warmed the surface of the pool so that it appeared twinkling and glossy, the room cozy and intimate. The floor and ceiling were tiled in a deep blue, and she felt as if she'd entered some hidden pocket of the ocean.

Arch looked so hot and manly slicing through the water. She stood beside the pool, happily gazing at the sight until he must have felt her eyes on him. He slowed his pace and then swam over to the shallow end, water streaming off his skin, his hair slicked back.

"I thought you might have changed into a bathing suit," he said. "A very small one, with little strings I can untie with my teeth."

The image reverberated through her, sending a shiver of excitement along her nerves. But no. As much as she wanted him, she couldn't abandon her role as caregiver.

"Exercises first," she reminded him, sounding a lot cooler than she felt.

She took a seat halfway down the pool deck, determined to keep it together. "Let's start with some leg sweeps. We want to target your inner thighs. Lift one leg out in front of you and sweep it to the opposite side. The goal is to feel the squeeze in your inner muscles."

"I'm not sure I got that," Arch said in a teasing tone. "Maybe you need to get in and show me."

She shook her head, barely fighting back the urge to slip into the water with him, and repeated the instructions. Arch performed the exercise dutifully.

"Now how about we get those hips moving?"

"Sure thing." He gyrated his hips in the water, and she remembered the way they'd moved last night as the most exquisite pleasure shook through her.

"Your glute medius is an important muscle," she said, working to hold on to her concentration. "It helps to keep you stable. This exercise works the outside of the hips. Hold on to the edge of the pool for balance. Now lift one leg out to the side, aiming for hip level. Pause at the top… Yes, like that, and then come back to standing."

It took everything she had not to drool as she watched his impressive flexibility. Even his look of concentration made her feel hot all over. The water supported his healing leg and offered resistance as he pushed through it.

As he completed the rest of the exercises, Tessa couldn't help but reflect on how well they worked together. No doubt about it, they were a good team.

"I'm exhausted," he said when they were finally finished. "You've worked me to the bone." He huffed in and out. "I don't think I can even manage getting out of the pool by myself. You'll have to help me."

He moved toward the stairs, where he lifted two dripping arms out of the water. Tessa stood to grasp them. But no sooner had she reached for him than Arch grabbed her by the waist, effortlessly lifted her into the air, and pulled her into the water.

She gasped as the water soaked through her clothes. It wasn't cold so much as unexpected. Then she glanced into his eyes and found him holding her gaze with the sexiest expression she'd ever seen.

How tenderly, how carefully he held her in the water. So while his move had been cheeky and playful, he made sure he hadn't hurt her.

At long last, she gave in to the longing she'd felt since he'd gotten into the pool and happily wrapped her legs around his waist.

"I've finally got you right where I want you," he said and then kissed her deeply.

She moaned with pleasure into his mouth as his hands slid down her back and over her hips. With his arms around her, she felt weightless, as if suspended in a dream. And then his lips moved from her mouth to her neck. He bit the flesh there gently at first, then more roughly.

He was as hungry for her as she was for him, and she could feel the swell of him grow against her thigh.

The fabric of her leggings and T-shirt clung to her skin. She couldn't bear them a moment longer. "You'd better get me out of these clothes."

Arch didn't need telling twice. He set her down so that her feet touched the cool tiles and then dove under the water. She felt him pulling at the waistband of her leggings and then at her panties. When he came up for air, he looked very pleased with himself.

He flung her soaked leggings and panties to the edge of the deck and then slowly, looking into her eyes the whole time, peeled the T-shirt from her wet skin. She lifted her arms, happy to have him take control as he pulled the wet fabric over her head, tossing the shirt to the pool deck. Immediately, he buried his face between her breasts, kissing one then the other through the lace of her bra.

The sensation was heavenly. The water made everything feel like silk on her skin.

He spent forever worshipping her breasts. Kissing her skin, rolling the taut peaks where all of her pleasure seemed to center. Finally, she felt his hands move around her back to unhook the clasp of her bra.

It was so good to be skin to skin with him. She wanted more. Her fingers instinctively played around the elastic of his swim trunks, and then she tugged them down. He wriggled free, but stopped just short of tossing them to the side to reach into the pocket and pull out a condom.

She smiled at him. "Always two steps ahead, aren't you?"

"No," he said, "that's you. But I was hoping that we would end my workout with my new favorite thing in the whole world." He gazed hungrily down into her face. "Making love with you."

Once protection was on, he was inside of her. And she swore nothing had ever felt better than their two bodies naked in the water.

Together, they began to move. It was slow and intense, a gentle, rhythmic rocking. And then it was fast and hard and oh so good.

The pleasure from her climax was so strong it felt like it came from the deepest part of her. A part that refused to believe that what they were sharing would inevitably have to end. The same part of her that wanted to believe their connection was too true, too real, for their relationship to *ever* end.

And though she knew better, just for these few moments when he called out her name as he fell over the edge into pleasure, she let herself believe that the two of them—and the deep connection they'd forged—could last forever.

Chapter Twenty-Six

Arch was floating on cloud nine. Everything about his weekend with Tessa had been perfect. The way she fit into his family, how independent and creative she was going off to the beach to paint for a couple of hours, and then the incredible way her rehab exercises had turned into the best sex of his life. Afterward, she'd made another of her delicious meals, and they'd cuddled up on the couch to watch a movie before some more hot sex.

Talk about bliss.

And now here they were, on the beach early Monday morning. Everything about Carmel-by-the-Sea's picturesque beach set his imagination on fire. The air was different at this time of day—cool and crisp, with a breeze off the ocean. If only he could get in and surf with his siblings, he'd be flying over those waves without a care.

But Tessa had insisted he stick to pool exercise only.

There was a time when her telling him he wasn't

ready would have been enough for him to get on a board to prove her wrong. Maybe he'd learned a thing or two since he'd broken his leg. Or maybe he was too besotted to ignore her wishes.

No, not besotted. The word might be *enchanted*.

Or maybe… just maybe… what he felt was even more than that.

It wouldn't be long before he'd be able to join his siblings and get back on a board again. He'd managed to walk from his house to the spot where his brothers and sisters were surfing without linking arms with Tessa for support. Although secretly he'd wanted to reach out and hold her hand and show everyone on the beach that they were *together* together, he was respecting her wishes about keeping their relationship private.

The thing was… he didn't plan to keep it private forever. At some point in the not-so-distant future, he hoped she'd change her mind about going public. Otherwise, there would have to be a day of reckoning—one where he hoped like hell that he could allay all her concerns about being with him.

He followed Tessa's gaze and saw an Irish setter chase a yellow ball across the sand. The dog was majestic and lithe, and it caught the ball between its teeth in no time before happily bounding back to its owner to do it all over again.

"I love dogs," Tessa said wistfully. "I always wanted one growing up, but we were never allowed. 'Too much mess,' my mom said. 'You kids would leave it all to me.' But I knew I'd love whatever dog we got with all my heart and *would* spend my time taking care of it." She paused. "I'd love to have a dog now. But given that I live in my clients' homes, I couldn't exactly bring it with me."

He thought of the family dogs they'd had, including Buster, who would be here now if he didn't bark when the Davenports went out surfing. He'd try to swim out to them, assuming in his doggy brain that they were hurt and needed to be saved.

It took every ounce of his willpower for Arch not to say, *We can get a dog together.* Because he could so easily picture the two of them walking their own dog on the beach.

But even more than that, he loved that she was sharing something more about her childhood. Little by little, she was letting her guard down and revealing herself to him.

"I bet you'll have the dog of your dreams one day," was all he allowed himself to say. And Tessa turned to him and smiled, making him feel happier than he could ever remember being. All because of her smile.

"There they are," he said, pointing to his siblings on their surfboards. They'd come out early when a text from Mila reminded him all the Davenport kids would be hitting the waves this morning.

All except him.

He could see Erin's petite silhouette and Mila's white-blond hair haloed by the rising sun. Damien and Finn were crouched on the sand, tending to something on one of their boards. Nick had his board under his arm and was walking into the surf. Arch called hello, and they all turned and waved. He smiled at them broadly, glad to have all his siblings in one place. It didn't happen as often as he liked, so he really appreciated it when they all were able to do something like this together.

As he and Tessa approached the tide line, he couldn't help but feel a twinge of jealousy. It was a perfect morning, the waves coming in nice sets. No wonder all the Davenport kids were suited up and ready to go.

But patience was key. He'd be out there soon, the waves rolling beneath his board, the sun glinting on the water. And the next time he went surfing, he'd be teaching Tessa.

As if she could read his mind, she said softly, "Don't worry. You'll be out there with them again soon." Briefly—far too briefly—she took his hand and gave it a squeeze, before dropping it, just in case anyone should see them touch.

His siblings grabbed their boards and headed into the water. When she was ankle-deep, Mila turned to Tessa. "Next time, we'll take you out too. You definitely want me as your teacher, not Arch."

Arch rolled his eyes as the rest of the Davenports paddled out into the ocean. He threw out the blanket they'd brought with them, and Tessa unpacked the Thermos flask of coffee.

It was still early enough that only the most dedicated surfers were out. Mila, Damien, Finn, Nick, and Erin paddled out toward the break. They got in position in a ragged line, then straightened and easily navigated the waves.

Growing up by the beach, his siblings had become experts on the boards, but Mila was clearly the best surfer, even post-career-ending injury. Her stance was the most natural, as though she was in communion with the movement of the ocean. Her style was so unique that it was hard not to be impressed with how effortless she made it look, when he knew surfing was not easy at all. He'd certainly had plenty of gnarly wipeouts in his time.

He took a sip of his coffee and relaxed back on his elbows. Now that he was healing well, he could appreciate chilling out a bit. No early call time, no huge crew waiting—each of whom needed him for something at the same time. No eighteen-hour days.

He loved his work, but the truth was that it felt good to relax. He'd thought he'd be bored stiff by a slower pace of life, but everything he did with Tessa took on a magical quality. He watched her concentrating on the surfers. She seemed genuinely captivated.

"It's so inspiring," she said, awe in her tone, not tearing her eyes away. "Especially Mila. I'd love to capture the fluidity of her movement in watercolor."

Arch smiled broadly. How he loved seeing the world through Tessa's eyes. Everything looked brighter that way and full of artistic promise.

His siblings caught wave after wave, riding in, showing off for one another—but mostly Tessa—each of them clearly having a great time, then turning and paddling back out to catch another wave. Between sets, he knew they'd be chatting about whatever came into their heads.

"Mila outshines everyone," he said, "but look at Damien go. He's getting some amazing rides, especially for someone who's been on the road for so long that he hasn't been able to get to the ocean."

They weren't out for much more than an hour. It was a workday after all. Mila caught a last wave and rode it all the way in to the beach. Damien was hot on her tail, and then all the others followed, walking up the beach, talking and laughing together with their dripping boards under their arms.

"Damn, those were some great rides," Damien said, his black hair slicked back, dark eyes sparkling. "I can't believe how much I've missed this."

Erin turned to smile at Arch. "You'll be back on the board soon," she said, just as Tessa had earlier. His youngest sister always thought about other people's feelings.

Tessa and Erin were right. Between his determination and Tessa's guidance, he'd be out there soon, chasing the perfect wave with her.

★ ★ ★

"You did well walking on the sand," Tessa praised as they made their way back to his house.

"Thanks," he said, holding the front door for her. But then had to add, "Although walking on sand doesn't seem like great progress when there are waves to surf."

"Trust me, you are doing incredibly well."

"Thanks to you. And I don't want to waste any more time whining. So what's the plan?" he asked in a deliberately sexy voice. "Some more rehab therapy? Or, after yesterday's successful workout in the pool, maybe we could try out the bed for some new moves?"

She was about to answer when she heard a male voice calling Arch's name. She'd become accustomed to his family coming in without knocking, but this was a voice she didn't recognize. When a couple walked into the living room, she was so surprised, she blinked as though she were seeing things.

To her total disbelief, there stood Smith Sullivan, the world's hugest movie star. And with him was his beautiful wife, Valentina.

"I hope you don't mind us dropping over like this,"

Smith said. "We're staying at Ian's place. How's the leg? I see you're out of the cast."

Tessa knew almost as much about Smith Sullivan's career as she had about Arch's before she'd met him in real life. Like Arch, Smith came from a big family. She was pretty sure that the Ian he referred to was his cousin Ian Sullivan, a billionaire who apparently had a house nearby. Smith Sullivan was a year or two older than Arch, with dark eyes, a masculine jaw, and a physique to make his fans sigh.

Valentina was lean and tall and equally gorgeous. Her thick hair was tied back in a ponytail, and her hazel eyes shone behind her glasses. She was wearing a dress the color of pearls, but it was the glow of happiness on her high cheekbones and full lips that really wowed Tessa. She'd seen them both on TV before, of course, but up close, the famous couple were even more dazzling.

Among the three Hollywood heavyweights, she felt damp and sandy and so very ordinary.

Smith and Arch embraced like the old friends they were, clapping each other on the back. "My leg's getting better every day," Arch answered.

Then he introduced Tessa.

"Hello," Valentina said. She extended a hand. "It's so nice to meet you. I heard that you're coming to the Moonrise awards ceremony. I hope we can sit together. It's always good to know a friendly face at these

Hollywood events."

Tess took a deep breath and tried to swallow down her anxiety. These were Arch's friends, and she'd be sitting at a table with them all. They were so close, they were able to wander right into his house without calling, and Arch was thrilled to see them.

She felt like she might need to breathe into a paper bag in a minute.

She put on her best breezy smile, the one she reserved for her most stubborn clients, and shook Valentina's hand warmly. "It's nice to meet you too," she said. "I'll be accompanying Archer to make sure he's steady on his feet and feeling up to presenting the award."

Was that a little flicker of amusement on Valentina's face, as though she'd already guessed that Tessa and Arch weren't just caregiver and client?

Thankfully, Arch diffused the moment by saying, "I'm so glad you could meet Smith and Valentina here, so you'll already know them when we sit together at Moonrise. It's going to be a great night."

From what Tessa knew about Valentina, she was a fascinating woman. Sister to the movie star Tatiana Landon, she was also her business manager, as well as a screenwriter. Her wedding to Smith Sullivan had been the subject of much Hollywood speculation, but Valentina herself had remained quite private, which Tessa really respected. How had Valentina managed to stay out of the limelight? Granted, Tessa had only just met her, but she got the feeling that Valentina definitely wasn't with Smith for fame and celebrity.

Arch motioned for everyone to take a seat in the living room, and Tessa offered coffee and tea. "I'll help," Valentina said quickly and joined Tessa in the kitchen. "Do you mind if I have an herbal tea?" She moved around the kitchen with ease, knowing exactly where things were kept.

"I'll have some too," Tessa said. "I've had too much coffee today."

Valentina flashed her a warm, genuine smile, and Tessa felt some of her trepidation melt away. While they prepared coffee for the men and Valentina made them mint tea, she returned to the topic of the awards ceremony.

"I'm quite nervous about it," Tessa admitted. "I've never been to anything like that before."

Valentina nodded. "Believe me, I totally understand where you're coming from. When I first entered the business—and especially when I started dating Smith—I was terrified of the limelight." She paused before adding, "It might help you to know, though, that while red-carpet events look dazzling when you see the highlights on TV, when you're there it's quite boring, really. Hollywood is all about illusion, but as I'm sure you've seen yourself, even the biggest stars are just normal people at heart." She touched Tessa's arm.

"I've always thought that Arch is one of the nicest men in Hollywood. He and Smith are alike in that way."

It was kind of Valentina to reassure her, but Tessa couldn't quite believe that she'd be bored at the ceremony. Glitz and glamor and the constant flash of photographers' cameras must be second nature to someone like Valentina, who'd spent most of her life working in Hollywood with her sister and now with Smith too.

Tessa put the tea and coffee on a tray, and the two women walked into the living room. Arch and Smith were doubled over with laughter. It was clear that these two went way back.

"Classic Frankie, right?" Smith was saying.

Arch was still laughing so hard he could only nod in response.

"You must miss being on set," Smith said to Arch. He turned to Tessa. "This one's a hard worker, you know. Never late, always ready to do another take. His energy is incredible." Smith smiled at his friend fondly.

"You're the same," Arch said.

Tessa put coffee mugs in front of the two men and cream and sugar on the table. She and Valentina settled with their tea.

Arch said, "I've been so focused on getting my strength back that I haven't had all that much time to think about being on set."

"How's the *Shock Tactics* script?" Smith asked.

Arch paused to think over the question. "Solid. Some nice humor, and the writing's better than I expected. I'm looking forward to getting started." He glanced down at his leg. "Thankfully, I'm getting stronger every day." Then he smiled at Tessa, a smile that was a little too twinkly, if you asked her. The kind of smile that just might give their secret away. "It's all down to Tessa. She's a taskmaster, but in the best possible way."

"To be perfectly honest," Smith said, "I didn't think you had a snowball's chance in hell of recovering from a broken leg in time to start shooting *Shock Tactics*." Then Smith smiled at Tessa. "But I hadn't counted on you coming into Arch's life and doing such an amazing job."

Tessa felt herself turn pink at the compliment, but had to tell the truth. "I can't take all the credit. As you say, Archer is a hard worker."

"Stubborn too," Smith said, shaking his head. "Stubborn, opinionated, and determined." He grinned at the group. "Did I leave anything out?"

Though Tessa's brain immediately thought, *You left out how amazing he is in bed*, she said, "He is one thousand percent committed to getting better." With a grin, she added, "And also stubborn, opinionated, and determined."

Valentina laughed. "We imagined he'd be a difficult patient. But he's clearly in good hands. You've been so lucky to have found the perfect caregiver, Arch."

He nodded. "I absolutely have."

Then Smith said, "Did Jay send you the script for the Moonrise festival? We don't have to say too much, but there's a bit of cheesy banter at the beginning before we present the award."

"Yeah, I got it. Haven't had a chance to look at it yet, though."

"We should rehearse," Smith said.

Tessa could tell how important it was to both actors to do their best work, even if they were simply presenting an award.

"That's our cue," Valentina said to Tessa. "Want to go upstairs and check out the view with me? I love Arch's telescope."

Tessa nodded, happy to spend more time with such a fascinating woman.

They climbed the stairs, and Valentina said how much she loved visiting Carmel-by-the-Sea. "It's so calm and peaceful here." She settled into the chair by the telescope. "I could watch the waves for hours."

Tessa agreed. It was exactly why she felt so inspired to paint here. Well, that and a certain someone giving her all the feelings.

"Do you know yet what you're wearing for Moonrise?" Valentina asked, still gazing through the window.

Tessa was glad Valentina couldn't see her expression. "I'm not quite sure. It's not my usual kind of night out." Truth be told, she never did nights out, but she didn't think Valentina was dying to know all about her ordinary life.

Nor had she said she couldn't afford a gown for an awards ceremony, but Valentina must have picked up on her hesitation. "You're more than welcome to borrow something of mine. We're not far off in size, and I have a special 'not for real life' section in my closet." She turned back to face Tessa. "I'm sure I have something that would look lovely on you. You're so pretty you could wear a trash bag, and it would look good."

Tessa blinked in surprise. Valentina thought *she* was pretty?

"Wow," she said, suddenly shy, "that's so kind. But I've got it handled." Tessa was determined to find herself something at a thrift store, something that didn't make her feel like another person entirely. But she couldn't tell Valentina this.

Valentina flashed her another smile. "Well, the offer's open if you change your mind." Then she sighed with pleasure as she turned to look back out the window. Her hand settled over her belly, and she rubbed it absentmindedly. "What a view," she murmured. "Watching the dogs running on the beach, and the birds, and the waves, is so relaxing. Smith and I should really visit more often. Hollywood feels like a world away. Which is a very good thing."

Just that quickly, Tessa found she couldn't stop herself. "What's it like to be in a relationship with a movie star?"

Oh no—she hadn't meant to ask that! Talking about giving away the secret that she was falling hard for an A-lister herself. And she didn't want Valentina to think she was prying into her marriage to Smith either.

But Valentina looked pleased to be asked. She was thoughtful for a moment and gazed down to where her hand still rested on her belly.

"It's not always easy," Valentina replied. "But when you're in love, it's worth it."

★ ★ ★

Arch and Smith rehearsed their part for Moonrise, which didn't take that long. Then Smith drained his cup and leaned forward in a way that told Arch his friend was preparing to ask a tricky question.

"So. Tessa." Smith paused a beat. Always brilliant at holding people's attention. "She's a natural beauty. Down-to-earth. Patient. And she seems to put up with you pretty darn well." He raised a questioning eyebrow as he waited for Arch to pick up the thread. "Anything you want to tell me?"

Arch grinned. Though he had promised Tessa he'd keep their budding relationship a secret, he couldn't hide his true feelings from Smith. His friend had likely picked up the energy between them the minute he walked in—especially when he'd told Smith and Valentina that Tessa would be attending the awards ceremony with him.

Although the women were upstairs, he lowered his voice as he said, "She's all of those things and more. Smart, thoughtful, gorgeous inside as well as out, and really talented too." He stopped and smiled. "She's under my skin, Smith."

Smith grinned back, his eyes creasing with pleasure. "I can see that. Even with a broken leg, you look so *happy*. I'm happy for you."

"Thanks, but I need your advice," Arch said. "Tessa comes from a totally different world. She values her privacy above all else. She doesn't want anyone to know there's anything between us—whereas I want to shout it from the rooftops. I know you had a hell of a time getting Valentina to be with you in the beginning. She had the same kind of reservations Tessa does." He paused. "How did you sway her?"

Smith blew out a long breath, one that seemed to speak to just how difficult it had been to win Valentina over. "When we first met, I felt like I was never going to convince her to see me as any more than a spoiled-rotten movie star. I had to be completely open and honest with her and show her, time and again, that I would always love her, heart and soul." Arch had never seen Smith look as serious as he did when he said, "The key is not to give up and to always be honest about your feelings for her. That's your best chance for her to come around. For her to see that even though your jobs are different, and she'll have to spend far too many nights in the spotlight, in the end it's just about what the two of you have together. Because that's all that really matters."

Smith's advice was sound. But Arch needed him to know more. "I'm worried that being honest about my feelings will scare her off."

Smith wasted no time. "Are you telling me you're in love with Tessa?"

Arch remained quiet for a long moment. His heart felt huge in his chest. Then he finally said, "I think that's something *she* should be the first to know."

Smith gave a low whistle. Because he clearly already knew the answer. Then he grinned broadly. "This is a great day for news." Then he yelled up the stairs. "We're finished rehearsing. Come on back down."

He heard female voices, and then the two women came down to rejoin the men.

Smith held out his arm, and Valentina walked forward and snuggled against her husband. The two of them looked so damned happy, Arch found himself leaning forward, wishing he could walk over to Tessa and pull her in that close to him.

"We wanted to tell you ourselves, before news gets out." Smith's eyes were bright with joy. "Valentina and

I are expecting a baby."

Arch let out a whoop of excitement. Then he said, "That's fantastic news. I couldn't be happier. You're a lucky man."

"Don't I know it," Smith said, giving Valentina a kiss.

"Congratulations," Tessa said.

"You guessed, didn't you?" Valentina said, turning to Tessa.

"Between the herbal tea and the way you've been resting your hand on your belly, I was beginning to wonder."

"We should celebrate," Arch said. "And with more than herbal tea."

"I think there's some sparkling apple juice in the pantry," Tessa said.

And so they toasted Valentina and Smith's baby with sparkling apple juice, and the four of them were soon chatting like old friends. He felt as though Tessa had always been part of his life.

He glanced from one beautiful woman, who was glowing with new life, to another beautiful woman and tried to picture Tessa and him one day announcing their pregnancy to Smith and Valentina. The thought made Arch's heart skip a beat. Because Smith had been right.

Oh yes. Arch was head over heels in love with Tessa.

Chapter Twenty-Seven

As soon as Tessa left the house that afternoon to paint, Arch texted Mila.

The coast is clear.
There in five ;)

Mila wasn't going to be able to resist teasing him all afternoon. But it was worth it. Along with her great sense of fashion, Mila would know the right outfit to suit Tessa's taste and shape, but not make her feel like she was playing a part.

He wasn't blind to Tessa's total reluctance to be his date for Moonrise. It was in her eyes every time he mentioned it and had only become more apparent after Smith and Valentina's visit.

Mila came to collect him in a white Porsche SUV, suitable for driving her clients around, yet with plenty of room for surfboards during her leisure time.

He maneuvered himself into the passenger seat, swinging his booted leg in.

"Did you have a good rest of the morning?" she asked brightly.

As his sister drove them into town, he told her how Smith and Valentina had dropped by and how they'd prepped for the awards ceremony. He didn't share their news, knowing that Smith wanted to keep the pregnancy private for as long as possible.

"Now, there's a couple deeply in love," Mila said, sighing a little.

Arch couldn't tell whether his sister was hinting at something going on between him and Tessa, or whether she was thinking about herself. So far, his sister hadn't been very lucky in love.

If only he could tell her that it just took one person, one magical person, to come into your life when you least expected it. But this would break his promise to Tessa. Because unlike Smith, Mila was *not* discreet.

Arch murmured his agreement and then swiftly changed the subject. "Where are we headed first?"

Mila turned left. "Dominique's, my absolute favorite boutique in Carmel. They have exquisite gowns I've always admired, but have absolutely no place to wear. Movie stars don't invite *me* to fancy events."

"You have been invited to every premiere of every movie I've ever made," he reminded her.

"I know. But presenting at Moonrise is taking things up a notch. So this is like a dream shopping experience for me." She sounded so excited about choosing a dress that he stopped arguing. If the dress could make Tessa even half as happy as Mila was right now, he'd have done a good job.

She parked as close to Dominique's as she could, and they walked the short distance to the fashionable boutique. She stopped at the window display before going inside.

"See?" she said, turning around triumphantly. "There's a gorgeous dress right there in the window. They must have gotten new stock in, because it wasn't there yesterday."

Arch joined his sister and looked through the glass.

At exactly the same time, they both said, "That would look great on Tessa!" And then burst out laughing.

The dress was one-shoulder, long, made of a shimmering silver silk that would look amazing with Tessa's long dark hair and piercing blue eyes. It was simple and formfitting, but not so tight that she'd feel uncomfortable or restricted.

"Come on," Mila said, taking Arch by the arm and leading him into the store.

Arch was extremely glad he'd enlisted Mila. This had been even easier than he'd thought.

Inside the shop, two women were looking through the carefully curated racks, their polished fingernails tapping against the hangers. Two glamorous sales associates stood behind the glass counter as a third walked toward him and Mila.

Arch immediately pulled his baseball cap farther down, until his eyes were partly shaded. Although people in Carmel-by-the-Sea were used to seeing celebrities and respectfully left them in peace, you could never be sure that the odd opportunist wouldn't break this unspoken code of conduct. The last thing he wanted was for anyone to recognize him and snap a photo of him in a women's clothing boutique that would be splashed all over the Internet within the hour.

"We should look at all the options," Mila said in a low tone that only he could hear as the sales associate approached. "Shall I pretend it's for me?"

Arch nodded, thankful Mila was so on the ball.

Mila returned the smartly dressed woman's greeting and said she was looking for a special dress to wear to a gala.

The woman barely glanced at Arch. "I can certainly help you. Do you have anything particular in mind? A color or style?"

"I was wondering about the dress in the window."

The sales associate immediately said, "The one-shoulder? It arrived just this morning from Milan."

Mila said she'd try it on and also wanted a couple of other options. The sales associate picked out a deep burgundy three-quarter-length gown and a marine blue silk that Arch thought would go with Tessa's eyes, although it had some ruffles he didn't think she would like.

Mila took all three into the changing room, and Arch took a seat outside. As he waited for her, he pictured Tessa's response when he presented her with an expensive gown.

He knew she planned to go thrifting for something to wear, but he hoped his impulse to surprise her with the dress wouldn't backfire. It wasn't that he wanted to undermine her wishes. He just couldn't help wanting to do special, out-of-the-ordinary things for her. To make her feel like the center of the universe.

Because she was certainly the center of *his* universe.

Mila pulled back the curtain with a flourish and stepped out. She was wearing the silvery dress and a smile so wide he grinned right back.

"It's perfect, right?" she said. Lowering her voice, she said, "It's a little tight on me, but Tessa is more willowy, so it will glide right off her curves. The silk is incredible, and the tailoring is masterful."

Arch found himself nodding, speechless as he imagined Tessa in the dress. It was a stunner and would look even more striking on Tessa, with her dark hair, than it did with Mila's sunshine blond. His sister was right that it was a little tight on her—she was more muscled from surfing and working out—but he could see how it would be just right on Tessa.

"It's the one," he agreed.

"I'll try on the others, just in case," she said. "We need to be sure."

Both of the other dresses were great, but they lacked the *wow* factor of the silvery-pearl dress.

"I think we have a clear winner," Mila said, back in the navy slacks and white blouse she'd worn into the store. She looked at the tag and then showed it to Arch.

Arch shrugged at the $5,000 price tag. He'd been expecting a hefty price for something so well crafted, and he was lucky enough to be at a point in his career where money wasn't a concern.

"The money doesn't matter," he said softly to his sister, "but you've got to promise never to tell Tessa." No question, she would freak out if she knew he'd spent that kind of money on a dress for her.

Mila narrowed her eyes. He was waiting for her to say something sarcastic about having more money than sense, but then her expression changed. She left the dress hanging on the rack and took a seat next to him.

Her voice still low, she said, "Don't mess this up. Tessa is not like the usual women you date—the ones you love, then leave. She could get hurt. *Really* hurt. I can tell you have a thing for her—it's totally obvious—but I'm not sure whether it's because you're bored and she's available."

Arch's eyes widened. So, his sister really did think

he was arrogant—and misbehaved—when it came to women. He might not have been perfect in the past, but who was? He'd always tried to treat the women he dated with respect for as long as they were together. Okay, maybe that often wasn't for long, but his work was usually to blame. He was never in one place long enough to make a deep commitment.

But with Tessa, everything felt different. It wouldn't matter if he had to spend weeks away on set—he'd find a way to keep them connected.

Since Mila had already guessed, he saw no point in pretending that he wasn't involved with Tessa. "You don't need to worry about that," he said. "I have a big thing for her."

"How big?" Mila raised a brow. Clearly, she was still suspicious. "You've always been so focused on your career. Women always come second."

He couldn't argue with that. She was right. It had always been career first. And he couldn't play games with Tessa the way he had in the past with others, enjoying their time together, however brief, with no hard feelings when it ended.

Tessa wasn't the kind of woman he could put second to his career. But more important, he didn't want to.

He was in love with her.

Completely in love.

But how to respond to Mila? As he'd said to Smith,

he had to tell Tessa he loved her before he told anyone else. "You're going to have to trust me on this one, sis. Tessa is different. Everything is different. She's not like anyone else I've ever met. I'm no fool. She's the real deal."

Mila's expression softened as she nodded. "I can't tell you how glad I am to hear you say that."

The sales associate cleared her throat and approached them. "Just wanted to see how you're getting on," she said, smiling. "I imagine they all looked stunning on you."

Mila grinned. "We're taking the silver one. It's perfect."

"Great choice," the woman replied. "I had a feeling you might say that, so I brought these to show you."

She lifted the lid of a cream and gold box and took out a pair of delicate silver heels. They were subtle, understated, and not too high, but sophisticated enough to set the dress off perfectly.

Mila looked at Arch, and when he nodded, Mila gave the woman Tessa's shoe size.

Together, they walked to the register, and Mila browsed the sunglasses while Arch paid. "Do you want anything?" Arch asked his sister before the woman took his credit card.

But Mila shook her head. She was too stubborn to accept a gift. She preferred to pay for things out of her own hard-earned cash, and he respected her wishes.

He'd find another way to thank her for her help today.

At the car, Mila carefully hung the dress from a hook and set down the shoe box. She chatted amiably as they drove to his place, but Arch had trouble focusing. All he could think about was Tessa on his arm, heart-stoppingly gorgeous in her new dress and heels, at the kind of event he usually dreaded, but was now actually looking forward to.

"Thank you," he said to his sister as he collected the dress and shoes. "I really appreciate your help today—as well as the advice. I know you're only looking out for Tessa, and I promise I won't let either of you down."

Mila's white teeth flashed against her tanned skin. "Wow... maybe you have grown up, Archer Davenport." And with that, she drove off, waving.

He let himself into the house and checked the time. Tessa would be back any minute. As fast as his leg would let him, he rushed to his bedroom and stashed the dress in its protective zip-up bag and the shoe box at the back of his closet, just as he heard Tessa come in through the front door. She called his name, and he went out to the hallway, excited to see her, even though they'd been apart for only a couple of hours.

"Hi," she said as he came to kiss her hello. "You look pretty happy about something."

He kissed her again and stood back, enjoying the sight of her. She was wearing battered jeans, her long dark hair was windblown, and there was a smudge of green paint on her cheek. He knew that she'd look amazing in that $5,000 dress—but right now, she was still the most beautiful woman he'd ever seen.

She didn't need a fancy dress to make her shine.

He was, he realized, deeply and forever in love with Tessa.

His heart was beating double time, but he managed to keep his cool. "Just seeing you, and being with you, makes me happy."

She smiled, a smile that started in her eyes and spread to her rosy cheeks. "Let me put my stuff away, and then I'll be right back,"

But Arch shook his head. He couldn't wait even a minute. He wanted—*needed*—to make love to Tessa right now. If he couldn't tell her yet that he was in love with her, because he still didn't think she was comfortable enough with their relationship for such a declaration, then at least he could show her with his body.

Planning to bring her to the heights of new pleasures she hadn't even imagined, he took her hand in his and led her into his bedroom, leaving her backpack in the hallway.

She followed silently, and when he looked at her, he could see the same desire that he knew was in his own eyes. Clearly, she was feeling this connection as deeply as he was. The thought made him stir.

He ran his thumb tenderly across the paint smear on her cheek, the words *I love you* on the tip of his tongue. He kissed her then, for fear of blurting them out, but let the loving sensation travel from his chest to his fingertips, trying to will her to feel the love in his touch as he undressed her and slowly began to caress her.

He wanted to spend hours on her body, but within a few minutes, she whispered into his ear, "I need you inside me. *Now.*"

A few simple words from her lips were almost enough to tip him over the edge.

He stripped off his clothes, then reached into the bedside drawer for a condom. He entered her slowly, willing himself to stay slow and deep so that she could feel every inch of him. Her moans of pleasure aroused him so much he struggled to control himself as she grabbed his hips and pulled him farther inside.

Her eyes flickered open, cloudy with desire. "I feel like our bodies were made to fit each other," she whispered.

"I *know* they were," he whispered back, gently kissing her mouth as they began to rock together in unison. The sensation of her hips shifting upward to meet his, eager, wanting more of him, sent those three words rushing into his brain again.

I love you so damned much, he wanted to cry out.

Instead, he let his body, his hands, his mouth, all

say the words for him as they moved together with increasing urgency, and soon the rolling, swelling feeling of pure pleasure took him over. and he lost the ability to think.

His entire world became Tessa and her body, and as he felt her shuddering climax, he allowed himself to let go of the final thread of his self-control to join her as they came together.

Sweaty and happy, he opened his eyes to gaze at Tessa's blissful, beautiful face. He kissed the tip of her nose and felt her eyelashes flutter against his cheek as she smiled.

She was precious.

She was *everything*.

Chapter Twenty-Eight

They were coming to the end of the morning's exercises, and Tessa could see just how much strength was returning to Arch's body. He was able to lift heavier weights and for longer, as well as comfortably hold his legs in poses that before had had him grimacing in seconds. His appetite had almost doubled—not to mention his appetite for sex.

In bed, he was able to go for hours, which she certainly appreciated given that until Arch had entered her life, it had been *years*.

The only problem with how well he was doing was that it made her all the more aware that he needed her less… and soon she'd be gone. On to another client somewhere in Monterey County—and he'd be returning to Hollywood.

The thought of it made her panic, so she pushed it from her mind. *Stay in the moment*, she urged herself, though it was getting harder to stop thinking about the future. One without Arch. Just thinking about it made her heart ache. So yet again, she had to remind herself,

Just enjoy the time you have together.

She flexed his feet and then gently set down his leg. "Five gold stars, Mr. Davenport," she said. "Soon you won't be needing my assistance to complete your exercises at all."

Arch frowned. "I wouldn't say that." He sat up and rubbed both legs vigorously with his strong hands. "I still don't feel entirely myself yet."

For a moment, she wondered if he was saying that because he felt as panicked as she did that their time would end soon. But again, she couldn't allow the thought to penetrate. It was too painful, and hadn't she had enough painful thoughts when it came to men?

After strapping on his boot, Arch got to his feet. "I'm dying to get out of the house. I know we had the day out that I planned, but let's do something *you* want to do today."

She smiled. As if he didn't always inquire what she'd like to do with any shared time they had. He was always thoughtful.

"I did promise to take you thrifting with me one day, so would you like to do that? There's this one store in downtown Monterey that I've been wanting to check out."

If the idea of shopping sounded boring to Arch, he didn't show it. She saw only affection in his face, and it helped her relax, helped her stop worrying about losing him. At least for one more afternoon. Especially when he said it was a perfect plan and went to shower and change. He tried to convince her to join him—and of course she wanted to soap up his back and have more delicious shower sex—but she was worried that he was already overdoing it with all the hot sex as it was.

She went to her room, showered quickly, and slipped into a blue T-shirt dress and slip-on sandals that would be easy to slip on and off in the changing rooms.

The little bubble of excitement that always came at the prospect of thrifting rose in her belly. She loved the prospect of a hidden gem she might discover. And this trip would be extra special because it was with Arch.

Here was another pastime she had never shared with a man, and she was about to let Arch in on it. To her surprise, the idea didn't feel weird at all, even though he was a kazillionaire and could drop thousands on clothes without his bank account even noticing.

Taking Arch thrifting felt completely natural. She was certain she'd find a dress she could wear to the Moonrise award ceremony. After all, no one would expect the caregiver to be wearing couture. So long as she didn't embarrass Arch, that was all that mattered, she thought as she ran a brush through her hair.

They met in the hallway, his hair still wet from the shower. Little droplets of water ran over his ears, and she couldn't help it—she kissed them away.

"You're so sweet, Tessa Taylor," he murmured,

slipping his hands down her back in such a sensual way that she shivered with pleasure.

When she pulled away from his deep, passionate kiss, his expression was so loving it brought a lump to her throat. She stared into his eyes for a moment and then looked down, afraid of the words on the tip of her tongue. Afraid to even *think* the three little words… let alone say them out loud.

"Shall we head out?" she said brightly. Maybe too brightly. Maybe Arch could see straight through to the very heart of her and know exactly what she was thinking.

Because there was no way that she was the first woman who had ever wanted *all* of him. No doubt he'd move on as soon as he was back in his regular world, while she'd be back in hers, taking care of someone else who needed her skills.

But all he said was, "Let's do it!" in just as bright a tone. "And let's take my Porsche. It's been sitting in the garage too long."

Tessa had never even seen Arch's Porsche. Didn't know he had one.

She must have been frowning, because he laughed and said, "I'll admit it is a bit of a boy's toy, but it's so fun to drive—you have to try it."

He grabbed his keys from the hall table and led them out to the garage. It was a gorgeous afternoon. She breathed in deeply, closing her eyes for a moment and enjoying the warmth on her face.

Arch clicked a fob, and the white garage door slowly opened. She walked to his side and saw three cars housed inside, each cloaked in a cloth cover.

"Let's take the Porsche Carrera Cabriolet," Arch said. "It's sporty but timeless. Drives like a dream."

He went to the smaller of the three and took off the cover. The car beneath was a two-seater, sleek and metallic gray.

Tessa laughed nervously. "I don't think I've ever been this close to such a nice car, let alone driven one."

Arch tossed her the keys. "First time for everything. Until my boot comes off, you're in charge behind the wheel. And don't worry, you're gonna love it. She's easy to handle."

Tessa slid into the black leather driver's seat as Arch put down the roof. He was nuts to let her drive a car this rare and expensive. "I'm not so sure about this."

Again, he reassured her that it would be fun. "You're an excellent driver, and it's such a gorgeous day. There's nothing like the feel of the open road with the wind in your hair."

With trepidation, Tessa adjusted the seat and mirrors, then put the key in the ignition. The engine roared, and it took all her strength not to jump in surprise.

"Listen to that beauty," Arch murmured. "I've

missed this. Thank you."

Tessa carefully pulled out of the garage and into the driveway before turning onto the main road into downtown Monterey. At first, the power of the car unnerved her, but as they joined the flow of traffic, she found she was actually enjoying herself. With the top down, her hair flowed behind her and her cheeks cooled with the breeze. The car was fluid, and it felt like she was driving on silk. When Arch put his hand on her knee, she was in seventh heaven.

Soon, they reached Monterey, and Arch guided her to where to park.

"Fun, right?" he asked as she turned off the engine.

"*So* fun!" she replied, and he kissed her, clearly not at all worried that someone in the parking garage would see them.

Downtown Monterey was one of her favorite places to shop, and Tessa was as excited to show Arch her special spots in Old Monterey as he had been when they'd gone to the aquarium. Downtown was a real hot spot of cultural and historical diversity, and its thrift stores reflected this.

She wanted to take his hand, but resisted the urge. There was no reason to add fuel to a fire in public that was burning down to its last embers. Tessa led him along a series of cobbled streets off Alvarado Street until they reached Angel's.

"I love this spot. It's more curated than other boutiques, and they have some really special things."

Arch smiled and followed her inside.

An old disco song was playing on the vintage jukebox by the customer service desk, and the sales associate was dressed like a fifties pin-up, with ruby-red lips, figure-hugging black pedal pushers, and a white crop top. She greeted them both and let them know she was there to help. Immediately, Tessa felt the thrill of their impending bargain hunting. She eagerly approached the dress section, ready to rummage through the colorful racks. She also appreciated that the sales associate didn't make a big deal about Arch. Tessa got the sense the woman didn't even know who he was. Amazing, but thankfully, true.

Arch followed Tessa as she carefully combed through the offerings for the perfect find. He looked a little bemused, but in good spirits. As for Tessa, she was determined to show him that you didn't need to pay a small fortune to look good.

"This place is wild," he said as he drifted to the opposite rack and showed her a men's white tuxedo. "This looks like something Fred Astaire wore onstage."

Tessa laughed. "It may well be! You should try it on."

"The pants are too short," Arch said, laughing. "But I do like this red top hat."

She loved how much—and how quickly—he was getting into the fun of thrifting. She'd been a tiny bit nervous that he'd turn up his nose at secondhand clothes, but he placed the hat on his windblown hair and kept it there.

"Somehow, you make it look good," she told him as she turned back to the dresses. A deep-red silk caught her eye. She held it up and admired the flowing bias cut. It was a classic shape and very understated.

"What do you think? Would it be suitable for Moonrise?"

For a moment, she saw his expression falter. Was the dress too flashy for a caregiver to wear? Should she go with something plainer? But Valentina had told her they'd be sitting at the same table, so she wanted to look as though she fit in.

"It's gorgeous." Arch held it up against her. "Maybe a bit long for you, but we can have it tailored."

He had a good eye—it was at least an inch too long, but she could adjust the hem herself. That must be why he'd looked at her so oddly for a moment. He obviously thought it wouldn't fit her. Arch took the dress from her arms, and when she protested, saying she could carry her own finds, he insisted he was there as her assistant.

She was surprised by how much she loved having him with her, when previously thrifting had always been her private thing. But it was nice to have an accomplice—and it was a whole new experience to have a second opinion from someone who really knew fashion and to have a special occasion to shop for.

She found two more dresses, both black, one strapless and falling to her knees, the other lace with short wide sleeves and cut very low in the back. Arch gave both the thumbs-up and showed her a vintage Levi's denim shirt he'd found.

"Perfect for horseback riding," he said, laughing, the top hat still on. "When I eventually get back on a horse, that is. But I think you should also have some fun." He took her to the other side of the store and picked out a pink ballerina's tutu.

"You're kidding, right?" She laughed.

He shook his head solemnly. "Maybe this is the moment you realize your true destiny is to be a ballerina. You have to be open to all avenues, Tessa," he said in a mock serious tone.

Even though he was making her laugh, she had to concede he was a very good actor. Even when he was just messing around with her in a thrift shop.

A glint of silver high on a shelf caught her eye. She reached up and retrieved what turned out to be a man's walking stick with a silver top. It must have been the height of elegance in its day, but its day had passed. The silver was tarnished and the wood scratched. But it was still a beautiful piece.

She handed it to Arch. "More interesting than a cane from the medical supply place," she said, joking.

But he turned it over in his hands, studying it carefully. "This is exactly what my character would have used in the Western." He sounded quite excited. "I can get my dad to polish up the wood."

She loved that he was totally getting into the world of thrift stores. "Absolutely. And the silver will gleam like new with some polish."

He tested it, walking a few steps, and it took his weight without any problem. In fact, the stick could have been made for him. "It's perfect," he said. "I'll use this at Moonrise. I can't believe you found it."

She gave Arch one of her best thrifting tips. "Always look up high or down low in a thrift store. Everybody looks in the middle, but most of the real treasures are tucked on the highest and lowest shelves."

"Noted, my thrifting queen."

They took their wares to the changing rooms, and on the way, Arch grabbed a green dinner jacket and a plaid bow tie.

"Some interesting choices you've got there," she teased.

"I'm an actor, so I can't resist a little dress-up," he explained, pulling open the curtain to a changing room. "It's one of my favorite things about my career—pretending to be someone else for a little while."

In her own dressing room, Tessa slipped into the red dress first. The fabric was sensational, but it was too long, as predicted. She stepped out to show Arch.

He was wearing the dinner jacket with no shirt and the top hat, while leaning on the cane.

"Oh my gosh… it's so you," she said.

"Why, thank you, madam," he replied in a British accent, taking a small bow and doffing his hat. "And may I say, you look incredible in red silk."

Tessa turned from side to side in the mirror. There was a lot to like about the dress, but it didn't feel quite right. "I'm going to try the others."

She slipped into the black strapless first. It fit like a glove, clinging nicely to her curves. But to her mind, it wasn't quite special enough for a red carpet.

She came out in the dress to see that Arch had found another hat, this one a wool flat cap, and had paired it with the denim shirt. "I'm calling this look 'sexy farmer who found himself at the rodeo.'"

She laughed and said, "The shirt looks great." It was so nice to see Arch this relaxed and playful. She'd been worried that he'd be bored, but of course it made perfect sense he would like trying on different costumes.

"What do you think?" she said, doing a little twirl. "I could dress it up with some red lipstick and some nice shoes, but I'm still not sure if it's red-carpet worthy."

Arch was complimentary, but said she could wear something more showy if she wanted.

The idea made her panic a little—the last thing she

wanted was attention at this ceremony, but she also didn't want to look underdressed. She tried on the last dress, but it wouldn't fasten over her bust. She slipped back into her T-shirt.

"The last dress was no good?"

"I couldn't get the zipper up over my chest."

He shook his head sadly. "You should have asked for some help... I'd have enjoyed that."

She wanted to lean in and give him a kiss, but though there was no one in sight, she was too conscious of being spotted.

★ ★ ★

"I'm going to get the shirt," Arch said. "You're right, it's a great fit. And the walking stick, obviously." He tossed it in the air and caught it like Fred Astaire. "What about the red dress? Did you want it?"

He hoped Tessa would say no. She looked great in it, of course—she'd look great in anything—but the dress Mila had found was something truly special, and he wanted to surprise her with it.

She shook her head. "It's not quite right. I'll keep looking."

"I want you to be happy with whatever you wear."

He'd loved watching her consider all the dresses so carefully. She'd looked fabulous in the two she'd shown him, but he was secretly glad she hadn't found the perfect one.

As they approached the sales counter, she suddenly stopped—her attention caught by something on one of the shelves. She reached to the top shelf and brought down something shiny. It was a little beaded evening bag, white, with a Deco vibe.

"This is gorgeous." She looked at him quizzically. "Is it weird to buy the bag before I find the dress?"

Arch shook his head. He couldn't believe how well what she'd chosen would go with the silvery dress. He and Mila hadn't even thought to buy a bag. "It's perfect."

She opened the purse, showing him the original silk lining. She turned the price tag over and then nodded with satisfaction. "Ten dollars."

His eyebrows shot up. "No way. I'm about to spend that on iced coffees for us."

"Way," she said, clearly pleased with her find. "Told you I'm good at this. And see? It was on a high shelf. There's nothing quite like a bargain."

He hadn't even looked at the price of his shirt. Twelve dollars. He was stunned. The walking stick was thirty-five bucks—and he'd be using it with a tux custom-made for him by Dior.

He went to add the bag to his pile of finds, but Tessa shook her head. "These are on me," she said. "You can buy the coffee if you like."

But he held firm. "You wouldn't even need that purse if you weren't doing me a favor. So I'm buying it—and your dress when you find one."

His hope was that if he could convince her to let him spend ten bucks on a handbag, he had a better chance of foisting a dress that cost five grand on her. Many of the women attending the event would be wearing gowns that cost ten or twenty times that. Nonetheless, he had to move carefully. He'd start with a ten-dollar bag.

As they headed toward a coffee shop, Arch realized he'd never been this relaxed with a woman—ever. Even at the aquarium, he'd been focused on how to impress Tessa and make sure she had an amazing day. But now he was just having fun, pure fun, and she was too.

"I love getting to know you better. Thank you for taking me shopping and letting me see more of your world." He paused as they entered the coffee shop. "And I want to see more of your life. When you go to the beach to paint later, is there any chance you'd let me come with you? I won't bother you. Maybe I could bring my script, and we could work side by side. What do you say?"

She turned to him, and for a moment, he thought she'd turn him down, keep him locked out of the work she was so passionate about. But then—thankfully—pleasure suffused her face.

And when she said, "I'd love that," he felt like he'd just won an Oscar.

Chapter Twenty-Nine

At the beach, Tessa set up her easel slowly, with more care than usual. She couldn't shake the sensation of eyes on her, even though Arch was already settled on a nearby bench, buried in his script. He wasn't even looking in her direction.

When he'd first suggested coming along, her first instinctive thought had been, *No way. Not a chance.* Arch might be the only living person who knew about her painting, but she truly did consider it a private, personal pursuit. It was a fanciful dream, painting. Her escape from reality and a way to process her feelings.

It was *not* a group activity. Especially with a man whose body made her wild with desire. How would she be able to concentrate?

But then she recalled meeting Mylene Fraser, who'd seen her work in this very spot, and had told Tessa that it was good enough to enter the Carmel-by-the-Sea *plein air* competition. Tessa had put the moment out of her mind, banishing it to some far-off place inside her. But what if Mylene had a point? She was a renowned artist after all. And hadn't Arch echoed her praise, displaying one of her paintings in the same room as a Picasso?

When Tessa had let his request to come with her sink in, even though it felt fraught with risk, at the same time there was nothing she wanted more than for him to share this space with her, to be part of her world.

Every inch of it.

Yes, the idea scared her to bits, but in a secret part of her heart, it thrilled her too.

Frankly, she didn't want to be alone this afternoon. Or, more accurately, she was having too much fun with Arch to leave him alone at home while she painted, also alone.

She'd spent so long keeping her true self hidden. She never could have imagined how beautiful it was to fully open up to another person, let alone her teenage crush.

But every step of the way, Arch had shown her that she could depend on him. Nothing about her or her life story had shocked him. Instead, he'd given her such beautiful things—kindness and understanding.

So even if they could never be a forever couple, at least he was hers for now.

And *now* was absolutely amazing.

What's more, given that she trusted him enough to be intimate physically, it made sense to her that she should trust him with her art.

Arch was engrossed in his script, a pencil in his mouth, ready to make notes in the margins. She smiled out of the pure happiness being near him brought her, then threw herself into her work.

As always, the physics of time changed as she painted. She was able to achieve a focus so complete, so absolute, that she had no idea whether fifteen minutes or two hours had passed before she was brought back to the present by the sound of a dog happily barking. She blinked several times, then saw Arch on the beach, playing with a chocolate Labrador puppy.

The dog bounded across the sand, chasing an old tennis ball, and then dropped it at Arch's feet. He picked it up obligingly and threw it again. And again.

Watching him, Tessa was filled with warmth. Arch really would love having a dog. It was clear that he fed off their positive energy, and vice versa. She could easily see him with his own dog at home, curled up on the couch or bounding along the beach, ball in its mouth. A gray-haired couple, no doubt the dog's owners, approached Arch, and she watched as they talked with one another. From where Tessa was standing, it seemed that if they knew he was a famous movie star, they didn't let on. He was easy to chat with, and the locals responded to his down-to-earth nature.

She'd been so engrossed in her work she hadn't even noticed Arch leave his spot on the bench. Turning to her painting, she stood back from her easel and studied her new additions.

Mylene was right: Her painting *was* good. And Tessa was in the zone. A few more strokes to capture the light on the leaves, and she'd be finished.

She quickly became reabsorbed and didn't realize Arch was standing beside her, watching, until he said, "Wow, Tessa."

She startled, but when she saw his expression of wonder as he took in her painting, she softened. He didn't need to say more. She'd impressed him, and that made something deep inside her glow golden and bright.

"The light on this is exquisite," he said. "Your colors are so soft. Did you underpaint this?"

She nodded, surprised he knew the term. "I never skip that step, or a value study, although I know many *plein air* painters do. I find that laying a good foundation serves as a guide for what's to come."

"Do you underpaint in monochrome, or do you go straight in with color?"

Again, she was surprised that he'd know the difference between underpainting with just one pigment or more. "I'm still finding my way, so I find it easiest to start with one color to separate the underpainting from the painting's color development. The process feels more manageable that way."

He nodded thoughtfully, still staring at the painting. "I think it's sensational, Tessa."

She was about to object and say something self-effacing, the way she always had before, but she caught herself. If there was one thing she'd learned from Arch, it was the power of belief in oneself. He didn't apologize for knowing that he was a great actor. On the contrary, he owned it.

Right then and there, Tessa saw how her attitude needed to change. Yes, her husband had been cruel about her painting. But that didn't mean he'd been right, though she'd taken his word as gospel for far too many years. It was long past time that she learned to accept praise as well as criticism.

Turning her smile to Arch, she simply said, "Thank you."

She could tell that Arch wanted to kiss her then. His eyes had gone misty with affection and desire. And oh, how she wanted to kiss him back.

But there were so many people on the beach, so many sets of eyes. She could feel him holding himself back and knew it was for her sake, because she had insisted on privacy, on secrecy.

But it seemed that today was a day for throwing caution to the wind. Not only with her new belief in her own talent, but also with her relationship with Arch. So she leaned forward and kissed him gently and tenderly on the lips.

He responded immediately, yielding to her and bringing their bodies closer. As she responded to his delicate touch, she could no longer deny that she had fallen hard and fast for him.

When they finally parted, she felt deep within her that something had shifted. Something big.

But, that little voice in her head that wanted to keep her safe said, *is the shift big enough? Can you really do this? Can you actually date a movie star without losing yourself in his world? And can you handle the people around the world who will wonder why he chose you when he could have a far prettier and more successful woman at his side?*

"Are you close to being finished?" Arch asked.

"I'm done. And we should head back soon. We still have your exercises to complete before dinner."

"I'd like to help with cooking," he said. "It would be nice to make food together."

She nodded, looking forward to another comfortable evening stretching out in front of them. She could easily picture them chopping vegetables together and then maybe snuggling up on the couch to watch a movie.

Even though movies were his profession, he loved to watch a good film and always waited until the credits rolled to comment on the acting, direction, and anything else that had struck him about the craft. It was fascinating to hear his views. Plus, he was genuinely interested in her views, as well, since she saw a movie purely as a fan, not a professional.

It was so easy to fall into playing house with him.

And so simple to wish that it could be like this forever.

Chapter Thirty

The next morning, Tessa made her way to Saint Anna's for coffee with Mila and Erin. Arch was on a conference call all morning, so she had a little more time than usual. She chose to walk rather than drive, wanting to savor the peace of the early morning and inhale that special Carmel-by-the-Sea air.

She was coming to love these Tuesday morning get-togethers and the warm way the Davenport sisters had welcomed her into their fold.

She'd made some overnight chia and mango pudding for breakfast, but had decided to skip her portion and have one of the café's infamous pastries instead. Looking in the window now, the options seemed as tempting and endless as always, but her eyes were drawn to an almond croissant.

Both sisters were at their usual table in the corner, and after hugging them hello, she slid into the chair next to Erin.

"It was so nice to see you both out on the waves. You make surfing look so easy."

Mila smiled broadly. She had caught the sun, and a smattering of new freckles had appeared across the bridge of her nose. "You'll be fine." Then she said, "I sealed the deal on a big sale yesterday."

Erin laughed, flicking her glossy hair over one shoulder. "Your eyes are flashing dollar signs, Mila."

"Nothing better than the thrill of the chase—unless it's winning," Mila replied, shrugging but happy to laugh at herself. "Plus, it means I can buy this gorgeous bag I saw the other day at Dominique's. A gift to myself."

Erin groaned. "Dominique's again? That place is insanely pricey."

Mila shrugged. "It's pricey because everything is beautiful and made in Europe. Worth every dollar."

A waitress appeared, and Tessa ordered a cappuccino and the pastry she'd spied in the window. Mila ordered another Americano, while Erin was happy with her iced matcha and beignet.

"I had a bit of a shopping disaster yesterday," Tessa said. Omitting the part where Arch accompanied her, she told the girls about her visit to her favorite thrift store. She'd been sure she'd find something to wear to the awards event, but had come away with nothing. "The three dresses were all lovely in their own way, but either the fit wasn't quite right, or it just wasn't special enough. All I found was a little beaded bag, which I do love. But I'm in a real dilemma over what to wear now that the ceremony is just a few days away."

Erin nodded in sympathy. "Don't worry, I'm sure you'll find something perfect."

"I'm going shopping again this afternoon." With the picture completed, she could give up an afternoon of painting to try to find the perfect dress. "There's this thrift store a forty-minute drive away that always has unique stuff."

Had Tessa imagined it, or had a conspiratorial look just passed between the sisters? She didn't think they were judging her for sticking to the thrift store idea. Especially when they both knew she couldn't buy a dress at a fancy boutique. Her wages, although higher with Arch than with her previous clients, didn't justify spending that kind of cash.

Mila leaned across the table. "You can't possibly want to drive that far for a dress. Why don't you come and raid my closet? We're not so different in size, and I have a ton of dresses that I've treated myself to but never wear."

Erin clapped her hands. "That's a great idea. Can I come? I love playing dress-up."

Tessa was about to refuse, as she had Valentina's kind offer a few days ago. She might not be in their league financially, but she didn't take charity. However, before she could say no, Mila grabbed her hand.

"Please say yes," Mila urged her. "I have a bad habit of impulse-buying fancy dresses and then having no place to wear them. I feel so guilty. You'd be doing me a huge favor."

Erin nodded. "She's not joking. Mila has a bit of a shopping problem. At least if someone wears one of her gowns, it will finally see the light of day. Finish up that pastry, and we'll get going!"

Mila really was a great salesperson. Tessa had intended to say no, but now found herself nodding in agreement.

With Mila and Erin's insistence that it would be fun to play dress-up, if nothing else, Tessa was glad. Wasn't it better to hang out with her new friends than to drive a long way to shop by herself?

Mila jumped up and insisted on paying the bill—she felt flush and wanted to treat everyone after her big sale.

The three of them piled into Mila's white SUV, and she drove the short distance to her place. Tessa imagined Mila's home would be fabulous—she had great style, an eye for fashion, and the experience of a Realtor all rolled into one. Despite how companionable both sisters were, they lived a very different life to Tessa's, and she couldn't quite forget it.

But as they pulled up to Mila's place, instead of feeling intimidated by it, she was charmed. Mila's two-bedroom was a quintessential Carmel-by-the-Sea home. A fairy-tale cottage.

"Your place is *lovely*," Tessa breathed.

Mila thanked her. "It was built by a local craftsman," she explained. "I fell in love with his attention to detail, and then when I set eyes on the soaring ceilings in the living room and the doors opening out onto the flower-filled patio, I knew it had to be mine."

"Close to surfing too," Erin reminded her.

"Absolutely. I *had* to live somewhere I could walk to the beach with my board," Mila said. "The great thing about being in my business is I see homes as soon as they come up for sale. I'd been saving for a while and grabbed this cottage the second I saw it."

They went straight up to Mila's bedroom, where she ushered them into a walk-in closet packed with clothes.

Tessa had never seen so many clothes in one person's wardrobe. The shock must have spread across her face, because Erin said, "As you can see, my sister is a fashionista. It's because she's built like a Greek goddess. She got all the female height genes in the family, so clothes always look amazing on her."

Mila brushed away the compliment. "I got used to being in the limelight from a young age, when I was surfing professionally. Did a lot of photo shoots and had some sponsorships. I don't miss always having to be 'on' the way Arch and Damien so often are, but I do appreciate that it gave me a taste for fashion."

It was the first time Mila had ever mentioned her

previous career to Tessa. All she knew from Margaret Percy was that she'd had a terrible accident that had ended her surfing success, and then she'd had to rebuild her life.

Tessa could sympathize with Mila's predicament. Remaking yourself when you thought you had it all figured out was a long and often excruciating process—but when you came out on the other side, you were all the stronger for it.

Mila began rifling through her dresses. Tessa felt a little apprehensive. She was of a similar height, but nowhere near as sculpted and toned.

"Come look for yourself," Mila said over her shoulder. "So many of these will look amazing on you."

As Tessa looked through the clothes, she felt more like she was in a boutique than someone's home. How could one person own so many beautiful clothes? It was a far cry from Tessa's own meager wardrobe that filled the suitcase stashed away at Arch's.

Mila held up a floor-length, deep-green dress that was so figure-hugging it made Tessa blush. She'd never worn something that revealing before.

Erin looked up from her phone, where she'd been typing a message. "Love it," she said, "but I'm not sure if it's really Tessa."

Tessa breathed out a quiet sigh of relief, but agreed to try it on for fun, along with a slinky black number that was backless, with a sexy draped neckline.

Mila told her to go ahead and change in the bathroom while she and Erin remained in the bedroom. As soon as the door was closed, Tessa slipped out of her jeans and white shirt and into the green dress first. It was, thankfully, looser than she'd imagined, but still so sculpted she couldn't imagine actually wearing it.

"Oh, Tessa," Erin said as she went into the bedroom to show the girls. "You're such a knockout, and you don't even know it."

"Totally," Mila agreed, appraising her. "You'd look good in anything."

Tessa flushed deeply, and Mila steered her around to face the full-length mirror. "See?" she said. "This is your Cinderella moment."

"Your *sexy* Cinderella moment," Erin amended.

Tessa wasn't used to seeing herself in something so figure-hugging and glamorous. It didn't really suit her windblown hair and makeup-free face. She had to admit, though, that the dress looked like something you'd see on a red carpet.

"I'd say that's a definite possibility," Mila said, walking around Tessa and studying her. "Let's try the black."

Erin sighed. "I wish I had somewhere fancy to go in a fancy dress. But I can't even get a date to the local Italian restaurant for a pizza, let alone a date with a movie star to an awards ceremony."

Tessa whipped around. "It's not a date. I'm just there to help out."

Another look passed between the sisters, one she couldn't miss this time. Oh no… they must have guessed something had happened between her and Arch.

She felt the familiar panic set in. They were really nice women and had been nothing but kind and welcoming, but surely they must think Arch was way out of her league. And they'd be one hundred percent right.

To deflect, she said she'd try on the other dress and raced back into the bathroom.

As Tessa shimmied out of the green dress, she heard Mila ask Erin about her love life.

"What about that photographer guy?" Mila was saying. "I thought he had potential."

Erin scoffed. "The forensic photographer? He spends half his time capturing awful crime scenes. And he really enjoys it. Too macabre for me."

Mila sighed dramatically. "Your standards are too high sometimes. You rarely date, and when you do, you find ten things wrong with the person before the main course has even been served."

"That's something of an exaggeration. But I just can't date as casually as you. You can go out and have fun without ever seeming to get too attached. You manage to keep your focus on your career and surfing and being there for the rest of the family. I don't know how you do it."

Mila said, "I guess that's all true. Well, apart from you-know-who... but that was another lifetime."

There was a pause, and then Erin said, "I think Mom and Dad have spoiled me for real life. Their love story is such a perfect fairy tale, and all these years later, they still crush on each other like teens."

"You've always been a sucker for a good story," Mila said. "Ever since we were kids. Go figure you ended up a journalist. But don't you want some excitement in your life? Someone who makes you shiver with anticipation when you see his name on your phone?"

Tessa took her time zipping up the dress. That was exactly how she felt whenever Arch sent her a message—like a bubble of excitement was bursting inside of her.

She walked back into the bedroom where the Davenport sisters were waiting. Erin was staring dreamily into the distance, a faraway look in her usually lively eyes. "Sex and love aren't everything. I'm comfortable being single, and I like my life. I know I could be a journalist anywhere, but I like working at the *Sea Shell*, and I'm happy in Carmel. I know the rest of you think I'm boring, but for me, being safe feels good."

"I can totally empathize," Tessa found herself saying as both of the women realized she had come back into the room. "Sometimes it's nice to just stay in your lane and know what's coming."

Another look between the sisters. But then Mila jumped up. "The green was amazing on you, but this little black dress is classic."

Erin nodded. "Elegant and understated. And yet, still sexy."

"That's Tessa's figure," Mila said. "She'd look sexy in anything."

Tessa looked in the mirror. She felt more comfortable in this dress. It had a halter neck, black bugle beads to give it sparkle, but the cut was classic *little black dress*. It hugged her figure without overtly advertising her wares.

Erin came closer so she was also reflected in the mirror. "It looks amazing. Much more subtle. And we can liven it up with accessories. I can do your makeup, too, if you'd like. And Mila's a genius with hot rollers. We could have you looking old-school Hollywood glam before you go to the airport. It'd be so much fun."

The sisters were both so excited that Tessa agreed to all of it—the dress, the makeup, the hair. If she was going to play at being glamorous for this event, then she should accept all the help she was offered. It would take a whole team to complete her for-one-night-only transformation.

"What about shoes?" Mila asked. "I'm two sizes

bigger than you."

Tessa was surprised. "How do you know my shoe size?"

Mila stuck out her foot in its gorgeous tan pump. "I have eyes in my head. I'm a size eight. You're what, a six and a half?"

"Good guess. I'm a six." She'd never have noticed the other woman's shoe size. Mila was amazingly observant. "It's okay. I've got nice black shoes. I'll polish them, and they'll work fine."

Chapter Thirty-One

When the day of the awards ceremony arrived, Arch was surprised to find he was excited about it. He'd been to countless events like these, and although they could be fun, they usually dragged on and involved a lot of smiling and staying on your best behavior, even when you were bored to tears and dying to leave. By the end of the night, he would have been kissed and hugged so often he'd carry the scent of other people's colognes and perfumes on him until he showered it all off.

His excitement was all down to Tessa. He was so eager to be out with her in public and introduce her to some of his friends in the business. And he couldn't wait to see her in the dress. He knew she was nervous about the whole thing, but with any luck, the dress would make her feel like the timeless beauty she really was. She fit into his world, and it was time she knew it.

They'd awakened together, and he'd had a few minutes to gaze at her beautiful face before she opened her stunning blue eyes to greet the day.

And oh, how they'd greeted it…

He still couldn't believe how much he longed for her when she woke, even after a night of great sex. They'd been slow and lazy, which was wonderful. She'd reached for him as though it was the most natural thing in the world, and he'd hardened instantly as her hand wrapped around him. He leaned over, finding her already wet, and they'd caressed each other until he couldn't stand it anymore and slid inside her, taking his time, until slow and lazy became urgent and energetic.

Every time they made love, it was better. Which was crazy, considering how great the first time had been. It was like she'd cast a magical spell over him. One he had no intention of breaking.

After a super sexy shower together—they simply couldn't get enough of each other—she'd prepared breakfast and then made him complete his exercises as usual. There was no day off with Nurse Tessa. They'd worked on balance, because he had to walk down a carpeted aisle, then up some stairs at the theater. He'd walk with his new thrifted stick, absolutely refusing to go back to crutches. He was determined not to fall on his face. If anything did happen to make him lose his balance, however, Smith wouldn't let him fall.

And now was the moment he'd been waiting for. It was time to start getting ready. He went to his bedroom and took out the dress, concealed in its protective bag, and the shoe box.

Smiling, he returned to the living room, and then the smile turned to a grin as Tessa looked up at him, confused.

"Is that your tuxedo?" she asked. "Do you need help getting dressed?"

As always, she was thinking of him and not herself. He swallowed, suddenly nervous. He hoped that this was going to go the way he'd planned. "No, this is for you… if you want it. No pressure."

The confusion on her face deepened, and she wrinkled her nose adorably as she always did when she wasn't quite sure what was happening.

"It's a dress," he said. "And some shoes." He put the box down beside her. "I know you didn't find what you were looking for when we went thrifting and that Mila lent you something, but I saw this in one of the local boutiques and thought it would be perfect for you." He paused a beat, but when she said nothing, he added, "If you don't like it, you don't have to wear it. If you *do* like it, there's a seamstress on standby in case it needs alteration."

Tessa's eyes widened. "Wow," she said. "What a lovely thought. I don't think anyone has ever bought me clothes before, let alone an evening dress. Thank you."

"Wait to thank me after you've seen it." Arch laughed, his nerves really kicking in now. He was so desperate for her to love the dress and feel special. He unzipped the bag and carefully took it out, his eyes on Tessa the whole time.

She gasped when she saw it, and her hand flew to her mouth. "Arch, I—I don't know what to say." She looked awestruck. "It's the most beautiful dress I've ever seen."

Relief flooded through him. "You mean it?"

In that moment, he realized there was literally no better feeling on earth than making Tessa happy. He now acknowledged that he'd been afraid she'd refuse to wear it, letting her pride get between them. But, thankfully, she was doing the exact opposite.

She got up and came to touch the fabric. "It's exquisite. Classic but modern too. I love it. I can't believe you picked out such a perfect dress. It's so..." She trailed off, clearly searching for the right words. "I'm just speechless. You really didn't need to do this for me." She looked a little shy. "But I'm so glad you did."

"You deserve it," he said quietly but firmly. "And it's just a dress. Something for you to enjoy and a way for me to say thank you for coming with me. You're doing *me* the favor, remember?" He gestured toward the shoe box. "Open it," he suggested.

She lifted the lid, and there was that delightful little gasp again.

"Gorgeous," she breathed. "They're a perfect match with the dress." She turned the sandals over in her hands and then looked up at him. "How did you know my size?"

"Don't get mad, but I snuck into your room the other day and looked in your closet. I hope you don't mind. You nearly busted me, in fact, when you came in from painting. Mila helped me choose the dress and shoes."

She laughed. "Ah, I remember! I thought something was up, but then you seduced me, and I forgot all about—" She gave a little gasp. "*That's* how Mila knew my shoe size. She and Erin totally had me fooled."

He grinned and asked her to try on the dress. "In case we need to alter it."

She thanked him again, then kissed him, and in a move so bold and beautiful it took his breath away, she stripped down to bra and panties right there in the living room.

Arch let his gaze rove over her perfect body. "You're killing me."

"In a good way?" she teased.

"In the best way imaginable."

She took the dress from his arms and seductively stepped into it. She turned around and asked him to fasten the zipper. He slid it up her back, enjoying the softness of her skin as he let his fingers brush against it. "It's a perfect fit," he said. "Come into my bedroom and look."

She slipped on the shoes and then headed toward

his room. She gazed at herself in the full-length mirror while he watched her turn this way and that, admiring how the fabric caught the light.

He had already known the dress was perfect, but he was still blown away by how incredible she looked. It didn't need alteration. The dress could have been custom-made for Tessa.

"It's beautiful," she said. "I can't believe how beautiful it is." She caught his eye in the mirror and then frowned slightly. In a quiet voice, she asked, "How much did it cost, Arch?"

He ran a hand through his hair, weighing his options. He'd been hoping she wouldn't ask about money or where the dress was from so he wouldn't have to lie.

But if he told her the truth, she might insist that he return it. He wanted her to have it, to shine and feel special.

He thought about telling her a little white lie—that he'd found the dress at another thrift store. But he couldn't do it. Couldn't bear to lie, in even the smallest way, to Tessa.

"I asked Mila to come shopping with me. And this was the one that we both knew would look incredible on you."

Tessa was silent for a moment. "It must have cost a fortune."

Again, he couldn't lie to her. "A fortune to some, but not for me." Before she could protest, he held up a hand. "I'm not saying you can't refuse it, if you're not comfortable with the idea of my buying you a dress. But I'm hoping you'll agree to wear it. Because I love—" He stopped before he said too much. "Because I love that, for once, I can do something nice for you, when you've been bending over backward all these weeks doing nice things for me."

"But that's my job. To help you with anything you need."

"Yes, it's your job. But can you look me in the eye and tell me it hasn't turned into more with me?"

She swallowed hard. Then she turned to look at herself in the mirror again. Instead of answering his last question, she simply said, "Thank you for the dress. I love it. And I'll wear it… even if it costs more than all of my possessions combined." She gave him a small smile in the mirror, and his heart finally started beating again. "And while you're right that I don't want to know how much you spent because it will likely freak me out, the truth is that you've made me feel really, really special. Not just tonight. But so many times since I came to stay and work with you. You'll never know how much I appreciate it."

He was about to pull her into his arms and kiss her, when he heard Erin's voice calling hello from the hallway. She and Mila were early.

"Your hair and makeup crew are here," Mila announced.

She strode into the bedroom ahead of Erin, armed with an expensive-looking hair dryer and a black case of what Arch assumed to be other hair-related tools.

Her eyes widened when she took in the sight of Tessa. "Oh wow," she said, sighing in admiration. "The dress is perfect."

Tessa did a little twirl. "Thank you for helping to pick it out." She gave Mila a special smile of thanks.

"I love it!" said Erin, coming into the room. "Tessa, you're a mega babe."

Arch felt a contented warmth flood through him. This was going even better than he'd imagined. Erin was carrying another clothes bag and handed it to Arch.

Tessa thanked his sisters. "I washed my hair and blow-dried it, but you've got carte blanche to style me however you like."

Mila's eyes glowed. She loved a makeover, and Arch knew that Tessa had all the natural beauty to make a truly jaw-dropping red-carpet entrance.

Tessa excused herself to take off the dress and shoes and went upstairs, grabbing her clothes from the living room as she went.

"Coffee?" he asked his sisters, leading the way into the kitchen. There was time before their ride came. Another surprise he hoped Tessa would like.

"Always," Mila said with drama, as though she could barely make it through the next five minutes without a hit of caffeine. Arch set about making coffee for his sisters. He also brought out some of the black sesame cookies he knew they both loved and put them on a plate.

Erin and Mila slid onto the counter stools and watched him with what he realized was bemusement.

"Are those the sesame cookies from that great Japanese store in Los Angeles?" Mila asked.

Arch smiled. "I wanted to say thanks for doing all this for Tessa. It means a lot."

Even though Tessa was upstairs, Erin lowered her voice and said, "We can see how much she means to you, Arch."

He nodded seriously, knowing full well that he was no longer capable of concealing his true feelings. He might be a good actor. But pretending that he didn't love Tessa?

Well, that was simply impossible, no matter his acting skills.

★ ★ ★

Tessa put herself in Mila's and Erin's hands, comforted by the knowledge that they'd do a great job with her hair and makeup. They wouldn't have offered if they didn't have the skills.

All she wanted was to look nice enough not to let Arch down. Plus, she was hoping she'd be able to avoid too much attention and just let Arch do his thing in the limelight. Every time she thought about walking a red carpet with him, a flutter of panic took over. She'd been pushing the idea out of her mind all week, but now that it was here, she was going to have to face it.

In a gap between the sisterly banter Tessa had grown to recognize was born of affection between the siblings, she said, "I'm feeling pretty nervous."

Mila was winding her hair into hot rollers, and Erin was applying shadow to her eyes, and so she kept them shut, waiting for one of them to reply.

"There's no need to be nervous," Erin said in a soothing tone. "Arch will be with you the whole time. Just imagine you're at a big wedding. You're more used to being at events where you don't know people than you think."

"Erin's right," Mila said. "When I was younger, I went to loads of sport events. I learned that everyone was too busy making sure their own outfits were okay to worry about anyone else's."

Tessa was grateful for their kind comments, but she still needed to explain. "It's less about my dress and more about how to behave. I've never been to anything like this awards show before."

"You just smile and make small talk," Mila said. "Seriously, Erin's right. It is just like a wedding. You'll be fine!"

Tessa had a flashback of her own wedding, which had been too big, more about showing off than declaring her love to Lewis. The memory made her so uncomfortable that she shivered.

"Arch wouldn't take you anywhere you'd hate," Erin said softly. "He wouldn't put you in that position."

Tessa let their soothing words sink in and told herself that they were right—she had nothing to worry about. *Just act like it's a big wedding. A big wedding with some famous faces…*

Before long, Erin said she could open her eyes. "Perfect," she said, appraising Tessa's face. "Even if I say so myself. And you've done wonders, Mila. Tessa's hair looks so full and bouncy."

Tessa let herself be guided over to the mirror. When she saw herself, she almost didn't recognize the reflection staring back. It was her face, but her features had been so carefully enhanced and emphasized that she almost resembled a Hollywood star.

"What do you think?" Mila looked proud of herself, as though she already knew the answer.

"You've done an amazing job!" Tessa said, delighted. "Both of you have. I never knew I could look like this."

"Your features are so beautiful it was easy to make you look like a movie star," Mila said.

Erin added, "Now put on your dress and shoes and come downstairs to show Arch. I can't wait to see his face."

She sounded so excited about it that Tessa felt her

own excitement rise. Arch had seen her in casual clothes and the barest minimum of makeup. And also completely in the nude, she thought with a thrill deep down inside. But there was still a part of her that wanted Arch to see her at her prettiest.

She slipped into the new underwear she'd bought for the evening, a secret splurge no one else knew about. Then she carefully stepped into the dress and slipped on the shoes.

Her reflection told her that she looked her very best. The dress fit her curves to perfection and shimmered when she moved. Her hair and makeup were better than she could have imagined.

Maybe she wasn't Valentina Sullivan or Sonia Montefiore, but she felt, for the first time, that she wouldn't look out of place on a red carpet next to Arch.

When she descended the stairs, she found Arch standing at the bottom looking up, clearly waiting to see her makeover.

She glanced at him nervously, hoping he'd approve. The expression on his face told her everything she needed to know.

His mouth opened and closed again, as though he couldn't find the right words. Finally, he went with a low whistle.

When she reached him, he said, "You will be the most beautiful woman there tonight. I'm a lucky man." Then in a lower voice, he said, "I want to kiss you so badly right now, but I'd smudge you." Instead, he took her hand, raised it slowly to his lips, and kissed it, which had to be the most romantic thing any man had ever done.

Then she walked into the living room, where she could hear the women talking. To her surprise, Betsy Davenport was sitting with her daughters.

"Tessa," Betsy said, "you look sensational. That dress is fabulous, and you're as pretty as a picture."

Tessa blushed deeply as she thanked her. "Everyone has been so kind."

"We all rally around one another in this family," Betsy said, smiling. "Which is why I've brought you these." She opened her leather handbag and took out a small box. "I have to admit, we all knew about the dress. I thought these would be the perfect finishing touch. These earrings belonged to my grandmother. They're something of a family heirloom."

She opened the box and turned it toward Tessa. Inside were a pair of large pearl drop earrings, each pearl hanging from a chain of small diamonds. They were simple and elegant and absolutely gorgeous.

"I don't know what to say," Tessa murmured. "I love them."

She couldn't get over how kind everyone was. The warmth of the Davenports was like nothing she'd ever experienced.

She hadn't bothered with jewelry, as nothing she

owned was fancy enough for the dress. She crossed to the mirror and slipped on the earrings, loving the way they looked, then turned to show the family.

"I wore those at my wedding," Betsy said, sounding dreamy, "and my mother wore them at hers. There's a lot of happiness and history in those earrings."

She turned to Arch, who still looked like he was in awe of her makeover. Realizing she hadn't told him yet how great he looked, she said softly, "You look really handsome, Arch."

He was dressed in a full black tuxedo, his hair recently cut and neater than usual. He looked like a heartthrob, and her heart beat wildly.

Even though they'd had sex time and time again, she couldn't believe he was her date. He was also carrying the very suave-looking silver-topped cane, which looked amazing after Howie had fixed it up. She hoped he'd use her arm, too, if he needed it.

"Yes, he certainly is my handsome boy," Betsy agreed.

"You scrub up pretty well, bro," Mila said.

Tessa knew that she and Arch were staring at each other in front of his mom and sisters, but she couldn't tear her eyes away from him and neither could he from her.

Finally, he said, "You look like a dream, Tessa. Just as I knew you would. I'm so proud to have you on my arm today."

The moment felt so special that Tessa wasn't even worried about how openly he was complimenting her in front of his family and whether they'd cotton to her sexual relationship with him. Instead, she savored feeling like a princess. Or maybe more like Cinderella at the ball? All she knew was that every part of her being glowed.

Arch turned to his mom. "Are you sure you're happy to drive us to the airport? I can order a car."

"Of course," Betsy replied. "I feel like I'm taking you both to prom!" she added in a teasing tone. "Except this prom involves a private plane."

Tessa gulped. Of course Arch would fly on a private plane. She had no idea what the inside of one even looked like. It was the perfect reminder that, just as Cinderella's magical night had to end at midnight, so would hers as soon as he was fully healed and she was sent off to her next client.

Although, for the first time, Tessa couldn't quite squash the hope that it might all work out for her the way it had for Cinderella…

Chapter Thirty-Two

Tessa touched the smooth black leather seats in the limousine. There had already been so many firsts today. A hair and makeup team, the surreal experience of flying in a small but luxurious private jet, and then being picked up at the private airfield near Moab by a limo. It was as if she'd stepped into someone else's life entirely.

And yet, here she was—Tessa Taylor, in an outfit so glamorous she did a double take every time she caught her reflection.

Arch was holding her other hand as he looked out of the window. The passing scenery was stunning. The desert was beautiful—rusty reds, ochres, and a thousand shades of gold, the shapes of rock formations from ancient caves and canyons, swirls and flowing arches that looked like rainbows. She was completely enchanted, and her fingers yearned for paints and brushes. How incredible it would be to paint out here, to capture the majesty of this place, although she was certain she'd never be able to do it justice.

Being surrounded by nature as powerful as this was a welcome reminder of how small her worries were and how much joy there was to be taken in the simple, natural things life had to offer.

"It's incredible, right?" Arch asked.

She nodded. "I've never seen anything like it. It's so… humbling."

Arch smiled. "You're right, 'humbling' is the word. As much as I love the ocean, there's something about the desert that ignites a different part of me."

He leaned in and kissed her gently on the lips. The screen between them and the driver was up and tinted for privacy, so she let herself relax into Arch's embrace. It would be a while before she got to touch him again in the way she liked to. No… the way she *needed* to.

Luckily, Erin had packed her off with enough makeup for touch-ups during the event. Besides, he smelled so incredible there was no way she could resist.

By the time their kiss ended, the road had widened, and there were several other limos in the flow of traffic.

"We're getting close," Arch said, following her gaze.

She grew nervous again, the bliss of their embrace rapidly fading, but Arch squeezed her hand. "It's going to be great," he assured her for about the third time that day.

She swallowed. It was fine for him to say that—

he'd been to countless awards ceremonies. But everything about this was new to her. It was unsettling.

And then as the road curved, she spotted the venue—and the waiting crowd—and the red carpet, lined with TV interviewers brandishing microphones and so many photographers she instantly felt faint.

She turned to Arch, aware her eyebrows had shot up to her hairline, and in a high-pitched tone said, "You told me this was going to be a small event. No big deal, you said!"

A flash of concern crossed Arch's face. "It *is* a small event. It's one of the smallest ceremonies I've been to. It *is* no big deal."

She looked out the window again at the grand building and the *huge* crowd of people. The flashing lightbulbs startled her, and she feared she was about to seriously freak out.

"Tessa," he said, his voice suddenly commanding, "look at me."

She turned back to face him.

His expression was full of kindness and understanding. "I promise you I meant it when I said it's a small event. But I should have been more thoughtful about your coming to it with fresh eyes. You know I would never want you to be uncomfortable. I'll be with you the whole way. Can you forgive me if I didn't think this through properly?"

His words were so sincere, and he was so quick to

assume responsibility, that she felt her panic melt. Well, most of it, anyway. As long as she was here with Arch and he stayed by her side tonight, she would be fine.

"Okay," she said. "I forgive you. If you say this is small-scale, then I'll believe you."

He squeezed her hands. "Thank you. Thank you for being here with me. I always feel stronger when you're around."

His sweet words touched her heart just as deeply as his kisses touched her body.

As their limo joined the queue of other sleek vehicles, she spotted Roxy Thanton, the Hollywood reporter who had come to the house to interview Arch. She wore a skin-tight turquoise dress, her hair piled high, her lips shining with gloss. She was talking with a film director so famous that even Tessa, who was usually clueless about these things, recognized the woman.

She turned to Arch. "Even Roxy Thanton is here."

Clearly seeing that she was still nervous, he squeezed her hand again. "I'll tell you what my agent, Jay, told me the first time I did one of these. Just pull your shoulders back and smile. Works every time."

She was about to protest that approach seemed a little too simple to work, but there wasn't time for more. The limo had come to a standstill, and all of a sudden, she realized they were at the red carpet.

Someone opened the door. Arch flashed her his winning smile, then said, "Here we go," before stepping out.

He held out his hand. This was it—she was about to walk onto her very first red carpet.

Tessa slid out of the car and into a dazzling array of cameras, lights, and people everywhere. She blinked several times, a little stunned.

When her vision cleared, she saw fans cheering and clapping across the street. They were cheering for Arch, and he gave them a friendly wave with his free hand, holding on to the cane with the other. Their cheers turned into whoops, and he waved again before turning back to her.

"You've got this, Tessa Taylor," he said in a low voice and then slipped his arm around hers and led her along the red carpet.

It seemed like a matter of seconds before they were stopped by a woman from an entertainment news show. She thrust her enormous mic in Arch's face and said, "Archer Davenport, glad to see you looking so healthy after your accident. How's the leg? And how are you feeling about tonight's ceremony?"

"Very glad to be here," Arch replied with a huge smile. "My leg's healing well, and I'm looking forward to celebrating everyone who is nominated tonight."

"I hear you're presenting the best picture award with Smith Sullivan. You guys just wrapped your own film. Can you tell us about it?"

Tessa stood beside him, not knowing where to look or how to act. She hadn't really thought about what it would feel like *on* the red carpet, standing still while Arch was interviewed. Instead, she'd simply imagined the craze of photographers and the noise of fans while they were being ushered into the venue itself. She should have known Arch would be stopped countless times along the way and that it would take an age to actually get inside.

Trying not to feel like a spare wheel, she remembered Arch's advice and pulled back her shoulders and smiled until her cheeks hurt. Just when she thought the interview was over and she was about to drop her pasted-on grin, the interviewer turned toward her.

"And who's your escort for the evening, Archer?"

Before Tessa had a chance to panic, Arch said, "This is Tessa, a good friend helping me navigate the red carpet and the stairs with my cane." He excused them both, leading her along the carpet.

She breathed a sigh of relief, glad to have the matter taken out of her hands. Arch was such an expert at knowing the right thing to say. It was an admirable quality, and she was thankful for his composure. She did her best to stay smiling and poised as he posed for a couple more photos and did three more short interviews. Then he said, "Let's head inside, shall we?"

Arm in arm, they took the steps up to the main

building. There was so much commotion and buzzy chatter as people greeted one another that it was hardly a reprieve. She'd never seen so many gorgeous and fashionable men and women in one place before. Some of them she recognized from their movies. Arch was stopped quite a few times by people wanting to say hello and ask about his injury.

As quickly as he could, Arch guided her into the grand auditorium. Once inside, she was instantly soothed by the dimmed lights and red-curtained stage. It felt a bit like stepping inside an old theater—albeit a gigantic one.

"Look, Smith and Valentina are already here." Arch pointed to one of the circular tables to the right of the stage. "As presenters, we get prime seating, and with my bum leg, they gave us a table close to the stage." She could almost see him measuring the half-dozen or so stairs he'd have to climb to get there.

"Do you want me to walk up there with you?" She'd do that for him, though she'd hate it.

"I'll be okay. I've got my cane, and I'll hang on to Smith if I have to."

Speaking of Smith, he was standing to greet them. She was instantly glad to spot their familiar faces in a sea of strangers, especially Valentina, who had been so warm and friendly when they'd visited Arch earlier in the week. Tessa had been honored to hear their news along with Arch, knowing how much they wanted to keep it secret from Smith's fans for a little longer.

The famous couple looked gorgeous and glamorous, as if they'd just stepped out of a *Vogue* double spread. Valentina was all Grecian goddess in a flowing, floor-length gown of emerald-green silk that drew out the green in her extraordinary eyes. The loose fit also hid any baby bump from sight. Still, Tessa thought the glow of happiness on both their faces would be a dead giveaway. Smith was handsome in a tux so classic he could have been playing James Bond.

The two men clapped each other on the back, and Valentina kissed Tessa's cheeks. "You look incredible, Tessa. What a gorgeous dress."

Tessa blushed, bowled over by the compliment from such a stunning woman. "Thank you. Yours is beautiful too." Tessa wanted to tell Valentina that Arch had surprised her with the dress, but worried she'd read too much into it.

Just then, an announcement was made for everyone to take their seats. The ceremony was about to begin.

Arch pulled out her chair, and as she took her seat, Tessa realized that her nerves had finally started to recede a little bit. She'd made it down the red carpet unscathed, with just one interviewer asking who she was. Yes, she'd been photographed and filmed beside Archer Davenport, but she was certain the TV editors would cut her out of the shots, since she clearly couldn't be dating a movie star.

Now all she had to do was watch the event with a couple who were good friends, who just happened to be super famous. As she watched the scene unfold around her and accepted a glass of champagne, she couldn't help but enjoy the buzz and feeling of being a Hollywood insider, even if only for an evening.

The lights changed to a warm orange glow, and then a well-known comedian came on to host the night's proceedings. In his opening monologue, he managed to make fun of many of the famous actors and presenters in the audience. At one point, he turned to Arch and said, "As for you, Archer Davenport, no *horsing around* this evening." The camera swung toward their table, and Arch gave a good-natured grin, lifting his cane in acknowledgment of the joke.

And then the awards began. Tessa's nerves dissolved, and she simply enjoyed watching people celebrate a business they all loved.

Soon, an usher approached the table and told Smith and Arch it was time for them to head backstage. Tessa wanted to kiss him and wish him luck as calmly and easily as Valentina did for Smith, but instead, she gave him a look she hoped communicated how she was really feeling. It was a brave move for him to use only a cane for support, and she was more than a little nervous for him. A public tumble could ruin his prospects of going ahead with his new action movie, and she knew how much it meant him to shoot that film and take his career to the next level.

When it was time for Arch and Smith to present, there was a hush and then a burst of loud applause as the men's names were announced. Tessa was proud at how warmly the audience was responding. Arch was so well regarded. The applause grew as they walked forward, Smith slowing his pace to keep in line with Arch. Seeing him up there, so determined and dignified with his thrift-store cane, she felt her heart swell with love.

Arch and Smith reached the twin mics. As the applause quieted, Smith turned to his friend and said, "I've been upstaged by beautiful women and upstaged by beautiful horses, but I've never been upstaged by a guy with a broken leg."

There was a ripple of laughter.

With his charismatic winning smile, Arch replied, "What can I say? I suffer for my art."

Tessa knew they were reading from a teleprompter, but the men's obvious friendship and respect for each other made it feel like they were just riffing on each other's personalities.

And then Arch said, "Speaking of suffering for art, this year's nominated filmmakers worked in difficult conditions, often with small budgets, but triumphed over each challenge to produce a spectacular range of unique works that have captured our hearts and imaginations."

Smith read through the list of nominees, and then, after a video montage was screened and time made for the all-important dramatic pause, Arch announced the winner of this year's Moonrise Festival best picture award.

There was more applause as the winners ascended the staircase and were presented the award, at which point Arch and Smith exited the stage.

And then the comedian came back to wind things up, and just like that, it was all over.

Of course, Valentina had sat through many events like this, so was used to seeing Smith up onstage, but Tessa felt like her heart could burst with pride.

When the men returned to the table, Valentina kissed her husband and said he'd done a wonderful job. Tessa told Arch how well he'd done.

She couldn't help reaching out to touch his arm, even though she wanted to touch all of him and kiss him as easily as Valentina kissed Smith. In a soft voice, she said, "Part of me was afraid you might stumble, but you looked so solid and strong up there."

Arch let out a breath and then accepted a glass of champagne, the first he'd allowed himself all night. "I might well have stumbled if you hadn't given me my strength back in rehab. I couldn't have gotten here without you, Tessa."

She squeezed his hand once under the table to

acknowledge his lovely words, then let go so that no one would see. Now that Arch's part of the evening was over, she could fully relax and enjoy getting an insight into this completely new world.

As the night wrapped up, various movie industry people came by to ask how Arch was doing after his accident and about his next project. She saw how easily he got on with everybody, remembering names and asking after family members. She also couldn't help but notice how people eyed her with curiosity or outright asked for an introduction. Arch was always charming, but never gave anything away.

A lot of them said, "See you at the after party." To which he didn't reply.

Valentina had been drinking sparkling water all evening, and Tessa had caught her stifling more than one yawn. Smith obviously noticed, too, for he said, "Let's get you home to bed."

After Smith and Valentina said their good-byes, Arch leaned closer and said, "Do you want to go to the after party? It's totally up to you. They are a lot of fun, but tiring too."

All she wanted was to be at home in Arch's arms, but she understood he might feel differently. Softly, she asked, "Do you?"

"Like I said earlier, I've been to lots of award shows, and this is one of the smaller ones. The after party won't be so spectacular, and it's been a long day for both of us. Plus, I'm still in rehab, right?" Then he leaned in so that he was out of Valentina's and Smith's hearing. "What I'm trying to say is that I'd much rather be alone with you than at any party, big or small."

Her heart swelled at his words, and the affection in his eyes was undeniable.

As undeniable as her feelings were for him.

Chapter Thirty-Three

The journey home had never gone more slowly. Arch wished now he'd booked them a room in some fancy hotel close to the Moonrise Festival venue, but he'd wanted to get home, with Tessa.

At last, they made it back to Carmel, and as tired as he was, he couldn't stop his excitement that now it was just the two of them.

"Are you very tired?" he asked her, hoping she'd say no, that she was as energized as he was, wanting to make love for what remained of the night and greet the dawn with her beautiful body wrapped around his.

She slipped off the earrings his mother had lent her and placed them carefully in their box. "I've never had my photo taken that many times in my entire life."

Not completely the response he'd been hoping for. But he understood how she felt. "I've been in this world so long, I never thought about the photographers. But they loved you. You look as good as the biggest stars out there. Better, because you're not playing a part. You're you." Then he kissed her, loving the feel of her lips softening under his. "I'm sorry if it was all too much for you. I just wanted you by my side."

She tilted her head back. "You're forgiven. And you know what? I had a good time. Much more than I thought I would. You were right—once you get past the hype and the glamour, they're all people doing work they love."

"I'm used to the whole Hollywood machine by now, but I remember how exhausting it was the first few times on the red carpet. You did great, Tessa." A wicked glint shone in his eyes. "Come on, let's get to bed."

He hoped she'd join him in his room and was beyond happy when *she* took *his* hand and drew him that way. Then he turned her away from him. "Let me help you with that zipper."

He slid the zipper slowly down her back, so slowly it was a caress. The sound of the enclosure opening, revealing her naked back, had him roaring to full arousal.

How did she always do this to him? And from the very start? From one simple hello on the beach all those weeks ago?

No woman had ever made him feel this intense need.

He'd be a gentleman if she was exhausted and would let her sleep, but based on the way her skin was warming as his fingers slid slowly down her back and the way her breathing was changing, he had a suspicion she was as aroused as he.

He slid the dress off her shoulders and let it slide down her body to puddle on the floor. He turned her slowly to face him and stepped back. She looked as though she were standing in a pool of moonlight. A goddess in nothing but a whisper of silk.

"Take your clothes off," she commanded in a husky tone that had him aching for her even more. She would never have given him such a sensual command in their early days. But now, she was bold. And so damned beautiful it made everything inside of him marvel that she was here with him.

He took his time, hoping it would only inflame her arousal. He stripped slowly, letting her watch as he removed jacket, bow tie, the studs, then the shirt, his socks… and finally his trousers.

She eyed his crotch and raised her brows as though to say, *You're not done yet.*

Sweet Lord. She was making him half crazy. No, not half. *Completely* crazy!

But he complied, slipping off his boxers over his raging erection. When she saw it, she gave a sharp intake of breath, and it was like a spell broke as they sprang to each other.

His cane fell to the floor as she pushed him back onto the bed.

She kissed her way down his body, loving him with her mouth until he couldn't hold back. He wanted to be inside her beautiful, hot body too much. He could barely stand to take the time to put on protection. He pulled her up so he could kiss her hungrily, and then she slid onto him, slick and so hot he could barely control himself. He thrust up, up, up—and she rode him until she dropped her head back with a cry, her body gripping him, causing his own cry of release as they came together.

For a long time, they lay entwined, waiting for their hearts to slow down, both spent and happy.

Arch wished the moment could last forever.

★ ★ ★

Arch wasn't surprised to hear from his agent the next morning, given that Jay always monitored the news and social media after an event that Arch attended. However, instead of giving him feedback, Jay's first question was, "Who's this new woman on your arm? Is she an actress I should be signing? Because she looks great on camera." Almost as an afterthought, he said, "Oh, and you were great last night. The silver-topped cane was a nice touch."

They'd eaten breakfast, and he and Tessa had been enjoying an unusual lazy morning, lingering over coffee, so she was sitting beside him. Though his cell phone wasn't on speaker, she could likely hear every word Jay said. He was not a quiet man.

He glanced at Tessa, who wasn't even pretending not to be listening. "She's—"

He couldn't lie and say they were just friends. It wasn't true, and he didn't want to pretend anymore. Tessa belonged beside him on the red carpet. And in every other place he'd ever walk, he wanted her by his side.

In the silence, Jay said, "What do I tell reporters about her? If she's not a starlet, they're going to think she's your new girlfriend."

"I'll call you back," he said and ended the call. He turned to Tessa. "You heard him. Everyone's dying to know who the mystery woman is."

"But people weren't looking at me. They were looking at you." She seemed genuinely puzzled.

He pulled out his laptop and within seconds found footage of the red carpet last night on every entertainment website. In every shot, Tessa was beside him, looking as though she belonged there. He clicked through several sites, and there they were, always together.

"I love this one," he said and turned the laptop so she could see better. It was a still photo where he had his arm around her, and they were both smiling for the camera.

"Can't you ask Jay to tell them that I'm your rehab nurse?"

"Nope." He didn't so much as pause before saying it. "Because no one will believe it. You know as well as I do that we look like a couple." He was silent for a beat. "We *are* a couple."

There was a pause while she remained speechless, and his heart began to pound. He was about to take the biggest gamble of his life. Archer Davenport, who'd always been so confident with women, was so nervous that his palms were sweating.

He was about to say words he'd never said before. But it was time. And it was his ultimate truth. The one thing he knew with more certainty than anything else.

"Tessa, I'm in love with you."

That was all he had. The bare truth. There was so much he wanted to tell her, but in the silence, he was suddenly frightened out of his wits.

What if she doesn't feel the same way?
What if she doesn't love me back?

She looked stunned and just stared at him with those gorgeous eyes of hers.

He took her hand. "I want to call Jay back and tell him you're the love of my life. I want to shout from the rooftops that you're mine."

This was the most vulnerable he'd ever been. She opened her mouth, and he waited for what she had to say... but it was like she couldn't find the right words. He was praying she'd say *I love you too*, but the longer he waited, the more awful the silence became.

Finally, she took a breath. "Why does your agent have to tell them anything? What you and I are building right now is just between us." She squeezed his hand. "I've never felt like this with anyone, Arch." Another pause. "But I'm scared."

He knew exactly what was holding her back. Not just the circus that came with his fame, but the emotional scars left by her husband. A man she'd clearly never felt true love with, given what she'd just said.

How could he let her know he was nothing like that cold, controlling man? He might be dead, but there was no doubt in Arch's mind that he was still messing with her, even from the grave.

"I've never felt like this either, Tessa. Only with you. And I've never told any other woman that I love her. Only you." Though she hadn't said the three little words back to him, he slid his fingers through hers. He understood that she wasn't where he was. Not yet. But hopefully she would be soon. "You don't have to say it back. I just feel that what we are sharing together is too special to be one-sided. At least I hope so."

She stared down at their joined hands. "I swore I wouldn't get emotionally involved… but I can't lie to you and say I haven't."

Thrilled that she might actually feel the same way, he couldn't help pushing a little. "Are you telling me you're getting closer to the idea that you could one day love me back?" It wasn't exactly an enthusiastic *I love you*, but if there was hope that she'd love him one day, he'd pull out all the stops to show her that he was the man for her. And that he would love her forever, into eternity.

When she answered his question with a nod, it was one of the best moments of his life. He could wait for *I love you* as long as he knew there was a chance it would come.

Just one nod and then a kiss that made him feel better than he ever had before. That was always how he felt with Tessa. As though colors were brighter, and roses smelled better, and the entire world was their oyster. As though everything he truly wanted in life was right here beside him.

Chapter Thirty-Four

Tessa laughed at herself when she got ready later that day to pick up a few things for dinner. She did not look at all like the glamorous woman in the clips and photos online. Today, she had her hair in a ponytail, an old baseball cap jammed on top, and sunglasses hiding her eyes. Not a scrap of makeup, and no one would call her jeans and T-shirt *designer*.

Arch had said *I love you*, not to the glamorous woman last night, but to the one she was looking at now in the mirror. Ordinary, everyday Tessa. He'd said those magic words over and over as they'd made love. And had she thrown herself into his arms and said them back? Like any normal woman who felt the way she did would have?

No. She hadn't.

Couldn't.

She'd been wrong before, thinking she was in love with a man who'd turned out to be cold and controlling. And though Arch was the opposite, there was a part of her—a deep, sensitive, frightened part—that couldn't accept the love of a good man. A part of her that thought she wasn't good enough for him. That there surely must be someone better for him. Someone from his glittering world.

She didn't want to say *I love you* until she could do it with her heart open and unafraid. After she got the groceries, she'd get out her paints. Hopefully, a few hours at the beach would calm her and bring clarity.

Maybe she'd make something extra special for dinner, something romantic, and if she found the words, she'd tell Arch tonight.

Because she *did* love him.

She'd known it for weeks. And for weeks she'd let fear be stronger than love. At the beach with her paints, would she finally find her way to taking such a massive risk as telling Archer Davenport that she loved him?

Waiting in line with fresh milk, a couple of avocados, and a lemon, she noticed that one of the gossipy papers in the rack in the checkout line featured a photo of Archer and her at the awards ceremony.

Two women ahead of her were chatting while they waited. One said, "Archer Davenport is so handsome. And he's so down-to-earth for a movie star. He has a place here in Carmel, you know."

Tessa was secretly thrilled that neither of them noticed that the woman in the picture was standing right behind them. She couldn't wait to tell him. He'd laugh so hard.

Then the second woman pointed to the photo of Tessa. "Who's that? His new co-star? I haven't seen her before."

Her friend said, "I read online that she's his new girlfriend. I don't even think she's an actress."

The second woman picked up the paper and studied the photo more closely. "I'm surprised he would dump Sonia Montefiore for someone like this. This girl is so *ordinary*. I bet she's a struggling actress, and he did her a favor. They do that in Hollywood, you know."

That moment was all it took for Tessa's dream to die.

The two women were right—and they were literally speaking her fears out loud.

Why would he want to be with someone so ordinary when he could have a gorgeous movie star who understood his world and knew how to stand on a red carpet without being coached?

All the sunshine had gone out of her day. And she wasn't sure it would ever come back.

She got home with the groceries, and when he said, "Do you want coffee? I was just going to make some," she blurted, "I can't do it. I can't be with you."

Arch turned, holding on to the kitchen counter for support. He searched her face, looking both puzzled and sad. "Why? What happened between your going out for milk and coming home?"

But all she could do was shake her head. "I can't talk about it right now. I need some time." She didn't even unpack the groceries. She simply walked up the stairs to her bedroom, trying not to cry. Trying not to scream with frustration. Trying not to wish that she didn't love Archer Davenport.

But Arch didn't wait. He followed her upstairs. "Tessa. Please. Talk to me."

"I can't," she told him again. "Not yet."

And even as he stood in her doorway, she pulled out her paints and easel and taped up a blank piece of paper. And like a waterfall, all of her emotions poured out onto it. It was like a huge crying fit made of blue, black, purple, and a thick, furious red. There was no subject, no focus. She wasn't normally an abstract painter, but she didn't care. She just let the feelings flow through her arm, through her brush.

She had no idea how much time passed before she finally ran out of steam. She might actually have collapsed right then and there if Arch hadn't come up behind her to hold her up. To be her strength when she had none. To be her calm when all she'd known in her marriage was fury. To be the embodiment of love when love had never truly been hers before now. Before coming to Carmel-by-the-Sea.

Before Arch.

"I don't know much about art, but I know pain when I see it," he said as he gently turned her in his arms to face him. "Your painting pretty much expresses how I feel right now too. I love you so damned much, Tessa. Please tell me what happened to make you feel this way."

There was no point in lying. She told him what she'd overheard at the store.

"And don't say it was only two strangers whose opinions don't matter. It's what *everyone* will say. And it's true. You could be with anyone. You're grateful because I helped you heal. One day, you'll realize that's what you're feeling. Gratitude, not love."

Though she could tell that her words had angered him, he didn't pull away. If anything, he drew her closer. "Don't tell me what I feel," he said. "I know my own damn feelings. Am I grateful to you for taking care of me? Of course I am. Just like I'm grateful to the woman who cleans my house, or the woman who does my taxes. I'm grateful to the women who pretend to love me on-screen, because they're good actresses, but I don't *love* any of them. I don't think of *them* when I wake up. I don't want to hold *them* in my arms when I drift to sleep. I don't want to have children with them. I don't want to choose a damn dog with them. I want those things with you. Only you, Tessa. *Only you.*"

When she would have tried to protest, he held up a hand so she found herself listening carefully, to hear the truth.

"Once and for all, I'm telling you that Sonia Montefiore and I were never an item. *You* are the woman I've waited for my whole life. Ask my family, if you don't believe me. Even though we tried to keep it a secret, they all know I'm hopelessly in love with you."

"But I don't belong on a red carpet."

"If it will make you feel more comfortable, then I will make a promise to you now that you never have to go to another of those things with me again."

She waved her hands in frustration. "It's not the red carpet. It's what it means. It's *everything*."

A voice boomed out from below. "How's my wingman today? Valentina and I are heading out tomorrow. Came over to say good-bye."

Like most of Arch's friends and family, Smith Sullivan hadn't bothered to knock.

Arch said, "I'll tell him to go. We are not finished here."

"No. Have a visit with your friend. I need to think. Please, Arch. I need some time."

And though it was clearly the very last thing he wanted in the world, he took her at her word and gave her space and time.

Chapter Thirty-Five

Tessa waited until she could hear Arch and Smith talking downstairs. Maybe it was rude, but she couldn't see Smith Sullivan right now when her head and heart were such a mess. She was glad he hadn't brought Valentina with him, or she'd have felt even worse about sneaking out of the house.

She didn't even take her painting things with her. Her mind was a tangled web of love and fear, and her nerves were frayed. But she needed the beach, the smell of the water, the feel of the sand between her toes. Even some happy dogs who might lift the heaviness in her chest.

She ran quietly down the stairs and let herself out the front door. Then, taking a deep breath, she walked toward the beach. She didn't head for her usual painting spot, just walked straight out of Arch's home until she found herself on the sand.

There were no surfers out. The swell wasn't high enough. There were no swimmers either. The water was too cold. But there were a few dog walkers in the distance and a couple jogging along the sand. A small boy, and possibly his grandfather, flew a kite, a green one shaped like a dragon's head.

She felt jumpy and unsure of every single thing.

But no. She was sure of *one* thing.

She was absolutely sure that she loved Archer Davenport, loved him with all of her heart.

But was that enough?

She took off her shoes and socks and set them out of reach of the waves. Then she walked forward to the edge of the surf and let the waves lick her toes. The water was chilly but good. Cold enough to help cool the heat of her fears.

She stepped deeper into the waves, letting the water hit her. Somehow, the cold shock was exactly what she needed. Without realizing she was doing it, she walked deeper. Now she was up to her knees. Her jeans were heavy with water as she waded forward.

A gull wheeled overhead, screeching, as though asking her what she was doing.

Truth was, she had no idea. She just needed to feel the freezing water as the waves washed higher and higher against her. She couldn't shut her emotions down the way she had for so long. Being in the ocean, especially one with such a cool bite, made her feel present inside herself in a way she'd rarely been comfortable with.

Lewis had always taken advantage of any vulnerability. But out in the ocean, she was nothing *but* vulnerable. It was stronger… yet here she was. Up to her hips in the waves.

Not falling.

Did that mean that she was strong too? As strong as an ocean? Because that was what she'd have to be if she took her place at Arch's side as his lover, his woman, maybe even his wife one day.

She thought back to the day they'd sat on the beach watching his siblings surf. They had been in wetsuits, but they had also all dived headfirst through the waves to get out to where the curls were.

She was in up to her waist now. A small wave came rushing toward her, and she dove into it, relishing the cold shock as her whole body went under. When she came up, her hair was streaming down her back, and she gasped from the cold.

Then she laughed. Full, deep, throaty laughter.

"I am not ordinary," she said to the waves, the gulls, and the fish in the sea.

She gazed up at the sky and laughed again. *"I am not ordinary,"* she screamed to the beautiful blue above her.

In fact, she was stronger, and far more unique, than she'd ever given herself credit for. She hadn't given up hope when she found herself both widowed and destitute. She'd asked no one for help. And yet, she'd managed to build herself a new, successful life.

If she could help injured people heal, if she could convince people like Margaret to do their exercises, then she could certainly cope with magazine covers or strangers saying she wasn't pretty or famous enough for Archer Davenport.

None of that mattered. She knew it with all her heart.

The *only* thing that mattered was that they loved each other.

She loved Arch so much, but she'd still had trouble believing him when he'd professed his love for her. But now, the waves nudged her in the direction of the beach, as though reminding her how great she and Arch were together.

At long last, Tessa saw her own strength. Not only in getting over her difficult past, but in letting herself open up again. At last, she realized how incredibly brave it had been to be intimate with Arch, knowing she was risking her heart. Even going to Moonrise as his date had taken courage.

If anyone had asked her two months ago how she felt about herself, she would have said she wished she could be stronger.

But she no longer had to wish for that.

She was already strong.

In fact, she always had been—but was only now finally seeing her own worth.

Arch had helped her see that she was extraordinary.

He'd supported her dreams, believed in her art, treated her as though she was vitally important to him.

Now she was able to blossom in every way—artistically and emotionally.

It was time—long past time—to let him know.

Taking one last, deep breath of the salty air, she shivered and waded out of the ocean.

Time to head home.

★ ★ ★

Arch could hardly stand it. He'd gotten rid of Smith by saying he had a phone interview scheduled, which was a total lie. But he couldn't joke around with his buddy when his mind was in turmoil.

He'd watched from the living room window as Tessa headed out to the beach. He'd seen her walk a little, stand there undecided for a moment, and then walk into the water fully clothed.

He wanted to run out there, make sure she was okay—but he had to respect her wishes to have some time to process. He also knew how healing the ocean could be, and he hoped it would help heal the wounds from her marriage.

Despite his resolutions, he never took his gaze off the woman he loved, ready at any moment to run to her if she needed him. Well, he'd be limp-hopping on his still-healing leg, but he'd get there.

She must be so cold. The water temperature wasn't

that high, and she wasn't doing anything to stay warm, just bobbing on the swell, looking out at the horizon.

At last, when he couldn't stand it another second, she turned. She waded out of the surf, soaking wet and more beautiful than ever. She paused to put on her shoes, not even bothering with the socks, and then walked up toward the house.

As quickly as he could on his booted foot, he went into the bathroom and gathered a thick, warm towel and his bathrobe.

When he got back to the window, she was nearly home. And even from this distance, he could see that there was something different about her. Even the way she walked was different, almost as though she'd gained some power in the ocean, just as he'd hoped she would.

Just as he had so many times in his life.

When she opened the door, he was standing there with the towel, which he wrapped around her. But she barely seemed to notice. Droplets fell from her hair and her wet clothes, but she only had eyes for him.

"I love you, Arch. I love you more than I ever knew I could love anyone. And I don't want to lose you. So if I have to wear pretty dresses and smile on red carpets with you every day of the week, that's what I'll do."

Arch had never believed he could feel this happy, just from hearing her say *I love you*.

He pulled her into him and kissed her lips, tasting seawater and then her. He wrapped his arms around her, giving her his warmth and getting very wet in the process.

"All I need is you, Tessa. We can skip every red carpet in the world from now on if that will make you happy."

She kissed him again. "*You* are what makes me happy. It took so long for me to allow myself to see or feel it, but you did the impossible—you broke through all my walls. I never thought anyone could, but you did."

He couldn't stop his smile, one that started deep in his center and blossomed all the way out to his lips. "I knew from the first moment I saw you on the beach with Margaret that you were going to be mine." He remembered how struck he'd been by Tessa, and every moment since, she'd only become more precious to him.

Another kiss, and then she said, "You can call Jay now and tell him I'm your girlfriend."

"No."

She looked confused. "No? But I thought—"

He stopped her sentence with another kiss. "When I call Jay back, I hope to say that the beautiful woman by my side is my fiancée."

She gasped. "Wait—what? Are you saying you—"

"Yes, Tessa." He couldn't stop kissing her, even on

the verge of proposing. "I'm saying I want to marry you. You've healed more than my leg. You've made every part of me better. And I don't want to live the rest of my life without you. I can't even imagine it now, not after all you've come to mean to me."

It wasn't easy getting down on one knee when his left leg was in the boot, but he managed to get down on his right knee. Then he looked up and said, "Tessa Taylor, love of my life, will you marry me?"

Without missing a beat, she knelt beside him to kiss him. And right before their lips met, she whispered, "Yes, I'll marry you. I am yours, Arch. Always and forever."

Epilogue

Mila Davenport had never thought of herself as a patron of the arts, but here she was at Devendorf Park in Carmel-by-the-Sea, gazing at paintings and thinking of ways to increase sales.

They weren't just any paintings—they were the work of Tessa Taylor, her soon-to-be sister-in-law. This was Tessa's first time exhibiting her paintings in public, and she'd been thrilled to take second place in the *plein air* competition, which entitled her to her own booth at the Carmel Art Festival.

Mila had taken to the quiet but efficient Tessa right away. She couldn't have imagined her devil-may-care movie-star brother would fall for his caregiver, but he'd done more than that. A big diamond ring sparkled on Tessa's ring finger, and she'd never seen her brother so happy.

Even now, the man who normally tried to keep his identity on the down-low when he was in town, was openly greeting his fans as they came up for autographs and selfies. Then he neatly steered them toward

Tessa's art, telling them all that she was an up-and-coming artist of incredible talent, which was undeniably true.

Erin joined her. "I didn't think there could be a more devoted couple than Mom and Dad, but Arch and Tessa are right up there. He wants to get married as soon as possible, before the paparazzi get wind of the engagement."

"He's so proud of her for being in this show, he's nearly bursting," Mila said, feeling happy for both of them.

"And she's already booked for her first gallery show right here in town." Since Erin was a reporter for the *Sea Shell*, she always knew what was going on.

"That's great," Mila said, delighted that Tessa was getting the recognition she deserved.

"She doesn't need Arch pushing his fans at her, but it's kind of adorable."

They were standing outside the tented area that housed the local artists' work. People came by in running shorts and yoga outfits, walking dogs on leads, some dressed in business clothes like Mila. They wandered by to browse, chat with the artists, and to buy original artwork. It was exciting. As a Realtor, Mila loved sales. She was still thinking of ways she might help Tessa when Erin nudged her.

"See that guy in front of the booth with the abstract still lifes?"

"Is that what they are?" Mila asked.

She'd stared at the multicolored splashes of paint and wondered. However, she'd already noticed the man in front of the booth. Something about him had drawn her attention when he'd first arrived, though he wasn't her usual type. She'd always gone for the athletic surfer-dude types, whereas this man was a little on the geeky, intellectual side. He had short brown hair and a moustache, and he wore his casual clothes as though they were unnatural to him. As though he was usually in uniform. She'd bet he was in the military.

"Who is he?" Once more, she was happy to have a journalist for a sister.

Erin dropped her voice to a near whisper, as though the man who'd now moved to look at the next booth might have a superhero's hearing. "That's Herschel Greenfield. The astronaut."

Now Mila looked at the man with even more interest. "The one who almost died?"

Erin nodded. "He nearly drowned at sea when his capsule opened during splashdown in bad weather. The ship almost didn't get to them in time. He made sure the rest of the crew got out okay, and then he almost didn't make it. He was a real hero."

"Definitely a hero," Mila echoed. Then she added, "That had to be incredibly traumatic."

She'd suffered her own trauma when that surfing accident had almost killed her. She'd lived to surf again, but her career as a competitive surfer had died. She'd been ranked the number three female surfer in the world, with her sights set on becoming number one.

And then, just like that, it was over.

She'd rebuilt her life and loved selling real estate and, once her body had healed, surfed every chance she got. But part of her would always regret that her shot at the big time had been taken away from her.

Erin said, "I'm supposed to be covering this event, so I'd better go interview some of the artists."

"Sure. I'll see you later."

They were all invited back to the family home for a barbecue later to celebrate Tessa's show. She saw Mom and Dad chatting with one of the artists. They never missed the *plein air* competition.

Mila was about to join them when Herschel Greenfield stopped in front of Tessa's display. Tessa had fallen in love with Carmel-by-the-Sea, and her paintings showed her appreciation of the local scenery and the people. She'd painted the sea in many moods—even one with a dog on the beach in midair, Frisbee just out of reach. And she'd also painted Mila out surfing. Mila hadn't had any idea she'd inspired Tessa until she saw the painting. The weather had been bad that day and the waves fierce. Tessa had caught the angry sky, the towering waves, and Mila, crouched over her board, blond hair flying behind her in the curl.

She'd thought about buying that one herself—

Tessa had caught the excitement she felt in her belly when she was in the zone. But she'd hesitated, wondering if it was too vain to have a picture of herself on her wall. She'd see how she felt if it didn't sell during the show. Even better, maybe a few carefully dropped hints would encourage someone in her family to buy it for her as a gift. She couldn't be called vain if she displayed a birthday or Christmas gift, could she?

She'd imagined that Herschel Greenfield would move on after checking out Tessa's wall of art, but instead, he moved closer to the painting of Mila. He stood there for so long that other art lovers had to move around him, like waves around an island.

Even though Mila wore a wetsuit surfing, it seemed like he was checking her out. Her temper flared, and she decided to let the astronaut know that she was no centerfold.

She walked up beside him and said, "Interested in buying that?"

Still staring at the painting, he said, "No." He shook his head. "God, no. I couldn't have that in the house."

Then, as though realizing he'd been insulting, he turned to her, looking stricken. He had blue-gray eyes that reminded her of the ocean during a storm. "You're a very talented painter, but it's not for me."

She wasn't sure whether he meant to be rude or whether he had zero social skills, but she felt a little snarky. "Lots of men would be pretty happy to have this painting on their living room wall. I didn't paint it, but I am the woman in it."

He did a double take—at the picture, at her. "That's you?"

He seemed to fumble for words, and she didn't help him out, just stood there waiting.

Finally, he said, "It's not that I don't want you on the wall. I mean, obviously, you're very beautiful. Even more stunning in person." He turned back to the painting and shook his head. "It's just… that wave looks like it's trying to gobble you up."

When he turned back and said, "You see?" she recognized real pain in his eyes.

Then it hit her—had the angry waves in the painting taken him back to his near-death experience? Was that why he couldn't have it in the house, yet couldn't tear himself away from it?

"Have you ever surfed?" she asked, feeling kinder toward him now that she suspected the source of his pain.

He shuddered. "No."

She had an instinctive feeling that he had developed a fear of the ocean, but didn't want to embarrass him by asking. She wasn't a therapist, just someone who'd learned to get back into the water after she nearly died out there too.

Maybe she could help him, though. At least she could offer. "I teach surfing to beginners on Saturdays, if you ever want to drop in."

"Oh, I—I don't think… I mean, I never thought of surfing as a sport. I do a lot of running. And cycling."

His body was strong and athletic, so she wasn't surprised that he was into sports. She also thought he was very cute in a nerdy way. She could imagine a quick fling if he was on holiday here. She'd been without a man for too long, and a guy on holiday wouldn't try to tie her down, which suited her fine.

"Are you staying in the area?" Yes, he could definitely be fun in the short term. She had a feeling there might be a hot fire burning beneath those awkward social skills.

"Actually, I'm thinking about buying a house here."

"Really?" Short-term affairs were one thing, but business was another. She gave him her most winning smile and pulled out one of her business cards. "If you're not already working with a Realtor, I'd love to help you find the perfect home. Will you be moving with your family?" She'd assumed he was single, but maybe he had a wife and five kids to relocate to Carmel. She should have asked Erin more about him when she'd had the chance.

"No. It's just me."

"Perfect," she said, then realizing how that sounded, added, "It's easier to choose a home when you don't have to consider other people's opinions." She held out her hand. "I'm Mila Davenport."

"Hersch," he said. "Hersch Greenfield."

"Nice to meet you, Hersch. Call me if I can help."

Carefully, he tucked her card into his wallet. "I will."

She checked the high-end waterproof watch that never left her wrist. Time was important to Mila. She wanted to cram every second she could into a life full of activity and fun and laughter.

Time was also money, however, and she should get back to the office.

But first she wanted to say good-bye to Tessa and wish her well—not that she needed it. There were already a number of SOLD stickers on her paintings. She was clearly destined for success.

An older man beamed as Tessa put one of the stickers on a seascape. "My wife will be so thrilled. It's for our anniversary," he said, and then, after a last glance at his purchase, he moved on.

Before Mila could reach Tessa, Arch said something to his fiancée, then leaned in for a kiss.

Mila felt herself go mushy inside. Her brother and Tessa were so deeply in love. She thought it was beautiful, of course. But she also wondered how they managed it.

Beside her, a familiar voice said, "Aren't they sweet? The first of my children to get married. I'm so thrilled."

Mila said, "Don't look at me as the next one in line, Mom. I mean, it's fantastic for Arch and Tessa, and I bet you'll be knitting baby booties within the year. But you know I'm all about my career."

Betsy Davenport simply responded with that knowing Mom smile and said, "Your turn will come, honey." She glanced to where Herschel Greenfield was now studying a sculpture of a mermaid. "That man seemed quite taken with you."

She wasn't surprised her mom had noticed. But she'd never been short on male attention. She tended to play hard, get bored, and move on.

She'd definitely seen that look in his eyes toward the end of their conversation, though. There had definitely been a sizzle of attraction between them. She didn't say so to her mom, of course, but he could be an interesting distraction.

Then she remembered what a hero he was, making sure the other astronauts got out of the capsule first and nearly dying himself—and knew she could help him overcome his obvious fear of water.

If he'd let her.

She gave him another long glance. *I'll make sure he lets me help him.*

Smiling now, Mila kissed her mother's cheek, congratulated Tessa on her success, then headed to her office. But all the while, she was thinking about Hersch… while a tiny part of her wondered if he was thinking about her too.

★ ★ ★

ABOUT THE AUTHORS

Having sold more than 10 million books, Bella Andre's novels have been #1 bestsellers around the world and have appeared on the *New York Times* and *USA Today* bestseller lists 93 times. She has been the #1 Ranked Author on a top 10 list that included Nora Roberts, JK Rowling, James Patterson and Steven King.

Known for "sensual, empowered stories enveloped in heady romance" (Publishers Weekly), her books have been Cosmopolitan Magazine "Red Hot Reads" twice and have been translated into ten languages. She is a graduate of Stanford University and has won the Award of Excellence in romantic fiction. The Washington Post called her "One of the top writers in America" and she has been featured by Entertainment Weekly, NPR, USA Today, Forbes, The Wall Street Journal, and TIME Magazine.

In addition to writing "The Sullivans" series, "The Maverick Billionaires" series, and "The Davenport" series, Bella also writes the *New York Times* bestselling "Four Weddings and a Fiasco" series as Lucy Kevin. Her sweet contemporary romances also include the USA Today bestselling "Walker Island" and "Married in Malibu" series.

If not behind her computer, you can find her reading her favorite authors, hiking, swimming or laughing. Married with two children, Bella splits her time between the Northern California wine country, a log cabin in the Adirondack mountains of upstate New York, and a flat in London overlooking the Thames.

Sign up for Bella's New Release newsletter:
bellaandre.com/newsletter

Join Bella Andre on Facebook:
facebook.com/authorbellaandre

Join Bella Andre's reader group:
bellaandre.com/readergroup

Follow Bella Andre on Instagram:
instagram.com/bellaandrebooks

Follow Bella Andre on Twitter:
twitter.com/bellaandre

Visit Bella's website for her complete booklist:
www.BellaAndre.com

Nicky Arden (aka Nancy Warren) is the USA Today Bestselling author of mystery and romance who had sold more than 5 million books so far! She's originally from Vancouver, Canada, though she tends to wander and has lived in England, Italy and California at various times. Favorite moments include being the answer to a crossword puzzle clue in Canada's National Post newspaper, being featured on the front page of the New York Times when her book Speed Dating launched Harlequin's NASCAR series, and being nominated three times for Romance Writers of America's RITA award. She has an MA in Creative Writing from Bath Spa University. She's an avid hiker, loves chocolate and most of all, loves to hear from readers! You'll often find her in her private Facebook group, Nancy Warren's Knitwits.

Newsletter signup:
nickyarden.com/newsletter

Nicky's Website:
www.NickyArden.com

Printed in Great Britain
by Amazon